ON THE RUN

New York City, early 1990s: a young, rich, and well-educated Central American man on the run from the police and Colombian drug dealers. He is accused of crimes he didn't commit. Ready to do what it takes to survive, Pablo ironically embraces the very drug trade that threatened his life in the first place. Who is he? What is he really capable of? The question of identity is at the heart of On the Run. More than a contemporary story of survival, it's a journey of self-discovery.

Pablo's voice is funny, sometimes mean and merciless. He moves with nightmarish ease from recounting his adventures to recollecting his early life. Not always politically correct, On the Run gives you an insightful, twisted, humorous, and often disturbing view of conflicting worlds and beliefs: North and Latin America; black, brown, and white; rich and poor; rational and esoteric – and shows how they mix, match, and clash.

ON THE RUN

IZAI AMORIM

First edition: 2016
Published by Izai Amorim

ISBN numbers:
978-3982165646 — Hardcover
978-3000530395 — Softcover
978-3000534867 — Ebook

Cover photograph ©1990 and book design by Izai Amorim

Author's website:
www.izaiamorim.com

Book website:
www.ontherun.izaiamorim.com

Author's mailing list:
www.mailinglist.izaiamorim.com

Dedicated to Jo and Simone...

"Emancipate yourself from mental slavery, none but ourselves can free our minds." *

**...and to all those who never came back.
Gone but not forgotten.**

"In this great future, you can't forget your past." *

* Marley (1945 – 1981)

Disclaimer

On The Run is a work of fiction, inspired by actual events and actual people. All characters, other than those clearly in the public domain, are fictitious. Any resemblance to real persons is purely coincidental.

Those were the early 1990s. Times have changed. Don't attempt to perform the same or similar criminal activities depicted in the story, as personal injury, property damage, arrest, prosecution, conviction, or even death may result.

On the Run contains words and language that some readers might consider profane, vulgar, or even offensive. Characters make non-politically correct comments on race, gender, sexuality, religion, ethnicity, and politics that may be considered derogatory by some readers. The opinions expressed in the story are those of the characters. They do not reflect those of the author.

Last but not least, don't believe everything that you read. On the Run is for entertainment purposes only.

Contents

[1]

[1 / 1]

Some people say that when you're about to die, you see your whole life flashing before your eyes, like you're watching a movie. Others say that you see angels. Some talk about out-of-body experiences. These different theories have one common characteristic: it's supposed to be a cosmic experience.

It's all bullshit. I didn't see any movie. I didn't see any angels. No out-of-body experience. As the bullets were flying around me, all I could see and hear was Mom screaming at me. "Shame on you, Pablo! To die wearing dirty underwear! How could you do this to me?" There was definitely nothing cosmic about that.

I had picked a seat opposite to the entrance, with my back to the glass wall. That way I could observe the whole restaurant. I had been doing that since my nightmare started two days before: never sitting with my back to the door, always keeping an eye on everything happening around me, looking out for cops or killers.

The moment I saw the guy coming through the door I knew that he was trouble. Big trouble. His eyes looked weird. As he walked in, I scanned him from head to feet. I saw the bulge under his sweatshirt, and instantly knew that it was a gun. Bells started ringing in my head. "The Colombians found you, boy. You're dead. You can run but you can't hide." But then I noticed something strange: he was a redneck. Blond and blue eyed. Not the Latino killer I was expecting. Could he be an undercover cop? No, he didn't look like a cop. Unless he was a cop on drugs.

He looked me in the eyes and I froze. "Shit, I'm dead," I thought. "Redneck or not, cop or not, on drugs or not, he's here for me." To my surprise, he turned around and started screening the room. At that point my head almost exploded. I thought, "Look, that guy, he's weird, he's trouble, he's armed, he's probably a killer, he's looking for someone, and it doesn't seem to be you. Who else in this room is being chased?"

It took him a few seconds to screen the place because it was packed, probably due to the two-for-one promotion they had, which had actually gotten me there in the first place. I was starving and broke. They probably had that promotion often because their food was really bad. But people seemed to be enjoying their meals. They sat there chewing their burgers and not noticing the guy at all, who kept screening the room. When he was finished, he pulled two small machine guns from under his sweatshirt, holding one in each hand.

He was looking the other way, so I dove for cover under the table. Right after that he started shooting. I couldn't see much from the floor; I only heard shots and screams. Screaming the loudest, inside my head, was Mom.

"Pablo, how can you die wearing dirty underwear?"

Bang, bang, bang, bang, bang...

"You're a disgrace to the family! Shame on you!"

Bang, bang, bang, bang, bang...

"How could you do this to me?"

Bang, bang, bang, bang, bang...

Suddenly a guy fell down in front of me, interrupting the trance I was in. Where did he come from? Was he trying to reach the door? I couldn't tell. Anyway, there he was: big, fat, and dead. Shot in the head, among other places.

I had the silly idea to use his body for cover, as if his flesh could protect me from those bullets. Only luck could save me, and it was pure luck that saved me in the end. But at that moment I thought that it was a good idea, and I hid behind his big body. After that I didn't see or hear Mom anymore.

I couldn't tell how long it took; one, five, or even ten minutes. It seemed like the shots would never end. There were short pauses, probably when the guy was reloading his guns, but soon the shots resumed. Only the screams never stopped.

It was amazing how loud it was. The first shooting that I had witnessed only two days before had been very different. The killers had used silencers, and the guys died on the spot. I had seen their bodies pierced by the bullets and blood coming out of their heads and flesh wounds, but it was a silent affair. Here it was the opposite. I couldn't see anything, but I could hear gun shots and screams.

Eventually the shots stopped. Still lying on the floor behind the dead guy, I raised my head carefully and took a look. It was ugly. The floor in front of me was covered with bodies, including that of the shooter, who had apparently killed himself. I could see the two machine guns, a few handguns, and a lot of ammunition clips scattered on the floor around his body.

The wounded people were moaning loudly, but I didn't feel sorry for them. Instead, I felt a mix of relief, joy, gratitude, peace, and hope. The whole thing didn't concern me. It had only been a lunatic shooting people inside a fast-food restaurant. I had been expecting to be killed since I left California. When the guy had started shooting, I believed that the end had come. They had finally found me. It was over, and I was dead. But no! Those bullets weren't addressed specifically for me. They were only randomly fired. No Colombians or cops hunting me. Only a Texan redneck playing mass murderer. I was still alive, free, and on the run. When I understood that, I smiled.

But I couldn't stay there forever. I told myself, "Wake up, man! Focus! Get your ass out of here. The police are coming." I was about to stand up when I remembered that the guy I was hiding behind must have a wallet. He was dead and didn't need it anymore, and I desperately needed money.

I found the wallet in the back pocket of his pants, so I grabbed it and got up. Thanks to the bullets there was no glass wall behind me anymore. Good, that way I could avoid using the front door to get out. People from nearby stores on the strip were already gathering in front of the restaurant, too afraid to go inside. No one was at the back, from where I made my escape.

Moving very slowly to avoid calling attention to myself, I walked up a little hill behind the strip. From there, lying on the grass, I could watch the show from a safe distance. I saw the first of the wounded getting out, and police cars, fire trucks, and ambulances arriving.

* * *

I opened the wallet: four credit cards and $235. That was good. I looked for a password written somewhere but couldn't find any. I checked the driver's license for the guy's birthdate, since many people used their birthdates as passwords for their cards. He was John Thompson, born on September 30, 1948. I checked his address, and saw that he was from the town I was in. Since he was almost twenty years older than me, I wouldn't be able to use his driver's license as mine, so I threw it away.

I took off my jacket, which was soaked in blood. The clothes underneath weren't in much better condition. I had John's blood all over me. I needed clean clothes, otherwise I would never be able to hitchhike out of that Texas town. No one would stop for a guy covered in blood. Now I had money, but for the same reason

I couldn't just walk into a store to buy stuff. I had to steal clean clothes.

But how? Should I simply walk into someone's backyard in broad daylight and take whatever I want? I was scared. But I thought, even if someone saw me and called the police, would they come? Those small-town cops were probably too busy at the fast-food restaurant, finally getting some action after years of chasing drunk drivers. Anyway, I had no other choice, so I convinced myself that there must be a quota of bad things that could happen to a person on any given day. I'd had my full share. It was mathematically impossible for something bad to happen again. With that conviction I walked towards the residential area behind the strip.

It didn't take long to find clothes drying in the Texas sun. I stole a T-shirt, a flannel shirt, and a pair of jeans. Everything was a few sizes too big, but better bigger than smaller. I also got a towel to clean up with.

I found a place behind a bush where I could change my clothes. When I took my pants off, I noticed my mistake: I had forgotten the damn underwear.

That upset me a lot. Not because I forgot, but because I cared. Why should I? I sighed. "Focus, man! You're standing behind a bush, half-naked, thinking about dirty underwear. Why? You have more important stuff to worry about right now. You have to leave this town as soon as possible. Forget the underwear."

I finished changing and rubbed the towel on my face, hair, and hands to get rid of the bloodstains. Only the shoes were still covered with blood. I rubbed dirt on them and walked to the gas station in order to get a ride north.

[1/2]

Soon a truck driver going to Dallas agreed to take me. We exchanged small talk until the guy turned on the radio for a talk show. At about that moment we passed a television truck, one of those mobile units used for live broadcasting. It was almost certainly heading to that town to report on the shooting. Man, were they quick! "Television determines the time of the shooting..."

I remembered the shooting theory and had to smile. According to my best friend RW, a shooting inside a fast-food joint at lunchtime was the quintessential manifestation of American culture. It combined the three really important things in America: guns, dieting, and TV.

First there was a guy who was crazy for guns. He didn't have only one, but an arsenal big enough to arm a whole platoon; all the guns that his constitutional right allowed him to carry. And he wouldn't only carry them, he would fire them, like he had seen on TV all his life: bang, bang, bang, bang, bang...

Then there was dieting. Why did such massacres almost always happen inside fast-food restaurants? It wasn't a coincidence. It wasn't because you had a lot of people concentrated in one place. That was also true of streets or shopping malls, where shootings never happened. Streets were too open; no stage effect. The shopping mall was the place dedicated to the most sacred activity in American society. A shooting there would be a sacrilege, like shooting people in a church. The fast-food restaurant was the perfect place. While the whole nation starved to get in shape, those people were indulging themselves in high-fat, high-caloric junk food. Yes, they must be punished. Bang, bang, bang, bang, bang: die, you junk-food-eating scum!

Television determined the time of the shooting. Since you had to give reporters enough time to get to the scene, set up their satellite dishes, and get ready for live coverage, you had to shoot those junk-food-eating bastards at lunchtime, never in the evening. Otherwise you'd get no prime-time exposure, messing up your only opportunity in life, or in death, to be on TV.

* * *

RW's shooting theory was supposed to be a joke. Now it seemed that he had been right all along. I could only hope that he hadn't been right about the death joke as well, another story he loved to tell. A guy was walking down the street early in the morning when he saw Death. He didn't want to die, so he ran away to the opposite side of town. When he got there, he met Death again. Death told him, "Funny, I was supposed to meet you here today at exactly this time. I was surprised to see you this morning in that neighborhood so far away from here. I was worried that you'd miss our appointment. I'm glad that you made it in time!"

Had that happened to me? I had run away because I thought that death was looking for me in California. But had my real appointment with death been in Texas? And if so, why was I still alive?

When my nightmare started, I told myself, "Head east, young man, head east. Go to the East Coast. They expect you to head south and cross the border into Mexico. Don't do what they expect you to do. Go east instead." So in one and a half days I traveled about 2,000 miles through five states: California, Nevada, Arizona, New Mexico, and Texas, arriving in that small town in central Texas just in time to meet Death.

Why did I survive our encounter? Did the shooter screw up his assignment? Or was our meeting supposed to be somewhere else and Death was leading me to our final meeting place through shootings? There had already been two shootings in two days. California on Monday and Texas on Wednesday. Would there be a third, fatal one? And if yes, when and where?

* * *

On Monday I was leading a perfectly normal life, completely unaware that very soon it would change forever. I had classes until half past seven in the evening and got home at eight, longing for a shower and dinner. I almost had a heart attack when I found three guys inside my apartment pointing guns at me. I had never come so close to guns before.

At first I thought it was a robbery. Then one of the guys told me in Spanish, "Don't worry, Baldy, we're not going to hurt you. Take it easy. How were classes today?" He had a Mexican accent.

After I heard that, I flipped out. How did they know about "Baldy?" Nobody in California knew that nickname. Only my friend RW and others guys from my college years in New York City knew it. And only RW still used it.

If they knew my old nickname and what I had been doing that evening, then they had been observing me, checking my daily routine, maybe even tapping my phone. I called RW frequently. Was that how they had picked up Baldy? "Shit, it isn't robbery but kidnapping," I thought. They were after me, not my wallet.

The guy told me they were "cleaners" and were there for a "cleaning job." At around ten some people would show up with a special delivery for me. I was to open the door, accompanied by one of the cleaners. The other two would hide in the bathroom. I should let the delivery guys in and tell them to take the couch.

I had to sit in the armchair by the window, out of the line of fire. The cleaner staying in the living room would take the other armchair. If I stayed cool and didn't do anything stupid, they would let me live afterwards, they said. It was business between the cleaners and the delivery guys. I wasn't part of it.

I could only hope that they were telling the truth. But if I wasn't part of it, why should it happen inside my living room? The whole thing didn't seem real. That stuff only happened in the movies, not in real life, I thought.

* * *

We watched TV in silence while we waited. At the expected time the delivery guys arrived. Two cleaners went to hide in the bathroom. The third one went with me to open the door. The visitors were also three in number, and were carrying two suitcases. One greeted me in English. "Hi, Baldy! Nice to finally meet you!" That was very strange. All those people seemed to know me as Baldy. Why?

I invited them in and told them to sit on the couch. The cleaner and I took our designated places. The suitcases were placed on the coffee table and the delivery people opened them. They were full of cocaine. Shit, a drug deal.

It was bad that a drug deal was going on inside my apartment. It was even worse that the sellers thought that I was the one buying the stuff. But I could still live with that. Terrifying was the fact that those sellers were going to get killed in front of me.

I didn't stay terrified for long, though. All of a sudden the two cleaners came out of the bathroom, shooting. The cleaner in the living room started shooting, too.

It was frighteningly quiet but for the sound of the silencers. In the movies silencers sounded nice, but in real life they sounded very creepy. In a few seconds the three delivery guys were dead on my couch, covered in blood. I was shocked.

One of the guys noticed and smiled. "It's okay. There's no reason to fear. They're dead. Can't hurt you anymore!"

"At least it's over," I thought.

"Where are the keys to your car?"

Shit, they were going to steal my brand new BMW convertible! When I gave them the keys, they saw my watch, which Mom and Dad had given me for my eighteenth birthday.

"We wouldn't mind having the Rolex. Looks nice!"

I gave it to them. I thought, "Take everything and leave. I will then sit down and have a heart attack."

"Now move your ass! You're coming with us. When we get outside, if you try to run away, if you scream, if you do anything stupid, we'll shoot you!"

"I'm not coming!"

One of them walked over to me, placed his gun on my head, and smiled.

"You can stay if you want, but only as a dead body. So, what will it be?"

That wasn't part of the deal, but I didn't dare say anything. Why had I been so stupid to expect people like that to stick to deals? Maybe they only needed a hostage to get away, I hoped. They definitely weren't kidnappers.

They took the suitcases with the cocaine and we left the building together. We got into my car, two of the cleaners in the front, the third cleaner and me in the back.

The driver couldn't get the car to move because he couldn't shift gears manually. I hated automatic transmissions, and had paid extra to import a BMW with a manual transmission. It was much more fun to drive, and I had no intention of lending my car to anyone. I had never thought about carjackers.

"What the fuck is this?" the driver asked, pointing to the gear stick. "I can't drive this shit." The cleaner sitting next to him couldn't, either. The guy sitting next to me said that he could manage it. He and the driver changed places.

They were all very upset. Our getaway was taking much longer than it should have. The third guy didn't know how to shift into reverse. After five unsuccessful trials, I explained to him how to do it. He managed to back up and then to get the car moving forward, but it was a bumpy ride. Despite the life-threatening situation, I felt like crying. He was ruining my transmission.

But I was quickly reminded that there was much worse stuff to worry about. The guy sitting on my side put on gloves, cleaned his gun with a handkerchief, and handed it to me.

"Hold it, Baldy! Don't worry. It's not loaded anymore. It's just for the old fingerprint trick."

"You're not going to blame me for this shit, are you?"

"Just do what I say and shut up, man."

We drove in silence after that. After about an hour and a half on the interstate, they stopped and let me out. I checked the time on the car clock. It was almost midnight.

The driver pointed in the direction we had been traveling. "Listen, Baldy, if you keep walking this way, you'll reach a gas station soon. There you can get a ride south. Keep going until you reach Mexico. Don't go back to Stanford. Those people we killed have a lot of friends, not only in California but all over the country. If they catch you, you're dead. Take care, man. Nice meeting you."

So there I was, in the middle of the interstate, looking south. I had to disappear before the friends of the dead drug dealers started chasing me. I didn't know who they were, but they seemed to know me well, including my nickname. How many hours did I have until they heard about the shooting?

I tried to hitchhike, but no one stopped for me. The cleaners were right: I needed to get to the gas station and try my luck there. It wasn't close, though. I walked south for a long time. They probably wanted to be very far away when I finally got there. Were they afraid that I would call the police?

* * *

I reached the gas station at about two in the morning. I was tired and scared, but at least I had made up my mind about what to do next. I wasn't going to call anyone. I was going to disappear for a few days.

Going north wasn't an alternative because I wasn't going back home. I didn't want to follow their advice, either. If south was the direction they went, why should I risk meeting those guys again? They were dangerous. West was out of the question. I would hit a big ocean very soon. The only option was going east.

I had never hitchhiked in my life and didn't know how to approach drivers. It took me a very long time to get a ride. It was almost four in the morning when an old truck driver named Chuck agreed to take me to Las Vegas, his final destination.

I was tired but too excited to sleep. Probably too much adrenaline in my bloodstream. At first it was very difficult to keep a conversation going. I needed to invent plausible answers for questions like what my name was, where I was from, where I was going to, why I didn't have any luggage, etc.

But that didn't last long. As I would later experience many times, after asking a few questions, drivers lost interest in me and started talking about themselves. That was the reason why they picked me up, I supposed: to talk about their lives and their petty problems. I wasn't interested in Chuck's life. If he was going to talk, he should talk about stuff that I wanted to listen to. At that moment I badly needed an education in hitchhiking.

"Could you teach me a few things, Chuck?"

It was a long drive to Las Vegas, and Chuck taught me a lot: the dos and don'ts of hitchhiking; how to recognize drivers at a gas station willing to take you and how best to approach them; the best interstates to travel; and so on. He explained the layout of the interstate network. The highway numbering system was simple: north-south highways had odd numbers, growing larger from west to east; east-west highways had even numbers, growing larger from south to north. He said that after we arrived in Las Vegas I should move south to Arizona and get onto I-40. Once on I-40 I would be able to travel fast all the way to the East Coast.

Chuck didn't like eating in interstate restaurants. Bad food, he said. He had sandwiches and fruit, which he shared with me. I offered him money, but he refused. "You're my guest!" We only stopped to use the restroom and fill up the tank, and reached Vegas in the early afternoon. He let me off at a gas station outside the city.

I was lucky that the killers hadn't taken my wallet. I still had my driver's license, a credit card, a debit card, and $120. First thing I bought was a newspaper. But the shooting had happened too late Monday evening to make the Tuesday papers. Then I went for a quick meal at a fast-food joint close to the gas station. When I tried to pay with my credit card, it was rejected. I found it strange but didn't connect things at the time. I paid cash, found a table at the back of the restaurant, and ate my meal. All the time I was watching everything that was happening around me. I feared that at any moment someone would come in looking for me.

After lunch I tried to get money from an ATM machine at the gas station. The machine swallowed my credit card. It was very strange. Yes, I was nervous and maybe had entered the wrong password. But shouldn't the machine give me at least three chances before swallowing the card? I tried the debit card, and the machine swallowed it, too. Something was definitely wrong, but I didn't know what. "Well, I can call the bank later when I arrive in a safe place," I thought. They would wire me money. I still had my driver's license to prove my identity.

I bought a map at the gas station and started putting into practice what Chuck had taught me. I was lucky, and in less than half an hour I got a ride south to Arizona. After two more rides I reached I-40. Then I started moving east quickly.

I crossed the border into New Mexico at around midnight, only twenty-four hours after being let out of my car in the middle of I-5 in California. I was very happy with my progress.

[1/3]

At about six in the morning I arrived in Amarillo, Texas, where I could buy the Wednesday paper. I went to a diner to read it over breakfast, and quickly found a very long article on the shooting. The dead delivery men were part of the Gonzalez crime family, Colombian drug traffickers. Two of them were brothers, and the third one was an undercover agent of the Drug Enforcement Administration. A sting operation had been going on for months. According to DEA sources, the cleaners belonged to the Rodriguez crime family, Mexican traffickers. The Mexicans probably knew that the DEA agent had successfully infiltrated the Colombians. That would explain the killings.

So far so good. At least now I knew who would be hunting me: Colombians. I was still enjoying my breakfast. But then the information started getting weird. I was supposed to be a big shot in the Rodriguez family. That was offensive: me, a Mexican drug dealer. I was Central American, not Mexican. When would Americans finally learn the difference?

Before being killed that night, the DEA agent had reported a series of deals with the Mexican clan, and I, "Pablo, aka Baldy," was his contact. He had never met me personally. It was supposed to be our first meeting. "Hi, Baldy, nice to finally meet you..."

A Mexican drug dealer was pretending to be me. Who was he? One thing I knew: he was not only smart but also dangerous, as I had witnessed. Smart and dangerous was always a bad combination. I lost my appetite and stopped eating.

The paper reported that one of my neighbors saw me leaving the building accompanied by three guys. He noted how long it had taken to get the car moving and found everything very suspicious, especially the change of drivers. The police had found the car abandoned on I-5, outside Santa Clara. They also found the gun that I had "forgotten" under the seat. The ballistic tests showed that it was one of the guns used at the shooting. The fingerprints matched mine. "It's just for the old fingerprint trick…"

I wasn't the witness of a murder; I was supposed to be the killer, and a drug trafficker. How could I prove that I hadn't done it? And until I found out, what other option did I have besides running away? Not only were the Colombians after me, but the Feds, too.

But the bad news wasn't over yet. The Feds claimed that I had accounts at three banks that I had never even heard of. Bank records showed suspicious activity on those accounts, a classic case of money laundering.

Someone had opened accounts in my name to launder money, and I was getting all the blame. But how could that person have done it? I remembered that my wallet had been stolen a year before in Stanford, just as I started my MBA. Maybe it hadn't been the work of an ordinary pickpocket, but of someone who was after my driver's license to open those accounts. If true, then that scheme had been going on for one year already. How many more crimes were committed using my name?

Then came the icing on the cake. The Colombians had put a $100,000 bounty on my head for killing the two brothers. That would set a lot of bounty hunters on my trail, the paper speculated, who would probably get to me before the police did.

The setup was perfect. Whoever masterminded it was a professional. No matter how much I thought about it, I couldn't figure out who that person was or why he had let me go instead of having me killed. Was he someone close to me, who liked me and wanted me to live? Or had the cleaners felt sorry for me and disregarded their instructions to kill me? No, maybe that was also part of the plan. The cleaners let me go because they most likely had instructions to do so. The guy who had set me up probably hoped that I would run away. I did have a clean criminal record up to that point. By running away I admitted that I was guilty. That also set the Colombians on my trail.

Then it occurred to me that only the Feds could have blocked my cards. That made me aware of leaving a trail behind: an electronic trail. I remembered Vegas and panicked; the ATM machine had swallowed my cards in Las Vegas. The Feds would know by now that I didn't go south but east. I could be going east to New York City or Miami, but definitely not south to Mexico. What if they started checking the roads in those directions?

Chuck the truck driver would remember me. He had picked me up not very far from Stanford. What if he called the cops and told them about me? About our conversation, about my intention to go east, about how he suggested that I get onto I-40? Every cop in every small town along I-40 could be looking for me at that very moment.

I saw that my hands were shaking. I looked around, but no one in the diner seemed to have noticed my state of shock. Everyone was having their breakfast and minding their own business. I decided to leave I-40 immediately and move south instead. Down to the Gulf Coast, where I could try to board a ship out of the country. I checked my map. There was a road going south through Amarillo. I stood up and left.

I found a truck driver who had to deliver stuff to a small town about one hour north of Austin. He told me that from there I would be able to get a ride to Austin or Houston very easily. I accepted immediately, not knowing that I would be traveling to meet Death. The truck driver let me out on the strip shortly before noon. I was hungry and went to that fast-food restaurant. What bad timing.

* * *

But I had survived the shooting! I was still alive, and was now on a truck heading north to Dallas, back on the run as before. Well, not exactly as before, because something had definitely changed: I was awake again. Watching those three drug dealers getting killed right before my eyes had made me freeze. It turned me into a robot, and I sleepwalked for thirty-six hours. That sleepwalker considered himself an innocent victim of fate. Life was being nasty to him and people were doing mean things to him, but he was the good guy, not fighting back, not doing anything wrong, and not breaking any law.

The second shooting changed that. It must have been the loud shots: bang, bang, bang, bang, bang... That noise woke up the survivor in me. The caveman. Now that caveman was whispering in my ears, "Stop being a pussy, man! The caveman is no victim! The caveman has no fears! The caveman has no regrets! The caveman must do whatever it takes to survive!"

The caveman was wanted for murder, drug trafficking, and money laundering. What difference would it make if he committed a few more crimes? Stealing clothes from a backyard or taking someone else's wallet: that was only theft. There was much more that the caveman was able and willing to do. I decided to return to my original plan and go east, but not on I-40. In Dallas I got a ride east on I-20. After all, those cops could still be out there looking for me. The caveman had no fears, but he wasn't stupid.

[1/4]

After we crossed the border into Louisiana, I asked the driver to let me out at the first small town we came to. It was late afternoon, and time was running out. Sooner or later John's credit cards would be blocked. I had to move quickly. It was time for the caveman to commit fraud.

First I tried to get cash advances. I found an ATM machine and tried four possible combinations for John's birthdate: 3009, 0930, 1948, and 0948, one with each card. After what had happened in Vegas, I was afraid that the machine would swallow a card if I entered the wrong password twice, even though I knew that we normally had three chances. It was pure paranoia, but I wasn't able to control it. I couldn't lose those cards. People normally used the same password for all cards. I hoped that if I could get it right for only one of John's cards, I would get it for all of them. But all four passwords were rejected.

I moved on to plan B, which was to buy two hundred dollars' worth of stuff and charge it to the credit cards. I didn't need a password for that, I only needed to fake John's signature. In case none of the cards worked, I could still excuse myself and pay cash.

Having lived in America for so long, I knew that many people never paid off their credit-card debt. They only paid the minimum amount on the bill and requested a new card from another bank. Not only their debt but also their number of credit cards kept growing. Why they still carried the old cards with the used-up credit lines was something that I could never understand. If John was carrying four cards, he could be one of those people.

It was not uncommon to have a card rejected at checkout. It happened to me in Vegas, and it was no big deal. What I didn't know was how many rejected cards it took to make someone suspicious of you. I was ready to find out.

I went to a discount store. The first thing I grabbed was, of course, clean underwear: a dozen pairs. Then a backpack, T-shirts, shirts, two pairs of jeans, socks, a jacket, a towel, toiletries, and some food. Everything cheap, but you couldn't get much for $200. It was the first time in my life that I bought cheap stuff because I had to and not because I wanted to. What a difference! Counting your money was such a degrading experience. I was about to get depressed when the caveman intervened. "Focus, man! Control yourself. You still have to keep a straight face if the cards are rejected."

The cashier was a very young girl, maybe seventeen. She looked nice and bored to death.

"Two hundred seventeen dollars and thirty-five cents."

I handed her the first card. Rejected. I smiled. She smiled back. I was embarrassed and scared. I had to say something.

"You lose track of your spending when you're traveling."

"Sure! Where you from?"

Great, she showed interest.

"New York City."

"A long way from home. You enjoying Louisiana?"

The ice was broken.

"Oh, great place! Very friendly people. Much better than Texas!"

The second card was rejected, too. I was sweating, but she seemed relaxed and happy to have someone to talk to.

"Glad to hear that you like it here. I had the same problem with my cards when I went to New Orleans last year."

"New Orleans? That's where I'm heading!"

She talked about running out of money in New Orleans and having to call her dad to wire her some. I gave her the third card. It was accepted; what a relief. I signed the slip with a trembling hand. It was the first time in my life that I had faked a signature.

After that I only wanted to get out of there. But she went on talking. Had I heard about the shooting across the border in Texas?

"Nope."

Blah, blah, blah, blah, blah...

"How many? Oh, how terrible!"

Blah, blah, blah, blah, blah...

"I've gotta go."

Blah, blah, blah, blah, blah...

"Have a nice day!"

Now I knew more about John's credit cards. I had two lemons, a winner, and an unknown. I went to a shoe store and got a pair of sneakers and a pair of leather shoes.

"One hundred twenty-two dollars and ninety-nine cents."

I tried the unknown card. Rejected. The guy looked at me, at my shopping bags, and smiled.

"Seems that you've done too much shopping today, John."

He called me John. I couldn't believe that people would react to it so naturally.

"Try this other one, sir."

"Call me Bob."

It worked.

"Thank you very much, Bob! Have a nice day!"

Yes, I had a winner! How much more money would be left on the card's credit line? I was now relaxed enough to find out. I went on a shopping spree in that Louisiana border town. I bought stuff that I could possibly need on the road: a pocketknife, a plastic wristwatch with alarm clock, a Walkman, some tapes, batteries, sun glasses, a winter jacket, more clothing, more food, and a bigger backpack to carry everything. I spent more than $600, and the card was still going strong. Too bad there was nothing else that I needed. You should travel light, especially when on the run.

While shopping I had depressing feelings again. My twenty-thousand-dollar Rolex was gone. Now I was the proud owner of a plastic wristwatch made in Korea. I had left behind a fifty-thousand-dollar stereo and a collection of more than 1,400 vinyl records. Now I had a Walkman and ten tapes. How deep I had fallen.

* * *

It was almost seven when I finished shopping. I was very hungry but couldn't walk into another fast-food restaurant that evening. So I went directly to the town's motel, badly in need of a shower and a good night's sleep. I hadn't slept in a bed since

Sunday night.

To check into the motel I had to use my driver's license. Therefore, it wasn't possible to pay for the night with John's credit card. I had cash again, and the joint was less than thirty dollars a night so I could afford it. But I was afraid of being recognized. What if the person at the front desk had heard about the shooting in California? It had made the national papers, probably even the local papers in Louisiana. They had printed my name and my picture. Besides that, I also looked very suspicious, wearing over-sized clothes and carrying a lot of shopping bags but no luggage.

I hoped that the shooting in Texas would be my salvation. It had been much worse than the one in California, and it was still hot news. All the way from Dallas the radio talked only about it. The truck driver was very quiet, savoring every detail. The girl at the discount store was very excited about it. I hoped that the person manning the front desk at the motel would be interested, too. Probably too distracted watching TV to care about me.

Luckily, I was right. Check-in was quick and easy. The TV was on, and the guy had his eyes glued to it. He checked me in as quickly as possible.

The room was a real dump, worse than I had expected. I had never stayed in a cheap hotel before. But at least it had hot water. I urgently needed a hot shower. When I undressed, I couldn't avoid seeing my dirty underwear, and Mom immediately popped up in my head. "You're so vulgar, Pablo! So disgusting!"

* * *

Unfortunately, I had inherited Mom's dirty-underwear para-noia. She always said that it was a shame if you were caught wear-ing dirty underwear. People would think that you were a low-class person. Worse, they would ask, "In what kind of family did this guy grow up? Did his mother never teach him the basics of per-sonal hygiene?" In short, she would be blamed for my disgusting behavior. Therefore, I should never do it. "Never! Did you hear me, Pablo? Never!"

Useless to tell her that nobody would see your underwear un-less you wanted them to. After all, you decided when to undress or not. She always replied that it wasn't true. You could have an accident, be taken to a hospital, and have your clothes taken off. Then, if you were wearing dirty underwear, "Shame on you,

Pablo! It's so vulgar! So low class!"

I had learned this at early age, and I had always followed Mom's advice. Now for the first time in my life I had been wearing the same underwear for days. That was driving me crazy. How upsetting it was to watch those stains grow. They were not only disgusting. Those stains were a bad omen foretelling a very dark future for me. They reminded me of the undress-you-at-the-hospital scene. Suddenly I had an equation popping up inside my head: Dirty underwear equals accident equals emergency room. I knew exactly what the accident would be: a shooting. So the equation quickly became dirty underwear equals shot to death.

I had never been aware of the existence of that equation. It was certainly the result of Mom's brainwashing. How much more weird stuff from my upbringing was still buried deep inside my brain that I didn't know of?

In the few moments of sanity that I had before the second shooting, I kept telling myself not to worry so much about the whole thing. The dirty underwear had no meaning whatsoever, and it was probably normal to have such weird thoughts in the state of confusion and shock that I found myself in. But why did I have to think about the damn underwear at the very moment that I was going to die? Wasn't there more important stuff to think about? What about the movie? What about the cosmic experience?

* * *

I took a long shower and got dressed; what a great feeling to be clean again. It was around eight, and I was starving. I sat down to eat, thinking about how wonderful it would be if I could continue using John's credit card on the road, saving cash. When John's relatives eventually found out about his missing wallet, they would block all his cards. How many days did I have? One? Two?

John was a local, so the identification must have happened in the afternoon. He didn't come home after lunch, and so his wife or daughter or mother or whoever certainly went looking for him. Being such a small town, it probably took less than one hour for everyone to hear about the shooting, with all those police cars, fire trucks, and ambulances cruising around.

The lady rushed to the restaurant sometime in the afternoon and realized that John was dead. What did she do? Call her relatives? Cry like crazy? Call the funeral home? She certainly didn't ask, "Where is his wallet?" She would probably only realize that John's wallet was missing when she got his personal belongings back from the morgue.

So, next question: how long did it take to get the dead person's belongings back from the morgue? Nobody told you this stuff. I had never cared to know, either. It was not the first time since Monday that I wished I knew the answer to a very trivial question. It seemed to me that my survival depended on it.

I had never been to a morgue. Yes, I had seen them in the movies a lot of times. The at-the-morgue identification scene. The wife crying, "Yes, it's him..." Someone putting an arm around her shoulder. "I'm so sorry..." But after that there was always a cut, and they showed the burial. Never anything about personal belongings. Did the relatives get the stuff after the identification? Did the morgue hand everything over to the funeral home? Did the police keep it as evidence? I had no idea.

I finished eating and turned on the TV for news on the shooting. The known facts were very few. Sixty people had been inside the restaurant, they said. Only five didn't get hurt. Among the fifty-five people shot, forty-five were already dead, and the remaining ten were badly wounded and receiving intensive medical care. That was good news: I had escaped unnoticed. The shooter had been identified. He was a local; Vietnam veteran, unemployed, drug problems. He left no note behind, so his motives were unclear. Besides that information, everything else was speculation and drama, as always.

They showed crying relatives, who all looked alike and sounded the same. Amazing how tacky such tragedies could be. There were uncountable interviews with people who hadn't been there and had no clue. I asked myself why they didn't interview the town's undertaker instead. "Mr. Black, can your facilities accommodate this unexpected increase in demand?"

At some point they showed an interview with the big-bellied police officer who was running the show. I thought, that was probably the guy who told John's wife that John was dead. Then I had an insight: unless that cop had met John before, how could he know John's identity if I took the wallet with the driver's license? He couldn't. Therefore, they found out that John's wallet was missing when they tried to identify him in the restaurant, very early in the afternoon. When John's wife got there and asked, no one knew who John was because John had no ID on him.

"No one with that name, ma'am, but an unidentified body. Can you describe your husband?"

Blah, blah, blah, blah, blah...

"The description fits the victim, ma'am. I'm really sorry to tell you this. Could you please go to the morgue for a positive identification?"

Then the morgue movie scene was played.

Tears. "Yes, it's him..."

Arm around the shoulder. "I'm sorry, but why wasn't he carrying any ID?"

"He always has his driver's license in his wallet."

"No wallet, ma'am."

That was it. The relatives had already been informed, and all cards would be blocked very soon. I wouldn't risk using the good one anymore. What a waste to get rid of a card with such an apparent high credit limit.

I turned off the TV. I was very tired and needed to sleep. It had been a long day, and a very important one, too. On Wednesday, October sixteenth, 1991, I was reborn. I was now the caveman. I could steal. I could lie. I could commit fraud.

And I didn't feel guilty about it.

[1/5]

I didn't hear my wristwatch alarm clock in the morning. I overslept and woke up at two in the afternoon. Actually someone woke me up, trying to open the door. Luckily I had put the chain on. I jumped from bed, scared to death, thinking, "They found you, boy! You can run but you can't hide!"

But it was only the cleaning lady. She didn't know that the room was occupied since I had booked for one night only and checkout time was noon. If I was staying another night, I should tell front desk and pay for it, she said.

I didn't want to spend another night there. I convinced the front-desk guy to charge me only five dollars for overstaying and left at three. Now wearing clean clothes and carrying a backpack like a normal traveler, I hoped to get rides more easily.

At around four I got my first ride and continued my trip east on I-20, traveling the rest of the day and the whole night through

Louisiana, Mississippi, and Alabama, entering Georgia shortly before dawn on Thursday. I had breakfast in Atlanta, where I bought a newspaper, but couldn't find anything about the shooting in California. The one in Texas was now the only news people cared about. That was good.

I hit the road again after breakfast, this time traveling north on I-75. After studying my map carefully, I decided to change direction and move north first, all the way to a town in northern Ohio where I-75 met I-80. There I would get onto I-80 and travel east again on a straight line from Ohio to New York City.

If I had stayed on I-20, it would have taken me to South Carolina, to where it met I-95, which connected the whole East Coast from Florida to Maine. If the Feds thought that I was traveling to the East Coast, as I feared Chuck the truck driver had told them, then I-95 would be the next interstate to watch. I could have only two possible destinations: Miami or New York City, the only cities besides Stanford where I had lived in America and where I had friends. I could reach both of them on I-95. If there were cops out there watching I-95, it was safer to travel north on I-75.

* * *

If everything worked out according to my plan, I would arrive in New York City on Sunday, covering fifteen states in one week. I had already traveled through nine: California, Nevada, Arizona, New Mexico, Texas, Louisiana, Mississippi, Alabama, and Georgia. Ahead of me: Tennessee, Kentucky, Ohio, Pennsylvania, New Jersey, and New York.

What an education that trip was. I didn't see much besides the inside of trucks and cars, the endless road ahead, gas stations, and fast-food joints. But I met and talked to a lot of people, mostly poor rednecks. Rich guys in nice cars never gave me a ride. It was always the farmer in his pickup truck, the guy in the run-down car, the truck driver. They picked me up because they were lonely and wanted to talk. But they weren't real conversations. Basically they talked to themselves. They did ask me the few standard questions in the beginning: where I was heading to, where I was from, what I did for a living, and so on. After getting that part behind them, they started their monologues.

At first I loved it. I didn't want to talk about myself, so I appreciated my role as listener. But soon it became unbearable. How

I wished they would shut up. When they did, it was to listen to talk shows on the radio. And that was even scarier. I had never heard so much paranoia in my whole life.

Amazing that I had lived in America for seven years and had never known about those radio talk shows. I knew and loved the afternoon talk shows on television. I used to tape them to watch whenever I had the time. Afternoon television talk shows were trashy but entertaining. Those radio talk shows were simply scary.

We never traveled in silence. It was either the driver complaining about his petty problems or a paranoid talk-show host warning about dubious conspiracies. Worse, when the talk show was over, the driver started to elaborate on what the talk-show host had said on the radio, sometimes going on for hours.

I couldn't stop thinking about Carlos, Dad's new political adviser. I had met him when I visited my parents in the summer, on my last trip home. Carlos was a distant relative of ours. He moved to America in the sixties, went to college, and later made a career in politics as a consultant.

When we were forced to end our dictatorship and re-democratize the country, Carlos saw a window of opportunity and moved back. No one down there had his expertise, so he would have the market to himself. Dad became a client. He invited Carlos to our house for dinner so that I could meet him. Carlos talked a lot, like most consultants. He explained his concept of the "culture wars" and how to wage them.

Our dictatorship was gone. Now we had a bunch of left-wing people endowed with civil rights. How to stop them from pursuing their economic agenda? How to stop them from forming unions, going on strike, demanding handouts from the state?

The answer, according to Carlos, was to wage the cultural wars, like they did in America. It was very simple, he said: you just fired people up with irrelevant but very emotional stuff, and they spent all their energy getting very upset about it instead of fighting for their economic and political rights.

It didn't really matter what. Theoretically, anything would do. Carlos said that in America they used issues like gun control, flag burning, school prayer, etc. If it worked in America, it would work for us, too. The challenge was to find the right emotional issues to fire up our poor. And that would be his job.

He even had the guts to quote Karl Marx, a subject that always upset Dad. The mention alone of the guy's name made Dad mad. To Dad it was never only "Karl Marx" but "Karl Marx, the asshole who started all our problems." Marx once said that religion was the opium of the people. Marx was right, Carlos believed. People needed opium to stay docile. But why use religion if we had much more powerful tools? The culture wars were "opium on steroids," he said smiling.

Dad also smiled when he heard that. It was the first time in my life that I saw him smile in connection with Karl Marx. Unbelievable! Dad had totally fallen for that guy Carlos. How could Dad be so gullible? I couldn't believe any of it. Carlos was selling Dad snake oil. Culture wars? Bullshit! I had lived in America for so many years. How come I had never noticed those culture wars? People were not that stupid. Not in America, not back home.

It took me only a few days on the road to realize that I had been wrong and Carlos right. Even more upsetting was realizing once again that Dad never lost. He had found the perfect guy to help him. Carlos was a gift from heaven.

The whole concept was very simple, very clever, and it worked wonderfully. Flag burning was my first encounter with opium on steroids on Tuesday afternoon. Cruising I-40 in Arizona, one truck driver bitched and moaned about flag burning for almost two hours, as if it was the most important issue in his life. Didn't he have more pressing problems? Before the talk show he had told me about missing mortgage payments and how bad his job was: low wage, long hours, and so on. Shouldn't he concentrate his anger on improving his life? No, he was too busy fighting the culture wars, just like Carlos had said.

After the shooting in Texas, gun control became the one and only opium on steroids people talked about. Not for it but against it. There was fear that liberals would use the shooting to introduce stricter gun control. Gun control was not the solution but the problem, they all explained. If people inside the fast-food joint had been armed, they could have shot back and killed that lunatic. The poor innocent victims died because they were unarmed, not because the shooter was armed.

"If I had been there, I would have shot that bastard!" I heard that all the time, always wondering if I would have survived the carnage if there had been even more shooters in the room firing even more bullets.

* * *

Immersed in a non-stop lecture on the dangers of gun control, delivered by paranoid talk-show hosts and drivers, I crossed the rest of Georgia, the whole of Tennessee and Kentucky, and most of Ohio, arriving in northern Ohio at nine in the evening on Friday. I went to a motel and checked in for two nights.

It was a bold but calculated move. Staying in a motel meant showing my driver's license and leaving a trace. I hoped that if the Feds ever heard about my stop there, it would set them on the wrong trail. Louisiana motel on Wednesday night followed by northern Ohio motel on Friday night could mean only one thing: I was on my way to Canada. Someone going to New York City or Miami would never make such a strange detour. If they concluded that I had escaped to Canada, they could even stop looking for me in America.

Besides sending the Feds on the wrong trail, I urgently needed to catch up on lost sleep. After my motel stop in Louisiana I knew that I wouldn't be able to wake up early on Saturday. I also needed to go shopping. So I decided to spend two nights there, leaving for New York early Sunday morning. If traffic conditions were good, it took about twelve hours driving non-stop to travel from Northern Ohio to New York City, a few truck drivers had told me. Early evening would be a good time to arrive in New York. What I needed to do was best done after dark.

It was great to take Saturday off. How I enjoyed the silence! I slept until noon and went shopping in the afternoon. I bought two alarm clocks, a wool cap, and a toy gun, a perfect replica of a .38 for less than ten dollars. Back in the motel I made two holes in the wool cap for my eyes so that I could use it as a mask. I spent Saturday evening in bed, listening to music on my Walkman and reading the newspaper. There was nothing about the shooting in California, but a lot about the one in Texas.

Before going to bed I set up my two new alarm clocks to five in the morning. No way would I oversleep again. Then I went through my whole plan again. It had two parts. Part one, to be executed in my first twenty-four hours in New York, would be the quick and dirty one, bringing me money and a place to hide. Part two would be much longer and would depend on a lot of luck. I had to find the only person who could help me, and I had no idea how long the search would take.

Sunday morning I got on the road at around six in the morning. I traveled through Ohio, Pennsylvania, and New Jersey, getting to New York City at almost eight in the evening. I was nervous. Would I be able to do the job? And afterwards, would I find a safe haven?

[1/6]

It felt strange to be in New York again. I had been there for New Year's Eve, but it seemed like ten years had passed instead of only ten months. I took the subway in the direction of JFK airport. What I planned to do couldn't be done downtown. I got off at Rockaway Boulevard subway station and walked down Cross Bay Boulevard until I found the bank that I was looking for. It had a drive-through ATM at the back.

The plan was simple. I would hide in the dark and wait. A four-door car would eventually come by. The driver would open the car window to stick his card into the ATM. I would then put my mask on, run towards him, and put the gun on his head. I would open the back door, or make him open it, and sit right behind him. With the gun on his head, I would make him take as much money as possible from the ATM. Afterwards I would make him drive towards Coney Island. Somewhere, probably around Marine Park, I would make him stop, get out of the car, and into the trunk. With him inside the trunk, I would drive to Coney Island, park the car there, and take the train to Manhattan. It would take some time for him to free himself, so I would get away without a problem.

Looking back, how stupid that plan was. Why did I have a pathological fascination with ATM machines? Just because it was the way I used to get cash didn't mean that it was the only possible way. But I knew that people would have money after they had used the machine, and I wanted that money.

The first car was a minivan. No trunk. After a while, a car came with two people inside. I couldn't handle two people. I waited for the third car. Two doors only. That was out of the question. When I was about to despair, I saw a four-door car with a big trunk coming. Perfect. A woman alone. Wonderful. That was it!

She opened the window and stuck the card into the ATM. I looked around. There was no one to be seen. I put my mask on and ran towards her. She almost had a heart attack when she felt the gun on her head. So did I. Shit, she was one of those four-hundred-pound people you only met in America. She was huge. There was no way I could ever put that woman inside a trunk. The plan was flawed.

But it was too late now, so I opened the back door and jumped inside. I put the gun on her neck and yelled, "What are you waiting for? Get the money. I have a gun to your head, and if you don't do what I say, you're dead!"

She started saying something, but I interrupted her.

"Shut your mouth and get money from the machine!"

She gave me one hundred dollars.

"What the fuck? I want one thousand! Do it again."

"All I can get is three hundred a day!"

Damn, low ATM withdrawal limits. Not everyone's limit was as high as mine. How could I have overlooked that detail? The plan was severely flawed.

"Get the rest and give me your purse."

I was sweating. My shirt was all wet, like I had taken a shower with it on. What if someone drove up? We couldn't park there forever. She gave me the $200. I gave her another credit card. She had a bunch of them in her wallet.

"We'll try all your cards, starting with this one!"

"There is no money left on this card..."

"Why are you carrying it, then? Listen, ma'am, I want money. Do you hear me? Money! Here are all your cards. You know which ones you can use. Get me money, now, or I'll kill you!"

She was now trembling and crying. "I'll try this one; it's new."

"Give me one thousand!"

"I can't get more than three hundred!"

Shit. It was not enough, and the whole thing was taking too long. What if someone saw us and called the police?

She gave me the money.

"Try the others!"

"There's not much left," she protested.

"I don't care. Try them all."

"Maybe I can still get one hundred from this one..."

I saw another car coming. I lowered my head so that no one

would see me. It felt like I was in a sauna. I was having difficulty breathing because of the mask. My head was aching, and my hands were shaking.

"Listen, ma'am, now behave yourself. Don't do anything suspicious or I'll kill you. Get the money out of the machine and drive slowly out of here."

She did it. She was more nervous than I was. When we were on the road, I could get my head up again.

"Give me the money and the cards!"

I told her to get on the parkway and drive to Coney Island, according to the plan. Stupid plan. There was no way I could get her inside the trunk. I had to skip that part and go directly to Brighton Beach. I wouldn't be able to get away as easily as I had hoped.

All that trouble for $700. I was pissed off. Fear was turning slowly into frustration and anger.

* * *

We drove in silence for a long time. Jamaica Bay, Marine Park, Brooklyn. I told her to get off the parkway and drive towards Brighton Beach. When we were on Coney Island Avenue, almost at our destination, she started.

"Have you heard about Jesus?"

I froze. A born-again Christian? Please no, not now!

"Shut up, bitch!"

"Jesus loves you! He'll forgive you. I love you too, brother. I know that you're a sinner, but you have a good soul. You're doing this out of desperation. But you won't despair anymore if you let me tell you about Jesus."

"I've already told you to shut up!"

"He'll set you free. Let me tell you about Jesus."

I went berserk and started screaming. "Shut up, now! If you don't, I'll kill you! Shut up, bitch!"

I was pressing the gun so hard against her neck that she yelled, "You're hurting me!"

"And you are getting on my fucking nerves! Get off the road!" The beach wasn't very far. Maybe half a mile. "Stop here! Now! And give me the keys!"

I couldn't make any mistake. I had the keys, so she couldn't drive away. That was good. She was too fat to follow me. That was also good. But she could still make a car stop for her, get help from someone. That was bad. How much time did I have? It would take at least two or three minutes until someone came to her rescue. I would be gone by then, already on the boardwalk, out of sight. Once on the boardwalk, the subway station was about one mile away. I could make a run for it in less than ten minutes.

"Brother, why are you doing this? Can't you see that what you're doing is wrong? Let me tell you about Jesus!"

"Shut up, you fucking bitch! Just shut up!"

"Maybe Jesus planned this whole thing. He knew that I would tell you about him."

I couldn't take it anymore. I still had the gun on her neck, so I pulled the trigger. Once, twice, three times, four times, until I remembered that it was only a toy gun. And that made me even more upset. At that moment I really wished that it were a real gun. Man, what a monster I had become. I wanted to kill her just to make her shut up.

She was too excited to notice anything and kept mumbling about Jesus. I opened the door, took off my mask, and ran towards the beach, quickly getting onto the boardwalk. It was a cold evening and there weren't many people around, so I could keep running without calling much attention. But even if it looked suspicious, I didn't have a choice but to run.

I had always loved Coney Island. In my college years I used to go there whenever I wanted to see the ocean. I also loved that subway station; my favorite in New York. The place looked as if nothing had changed since the forties. But I had no time to enjoy the station's atmosphere. When I finally arrived there, I jumped on the train and got out of Coney Island.

If the gun hadn't been a toy, I would be a murderer. Not in self-defense, but to make someone shut up. That was scary. I was going to hell, I thought, and would burn there forever.

[1/7]

I could never understand born-again Protestants. Life was so simple when you were Catholic. You were born, and you became one automatically. You didn't have to "choose Jesus," like those folks did. You didn't have to be born again, either. Being born once was more than enough.

As a Catholic you had to understand one thing only: you were a sinner. It was your nature. There was nothing you could do about it. It was all Adam's fault, and you inherited it. The original sin. Once you accepted this fact, life became very easy. You went to church periodically and confessed, unloading your sins and making room for new ones. God always forgave you. He knew it was in your nature to be a sinner. He created you, after all.

One day you died. Provided you hadn't done anything really bad like killing someone, according to the credits you had you went directly to heaven or spent time in purgatory. Purgatory was bad, but eventually you got your upgrade. Not because you deserved it, but because God was merciful. It was a present God gave you. There was nothing you could do to influence God's decisions. He owned the place and called the shots.

Born-again people saw things differently. You could change your destiny regardless of what God thought about you. You could stop being a sinner and climb up your own private stairway to heaven. You just had to do the right thing. Go by the book. Follow the rules. It was a meritocracy. You went to heaven because you deserved it. You deserved it because you were good and righteous. Mercy was for suckers.

I had to admit that I enjoyed the funny sides of the born-again crowd. Like televangelists, for example. Great to watch, almost as good as the afternoon talk shows. Especially when they started praying like they had a direct line to God. They just dialed and got through. Then they went on for hours. Afterwards they asked people to send the money. And then there was their fascination with the apocalypse.

Back in Stanford in September, only a few weeks before my nightmare started, I saw a televangelist preaching about the collapse of the Soviet Union. He started the show saying that the apocalypse was coming. He had predicted many times in the past that the world would end when the red beast of the apocalypse, the Soviet Union, was destroyed. Now the beast was dying, the end was near, and Jesus was coming. I was pretty impressed by his performance until he started asking for donations. If the world was going to end, what did he need the money for? But as Dad liked to say, we shouldn't pass judgment on another man's business.

My problem with the born-again crowd started when you met them. They were a real pain in the ass, always trying to convert you at the most unexpected situations. Even the way they talked was annoying. You learned as a Catholic that God was Father, Son, and Holy Spirit. The Holy Trinity was a very big deal to us. Throughout history many people had burned at the stake for denying it. But the born-again people only talked about Jesus this and Jesus that, like they were talking about some buddy of theirs. No respect.

I got upset every time they tried to convert me. What for? There was no need for that. I was a sinner. If God was merciful, he would save me. If he didn't want to, there was nothing I could do about it. Actually, to tell the truth, I wasn't even sure if God and the related stuff like heaven and hell really existed. But Dad once told me that it was never stupid to hedge your bets, especially when hedging cost you nothing. Considering what could be at stake, it was worth seeing a priest now and then to confess and come clean.

That made sense only if God were stupid, I replied. But being God he could see through that. Dad answered that if God were that choosy, he would end up all alone in heaven. I should definitely hedge, just in case. "Nobody ever came back to tell how it is, Pablo." I saw Dad's point. Actually, a pretty smart and rational way to deal with a very irrational issue. Since then I had been hedging, but not really convinced.

Until the moment that I pulled the trigger, I was very optimistic about my chances of going to heaven and avoiding hell, if they existed. I was still hoping for and expecting forgiveness, even though I was doing a lot of nasty things: stealing, committing fraud, committing armed robbery. But God, if he was out there, knew that the circumstances had pushed me into that situation, and he would forgive me.

Then I pulled the trigger. Four times. Nothing justified killing. And killing only to make someone shut up was the ultimate transgression. Kind of a double capital sin. How could I be so vicious? And I had always thought that I was a good person. I hadn't known what I was capable of. Now I was getting a glimpse of the real me, and it was scary. Riding the subway back to Manhattan, I realized that it was over and I was damned: if hell existed, I had a one-way ticket, and I deserved it.

There had been a time in my childhood when I believed that I was going to hell because I was rich. I learned at school that rich people never went to heaven. It was written somewhere in the Bible, the religion teacher told us. A very confusing passage mixing camels, needles, heaven, and money.

But Mom and Dad explained to me that it wasn't true. I shouldn't take those Bible passages too seriously. It was one of many cases of bad translation. Camels and needles? It didn't make sense. "Bad translation, son! Obviously." Rich people were also God's children. Besides that, they created jobs and therefore spread the wealth, which was a good thing.

I was very confused, but I had to believe my parents. When I grew older, I found out that despite the jobs we created we actually kept all the wealth for ourselves. But I still felt on the safe side. Wealth alone couldn't be enough reason to be sent to hell. Everyone I knew was rich, and it couldn't be possible that all of them were going to hell. I thought that you only went to hell if you did something bad like killing someone.

So I was on my way. I was a potential killer. I was a violent, ruthless bastard. I had a monster inside of me. The caveman was in reality a thug, a murderer. In a few hours in New York I had committed armed robbery, followed by carjacking and attempted murder. Enough stuff for a century in jail and eternal damnation afterwards. And everything for only $700!

* * *

The train crossed the tunnel into Manhattan, and I got off in the Village. I remembered that I still had all the stuff with me: the gun, the mask, the car keys, the credit cards, and the woman's wallet. Shit, I was carrying evidence. I opened the wallet. Empty.

I walked around searching for trash cans to dispose of the stuff. I threw the wallet in one, the gun in another, the keys in a third one, and so on, but only after cleaning everything with the wool mask to get rid of fingerprints. The mask was the last item that I threw away.

As I passed a movie theater, I saw that a film was about to begin. I thought that maybe I'd be able to relax if I watched a movie. But I couldn't concentrate. After twenty minutes I gave up and went to the restroom. I started washing my face when I realized that I wasn't alone; a guy was taking a shit and whistling. I got upset. I didn't know if it was the smell or the tune that he was whistling, but I found the whole thing very annoying. I should have left, but I didn't.

Moving closer to the stalls, I saw his pants down around his ankles. His underwear had a big stain, really disgusting. How could someone who wasn't running away, who was leading a normal life, who had no excuse not to change clothes, wear dirty underwear?

Suddenly my paranoia came back. Dirty underwear is a bad omen... Soon you'll be wearing it again... You're playing a losing game... Dirty underwear is a bad omen... They're going to get you... You can run but you can't hide... Dirty underwear is a bad omen... It was as if I were going mad.

He noticed that I was standing outside.

"You got a problem, man?"

"Yes! Stop whistling! It's fucking annoying!"

"Listen, dude, I whistle wherever and whenever I want. Just get the fuck out of here and let me take a shit in peace, will you?"

"No! You'll stop whistling! It's fucking annoying!"

"Go to hell!"

That was it: he reminded me that I was going to hell. Son of a bitch. I had never, even as a kid, been involved in any fight, but now I couldn't control the urge to smash that guy's face. I took a step back and kicked the stall door. It opened, hitting him in the head. He tried to get up, but I kicked him and he fell back. I kept kicking and punching him until he stopped moving. He was almost unconscious, badly in need of medical care. I took his wallet and left the movie theater very quickly. The usher gave me a funny look on my way out.

I walked quickly away, looking for the next subway station. I saw a cab coming my way and waved it down.

"Penn Station."

I still had to get my backpack, which I had left in a locker. I was sweating, and my hands were shaking. The taxi driver looked at me with distrust.

"You okay, man?"

"I'm fine. Just took a strange pill. But I'll be all right."

He didn't look convinced.

"Hey, you don't have anything against drugs, do you?"

"Nope, as long as you don't do it in my cab."

He drove all the way observing me in the mirror. That made me even more nervous. They would find me. The usher saw me leaving. The cab driver picked me up close to the movie theater.

He noticed that I was nervous. He would tell the cops that he took me to Penn Station. They would come after me. You can run but you can't hide...

After retrieving my bag, I went to the subway station and boarded the first train that came by. I kept moving the whole night, changing trains. Bronx, Brooklyn, Queens, Manhattan: I went everywhere and nowhere.

I had the impression that since my ordeal started in Stanford I had been safe only when on the move. I moved for one and a half days between California and Texas, and nothing happened. When I stopped there, I was almost killed by a lunatic and stole a wallet from a dead body and clothes from someone's backyard. I hit the road, and again nothing happened. In a few hours in New York City, I had robbed, carjacked, attempted murder, viciously assaulted, and robbed again. I told myself, "Keep moving, man. Keep running. Every time you stop moving you go one step lower on your stairway to hell."

I had never thought that I would feel safe riding the subway that late at night. But I did. I must have looked very evil. People got on the train, took a quick look at me, and sat down as far away as possible. They must have read it in my eyes: murderer.

[1/8]

In the morning I got off the subway at Fifth and Fifty-third in Manhattan. I knew where I could get a good falafel to eat in that area: the Egyptian street vendor at Sixth and Fifty-first. It was early, and he wasn't there yet. I was hungry and tired, but at least I knew what to do next. I had to find a place to live for the next weeks.

I had money again. The guy I attacked in the movie theater had almost $150 in his wallet. Adding the $700 that I got from the woman and the money that I had left, I now had exactly $905. I could get a room in someone else's apartment for a few hundred dollars a month. I bought the newspaper and started looking.

Having lived in Manhattan for four years in the eighties, I thought that I should avoid the area. What if someone I knew recognized me? I restricted my search to Brooklyn and Queens. It was also cheaper to live there. I made many phone calls from a pay phone, but all rooms were either already taken or unsuitable. Some people wanted only roommates with day jobs. Others needed references. I had none of that.

On the sixteenth call I got lucky. A woman answered. It seemed that I woke her up.

"Yes, it's still available. Five hundred. You can come to see it later, but please not before one in the afternoon. Get off the F line at York Street."

She gave me the exact address and told me how to get from the subway station to the apartment. Five hundred was more than I wanted to pay. I continued to make phone calls, looking for a cheaper room, but I couldn't find anything else.

I went back and the falafel guy was finally there. I had the impression that he recognized me, but it must have been paranoia. He couldn't possible remember all his former customers. So many years had already passed. He probably only stared at me because I looked like shit. I ate two falafels and hit the road.

York Street was a funny subway station. I had never gotten off a train there before, only passed through. There was only one exit. I couldn't remember seeing that in any other subway station in New York. A perfect trap, I thought. If someone blocked that exit, I wouldn't be able to get out. Not a place to get off late at night. But then I remembered that I was on the other side now. Now people were supposed to be afraid of me.

Once outside, I saw that I was under the bridge. Scary. I remembered the advice that I had heard over the years, "In New York always avoid the areas close to the bridges." But that didn't apply to me anymore. Everything that I had learned about life in the city stopped making sense.

When I found the street, another surprise: the building wasn't located in a residential neighborhood. All I could see were warehouses and a lot of parked trucks. The building itself was also a warehouse, but on the upper floors there were some apartments. Only a cargo elevator. I climbed the stairs.

She opened the door and showed me around. It was a messy place. She didn't ask any questions. There was only one rule: no noise in the morning. She never got up before noon. I thought about asking what she did for a living, but remembered that she could ask me the same question. Better avoid the topic altogether. I asked instead if it wasn't dangerous to live in that area, to walk home alone late at night. You could hear your footsteps when you walked down the street. Completely deserted area.

She smiled. "Don't worry. This is Mafia-controlled territory. In this area nobody messes around. Even the gangs stay away from here. And besides that, in New York you only get mugged if you look like a victim. That's not the case with you."

I had always loved that New York logic. She seemed to be very easy going, and I thought that I shouldn't expect a lot of problems sharing the apartment with her. I asked when I would be able to move in.

"Anytime. The room is empty. I want the money up front. Always cash. Always on the first of the month. If you don't pay, you move out." She looked me in the eyes. "In case you're thinking, yeah, she's a woman, I can do whatever I want, you should know: I got this apartment here because I have connections. If you don't pay, it's not me who'll kick you out. I'll let other people handle it. And it'll hurt."

"Is your family in the Mafia?"

"Why do you care? Mind your business. I'll mind mine. And keep away from me. Don't you ever try to touch me, or I'll have you killed!"

So uptight. It didn't sound convincing, though. If she was that well connected, what was she doing living in dump like that? Couldn't her Mafia friends get her a well-paid occupation and a nice apartment somewhere else?

"Today is the twenty-first. If I give you six hundred, would it cover the rest of October and November?"

"Kidding me? Ten days until the end of the month! A third of the month is more than one hundred. It's one hundred and..." She seemed to have trouble dividing five hundred by three. "One hundred sixty something. One hundred sixty will do. That's six hundred sixty dollars. On December first another five hundred."

I decided not to haggle and gave her the money. It was two thirty in the afternoon. I took a shower and went to bed. I hadn't slept since Ohio and was very tired. But I couldn't fall asleep. Too many thoughts were going through my head.

* * *

I had made it. I had survived two shootings. I had crossed the country in only one week. No Feds or Colombians had found me. I was now safely hiding in a room inside a warehouse in Brooklyn.

But my situation was still very scary. I was now dirty poor. A small criminal, hiding in a dump in Brooklyn with only $230 left for food.

I had no option but to continue executing the plan that I had made on the road. I had the first part already behind me. It hadn't been an astonishing success, I had to admit, but it hadn't been a total failure, either. The ATM job brought me only $700, and the room that I got was a dump. But I did get money and a room. That was what part one was about. Pulling the trigger on the woman and beating up the guy inside the restroom wasn't nice. But shit always happened. And I got an extra $150 from the guy, which I badly needed. So there was a plus side to that. If I had to grade my performance, I would give me a C minus.

Part two was finding Mad Dog, the only person I knew who could help me. He was the reason why I had come to New York and not to Miami. He was the only choice I had. The Feds knew nothing about him, so it would be safe to make contact.

I couldn't get help from anyone else. My best friend RW would take a bullet for me. If I called him, he would drop everything and come from Jamaica to help me. He would bring me money and help me get a fake passport to leave the country. But contacting him was not an option.

The Feds probably knew about RW by now. I had made a huge mistake, which I would never make again: I had left a trail behind. RW's name was in my address book, as well as the names and addresses of all the people I knew. When the Feds searched my apartment, they surely found the address book. If they questioned some of the people whose names were in that address book, they quickly got all the information they needed to make the necessary connections. They must have found out that RW was a good, old friend. They must have read the letters and seen his Jamaican phone number all over my phone bills.

Amazing how much the normal things of life could tell about you. Pictures, letters, address books, bank and credit card statements, school records, phone bills... You only noticed that you left a huge, undeletable trace behind when it was too late.

At least I had realized it before contacting anyone I knew. It would have been a big trap for me and for them. The Feds didn't know where I was, but they knew exactly where my friends were. They only needed to watch my friends and wait for me to make contact. I would let the Feds waste their time watching and waiting while I searched for Mad Dog instead.

But what if I didn't find him fast enough? Or not at all? It was a frightening thought. I tried to cheer myself up. Hey, it was somehow ironic that I had landed in that apartment, wasn't it? Where else should a criminal hide, if not in Mafia-controlled territory? If I couldn't find Mad Dog, maybe I could meet a Mafia guy and turn in my résumé.

[1/9]

To me, New York City would always be associated with résumés because of David and the résumé drill in my freshman year at Columbia; a good and happy time.

"Why do you write a résumé? To get a job interview! If your résumé doesn't land you a job interview, it's worthless. Got it guys?

"And why do you go to the job interview? To get a job offer! You might not even want the job, but you have to get that job offer. Otherwise your interviewing skills suck. Got it guys?

"Always have an updated copy of your résumé with you. You never know when you'll need it. You never know when opportunity will come knocking on your door. You never know who'll sit next to you on the plane and find you very sharp and interesting. If you don't have a copy of your résumé to give to that person, you'll miss a great opportunity. Got it guys?

"It has to be good. Only a good résumé will bring you to that interview. And when you are in there, you have to look that guy in the eyes and make him think that you're what he's been looking for all his life. He has to want you. Got it guys?"

Got it, David! Every single freshman English class he would repeat his why-do-you-write-a-résumé-and-why-do-you-go-to-a-job-interview act. The whole semester, three days a week: Mondays, Wednesdays, and Fridays. David was incredible. He knew all the tricks.

"Why do you write a résumé? Why do you write a résumé?"

Funny, despite all the crap about modern pedagogical methods, what I really remembered were the things that were repeated to me over and over again. Brainwashing, one could say. If I was asked what I learned during my four years of college in New York City, I would answer, "You write a résumé to get a job interview, and you go to the job interview to get a job offer. Then you decide if you want the job or not."

What did I remember from high school? A crazy trigonometry teacher who yelled every class, "What's a sine?" The first time he asked that question, a guy answered, "You get the sine by dividing opposite by hypotenuse." The teacher replied, "That's how you calculate it. Sine is a number. It varies from minus one to plus one. That's all it is, folks: a number!" After that day he kept asking, "What's a sine?" And each time everyone answered in unison, "It's a number!"

So sine was a number, and a résumé was an invitation to a job interview. You wrote it to get a job interview, and you went to the job interview to get a job offer. Sounded easy. Too easy to be true. But despite my initial skepticism, it did work. At least it always worked for me. I never had any problem getting job interviews, job offers, and good jobs. I always got internships in New York in the summer vacations. I got a great job after college at an import-export company in Miami.

At first I thought that it was only a coincidence. After all, it was the late Reagan years, and the economy was doing great. There were plenty of jobs around. I wouldn't be so naive to think that my résumé alone was doing wonders for me. In life one could discover a connection between the most unrelated subjects. One could find out, for example, that floods in Southeast Asia and an increase in the murder rate in Mexico City always occurred in the same years. They were correlated, and that wasn't a problem. The problem started when you mistook correlation for causality, when an idiot decided to kill people in Mexico City in order to cause floods in Southeast Asia.

So I was very skeptical in the beginning. Was there really causality, or was it only correlation? But even at the beginning of the year, with the economy stuck in the Gulf War recession, I still got invitations to interviews for summer internships much more easily than most of my colleagues at Stanford. I could choose the company I worked for. Many of my classmates had to take whatever was offered them.

So it probably worked. Or it used to work in the past. Good old days. You only had to go to the school's placement office, choose some good companies, do your research thoroughly, write a nice cover letter to attach to your résumé, mail both, and wait.

Soon the appointments would come.

"Mr. Green, your company has increased its presence in Mexico in the last five years. You recently completed a new plant there, doubling your existing manufacturing base. It shows a very strong commitment to the region.

"As a Central American national with an American education, I am very qualified to join your marketing department. I have already worked in the field, and I have a very strong academic record in both the marketing and finance areas. My language skills and my multicultural background can add strength to your already dynamic and diverse international marketing team..."

* * *

Since kindergarten I had almost twenty years of the best education money could buy. Dad had always put a high value on education. He always said, "You can lose everything in life, boy, but what's inside your head is yours forever. No one can take it away from you." When the revolution started, when the red bastards came hunting you down and you had to leave the country on the last flight to Miami, you couldn't take much with you. Only some cash, and there was a limit to that, plus whatever you had inside your head, which was your education. Everything else you left behind was nationalized by the red bastards.

The poor man had his reasons to fear. It all started with the Cuban revolution in 1959. Having to watch some distant relatives we had over there, from Mom's side of the family, flee to Miami with nothing scared the hell out of Dad. I grew up listening to him saying, "It happened to Antonio. It can happen to us." When he was starting to mellow with age, bang: the Sandinistas took power in Nicaragua in 1979, exactly twenty years after Cuba. He went berserk. It was getting closer to us. Cuba was an island. Nicaragua was on the continent and very close to us.

I was thirteen years old and his only child still at school. My other siblings, much older than me, were either in college or had already graduated. Dad took me out of my old school, a traditional Catholic school that my whole family had attended for generations, and transferred me to the small American high school attended mostly by American expatriates and some local rich kids we knew.

Before that day, Dad used to say that he couldn't understand why parents denied their children a good, traditional, religious education and sent them instead to an English-speaking school. He never repeated that. Now I was supposed to get an American education myself. The Reds were coming our way. We weren't going to leave for Miami as ordinary refugees. We were upper class, after all, and deserved respect.

It was already too late for him and the rest of the family, but I would learn to speak the language almost like a native, go to college in America, get a certified degree from a good university, and learn how Americans did business. Then I would return home and carry on with life. If anything ever happened, we could always start over with dignity in America. I would help the family settle down and start new businesses the American way.

Dad called it an insurance policy. He was right, at least theoretically. I wondered how angry he got when he found out after the shooting in California that he paid all that money for a worthless insurance policy.

After I finished high school, I came to New York City in the fall of 1984 for my BA in business administration. I had great fun for four years. I didn't want to go home after I was finished. I convinced Dad that I needed practical training, otherwise the money would have been spent in vain. He agreed and said that I should find a job where I could learn something related to one of our businesses back home.

I wanted to join a brokerage firm on Wall Street. Dad wanted me to go to Kentucky, of all places. The Japanese had opened a car plant there. Like everyone else at the time, Dad thought that the Japanese were the future. They were the kings of management, and I could learn a thing or two from them. No way would I go to Kentucky. We settled for an import-export company in Miami, where I could enjoy life, at least compared with who-knows-where in redneck country. We also had a big trading company back home, so it would be useful training.

After two years working in Miami, I convinced Dad that I needed an MBA. That was a great excuse to go to the West Coast for another two years. I had almost convinced him that I needed more practical training after graduation, which was supposed to happen in the summer of 1992. He wasn't very receptive to the idea yet, but I was sure that I would eventually convince him.

He wanted me to go back home and start running some of

our businesses. But he and my older brothers would be on my back, watching every move I made. "That's not the way we do business here, kid." Right! I would gladly continue my "practical training" and let them keep doing things their way.

* * *

But it was over now. The whole strategy turned out to be useless. There was a fatal flaw in the plan: it required that I kept my identity. Amazing that it never occurred to any of us that if I lost my identity, or if I changed it, then everything would be useless.

Sure, I still had the experience. As Dad always said, what I had inside my head could never be taken away from me. But I couldn't prove that I had it. The BA I got in 1988 had my real name on it. The MBA I was supposed to get in 1992 would also have my real name on it. All my school transcripts, letters of recommendations, and academic awards showed my real name. But now that name was useless. Worse, nobody had taught me how to survive on the streets. No lessons on how to steal, rob, forge, kidnap.

I could turn myself in. But what for? To rot in prison for something I didn't do? Actually, I had enough stuff on my back to go to the electric chair. But I wasn't sure if California had the death penalty or not. I had never cared to know. Trivia. I had never imagined how important trivia was.

I couldn't call Dad and ask for help. First of all, he was certainly devastated by the whole affair. His youngest son a drug dealer and murderer. How sweet. Second, the Feds were probably tapping his phone and controlling his movements. He couldn't do anything for me. Wire me money? I couldn't go to the bank, show my ID, and collect it. Send a private jet to pick me up? The Feds would arrest me at the airport.

Besides that, I couldn't involve him in the mess I was. What if the Feds tried to link him to the whole dirty business I had been dragged into? Every rich Latin American was a potential drug dealer. People were always suspicious of the origin of our money. Dad had a lot of money stashed in America. The Feds could try to freeze it or, even worse, confiscate it. Drug laws were very tough in America. The Feds could seize any asset remotely involved in drug dealing.

I didn't want to be responsible for making the U.S. government confiscate Dad's money. That would be very mean. Not from the financial point of view, since most of his money was hidden offshore, in Switzerland and on the Caribbean Islands. And having money, he could afford enough lawyers. Eventually he would prove that he had nothing to do with his wicked son's dealings. But it would be an irreversible blow to his deep-rooted beliefs, and I had to avoid that at any price.

Here you had a guy who spent his whole adult life fearing a Communist revolution that forced him to flee the country in a hurry, leaving behind all his assets to be confiscated by a "long-bearded son of a bitch," as he always put it in such a lovely way. Here you had a guy who had a deep admiration for America and what America stood for: freedom, democracy, and free enterprise.

You could easily mistake Dad for a Protestant because of his enthusiasm for hard work, self-improvement, and self-reliance. He loved cowboy movies. He thrived on watching those lone riders surviving in the wilderness with their big guns and beautiful horses, especially when they killed the bad redskins. Reds deserved to die, be it on a Western movie or in real life, according to Dad.

America was his dreamland. He would never live here if he didn't have to, but he admired it a lot. Democracy, freedom, free enterprise. The fact that he lived in a country where real democracy was non-existent and made most of his money ripping off the state, manipulating the markets, and operating together with a few friends what the free-enterprising Americans would call cartels, didn't bother him much.

"Democracy is good, but it requires a responsible and well-educated voter. It takes time, son. First we have to educate the masses. It's dangerous to have democracy with ignorance...

"Free markets are the ideal solution, but they only work in a country like America. It's big enough. Here we need to keep the markets closed, at least for the time being. Otherwise, we won't survive the foreign competition. It's a matter of sovereignty, of national interest..."

I doubted that he believed that crap. He was just cynical. Actually, I must have inherited his cynicism. It was definitely not Mom's. But although it seemed paradoxical, his love, admiration, and respect for America and what America stood for were very sincere. One could call it a platonic love.

Therefore, to have the United States, the sacred temple of

private property and the bastion of democracy, freedom, and free enterprise, confiscate his hard-earned money and do to him exactly what he had always feared the bad Reds would do, that would kill him. His whole ideological framework would break into pieces. I didn't want to be blamed for that. Not me. Regardless of how much I sometimes hated Dad, I just couldn't do it.

It had already been very tough when the United States pressed us to end our dictatorship right after the Berlin wall came down in 1989. We had to get rid of our butchers in uniform and hold free elections. Poor Dad. "Elections will bring those pigs into power. We have fought so long and so hard to get rid of them. With the gringos' help, by the way! Now we have to sit here and watch the Reds get elected! Fuck Bush! Nixon would never do this to us!"

Nixon had been Dad's favorite American president. "A good man," Dad always said. Like Nixon, Dad hated all Communists, but Dad considered a Communist anyone with any kind of social agenda, what in other countries people called social democrats or trade unionists. In Dad's opinion they were all Communists, and he hated them all, especially the ones in the church. He once asked his good friend the archbishop to remove a priest from a small church deep in the woods because he was indoctrinating the peasants. Dad was checking out a farm that he was planning to buy and decided to attend Sunday mass. The priest didn't know him and went on with his usual preaching. Dad didn't like what he heard and called the archbishop right after mass. On Monday the priest was removed, and he probably never found out why.

Actually Dad used to pray to God to make Communism disappear from the face of the earth. Every Sunday he lit a candle for that. After years of praying, God finally heard him and wiped out Communism in Eastern Europe and started dismantling the Soviet Union. Oh, the Soviet Union: how Dad hated it. "The birthplace of all evil!" Now the place was falling apart. They even had presidential elections in the summer. Elections for the Kremlin; who could have even dreamed? The Berlin Wall was also gone. Communism was as good as defeated in Eastern Europe, and we had won the Cold War. Wasn't that great?

No, that didn't make Dad happy at all. On the contrary. I was sure that deep in his soul Dad secretly wished that the Soviet Union had survived. Had Dad lived in America, he would know that saying, "You should be very careful what you wish for because you might get it." Suddenly, to his indignation and anger, our dictatorship wasn't welcomed in Washington anymore. Maybe Americans felt awkward to have right-wing dictatorships flourishing in their backyard while Communist dictatorships were being dismantled all over Europe. Dad screamed for weeks. "What's their problem? They helped us to set up the whole thing in the first place!"

But he didn't have a choice. He had to adapt to the New World Order. And he did adapt very quickly. He learned how to play by the new rules. After all, Dad was a survivor, a tough and mean fighter. In the spring we had free elections for Congress for the first time in thirty years. Presidential elections should follow in 1992, according to our new constitution. With the help of Carlos, his political adviser, Dad invested a lot of money electing trustworthy congressmen and senators for the new congress, which was also a constituent assembly. He and some friends created three political parties that they secretly controlled.

The people demanded a new constitution, to be written by the constituent assembly. Dad couldn't understand what was wrong with the old constitution, but he quickly realized the opportunities lying ahead. If things were done quickly, he would be able to influence matters to his advantage. An open-ended process would have been dangerous. Dad decided that the new constitution was to be written in only six months, which was a very short time. The generals, acting on Dad's demands, made this a condition for holding free elections and proclaiming amnesty for political prisoners. The opposition had no choice but to agree.

Dad rode the waves of nationalism and anti-imperialism very effectively. While all eyes were focused on civil liberties, freedom of press, freedom of assembly, freedom of this, freedom of that, Dad was working behind the scenes to establish new monopolies and cartels. The left, his hated Communists, was very happy to join the right, his puppets, to restrict foreign investment in major economic areas. Telecommunications, for example, was now out of reach for foreign companies. It was Dad's idea. He was set to make millions with that simple constitutional change.

Even areas where foreigners had been operating for years, like mining, were affected. The poor Americans now had to sell their mines, and they had only one year to do it. Who was negotiating to buy them out? Dad. How much was he offering? Peanuts. He would soon own the biggest gold mine back home, besides two or three smaller ones. It was Dad's sweet revenge. "You get your damn democracy, I'll take your mines! Don't like it? Go complain to Bush!"

The new constitution also restricted the activities of foreign banks. The country had only three big national banks, and it would remain like that for a long time. Dad had a major stake in one and minor stakes in the other two, just to be on the safe side. You had to make sure that you had cheap credit for your companies, he always told me.

⁕ ⁕ ⁕

All in all, Dad would become much richer after that mess eventually ended, the introduction of the so-called democratic system. As Carlos explained to him, the secret was to understand what made the Reds tick and to use their ideology against them.

Reds hated all capitalist pigs. But capitalist pigs came in a hierarchy of evil. Foreign capitalist pigs were right at the top, sucking the blood of the nation, like in the colonial times. "Neocolonial exploitation" was a great concept to explore, Carlos told Dad.

If you couldn't end all exploitation, you could at least end neocolonial exploitation by foreign capitalist pigs and settle for the lesser evil, which was exploitation by your native capitalist pigs. At least the profits stayed in the country and were reinvested, creating jobs. That was the common ground Dad found with the Reds when writing the new constitution.

Of course all were only biding their time. The Reds hoped to consolidate their power and then get rid of us, the local bloodsuckers. Dad hoped to keep them at bay and continue to send the money out of the country, exactly like the evil foreigners would have done. But these were irrelevant details in the big political picture. We ended neocolonial exploitation with the new constitution. Exactly what the people had asked for.

The last time Dad had called me at the beginning of October, two weeks before my nightmare started, he was very happy. He told me that he would recoup the investment he made in the elections sooner than expected. His minions in Congress had included in the 1992 budget the funds to build the new international airport. Who needed a new international airport if the old one was doing just fine? The construction cartel, of course. Capitalism was about growth. You had to keep growing and therefore keep building stuff. Otherwise all those construction workers would be without jobs. That wasn't good.

The construction cartel would rig the bidding process, as always. One company would nominally win the bid with an outrageously high price. All cartel companies would actually build the airport in a consortium. Since we owned one of them, Dad would earn a few million more, recoup the investment he made in the elections, and still have enough money to buy one hundred more representatives in the next election in four years, which he was already planning for with Carlos's help.

That was the beauty of democracy, Carlos told us. "Business as usual without those pathetic political prisoners to give you a bad reputation worldwide."

[1/10]

Yes, Dad would survive democracy. He would certainly survive free markets as well. With the amount of capital he had amassed, it wouldn't be a problem for our family to fight any competition. But Dad avoided them as much as he could. If our family ever had to deal with free markets, that wouldn't be his problem but mine, he told me many times. I had studied and worked in America, and therefore knew all about free markets.

Not my problem anymore. I wasn't going back home. Never. I would be safe from persecution there since we didn't have an extradition treaty with the United States, and Dad would make sure that it stayed that way forever. But the Colombians were my real problem. They believed that I had killed the two brothers and the DEA agent and disappeared with their cocaine. They would track me down anywhere and kill me. Why should I move back to Central America, so close to Colombia?

If Dad still needed an insurance policy, he should send my older brothers to America for executive education. I had other things to worry about, like staying alive and getting my good life back. Poverty was a nightmare. Mom hated all poor people, but I had never had any kind of problem with them before. The poor were servants you gave orders to. We belonged to different worlds, and that was all. Now I was living in their world, and it scared me to think that I could stay poor forever. That fear was even bigger than the fear of going to jail or being killed.

I had never had any problem getting money. You just inserted those small pieces of plastic called debit cards into those friendly machines called ATMs, entered a password, and the money came out. Work? I only did it for fun. Why on earth should I spend time back home if I could be in New York, Florida, or California? "No, Dad, I really need this job. It's important for my career." Dad, who apparently was a closet Protestant, probably felt very proud of his hardworking offspring. I never even worried about pay. I lived off my investments.

Suddenly I had nothing. No magic pieces of plastic. No good job. I couldn't even apply for one. Yes, I could play the undocumented immigrant and get a menial job. But what for? Surviving? I didn't need only to survive. I needed a lot of money to start a new life somewhere very far away, in a country where no Feds and no Colombians would even think about looking for me. A menial job would only prolong my disgusting state of poverty and keep me grounded in America.

I had to face the facts. I needed a lot of money, and under the circumstances I wouldn't be able to get it legally. I had to go into crime. Officially I was already a criminal with a very bad reputation. I had made all the headlines with style. "Cold-blooded killer." "King of Cocaine." I wouldn't be caught and make headlines like "California Drug King Arrested in NYC, Cleaning Toilets for a Living." That would be even more humiliating to Mom and Dad than the alleged drug dealing and killings. In our family no one had done any kind of menial job or manual labor for two centuries.

But what could I do? Armed robbery was too much risk for a very low return. The best and quickest way out of my misery was to use the same stuff that brought me in: drugs. I already had the right genetic background anyway. Latin Americans dealt with drugs. Everybody knew it. It even had marketing potential. Who would want to buy cocaine from a Norwegian or a Canadian?

I could see myself doing very well in the business. I could put into practice everything that I had learned in business school. Coke was basically a commodity. The major factor was price, of course, but as anyone selling premium mineral water knew, there were ways to make a lot of money selling what appeared to be a commodity. Service was a key point. Reliable, discreet, and efficient. Quality was also very important. And then the king of kings: marketing. Identify market niches, personalize the product, introduce innovative packaging, do buy-two-get-one-free promotions, print coupons, and so on. The sky was the limit.

There weren't many well-educated drug dealers around. I could make it big in the industry. If I could send my résumé to a drug dealer, I would surely get a job interview and a job offer.

"Mr. Green, reading the paper recently, I came across an article describing your organization and the problems you are facing due to the recent loss of very competent and loyal workers.

"I want to take this opportunity to express my indignation at this outrageous and excessive intervention in your business. Regulatory agencies will never learn that too much government intervention only leads to distortions in the markets, causing low productivity and high prices. It shows once again that the government bureaucracy is not interested in self-regulated and efficient markets, but only in increasing its own power.

"Since I assume that you have openings for the position of drug dealer, I would like to apply. Though I don't have any practical training in the area, I can assure you that I will perform my duties very well.

"As a Central American national with an American education, I am very qualified to target the upscale market, which generates the highest profits. My whole life I have attended the finest parties, dined at the best restaurants, and frequented the nicest clubs. I can socialize with rich and powerful individuals as one of their own. This puts me in a unique position to market your product to quality-conscious consumers willing to pay more money for a premium product. My language skills and my multicultural background can be very useful in dealing with your major suppliers and negotiating price reductions..."

* * *

But who should I write to? And where could I get the address? When I lived in New York in the eighties, people in the poor neighborhoods used to complain a lot that they had too many drug dealers around them. Their kids' only career opportunities were to become drug dealers. The neighborhood was awash in drugs. Back then I thought, what a sad destiny to become a drug dealer.

But I had been wrong. Actually drug dealer was the dream job. Pay was good, the job was easy, and the chances of advancement were enormous. You didn't have twenty-five layers of management above you. You didn't have to wait years until someone made room at the top so that everyone else could climb a single rung. It was the dream job in the ultimate lean and mean corporation. And it was easily available in the neighborhood. The contacts were there. The practical training was available twenty-four hours a day. All you had to do was join the business. Why the complaints, then? Some people really didn't know how to count their blessings.

It wouldn't be that easy for me. The only contact I had was Mad Dog, RW's childhood friend. He had moved from Jamaica to New York in the late seventies and became a drug dealer a few years later. RW was very close to Mad Dog, and the three of us used to hang out in the years RW and I attended college together. Mad Dog was already a very successful dealer at the time. He had people working the streets for him.

The last time I saw him was in the summer of 1988 at RW's farewell party, right after graduation. More than three years had passed; a lot of things could have happened in those three years. I didn't have any address or phone number. Mad Dog and his gang sold drugs in Brooklyn, but Brooklyn was a hell of a big place to search.

I had a precedent, which gave me a lot of hope. In our freshman year I had helped RW find Mad Dog in Brooklyn. But back then the two of us could move around freely, no cops or killers chasing us. Now I had to do it alone while watching my back.

The chances of locating Mad Dog again were very small, maybe one in millions. But after the shooting in Texas I had lost my faith in statistics. In a country of 250 million people, what had been the chances of being inside that fast-foot restaurant at the very moment when that lunatic started playing mass murderer? One in how many millions? And what had been the chances of surviving it?

Statistics meant nothing. I had found him once; I would do it again. The only question was, how would I get by until then? If I watched my money carefully, I would be able to live on ten to fifteen dollars a day. That would take me to mid-November. Then I would have to commit another armed robbery to raise money.

"Caveman, you have three weeks," I told myself before I finally fell asleep.

[1 / 11]

I slept deeply and long, just like in that motel in Louisiana. When I woke up, for a few moments I didn't know where I was or even which day it was. It took me a while to recognize the room: my own room on the top floor of a warehouse somewhere in Brooklyn, New York. The room was bathed in sunshine. Was it morning or afternoon? I checked my watch: three fifteen in the afternoon, Tuesday. I had slept for only one night after all.

I was starving, so I searched my backpack. I found a few biscuits, and proceeded to devour them. Then I went to the kitchen to see how much cooking I would be able to do in that place. It would be not only cheaper to eat my meals at home, but also much healthier. Junk food was killing me.

The apartment was very quiet. Either the woman was still sleeping or she had gone out. The door to her room was closed. What was her name again? Jane? Janet? I couldn't remember.

The kitchen was awful. There were a few pots and pans, and I would be able to do some basic cooking, but everything was filthy, including the fridge.

I went out to buy groceries. It took me a long time to find a small supermarket selling fresh stuff and not only packed food. I bought twenty dollars' worth of food and went back home.

Besides getting better nutrition, I also needed to work out again. The area I was living in would be great for jogging, with all those empty streets. I had bought a pair of sneakers, T-shirts, sweatshirts, and sweatpants in Louisiana, but I could wear them only indoors. I needed warmer workout clothing, but I couldn't afford it. I took the stairs, thinking that carrying the bags to the fifth floor would be good exercise. That gave me an idea. In such a deserted building nobody would notice or care if I worked out on the stairway. Climbing stairs was good cardio workout. I could also do sit-ups and push-ups there.

When I got back to the apartment, I had a pretty good idea of what my daily routine would be in the next days. Wake up at eight; work out on the stairway; take a shower and have a big breakfast; make a sandwich for the road; leave at ten in the morning; search for Mad Dog until four or five in the afternoon; buy a newspaper; return to the apartment; cook dinner; read the paper in bed; try to fall asleep before midnight.

When I got back, the woman was in the living room.

"Hi, John! Went shopping?"

It was strange to hear her calling me John, but that was the name I had given her. What was her name again?

"Yeah, Jane. I'm cooking a simple dinner later on. Pasta and salad. Do you want to join me?"

"Janet, please. Yes, I'd love to eat at home for a change. I never cook. I hate cooking."

As if I couldn't tell, having seen her kitchen and fridge.

She watched me unpack the groceries. "You didn't get any wine! You don't drink?"

I couldn't afford it, man... "I couldn't find a good bottle in the supermarket. By the way, could you give me some tips on where to buy fresh food here?"

"No idea, John. But I know where to get good wine. I'll get us a bottle for dinner. You bring the food, and I'll bring the wine. That's a fair deal, right? See you later."

She brought the wine and drank most of it. She didn't eat much. It seemed that she got most of her calories from alcohol, which was fine with me. I enjoyed eating. The more she drank, the more relaxed she became.

"Where you from, John?"

"Miami."

She frowned. "Been there. Didn't like it."

"Nothing compared to New York!"

"What brings you here?"

I told her that I liked to travel. I basically lived on the road, hitchhiking from place to place, doing odd jobs here and there. I lived rough when the weather was fine and took a room when it got cold.

"I'm planning to spend the winter in New York and to move north in the spring."

"So you're basically a bum?"

"Part-time bum! I work now and then. I'll probably get a job here."

She was an actress, but finding acting jobs in New York was really tough. She had tried L.A. but hated it. She came back from California after only one year there. Now she worked in a bar in the Village, from ten in the evening till four in the morning.

"If you want to work the night shift, I can ask around. I know a lot of people."

I told her that I preferred the day shift but might consider the night shift if I couldn't get anything else. But first I wanted to do some sightseeing. She left at nine. I did the dishes and went to my room to think about my next moves.

* * *

My long term to-do list was easy to draft: one, find Mad Dog; two, convince him to give me a job; three, make a lot of money and save a big pile of it; four, get new identity papers; five, move to a foreign country with the money and start a new life there.

I was pretty certain that I would find Mad Dog and get the job. It was only a matter of time. Saving money was problematic. Where should I keep it? I didn't have a bank account and couldn't open one without papers. I could hide the cash somewhere, but it could be stolen. And I wouldn't be able to take it with me when I left America. There was a limit to how much cash you could carry across borders.

Getting new identity papers was something that I needed to do at the very beginning. After that I could open a bank account and save the money. The best option was to hide it offshore, like Dad did. Out of the reach of the Feds. If I had to hit the road on short notice, I wouldn't leave any money behind.

I knew how to create an offshore structure. First, set up a company in a friendly jurisdiction like the Cayman Islands or the British Virgin Islands. Second, open a bank account for the company on the same island. Finally, transfer the money offshore. But the company needed a beneficiary owner and someone to manage the account. That person needed an identity, even if the offshore registry and the bank kept that identity secret.

How did you go about getting new identity papers? In the movies it was easy: Istanbul, a dark bazaar, a guy sitting in the corner. You walked in and said that you needed a passport. He asked for money and a picture and told you to come back the next day. Even if I knew where to do that in New York, it wouldn't be the right solution for me. A fake passport was good enough to cross a border, but it would be a problem in the long run. I needed a real passport that I could renew at a U.S. embassy in a foreign country when I moved abroad for good. I also needed a real Social Security number to open a bank account in America.

A fake one could be discovered. I couldn't take that kind of risk.

I once read a very good magazine article about fraud. It explained how people built the fake identities needed to do it. You only needed to get ahold of someone else's birth certificate, use it to get an ID, and start committing crimes in the guy's name. If someone found out, the real person would get the blame, not you. Pretty much what was done to me in California. Only that you didn't even have to steal the guy's driver's license, like in my case. You only needed a birth certificate, and you could get it by mail. Yes, in America you could get a copy of your own birth certificate by mail. All you had to do was write to the vital records office in the town where you were born.

Since I didn't want to take over someone else's identity for only a short period of time but for the rest of my life, not any birth certificate would do. I needed to find someone who died as a child and therefore left behind no paper trail whatsoever. The problem was, dead people didn't write letters. The vital records office cross-referenced birth and death records before issuing the birth certificate copy.

But there was no centralized office at the federal level and very little coordination between states. The solution was to find a guy who was born in one state and died a few years later in another. I would have to spend hours in the library searching for death notices in old newspapers.

Getting the birth certificate was only the beginning. To get a passport I needed a birth certificate as proof of citizenship, and a picture ID as proof of identity. To get a driver's license, a great picture ID, I needed a Social Security number. So the next step after I got the birth certificate was to get a Social Security number. But how could I go to a federal building and apply for one at my age? How could I explain that I had lived for a quarter of a century and never needed one? What if the dead guy's parents had requested a number for him? It wasn't common in the sixties, but not impossible.

Another tricky issue: to which country should I move? Europe was cool but difficult to immigrate to. Australia and New Zealand were easier to get in as long as one had skills that were needed. But my new identity wouldn't have any school records. Maybe Asia?

At Stanford all that people talked about was China's rise. Forget Japan, they said. China was the future, the new frontier, the place to make lots of money. But it was not easy for a foreigner to move there. They took no immigrants.

Most companies were using Honk Kong as a bridgehead to China, since Hong Kong would soon become part of it. The British were already negotiating Hong Kong's return to China in 1997. If you got into Hong Kong before 1997 and didn't leave after the transfer, you would then be living in China proper.

That sounded promising. Go east, young man. In Hong Kong I would be in the very deep east. Hong Kong also had a very interesting characteristic: like Berlin once, it was a capitalist city surrounded by Reds. Reds had always been a part of my life, as ghosts, so to speak. Why not have them as neighbors, in flesh and bones? And when Hong Kong returned to China in 1997, I would live among Reds. What about that, Dad? Right inside the lion's den. Yes, Hong Kong seemed the place to go. I had to check their visa requirements.

My to-do list was much longer and detailed now: find Mad Dog; get a job; save money; do library research; get a birth certificate, a Social Security number, and a driver's license; open a bank account in America; get a passport; save a lot of money; open an offshore company and its bank account; transfer money offshore; get a visa for Hong Kong; get out of America.

* * *

Now I had to plan my search for Mad Dog. The first time RW and I searched for him it took us seven months, from October 1984 to May 1985. We went searching once a week, always on Wednesday afternoons, for about three to four hours.

RW kept tabs on our trips. He had a big Brooklyn map where he marked the streets we had covered, adding date and trip number. We found Mad Dog on trip number twenty-two. I never forgot that because the three of us talked a lot about twenty-two being our lucky number.

Those twenty-two trips were my only benchmark. Now, searching for more than double the amount of hours per trip compared to the first time, maybe I would be able to find him in half the number of trips. That meant eleven days. I could make it before I ran out of money. That thought gave me hope.

I wasn't looking forward to doing it. I was again afraid of going to those areas, now for a different reason. In 1984 and

1985 I was afraid of getting mugged or beaten up. Now I was afraid of being recognized, which would lead to either arrest or death, depending on who found me, the Feds or the Colombians. The Colombians were my biggest worry. They probably went to their connections, dealers and street criminals, showed my picture, and offered them money. I had to assume that lots of people on the streets of Brooklyn knew that "Pablo aka Baldy" was worth $100,000 to the Colombians. Dead or alive.

I hadn't shaved in a week, and my beard was starting to show. With a wool cap and sunglasses, I hoped that anyone out there looking for the beardless Baldy of those pictures wouldn't recognize me.

I would have to find someone to bring me to Mad Dog since he wouldn't be hanging out on the streets selling drugs. I couldn't tell them my real name. I decided to use RW's name: Winston. Maybe the nickname "Winston Twenty-two" would ring a bell with Mad Dog.

On Wednesday, exactly one week after the shooting in Texas, I would start my search for Mad Dog. At ten in the morning I would get on the train at York Street heading for Crown Heights. A strange coincidence, I thought, to start on a Wednesday like in 1984. It was also a very ironic coincidence that I had to come to New York to solve my identity problem. When I first came to attend Columbia University in 1984, all I wanted was to leave it behind.

[1/12]

Mom and Dad wanted me to go to college in Miami. Closer to home, nice weather, Latin American culture, not too American. That was exactly what I wanted to avoid. I was tired of living in two worlds. I didn't want to hear any more complaints about how I had changed myself into a gringo. How I hated those two words: gringo and Yankee.

"What, you don't want to play soccer? You'd rather play football with your Yankee friends? You've become one of them. Yankee!" How I wished I had. At least I would know who I was.

My parents had given me such a hard time, but they were the ones who had sent me to the American high school in the first place. I had never asked for that. I had been pretty happy in the old one. But Dad thought that I had to get an American education. An insurance policy. He and his paranoia. One day the Reds took power in Nicaragua, the next day I was thrown into that different world: American culture; American language; American food; American music; American history; American world view, American values.

That was during the day. Late afternoon I was back home in what was supposed to be my world. My parents never realized how that double life was slowly screwing me up, in a big way. I was too young to learn the single concept that wrecked my personality: relativity. Not Einstein's theory of relativity, but life's relativity.

As I moved between two completely different worlds, looking at things one way during the day and another way in the evening, I realized that there was more than one legitimate way to see and understand things. As I kept crossing the borders between those two worlds, I couldn't even tell which was better. They both seemed good in their own contexts.

I learned to put things into perspective according to which world I happened to find myself in. In life, any change of position changed your point of view, both literally and metaphorically, making you change your mind about the subject, which in itself remained the same. Things stayed unchanged. It was your point of view that changed. All was relative.

After 1979 I became a gringo to my family and friends. But to Americans at high school I was a Latin American guy. I didn't belong anywhere. I hoped that when I went to college in New York I would finally have only one role: the Latin American guy living among Americans. All other Latin Americans would have that same role, too. We would on the same boat. I would finally belong.

I had always loved the city. I visited it with my family every summer. In the winter we went to Miami because it was much warmer. Mom loved to shop alone in New York. She moved from store to store on Fifth Avenue. I stayed with whomever was accompanying us on the trip: Dad, siblings, cousins. After 1980 I was allowed to move around alone. After all, I was already fourteen and could speak the language well, having attended the American high school for one year already.

In my new school I discovered rock music. I had a young biology teacher, Jimmy, who was a music fanatic. He had a huge record collection with all the great bands of the sixties and seventies. You couldn't buy even half of those records back home. Jimmy made us tapes, but I wanted to have the real thing: the records. After 1980 during all my trips to New York, I only wanted to go shopping, just like Mom.

No one in my family wanted to come along. "Why do you spend the whole day inside record stores?" Because it was fun. New York had the best and biggest record stores on earth. You could get a record at the very moment it was released. You didn't have to wait for months, like you did back home. I returned home with thirty or forty records each time. I couldn't buy more because there was a limit to how many records I could carry as hand luggage.

Then there was Madison Square Garden, where you had the coolest concerts. My teacher Jimmy used to tell us about the concerts he had seen there in his college years. What I had missed! But I wasn't allowed to catch up. In our family trips Mom never allowed me to go to any concert there, even if one of my older cousins offered to take me. I was too young; there were too many drugs; it was dangerous. The usual crap that mothers told you. Dad always sided with her.

That was ridiculous. My teacher Jimmy went alone to Woodstock when he was fifteen, and my parents wouldn't allow me to go to Madison Square Garden with an older cousin.

That made the place even more attractive to me. On each trip to New York I went to Madison Square Garden at least once to hang out outside, just for the atmosphere. I kept telling myself, "When you are older, you'll come for all the concerts you want, and no one will stop you."

The day I got my letter of acceptance from Columbia University was probably the happiest day in my life. Pretty soon I would be in New York on my own. I would do anything I wanted, any time I wanted. Mom, Dad, brothers, sisters, relatives, everyone else would be thousands of miles away. Free at last!

My happiness didn't last very long. Mom found out that Columbia was in Harlem and wouldn't let me go. "It's dangerous! All those black people around you! You could get mugged! Even killed! How can this be a decent school if it's located inside a slum?"

I argued that Columbia was located in Morningside Heights, which was another neighborhood. Close to Harlem but not in Harlem. Mom didn't fall for those technicalities. "Don't try to fool me, Pablo! Anything north of Central Park is Harlem! You know that!"

I should go to a safe university town, she said. The University of Michigan in Ann Arbor, for example. No way! I didn't want to go to the Midwest. I wanted to go to New York City. Mom then suggested Princeton or Yale. They were both not very far from New York, and I could make weekend trips. Columbia was out of the question. "How can you even think of it? Living among blacks?"

***

Both my parents had annoying color problems, but Mom's was absurd. Somehow I could understand Dad's. Reds were really dangerous. It wasn't only paranoia; there were real Commies out there trying to get him. Not that the Commies had a chance. Our generals had everything under control. The prisons were full. But as Nicaragua had shown, revolution was possible.

Mom's color problem had always puzzled me. Blacks weren't a danger to us. We weren't in South Africa, and we had nothing to fear. We didn't even have that many blacks in our country. Because the early Spanish immigrants were so successful at enslaving the natives, there had never been any need to import African slaves.

Cuba, where Mom's family came from, had imported a lot of slaves. Mom's ancestors had black slaves working on their plantations for generations. When slavery was abolished, most of the family left the island and came over to the continent. The slaves were gone, but for some reason the hatred remained. Every generation born in the new country was raised as if the family still owned slaves.

Our trips to Miami and New York were always a great opportunity for in-the-field training, since the blacks we lacked back home existed in such abundance in those two cities. Mom and Dad showed me all those black people hanging out on the streets, doing nothing. Lazy, dangerous, black people. "Watch out, kid. Never talk to them!"

Dad had definitely picked it up from Mom, because his brothers and sisters didn't have that obsession with blacks. Mom always said that Dad had a bad upbringing. But he learned quickly. It seemed to be one of the consequences of marriage. With time couples seemed to blur their personalities. Unfortunately my parents picked up only the worst of each other. After they got married, Mom learned to hate Reds, and Dad to hate blacks.

Though for Dad it was more of a pedagogical tool than real hate. His theories of self-improvement, hard work, and self-reliance were very well illustrated with the good example of the blacks. "Look at them, Pablo! They don't work. Just hang around, like lazy bastards. Which by the way is exactly what they are: bastards. No fathers to raise them. They only fornicate and have babies like rabbits. No families. No jobs. They live off welfare. Off other people's taxes. Bloodsuckers, just like the Commies."

Then he quickly moved to his favorite color mixture: black and red. "Look at Africa. The only countries that function are the ones that aren't Communist. Look at Angola. It was paradise until the Portuguese left and the Communists took over. Now it's a wasteland."

And finally he arrived at his real object of hate: Reds. That was the game, repeated over and over again. Mom would start with the blacks. Dad would pick up from that, stay on the subject for a while, move from "black only" to "black and Red," then further to "Red only," and stay there. Although Mom tried to raise me as a slave owner, to her despair it wasn't very effective. The big threat at home was the Reds, not the blacks. Dad had control over my upbringing.

* * *

Mom's racism had always been an irritant, since she never stopped talking about blacks. But up to that point it had never had any consequence for me. Now it was going to ruin my dream of living in New York City. So I did what I had to do. I "played marbles" with Dad. This was the code name for doing to him what he had always done to me: use manipulation, lies, and deceit to obtain what he wanted. The marble story illustrated that perfectly.

When I was a small kid, I loved playing marbles. The only problem with my favorite game was that with time marbles broke, and you had to replace them. But marbles were cheap and could be found everywhere. Until the day came when there were no marbles to be bought. I was desperate. All the kids were running out of marbles. Very soon we wouldn't be able to play anymore.

It was 1973, and I was too young to understand what was happening. The country was up in flames. Protests. Strikes. Violence. People wanted to get rid of our right-wing dictatorship. Once again. They were not successful, of course, but they tried hard until they were crushed. Once again.

The protests had started very small, almost by accident, in late 1972. Some students staged a demonstration on campus against Nixon's reelection. Demonstrations were illegal, and the police arrested dozens of them. One didn't survive the secret police's interrogation methods of choice and died. Things like that happened all the time. They just got rid of the body.

But that time the victim was the son of a very rich and influential man. The father demanded the body for burial. The generals couldn't refuse since the father was not only very rich, but also the finance minister's brother. Thousands of demonstrators came to the burial. Afterwards they marched on the streets, calling for the end of torture, free elections, and so on; the usual list of demands. The police dissolved the demonstration with rubber bullets, hurting lots of people.

Things escalated quickly, and the situation got out of control. There were protests and demonstrations on a daily basis. The police couldn't handle it anymore, and the armed forces were called in. They sent the cavalry to disperse the crowds, followed by the infantry to beat up whoever refused to go home. But crowds were not stupid. They realized that if they threw marbles on the streets, the horses and the soldiers would step on them, slip, and fall.

There were many bloody street battles. On one side were horses, soldiers, tear gas, batons, and guns. On the other side were students, workers, sticks, stones, Molotov cocktails, and marbles. The government always won, but the marbles brought down and injured a lot of horses and soldiers. Eventually the government outlawed the sale of marbles and confiscated all existing stock.

I didn't have a clue about all that. All I knew was that I was running out of marbles. Dad explained to me that the Communists, the Reds, were to blame. They were evil and took everything away, including marbles.

Years later I would hate Dad for that. He never missed an opportunity to indoctrinate me. It was a dirty trick. I was a small kid, only seven years old, and there I was, hating Reds because of marbles. I didn't even know what a Red was. I only knew that they took all the marbles away and were therefore evil.

I asked Dad why those people did that. He told me that they

used the marbles to hurt the poor horses and soldiers. Why were horses and soldiers necessary? To protect us. The Reds wanted to take everything away. They hated us because of our money, and if they could, they would take away not only the marbles, but everything that we had.

That information was too scary for a seven-year-old kid to deal with. But Dad promised me that everything would be all right; he would never let anything happen to us. And he would get me some marbles. He sent a special courier to Miami and had marbles smuggled in for me. One hundred beautiful American marbles. I was so proud of Dad. It was a good feeling to know that I was protected and taken care of.

Dad told me how much the courier trip cost. I didn't understand money at that age, but he made a good comparison. The money he spent to smuggle in those one hundred marbles would be sufficient to buy one truckload of the stuff back home. One truckload of marbles I could understand. It was a fortune.

Dad wanted me to learn how good it was to have money. You could fly in marbles from Miami if you wanted to. Money could buy you anything. It was the first time I understood the kind of things that money made possible. I told Dad that I was very happy to be rich, and that I hated all Reds. He was very moved to hear that. At that moment I learned that the magic words "I hate Reds" opened a lot of doors with Dad. Manipulation was the name of the game, and I had the best teacher.

It was easier to manipulate than to fight head on. But fight we did, a lot. My early teenage years were hell. I kept accusing him of brainwashing me since childhood. And I always mentioned the marble story. Eventually I stopped fighting and started playing marbles instead. It was much more effective.

* * *

If I wanted to go to college in New York, I had to convince Dad, who would overrule Mom. Obviously I had to play the Red card. I went to my biology teacher, Jimmy, asking for help. He helped me build my case, giving me the facts and the lies that I needed to make up a credible story and impress Dad.

Following the strategy that Jimmy and I developed, I told Dad that Princeton, Yale, Harvard, MIT, and other Ivy League universities were hotbeds of left-wing intellectuals. It was not a coincidence that the student movement of the sixties had started in those universities. Those students had hated Nixon, Dad's favorite American president. I didn't tell him that things hadn't been any different at Columbia. That detail was irrelevant to my story.

Roosevelt, that left-wing, tax-and-spend New Deal liberal, went to Harvard. He also attended Columbia, but that was not worth mentioning. John Kennedy, the guy who lost Cuba forever to the Reds, went to Princeton. Bob Woodward, the reporter who helped bring down Richard Nixon, the most honorable of presidents, went to Yale.

Columbia, on the other hand, was totally different. Dwight Eisenhower had been the university president, and you couldn't get more right wing than that, could you? Eisenhower had been Dad's second favorite American president.

I saved the big lie for the very end, to close the deal. "And Nixon, Dad, Nixon himself taught at Columbia!" Checkmate! Dad didn't have a clue, and there was no way he could check the facts. He swallowed everything.

"So, Dad, you're not going to send me to Princeton or any other liberal institution to be indoctrinated by those left-wing professors, those disgusting Commies, are you? In Columbia we do have a few blacks outside, and that's a bit annoying, but in the other universities we have lots of Reds inside. What's worse?" The beauty of rhetorical questions.

"I'll take care of it, Pablo. I'll talk to your mother."

They had a big fight that evening. I could hear Mom screaming, "If anything happens to the boy, I'll blame you forever!"

There were conditions, of course. It was mandatory to live on campus in the first year. Mom liked it. In her eyes it was safer that way since I didn't need to cross the "black slum" to get to classes. I wasn't supposed to hang out outside campus at any time of the day or night. For the rest of my college years I was to rent an apartment in Manhattan, never in Harlem, and stay away from the black danger.

I could live with those conditions. There were only two minor problems left. One was my music. When would I be able to bring my 500 records to New York? I had everything professionally packed and ready to ship to America. Would I have place for them in my dorm, or would I have to wait one year until I moved to my own apartment? The other worry was dorm life. I would have to share a room with a guy I had never met before. I didn't like the idea. Back home I had always had a room for myself. What if the guy was a jerk?

[1/13]

I arrived on campus on a sunny day in the beginning of September, 1984. Up to that day I had never believed in fate. Afterwards I wasn't sure anymore. But if there was really someone controlling our destinies, that someone had a very mean sense of humor. I walked into my room and there was a black guy standing there.

At first glance I thought that he was a cleaning person or a janitor, but he wasn't wearing a uniform. Actually, he was dressed pretty well. He saw me and smiled, and I smiled back. He walked over to me and introduced himself.

"Hi! My name is Winston. I'm your roommate. I'm from Jamaica. I heard that you're from Central America. I'm very excited, man! I can finally practice my Spanish!"

I froze. Shit, I would be sharing a room with a black guy! What would Mom do when she found out? I could just hear her. "I warned you! I'm bringing you back today! We're not paying all this money to have you sharing a room with a black man! That's a shame. What will our friends say? I told you that Columbia was a bad choice! I told you, Pablo!"

I could have gotten a black roommate in any college in America. It had nothing to do with Columbia, but Mom would never believe it. I was going to be sent to another city because of that guy standing in front of me, smiling like an idiot. How could anyone smile in a situation like that?

I didn't know what to do or say. I thought about leaving immediately, going back to the administration office, and asking for a new roommate. But what reason could I give them? I couldn't tell the truth. That would probably reflect badly on my reputation. I could be labeled a racist. That was not good. Not good at all. They could even kick me out of school. In America they were very touchy about race.

I was so immersed in those thoughts that I didn't even notice that the guy in front of me had extended his hand, expecting a handshake. I only noticed it too late, when he gave up and crossed his arms, looking very pissed off.

I had to say something. "You got a scholarship?"

He looked me in the eyes and spoke slowly and coldly. "I was offered one, but I thought it would be fairer if they gave it to someone who really needed it. I'm paying full tuition." Translation: I'm smart and rich.

I didn't know how to proceed with our conversation. I just stood there, looking at him. After a few seconds of very awkward silence, he dropped the bomb.

"You have a problem with me because I'm black, don't you?"

That direct question caught me off guard. "No, it's not what you're thinking."

"I'm not thinking anything! I can see it right there on your face. You're scared! What are you afraid of?"

"Sorry, man, wrong impression. I'm not scared of you. I don't have anything against black people. Never had. I'm just not used to them."

As soon as those words left my mouth, I realized that it had been a stupid thing to say. But it was too late. The guy was furious.

"Not used to what? What is there to get used to?"

He said that very loudly, almost screaming. The situation was deteriorating fast. What should I say? I couldn't come up with anything and remained silent. That made him angrier.

"Answer me, man! Why are you scared of me?"

"It has nothing to do with you! It's my mom! I'm scared of my mom, okay?"

"What does your mother have to do with it?"

"She'll kill me."

"Kill you for what?"

"For having a black roommate!"

"Your mother is a racist?"

"My dad, too."

"But not you?"

"No, never been."

"Why are you scared of me, then?"

"I told you already, man. I'm not scared of you. I'm scared of my mom. She'll kill me!"

"Your mom is not here!"

"It doesn't matter. When she hears about you, she'll make me leave Columbia, send me to Princeton, Michigan, who knows where. At any rate somewhere far away. But I want to stay here in New York."

"What the hell are you talking about?"

I told him everything about Mom's color problems. How much I wanted to study in New York; how tough it had been to convince Mom to let me; the Harlem problem; the threats concerning socializing with black people.

He calmed down. "Shit, man! I was afraid I'd share a room with a white racist. Now I got stuck with a brown one! It's even worse! I want the real thing or my money back!"

He laughed as he said it. He had very disarming laughter.

I protested. "What do you mean, brown? I'm white, man!"

He laughed again. "White? You kidding me? You're brown! Latinos are brown, not white. Everybody knows it!"

"Now you're the one being racist!"

He smiled. "Oh, you don't like being on the receiving end? You don't like prejudice? How sweet!"

I thought that maybe I should apologize. "Sorry, man! Why don't we forget this conversation and start again from the beginning?"

He smiled. "That's a good idea. Let's get out of here and have a beer. But you haven't told me your name yet."

"Pablo."

"Escobar? Pablo Escobar Junior?" he asked, tongue in cheek. "Your Dad is the drug dealer?"

I had deserved it, so I played along. "Yes, of course. And the beer is on me. You know, I must launder our drug money. By the way, where can we get a beer here? You're not allowed to drink in this country until you're twenty-one!"

"Heard about it. You have to know where to go."

He took me to his apartment a few blocks away from campus. In Harlem! The guy had rented a huge apartment for himself even though he had to live in the dorm. He had style. He told me that he was going to move in permanently in the second year. During freshman year it would be his weekend refuge. He winked as he said, "There are things you can't do in the dorm, you know?"

Smart guy; why hadn't I thought about it myself?

He had a huge record collection, bigger than mine. I was impressed. "How many?"

"Six hundred fifty."

"I didn't know that Bob Marley had made so many records."

"He didn't. Just a dozen are his. The rest are rumba and salsa records. Feel welcome to borrow them whenever you feel homesick."

All the bantering was a good sign. The mood was improving. I went though his record collection. We had similar taste in music.

"By the way, Pablo, drop the Bob. It's Marley only. He's the only Marley who matters on this planet."

"What?"

"'The stone that the builder refused will always be the head cornerstone.' Do you know the song?"

That was the beginning of my Marley education. Like most people, I had the Exodus album, which I really liked, but nothing else. A few months later I would know all Marley songs.

We had similar backgrounds: both from extremely wealthy families; both the youngest child; both getting the kind of education that their parents never had; both being groomed to join the family business someday; both considered different by other people. I was the gringo. Winston was the guy from Trench Town.

Winston's dad was a self-made man, what Mom called with disdain "new rich." He had gone from destitute to millionaire very quickly, and still had too much of his Trench Town background showing. Many of his childhood friends still lived there. Once in a while he took Winston with him to visit them, always accompanied by bodyguards. The other kids at school were upper middle class and looked down on Winston's family, even though they had only a fraction of their wealth.

"British colony equals British class prejudices, Pablo. We inherited the whole shit."

It wasn't only the Trench Town roots: Winston's dad had dropped out of elementary school. The other kids' fathers had all gone to college. So Winston was the son of the rich analphabet.

* * *

We hooked up very quickly. Someone witnessing our first meeting in the dorm would never have thought that we would later become best friends. We both majored in business administration and had almost the same classes. We were practically always together. There weren't many Jamaicans on campus, but a lot of Latin Americans. Since RW wanted to practice his Spanish, we ended up hanging out a lot with the Latin American crowd in our first months. It wasn't a very pleasant experience.

There were some exceptions. I did make a few good Latin American friends. There was the Argentinean son of a diplomat, who had already lived in half a dozen countries. There were the two Mexicans who, like me, had attended an American high school in their hometown. There was the Bolivian guy whose mother was American. What made us get along so well was the fact that all of us had been exposed to relativity, each one in his own way. We felt comfortable in America.

Not the others. They belonged to what the Argentinean called the Latin American ghetto. Like the guy from Peru, for example. The idiot used to walk around campus wearing a poncho. You could spot him miles away. I asked him, "Why don't you buy a normal coat like everyone else?" Nope, he was Peruvian. He couldn't deny his culture. He had to show that he was proud of it. Therefore, the poncho.

He said that his poncho disturbed me because I was a self-hating Chicano. I was ashamed of my culture and tried hard to become an American. I spoke, dressed, and acted like a gringo. I had "sold out to the gringos." In Spanish, "vendido a los gringos." I asked him, how could his whole culture be concentrated in a piece of clothing? His roots, baby, his roots, was the answer. Where were mine? "Vendido a los gringos, Pablo!"

One day I asked him when he would bring his llama to America. If a simple poncho was already such a powerful statement, could he imagine how much more pride he would be able to show if he rode his llama on campus? He stopped talking to me after that.

It was great fun to watch how the Latin American ghetto reacted to America. They had no idea about what they were getting into when they first arrived. They weren't aware of what RW called the asymmetry of knowledge. At school most people learned about their own countries and about America, the most important country in the world. Americans couldn't possibly reciprocate because there were almost 200 countries on earth. But ignorance was mistaken for arrogance.

Some foreign students knew by heart the names of all American presidents or all American states, and got very upset when Americans couldn't reciprocate and say anything about those foreigners' countries. Some of them then tried to fill the perceived gap in the Americans' education, only to get offended when after five minutes Americans changed the subject. Rightly so; what could be more boring than tales of a distant and unimportant place?

Many Americans didn't know or care much about the world. As far as they were concerned, the world started on the East Coast and ended on the West Coast. But the asymmetry of knowledge didn't make them better or worse than anyone else. Just different. Everyone had his way of looking at things. It was all relative.

RW loved to make fun of the situation, which didn't help us make friends in the Latin American ghetto. He made up the most outlandish theories to explain America to them, like the shooting theory. But the ghetto couldn't accept RW's wise explanations for the weird things they saw here. Maybe they lacked a sense of humor.

They convinced themselves that they had the duty to bring light into the perceived cultural darkness of the Yankees, to show them the real thing; real food, real music, real culture. For this purpose they organized the Latin American evenings. It was always very interesting and entertaining. A great opportunity to have fun, relax, and forget exams, papers, and school stress. RW called it folkloric entertainment, and the Latin American students doing it the folkloric entertainers.

A lot of Americans went there, not to be educated or indoctrinated but to have fun. With the exception of the few Americans who wanted to become Latin Americans. A very strange species. They learned Spanish and always hung out with Latin Americans, especially the folkloric entertainers. It was a beautiful symbiosis. Those Americans were more Latin American than I was. Some even started telling me that I wasn't a real one. They probably knew better: new converts were the most fanatic believers in any religion, RW kept telling me. One even bought a poncho. But still no llama.

They acquired the Latin American ghetto's worldview. They romanticized Latin America. Poverty was so cool. "Can't you see that people in Latin America are happy in poverty? Money and progress will only destroy their societies. People in America have everything and are unhappy!" Some even supported the Sandinistas and spent the summer in Nicaragua doing volunteer work to help the revolution. America was shit. Latin America was cool:

poverty, peasants, social interaction, solidarity.

That stuff made RW mad. His dad had been dirty poor, so he knew better. RW argued that poor people were happy despite poverty, not because of it. Poverty was not romantic, but humiliating. There was no dignity in starving. If you asked the poor about their dreams, they would answer that they wanted to live in big houses, eat well, dress well, send the children to school; in short, to improve their lives. "As Dad says, only intellectuals dream of poverty," RW said many times. But no one was listening.

That was the scene. My refusal to join the Latin American ghetto and become a folkloric entertainer myself was fatal. They started to ostracize me. Who cared about it, anyway? There was so much going on, so much to see, so much to experience.

"Open up your minds, guys! America is not as bad as you think. There's a lot to enjoy here."

"Self-hating Chicano! Sold out to the gringos!"

That was when RW started calling me Baldy. The nickname not only meant bald head; in the Rastafarian sense of the word, a person without dreadlocks. It was also a word play; an acronym for "Bendido A Los Diabolicos Yankees," Spanish for sold out to the diabolical Yankees. "Bendido" instead of "vendido" was an inside joke about Spanish speakers' troubles with the pronunciation of V and B. Baldy was therefore a typical, multi-layered RW joke.

I started calling him Rastaman Winston, just to tease, and it developed into RW. He also had a hard time on campus. Always the same stupid questions. "What, you Jamaican? You don't look Jamaican. Where are your dreadlocks, Rastaman? Do you smoke a lot of pot?"

After a couple of months RW and I drifted out of the Latin American scene into the left-wing scene. Another bad trip.

[1 / 14]

On campus there were a lot of students who called themselves Communists. RW told me that there were very cool women in that scene, and that we should check it out. I agreed. After all, it couldn't possibly be worse than the Latin American ghetto.

RW was right, at least concerning the women. After Christmas break I met a girl, a freshman in political science. She was hot, and Communist. But I couldn't care less. I was fascinated by her. RW teased me, "You fell in love, Baldy!" But I wasn't sure if it was love or only intense desire. Or maybe the fascination with the forbidden fruit, since Dad would disinherit me if he found out about the affair. Probably everything combined. We made love all the time. When we had some time left, she talked about Communism. I agreed with everything. Yeah, Communists made better lovers.

I didn't take it as seriously as she did. RW and I joked all the time about founding a Communist society in Jamaica. Free joints, free love, and reggae music. Stereotypical but very cool. Since I wasn't a native, RW would be the prime minister, of course. But I would be more than happy to serve as his right, or better said, left hand. Nice villas on the beach, Russian limousines, vodka, and caviar. Socialist paradise. Someone had to organize the socialist production. We could easily see ourselves as members of the ruling class in the classless society.

Things got bad when the girl convinced me to attend her study group meetings on Tuesday evenings. If she was part of that group, then it must be very cool, I thought. I took RW with me. Maybe he could meet a hot Communist girl himself.

Man, what a bunch of idiots. They asked, what in the hell did we want there? RW and I were rich guys. We exploited the proletarians. We were bloodsuckers. It was a class struggle, and we were on the wrong side. So what? Why couldn't rich guys become Communists? Should we first give our money away and then join the party? Rich people were also supposed to give their money away in order to become Christians. But who did it? All rich people I knew claimed to be Christians, and nobody cared. If the church didn't take it that seriously, why should the Communist Party do so? I guessed that they were only jealous because I was the one dating the hot comrade, not them.

A lot of the kids in that group were Maoists and believed in the Cultural Revolution. That at the same time when the Chinese were discovering the glories of capitalism. That was what happened when you didn't update your literature, RW kept joking. They talked with great pleasure about sending the bourgeoisie to be re-educated in labor camps. And who was going to run the country? The people, meaning the party, meaning them, those pimply-faced underachievers. Why should RW and I cut sugarcane in Jamaica while those idiots would be on the beach drinking our vodka and eating our caviar?

After a few meetings I got fed up and told them that they were only a bunch of lazy bastards who wanted to enjoy life at the cost of others. Then I realized that I was talking like Dad. That was it: I was out of there. They did what Dad had never managed to do in all those years: they made me see that Dad had been right all along regarding the Reds. And I hated when I realized that Dad was right. I sent them all to Siberia, since as atheists they didn't believe in hell. RW also left in solidarity.

Soon after, to my surprise and anger, the girl sent me to hell. She told me she had done self-criticism and realized that she couldn't keep seeing me, though she liked me a lot. Self-criticism, political conscience, class enemy: how I hated that crap.

She told me, "In the revolution your political convictions must be stronger than your feelings."

I couldn't believe it. How could she give up such a great relationship because of a stupid ideology? But she did. "Lighten up!" She wouldn't. That was it: ideologically merciless.

I was devastated. RW took me to his apartment that evening to have a few drinks. I was depressed and drank a lot. He kept saying, "It's only a pussy, Baldy. Only a pussy. There are thousands of others out there. Take it easy!" That was what friends were for. They helped you put things into perspective.

Since then I had never stopped disliking Commies. Not only they were lazy, envious bastards, as Dad always said, but they could also destroy your sex life.

* * *

This happened shortly before spring break. I had planned a trip to Miami with the girl. Now what? I asked RW if he wanted to go somewhere with me. He said, "Let's go home, Baldy! Let's check each other's hometowns. Three days in mine, three days in yours!"

"Are you out of your mind? I told you about Mom!"

"She invited me!"

"She what?"

Mom had called a few days before, but I had been out with my Communist girlfriend. They talked in Spanish, and Mom found it really sweet that I had a Spanish-speaking American roommate.

RW didn't tell her that he was Jamaican, of course. She invited him to come home with me anytime he wanted.

"Let's do it, man!" he said, grinning mischievously.

I refused. It would be a bad trip. She would treat him badly. She would get mad at me. She could even restart her argument about changing schools.

"Baldy, man, you told me that your father gave you one million dollars for your eighteenth birthday, remember?"

"So what?"

"You're all set, man! You're not underage anymore. You have enough money to pay for college. She can't do anything to you! It's time to start standing up to your mother!"

"She'll treat you badly."

"I can take any shit for three days. It'll be worth seeing it!"

"Seeing what?"

"Her face, man! Her face when she meets me! I'm dying too see it!"

Well, he saw it. We came unannounced and took a cab from the airport directly home. It scared the daylights out of my parents to see a six-foot-tall black guy walking into their living room. They were speechless and couldn't hide it. I was ashamed and wished I could disappear at that moment.

"This is Winston, Mom. My roommate. You invited him here two weeks ago, remember?"

"Thanks for the invitation!" RW said in Spanish, grinning.

Mom just stood there with her mouth open. I could almost hear her thoughts. "My son has been sharing a room with a black man since September!" She left the room quickly, saying that she had to prepare the guest room. RW asked to use the bathroom.

That was the chance I had been waiting for: to be alone with Dad for a few minutes. I could use my secret weapon, which I knew would work with him. I quickly told Dad that RW's father had made it from destitute boy in Trench Town to one of the richest men in Jamaica. Dad was surprised. I then said that actually, RW's dad had almost as much money as we did, and that he had amassed it in only one generation. Dad was impressed. Smiling, he told me, "Pablo, what a wonderful story! Thanks a lot for bringing your friend here!"

He had looked for something like RW for ages, he said: living and walking proof that blacks were really lazy. Because if RW's dad could make it, every other black guy also could. The fact that they didn't only demonstrated that they were lazy bastards. That was the way Dad's logic worked. During the three days we spent there, Dad didn't stop talking to RW, asking questions like an anthropologist on a lost island. Yes, there it was: the proof of the effectiveness of the vision thing.

Anyone who grew up watching Hollywood movies knew how important the vision thing was to Americans. If you had a vision and believed in your dream and worked hard enough, it didn't matter how long it took, eventually you would succeed. Easy, right? Dad, the closet American, was also into the vision thing.

Once, in my teenage years, I asked him a question, just to tease him. "Hey, Dad, listen. In order for the vision thing to function, it must work only for a few people, because to have a winner you need the losers, right? There must always be a lot of people, actually almost all of them, who'll never make it, regardless of how much they believe, dream, and work. Their failure is built into the system. This vision thing is all bullshit, isn't it?"

He looked at me, surprised. "You're starting to talk like a Communist! I worry about you, Pablo. But you're too young to understand it. You'll see what I mean when you get older. Just wait."

Anyway, Dad was very happy with RW. He even told me when we left for Jamaica, "You know what, this dark-skinned friend of yours is actually not a bad boy. Very bright and very charming, too." That was typical Dad. When he finally met a black guy who didn't fit his stereotype, he didn't change the stereotype but the guy's color. So RW wasn't black anymore. Only dark-skinned.

Actually, to be fair, it was not only Dad. That was something most people did back home. We changed the name to eliminate the problem. The police didn't torture people. People got hurt resisting arrest. We didn't exploit workers. We created jobs. It wasn't an underdeveloped country. It was a developing country. People weren't starving to death. They only had an acute protein deficiency. And so on. When I arrived in Columbia, I was surprised to see people on campus doing it, too. They even had a name for it: political correctness.

So Dad found that RW was a great dark-skinned guy. But Mom wasn't impressed. She hated black people, even if they were bright, charming, well educated, and rich. Actually, especially if they were bright, charming, well educated, and rich. How could they dare?

* * *

When I was back in America, Mom called to complain that the guest room stunk. She had to throw away the mattress and have the bathroom professionally disinfected. What did I think I was doing bringing RW to our house? And how could I go to Jamaica and spend three days with his family? The poor woman was shocked. RW was the first black person to enter her house who wasn't a servant. The first black person ever to have slept in the guest room and eaten at the dinner table.

Later I asked RW, "So, was it really worth it?"

"Of course," he answered, but it didn't sound very convincing. Then he added, "You know what, Baldy? You need a new girlfriend, right? I'll introduce you to a hot Jamaican girl I know. And then I'll take a picture of the both of you in bed and send it to your mom!"

We both laughed. I then knew that he hadn't taken it so lightly as he was pretending to. He was dreaming of revenge.

"RW, maybe we should send a picture of both of us in bed. That would kill her!"

"No way! That would kill my mother too, Baldy! She's already sick, as you know. Let's stay with the Jamaican girl, okay?"

"When will you introduce her to me?"

"I'm invited to a party in two weeks, and she'll be there. I'm taking you with me."

But it never happened. The Wednesday before that party we finally found Mad Dog. Trip number twenty-two.

[1/15]

RW told me Mad Dog's story a few days after we first met. At the time we didn't know him by that nickname; he was still Douglas to us. It was a very sad story. From first grade on, RW and Douglas were in the same class at school and became best buddies. But Douglas's parents didn't approve of the friendship. They didn't want their son playing with the son of the rich Trench Town analphabet.

Douglas's dad had gone to law school. He worked in the

attorney general's office, and was in charge of an undercover investigative unit. In the summer of 1977 he was shot dead while investigating a case of corruption in government. The police never found out who killed him. Douglas's mother had a nervous breakdown and had to be interned in a psychiatric hospital. Douglas and his three younger sisters went to live with their maternal grandparents.

Douglas didn't cope well. In only one week he had lost his father for good, and was separated from his mother for an indefinite period of time. He was only twelve, just starting puberty. The shock was too much for him; he started to make trouble. His grandparents couldn't control him and were counting the days to send him back to his mother. But his mother never came back from the hospital. She killed herself, cutting her wrists. Douglas went berserk. He started smoking marijuana and was always high.

Winston and his parents watched this deteriorating process without knowing what to do. They all liked Douglas a lot. Winston's dad went to see Douglas's grandparents and offered to raise the boy for a couple of years. Douglas needed a stable home and a friend he could talk to: Winston. If the boys lived together, maybe Douglas would be able to overcome his grief.

The grandparents refused. They wouldn't give their grandson away to be raised by strangers, especially that kind of strangers. They didn't like Winston's family. But they knew that the boy needed a stable home, preferably very far away from the drug scene he was now involved in. They had another daughter who had immigrated to America and lived in New York City. They begged her to take Douglas to America and raise him. She agreed, reluctantly. Her husband, also Jamaican, didn't like the idea very much. They already had two children.

It took many months to get the paperwork done. They had to adopt Douglas in Jamaica first, in order to get him a visa for the United States more easily. Eventually every problem got solved, every form got stamped, and in the fall of 1978, just in time for the new school year, thirteen-year-old Douglas moved to America for good.

Winston's parents tried to get a contact address so that the boys could keep in touch, but the grandparents refused. The sooner Douglas forgot Jamaica, the easier he would adapt to his new country. That was supposed to be the end of the friendship between Winston and Douglas.

But RW never forgot his friend. The main reason he chose Columbia was to find Douglas in New York City. One year before he finished high school, he started to track Douglas down with his dad's help. One private detective in Jamaica could get hold of a copy of the adoption papers, revealing Douglas's new surname and his aunt's address in New York at the time of the adoption. Another detective in New York could follow up on that and find the school he attended until he dropped out in 1982 and left home for good.

His aunt didn't know his whereabouts. His former schoolmates didn't know much about him, either. The detective could only find out that Douglas was now dealing drugs somewhere in Brooklyn, but had no criminal record yet.

* * *

I was pretty impressed to hear that story. Wow, private detectives! Winston really had style: an apartment to use on weekends, private detectives to find lost people. He knew how to use his money to achieve his goals. I had a lot to learn from him.

I asked him what would be the next move. Would the detective start searching for Douglas? Winston had asked the detective to do exactly that, but the guy refused, saying that he had only a desk job. Winston then asked if the detective could recommend someone able to do the job. The guy said that he knew a lot of people able and willing to do that kind of job, but he didn't think it would be a wise move.

Since Douglas was now a drug dealer, he would be watching his back. He wouldn't be found unless he wanted to. If detectives started looking for him, Douglas could mistake them for the police or people with a score to settle, and would certainly hide. That would be a waste of time and money. If Winston had the guts, he should do it himself. He was too young to be in law enforcement and looked too clean to be a criminal. He had a Jamaican accent and a reasonable story. With luck, it could work.

He should be careful and take a few precautions, though. Always go during the day, bring a friend to keep him company, expect to be robbed so never carry anything of value, and so on.

"Shit, Winston, he wants you to do it yourself?"

"He's right, Pablo. Would you come along?"

I found the idea scary but didn't want to admit it. "Why? Are you afraid?"

"Not really. Brooklyn can't be worse than Trench Town."

"You had bodyguards there!"

"I needed them. Everybody knew us there. Here I'm just another black guy."

"So you don't need me."

"No. You should do it for your own sake. It's time to get street smart, Pablo! See the other side of life!"

"I'll think about it."

"The best day is Wednesday. We can go in the early afternoon right after freshman English. We can start soon. There are only a few phone calls I have to make first."

He called all the people the detective had contacted in New York, starting with the aunt. She refused to talk to him. He then tried Douglas's former high school friends. The only useful information he could get was that Douglas wasn't called Douglas anymore. The name had evolved: first Doug, then Mad Doug, and finally Mad Dog.

At the beginning of October we started our search. I was scared, but Winston was right: I needed to get out of my cocoon. It was time to grow up. Almost every Wednesday we went to Brooklyn searching for Mad Dog. We left our watches, IDs, and credit cards in the dorm, taking only cash with us, one hundred dollars each. Winston told me that it was always good to have something to give to the guy trying to rob you. Criminals got really aggressive when there was nothing to take. Especially if they were on drugs.

We got mugged twice. The first time the guy was very high on drugs and held a knife to our faces. We gave him the money and he ran away. The second time three guys came and asked for money, their hands in their pockets. We didn't care to find out if they were armed or not. We gave them the money. Both times no one hurt us.

The search took forever. We got to know a lot of bad spots in Brooklyn. There were a lot of false leads. We met four or five Mad Dogs before finally finding Douglas. What a stupid nickname. There were probably hundreds of Mad Dogs on the streets.

* * *

"Come back tomorrow."

"Tomorrow we can't, but we can come back next Wednesday."

"Next Wednesday at three."

The following week the same guy took us to a corner. We stood there for a while, not understanding what was going on. Then we noticed that the guy was looking at a building on the other side of the street. We looked in the same direction and saw a person hiding behind the curtains, checking us out. A few minutes later another guy came out of the building and said to RW, "You the one looking for Mad Dog? Come with me. The white dude stays, though."

RW noticed that I was afraid of staying behind. "The guy is cool, man. He's my friend."

"I don't give a shit. You alone."

I saw how excited RW was to meet Douglas. "It's cool, Winston, I'll wait here. Go. I hope it's him!"

"I'll talk to him and send for you."

The three of them disappeared into the building. I was left behind, standing alone on a very mean street, in a very mean neighborhood, deep in Brooklyn.

Mario, a Puerto Rican guy who worked at a bookstore close to campus and who grew up in Spanish Harlem, used to say that when you went to a bad neighborhood, you should put your hands in your pockets and look cool. People would think that if you were crazy enough to be there, you were probably armed. Another jewel of New York City logic. I remembered that. But there was a small problem: all the other guys were armed too, Mario. And not only pretending. I decided not to put my hands in my pockets.

After about half an hour a guy came for me. "Mad Dog's calling you. Come with me."

We went. Second store left. There was a black guy at the door. After checking if I was armed, he let me in. There were more guys inside; all black, all armed to their teeth. I had to think about Mom and grinned.

One of them showed me a door. "They're in there." I opened it and saw RW and Douglas talking on the couch. Both stood up immediately. Douglas was even taller than RW.

"This is my friend Pablo. I call him Baldy. He's Latino, but he's okay."

I took that as a compliment. "Nice finally meeting you, Douglas!"

"If you call me Douglas again I'll kill you, motherfucker!"

I froze. The guy looked very angry.

Then he burst out into laughter. So did RW.

"You were right, Winston! He's scared! Don't worry, Baldy! It was a joke. Only a joke."

He told me that he didn't like being called Douglas anymore. Douglas was dead. He was Mad Dog now. It had much more style.

RW was beaming with happiness. "We found him, Baldy! Trip number twenty-two!"

Mad Dog seemed very happy, too. I got the impression that I was only disturbing them. "You two have a lot to talk about. I'll go back to the dorm. See you later, Winston."

"I'll send one of the guys to walk you to the subway station," Mad Dog said. "These are mean streets, man. A baby-faced Latino guy like you could get hurt."

I was about to refuse when RW said, "That's a great idea! Thanks, Baldy. I'll never forget your help. I won't go back to the dorm tonight. I'll sleep in my apartment. Mad Dog will come over on the weekend. You'll then have the chance to get to know him better."

The Saturday I was supposed to meet the hot Jamaican girl I spent with those two Jamaican guys smoking joints, listening to Marley, and talking. It was the first of many such evenings.

* * *

RW used to give wild parties in his apartment, which we called Sweet Jamaica: great music, great herb, and a lot of Jamaicans. I was one of the very few guys from college invited there. Mad Dog came to a few of those parties, but he preferred to meet us alone.

He didn't like to listen to Marley when strangers were around. Marley made him remember his childhood. His dad had been a great Marley fan, and Mad Dog grew up listening to Marley's records. He was listening to the Exodus album at the very moment when he was told that his dad had been shot. The album had come out that summer. He was in love with a girl at school. "From the very first time I rest my eyes on you, girl, my heart says follow through…" The Kaya album came out in his last summer in Jamaica, when he was waiting to be adopted and taken out of the country. "Oh, children, weep no more…"

His grandfather didn't let him take his Marley records to America. He thought that the music was a bad influence on Mad Dog. In his opinion Rastafarians were only dopeheads, and Mad Dog was on his way to becoming one. His aunt and adoptive mother, probably acting on her father's instruction, got rid of all Marley records and tapes in her apartment before Mad Dog arrived. When he wanted to listen to Marley he had to go to a friend's place. They smoked pot together and listened to the music for hours.

The music soothed his pain, but it also put him in a mellow mood, melancholic and vulnerable. He didn't want to be around strangers when he was in that mood, especially after he started dealing. He told us that a drug dealer had to be strong and mean, otherwise he wouldn't survive the streets. When he was working with his dealers, they listened only to rap. Most of the guys loved the gangster stuff anyway.

Mad Dog brought a lot of rap records to Sweet Jamaica, introducing RW and me to rap music. He could impersonate a street gangster very well. Listening to him doing the Brooklyn accent, you could easily believe that he had been born and raised in the ghetto. No hint of his upper middle class Jamaican background.

Mad Dog never became a close friend, but we got along well. Until graduation we saw each other about once a month, always in RW's apartment in Harlem. RW visited him in Brooklyn once in a while, but with only two or three exceptions I never went back to those mean Brooklyn neighborhoods again.

[2]

[2 / 1]

Six years later I was back in Brooklyn searching for Mad Dog, this time as the caveman, not the baby-faced Pablo. I wasn't afraid of getting mugged. As my roommate Janet had said, I didn't look like a victim. I had the impression that the drug dealers I talked to could see the caveman in me. They didn't seem afraid but somehow respectful, like they knew that they shouldn't mess with me. That made me happy. At least I was getting some kind of reward for all the suffering I had gone through. The caveman could inspire respect.

The caveman could attract cops, too. That was a completely new experience. I had never been stopped or frisked in my whole life. Now whenever I walked past cops, I could feel that they screened me for much longer than usual, as if they too were sniffing the caveman in me.

I thought that I was just being paranoid. I had reasons to fear cops, after all. But then I was reminded that even paranoid people could have real enemies. On my sixth search day, two plainclothes police officers frisked me.

I was walking down Brooklyn Avenue in East Flatbush. I saw two black guys standing around and thought that they were dealers. When I was about six feet away, they pulled their guns and screamed, "Police! Don't move! Get on the ground!" One of them flashed a badge.

I froze and just stood there, looking at the guns and the badge. One of the guys screamed again, "Get on the ground! Now! Hands on your head!" I had seen that scene so many times in the movies. Now it was happening to me. I got down and put my hands on my head. The sidewalk was wet and cold and I got my clothes dirty.

One of the cops frisked me. He couldn't find anything and asked, "What are you doing here?"

"Walking around. I didn't know it was a crime."

He kicked me in my left leg. "Watch your mouth! Why don't you have an ID?"

"Got mugged a few days ago."

The one frisking me told the other, "Only two dollars." Talking to me, he said, "Can't even get a joint here with two dollars."

"I don't do drugs."

"Get up and take off your sunglasses."

I did. He checked my eyes and told his partner, "Not high."

"I told you that I don't do drugs."

"So what the hell are you doing here? Got lost or what? Get out of here, or we'll arrest you for loitering. Go!"

I turned around and walked away. I was wet and dirty, and my leg was hurting; the bastard had kicked really hard. I could hardly breath because my heart was pounding like I had sprinted a mile. "Look at the positive side," I told myself, "at least they weren't Feds looking for you." But I was shocked to realize that there were plainclothes cops out there searching for drug dealers and drug addicts. I had to be extra careful.

* * *

More than a week later, on Tuesday, November fifth, I was feeling very depressed. I had missed my eleven-day deadline. It was already my fourteenth search day. I was running out of money, and Mad Dog was nowhere to be found. I had already met four wrong ones.

It was past three in the afternoon, very cold, and I was about to call it a day. I was walking down East Fifty-fifth Street on my way to the subway station Crown Heights when I saw a black guy selling dope to a young man. When I approached him, he smiled, probably expecting me to be his next customer.

"No, thanks. I'm looking for a Jamaican guy. Mad Dog. You know him?"

"Lots of Mad Dogs around here..."

"He doesn't work the streets. He's higher up."

He frowned. "Not scum like me, you mean?"

Shit, why did those guys get offended so easily? I tried to sound nice. "Never said that. Just said..."

He interrupted me. "I heard what you said. What do you want from Mad Dog?"

"Talk to him. He knows me. I'm Winston Twenty-two."

He laughed. It happened each time I told someone that my name was Winston Twenty-two. People found the name laughable but somehow believed it. Maybe it sounded credible exactly because it was laughable.

"Winston what?"

"Winston Twenty-two. Mad Dog and I went to school together in Jamaica."

He laughed again, and I had to smile. What was it with Jamaican guys laughing that way that always disarmed me? You couldn't get really mad at them when they laughed like that.

"You Jamaican, Twenty-two?"

"No, my family lived there in the seventies. Can you bring me to Mad Dog or not?"

"Maybe. What do I get?"

"Mad Dog's gratitude?"

"You're a funny guy, Twenty-two. Come back tomorrow in the afternoon."

"Here?"

"Right."

"What time?"

"Afternoon."

* * *

I went home very excited. Would I get lucky this time? What a coincidence it would be to find him on a Wednesday again. I started to feel hope. I came back the next day at two in the afternoon, but the guy wasn't there. I walked around the area searching for him in the nearby streets, but I couldn't find him. I kept coming back to our meeting point every hour, but he never showed up. I went home feeling very depressed.

On Thursday I went back at around three in the afternoon. I searched for the guy everywhere but couldn't find him. I was standing on the sidewalk, thinking about my next move, when I heard someone screaming, "Twenty-two!"

I turned around and saw two black guys walking my way. I couldn't tell from the distance if one of them was the same I had met two days before. Both had hoods over their heads. When they were about fifty yards away, one stopped walking and stayed behind. The other kept moving my way. He was the one I had met.

He smiled at me. "Long time no see, Twenty-two."

"Where have you been? I was here yesterday the whole afternoon!"

"Pissed off?"

I didn't think it would be wise to admit it. "No, it's okay. Is that Mad Dog standing over there?"

He shook his head.

"Can you take me to Mad Dog now?"

"Like in the movies? 'Take me to your leader'?"

Laughing, he took his left hand out of his pocket and gave me a sheet of folded paper. "Call this number today at six. It's a pay phone. If you're late, you'll miss him."

"Did Mad Dog give you the number?"

"Take care, Twenty-two."

He turned around and walked back to his friend. That was the first time in my search that someone had given me a phone number. I unfolded the sheet of paper and saw a number with a Brooklyn area code. Below the number it was written, "Answer only yes or no, or I'll hang up." The information was typed.

Was that really a pay phone number? Would Mad Dog answer the call? What if it was a practical joke, like the number of a police station? On the other hand, what did I have to lose besides the money for the phone call?

* * *

There was a pay phone on Jay Street so I headed home. I couldn't figure out what "answer only yes or no, or I'll hang up" was supposed to mean. That could be Mad Dog. He sometimes did and said strange things. Was he afraid of something? And if yes, afraid of what?

But whatever kind of games he was playing, could it be that I had found the real Mad Dog? Thursday, November seventh. Search day number sixteen. Full of hope, at around five I got off the subway at York Street. I had one hour to kill.

I thought about going home, but my roommate could be there, and I wasn't in the mood to talk to her. I walked up and down Jay Street, never getting too far away from the pay phone. At six o'clock sharp I dialed the number. It rang only three times. Someone picked it up but said nothing.

I said, "Hallo?"

"This phone line is not secure. Don't say anything but yes or no or I'll hang up. You understand me?"

It was him! I could recognize his voice. I felt so happy at that moment, so overwhelmed, that I forgot to answer.

He asked again, pissed off, "Understand me or not?"

"Yes!"

"Recognize my voice?"

"Yes!"

"Recognize yours, too." That made me even happier. He continued, in a rushed tone. "I can't talk long. I'll give you instructions on how to make a safe call. Tomorrow at ten in the morning."

Why was the line not secure? We were both using pay phones.

"Remember the first time we met?"

"Of course!"

"Yes or no! Or I'll end this fucking call!"

Man, what was his problem?

"Remember that you left early and I had a guy walk you back to the subway station?"

"Yes."

"Remember that station?"

"Yes." Church Avenue. I had been there just three days before.

"Get on a train at that station. Heading to Manhattan, count seven stations. The station where you get on the train is number zero. You start there and count seven. Understand?"

"Yes."

"At station number seven you get off the train. Walk the street named after the station, heading to Manhattan. Got it? Seven stops, street named after the station, walk direction Manhattan."

"Yes."

"Cross an avenue. Keep walking same street in the same direction. Cross second avenue. Then you'll find a pay phone. Again: cross two avenues, pay phone. Got it?"

"Yes."

"Be there at ten. I'll call you. Don't tell anyone about it. It's not safe. Understand?"

"Yes"

"Gotta go."

He hung up. It was probably the shortest phone call of my life. And the most important one. I had found him, on trip number sixteen!

When I started walking home, it happened: I didn't understand why, but I had an uncontrollable urge to cry. I burst out in tears and started crying out loud, like a little child. It was scary: I wanted to stop it, but I couldn't. I sat down on the street curb and cried and cried and cried. Was that what people called a nervous breakdown?

I didn't know how long I had been crying when I heard, "You okay, son?"

I looked up and saw an old lady standing in front of me. How long had she been standing there? I couldn't tell.

"Are you okay, son?"

I nodded, still sobbing.

"Anything I can do for you?"

I shook my head, but she kept watching me. That made me feel ashamed, so I stood up and walked quickly away, still sobbing. I could calm down only a few minutes later. I was scared; I hadn't cried like that since childhood. I went back to my apartment, getting there at about half past six.

Janet noticed something and asked, "You okay, John?"

I decided to tell a lie so that she would leave me alone. "Just heard that a very good friend of mine died last week..."

"Sorry..."

I went to my room and studied my Brooklyn map. The station he meant was Bergen Street. The street I had to walk was Bergen Street, and the avenues I had to cross were Fifth and Fourth. The pay phone would be on Bergen Street between Fourth and Third avenues. Why would that pay phone be safer than the one I had just used?

[2/2]

I didn't sleep very well that night. The next day I was too tired to work out, and could hardly eat breakfast. Afraid to be late and miss my call, I left home so early that I got to the pay phone at nine. To kill time, I looked around and examined every window to see if someone was hiding behind a curtain and checking me out. I couldn't see anyone. The phone rang at ten.

"How are you doing, Baldy?"

"Can I talk now?"

"This line is safe."

"I'm in deep shit, man!"

"Of course you are! Why would a rich guy like you go looking for my black ass if he wasn't in deep shit?"

He was right, and I felt ashamed. "Sorry, man, we lost contact after I left New York. But I always asked Winston..."

He laughed, interrupting me. "It's all right, Baldy. It was only a joke. I heard a lot about you in the last weeks. King of Cocaine!"

"I didn't do it, man! It's a big mistake. Believe me!"

He laughed again. "That's what criminals always tell the judge, Baldy. Have you been rehearsing? 'No, Your Honor, it wasn't me. It's a mistake.'"

"I was set up. Please believe me. I can tell you everything later. It's a very long story. You know I couldn't do that."

"Yeah, you were always mommy's little boy, right? Give me the short version. Who set you up and how?"

"Basically someone ran a drug operation using my name."

"No shit! What about the killings in your apartment? The fingerprints and stuff?"

"I was there but didn't do it. It was a setup. They got my fingerprints later to blame me."

"It worked. Everyone believes it was you."

"Yes, that's why I need your help. I have to hide. The cops know everyone I know. I can't ask anyone for help. You're the only person in my life they know nothing about."

"And let's keep it that way, Baldy! Let's keep it that way. But how can I help you?"

"I need a job!"

"Selling drugs?"

"Yes!"

He laughed. "You can't handle that, Baldy. The streets are mean."

"I don't need to do it on the streets. You already have people doing that. I can go places your guys can't."

He was silent for a few seconds. "Listen, Baldy, when I heard that you were looking for me, I expected you to ask just that. I thought that fate had brought you to me because I've been look-ing for someone like you for ages."

"Like what?"

"A white, well-educated dude. Someone who doesn't look like a dealer."

I smiled. Yes, he would help me! "You just found your man, Mad Dog!"

"But you're brown, not white. Remember?"

I sighed.

"Lost your sense of humor, Baldy? You used to laugh at this shit."

"I'm not in the mood. Do I have the job or what?"

"I'm not sure, man..."

"You just said that you've been looking for a guy like me."

"Yes, but I thought that everything I had heard about you was true. That you had joined the business, and that you had the experience. You need experience to do the job, man."

The conversation was getting on the wrong track. He was going to dump me. I got nervous. "Listen, it's okay if you don't want to give me a job. But you can still help me. I need money. I have only fifty dollars left. There's still Winston. He can't send money to me directly because I can't go to the bank and collect it. But he could send you the money. You'd give it to me. What about that?" I was on the verge of crying.

"Listen, Baldy, let's leave Winston out of this shit."

"Why? He's the only person in this world who can help me if you won't."

He sighed. "You're right. Are you sure you can do the job, Baldy?"

"Of course! I'm not the guy you once knew, Mad Dog. I've changed. I'll do anything to survive. I've already done a lot of bad stuff in the last few weeks. When you hear my story, you'll know that I can do the job."

"Okay, Baldy, I'll listen to your story. Let's meet and talk."

"When?"

"Today. Let's do lunch. Are you hungry?"

"Only if you pay. I can't afford eating out."

"It's on me. Do you see the supermarket across the street?"

"Yes. Are you in there?"

"Kidding me? I'm very far away. To the right of the supermarket there's a coin laundry. See it?"

"Yes."

"You go in there and look behind machine number three. I hid a pager there for you."

"Why do I need a pager?"

"So that I can tell you which number to call next."

That irritated me. "I thought this line was safe. You said so!"

"Safer than the last one, yes."

"What is this shit all about, Mad Dog? Why the pager? Why the yes-and-no thing? What are you afraid of?"

"You think I'm exaggerating?"

"Ain't you? I'm the one who's being chased, not you."

"Exactly! And I have no intention of being close to you when they find you, man. I want to live a bit longer. Those Colombians are mean motherfuckers."

"They don't know where I am."

"But they're looking for you everywhere."

"The Colombian family is not that big."

"It's the bounty, Baldy. Everyone is looking for you. One hundred fifty thousand dollars is a lot of money."

"It's only one hundred thousand. I read the papers."

"Papers? I was told that personally by one of my suppliers."

I felt bad. The bounty had gone up fifty percent.

"There are a lot of mean motherfuckers out there looking for you. You were lucky that nobody recognized you. And then there are the Feds."

More bad news? "What about the Feds?"

"Ever heard that saying, 'the enemy of my enemy is my friend'? They could be working together, Baldy. The Feds and the Colombians. They both want the same thing: your brown ass on a plate."

I sighed. "I thought I was the paranoid one, Mad Dog."

"Only the paranoid survive. We can't trust anyone. That guy you met on Tuesday? He's okay, but he'd sell your ass if he knew it was you. Why shouldn't he? He doesn't owe you shit, does he?"

"No, he doesn't."

"And we can't be sure that he didn't suspect anything, can we? He had the phone number and the time of the call. If he gave it to someone else, the call could be traced. That's why it had to be short. The Feds might know that we're talking right now."

"But they don't know where I am, Mad Dog. They can't tap all pay phones in Brooklyn!"

"Yes, they can, if they want to. You have no idea what the Feds can do. For that reason you'll hang up now, go inside that coin laundry, and get that fucking pager. Behind machine number three. I hope it's still there. I'll call back in ten minutes."

* * *

I went to the coin laundry, which was almost empty. I found the pager behind the machine, went back to the pay phone, and waited for the call. I let it ring only once.

"Did you get it, Baldy?"

"Easy."

"So listen to me. For the next two questions we'll play the yes and no game again. Just in case."

"If you insist..."

"Here we go. Yes or no only. Remember where I made the move on the drag queen?"

I had to laugh. Of course I did. It was on Washington Square. Mad Dog had been bragging to RW and me about how he could pick up any woman, how irresistible he was, and so forth. Then he saw the drag queen from the distance, thought that she was a real woman, and told us that he would go there and pick her up. He came back very quickly.

"Yes."

"Remember the spot where the drag queen was standing?"

"Yes."

"Okay, that's your destination. From that spot you can see a pay phone across the street. Use it to call the number on the pager. Go there now. But not directly. Lose your tail first."

"Lose what?"

"Your tail, man. The guy who's following you."

That scared me. "Who's following me? What do you know that I don't?"

"I don't know shit," he said in an aggravated voice, "but if there is someone following you, make sure you lose him, okay? Come to me alone!"

"How can I lose him?"

"Man, you have a lot to learn!"

"Then teach me! You're the only person I have left!"

He sighed. "You're right again... The subway is the perfect place to lose a tail. When a train arrives, normally the platform is crowded, right? The people inside the train get off and move away from the train. Then the people who were waiting on the platform get on the train. After that, when the train is about to leave, the area in front of the train is empty. That's when you get off. Understand why?"

"No."

"I thought so. You get off, turn around, and stand on the platform watching the doors. Check if someone else also leaves the train in a hurry. Either your tail isn't quick enough and stays on the train, and you lose him, or he must run to get out, giving away the fact that he's following you. Got it?"

"It could be a coincidence."

"Right. For this reason you walk to the other side of the platform and take the train in the opposite direction. If the guy does the same, he's your tail. Okay, this could also be a coincidence. That's why you have to do it a few times to be sure."

They did call him Mad Dog for a reason. "Okay..."

"You'll have two hours to travel around. Be there at twelve thirty. I call the pager, and you call me back. Easy, right?"

"I don't see the point, but if that's what you want me to do, I'll do it. My life is in your hands, you know?"

"Shit, Baldy, don't talk like that! It's depressing. I've gotta go. Talk to you later."

What was that saying again? You should be careful what you wish for because you might get it? That was my man, Mad Dog. The guy I had risked my life searching for. The guy who would save me. Was he sane?

[2/3]

Walking back to the subway station, I wondered why people said that there was a very fine line between high intelligence and madness. I knew Mad Dog well. He was very bright. He dropped out of high school, he said, because he realized that a formal education wouldn't take him very far. But he never stopped learning. He read a lot of books. I had to give him credit for his intelligence and his experience, even if that lose-your-tail thing seemed like paranoia to me. Had underground life done that to him? Maybe with time you didn't notice your paranoia anymore and acted like the danger was real. How could I know, anyway? I had been a criminal for less than a month; Mad Dog for almost a decade.

On the train to Manhattan I realized that losing a tail was a very simple thing to do. I should give it a try. I had time to kill anyway. Besides that, maybe he was following me or had someone doing it. It could be a test, and I didn't want to flunk it.

I got off at Fulton Street and went back one station to Wall Street. Then I went back to Fulton Street, where I changed lines. I went up to Bleecker Street, did a U-turn, went one station back to Spring Street, did another U-turn, and went up again to Aston

Plaza, where I got off the train and walked to Washington Square. I was pretty sure that no one was following me, and I didn't want to be late.

I found the spot and the pay phone. The pager started vibrating at twelve thirty. He might be crazy, I thought, but never late. The number had a Manhattan area code. I called him back.

"Mad Dog?"

"All right, Baldy. Good man. Hungry?"

"Very."

"Remember that Ethiopian restaurant we used to go, about two blocks from here?"

"Yes."

"You go in first and take a seat. I'll arrive ten minutes after you. See you there."

The place was packed, but I could get a table. When Mad Dog walked through the door, smiling at me, my eyes got misty. "Shit," I thought, "You're not going to cry like a baby again, are you?"

"Baldy, man, give me a hug!"

When I hugged him, I burst into tears. Man, how embarrassing; I was crying on the guy's shoulders like a sissy. And everyone was watching. Fortunately I could stop it quickly this time.

"Sorry, Mad Dog, I didn't want to. I don't know what's happening to me. Probably too much stress."

"It's good to cry, man. You're finally getting in touch with your feelings."

"Oh, no! You aren't going to give me that new-age crap of yours now, are you?"

He smiled. "I see that you're not there yet. But you're on your way, man. I'm proud of you."

We sat down, and he looked me in the eyes for a while. "You have changed, Baldy. Gone through a lot of shit, right?"

"Very bad trip, man."

The waiter came, and we ordered. Then Mad Dog asked me for my story. He listened mostly in silence, only commenting here and there or asking for more details.

I told him about the setup first. He was impressed. "A perfect plan, Baldy. The guy who set you up is a genius."

"Why didn't he keep going? Why the shooting in my apartment? Why stop a winning game?"

"Who knows? Probably something went wrong. Maybe he was tipped off about the DEA investigation. Maybe he had problems with the bank accounts. We'll never know. Suddenly you became a problem, and he had to get rid of you. But he was very professional. He used you until the very end, and then disposed of you in great style."

"You call that shit great style?"

"Come on, Baldy. In one single move he stole the Colombians' cocaine, sent two of them to hell, got rid of a dangerous undercover DEA agent, and you got all the blame for that and for all the other stuff that was going on behind your back. That's what I call style, man!"

"That's what I call an asshole, Mad Dog."

"You're too emotionally involved to appreciate the beauty of the plan. But he made one big mistake: he underestimated you. You were supposed to be dead by now, killed by those vicious Colombians. That was also part of the plan, but you never got the bullets marked for you. You got away. That's the only flaw in the guy's plan."

"They're still out there."

"But they won't find you, Baldy. I'll teach you how to go underground. Big way. But now tell me about your flight. How did you get from California to New York?"

I told him about my hitchhiking and the shooting in Texas.

"You were inside that restaurant? It was all over the news!"

"Remember RW's shooting theory?"

He laughed. "Yes, the shooting theory! Man, it was like Winston was predicting the future!"

I talked about how the shooting changed me, about stealing John's wallet and using his credit cards.

He loved the caveman thing. "Right! Caveman! That's it. That's what's different about you now. You're going back to the roots."

"Becoming a troglodyte?"

"No, getting in touch with your inner self. Your true self. That's great!"

"There you go again."

"Never mind. Tell me more."

I told him about the rest of the trip and the ATM disaster. The fat woman made him laugh. When I told him the Jesus story, he had a laugh attack. Everyone inside the restaurant started looking at us.

He noticed that I wasn't laughing. "Come on, Baldy! This is hilarious!"

"It would be funny if I hadn't tried to kill her. If I hadn't pulled the trigger."

"Kill her with a toy gun?"

I talked about my nervous meltdown, about wishing it were a real gun, about feeling like a murderer.

"Take it easy, man. I would have shot the bitch, too. You would be doing her a favor anyway. Sending her to meet her Jesus."

I finally told him about the guy I assaulted inside the movie theater. "I went though all this shit in only one week, Mad Dog. I have changed. I can do the job."

"Probably. Tell me the rest. What happened until today?"

I talked about finding the apartment and how weird my roommate was.

"Sounds like a good place to hide. For the moment. Just don't fuck her, okay?"

"I don't think this will happen, but why do you care?"

"You'd start talking. It's difficult to keep secrets from the woman you are fucking. Sooner or later you'll let something slip. You have to keep mum, Baldy. Your life depends on it."

I nodded, then told him about my search, the people I had met, the close call with the plainclothes cops.

"That's all, Mad Dog. Do I have the job or not?"

He smiled. "Yes, Baldy, I believe so."

I was truly happy. "Thanks, man!"

My eyes got misty again. I tried to control it. He noticed and smiled. "Let it flow, Baldy!"

I ignored his remark. "So, what will I be doing?"

"First thing, stop being so uptight. If you feel like crying, you should do it. Finally get in touch with your feelings, man."

Shit, I had forgotten how deep Mad Dog was into new-age and esoteric stuff.

"I'll try, Mad Dog. Maybe you could give me some lessons?"

"Of course I will."

It was supposed to be a sarcastic comment.

He smiled and added, "I know."

"Know what?"

"That you were being sarcastic."

Could he read minds, too?

"Tell me about my job, Mad Dog."

"Next week you'll learn more. Not today."

He gave me an envelope.

"Here's some money. A cash advance."

I took it, wondering how much would be in there.

He smiled. "Two thousand."

Maybe he could really read minds.

"You look like shit, man. A rich guy like you will never get used to life on the streets."

It wasn't only the cheap clothing I was wearing, he said, though I did look like a bum. It wasn't the fear I had of being killed, either. My problem was that I looked hopeless in a way that only rich people caught without money could look. If I kept the $2,000 on me all the time, I would feel much better.

He was right. Somehow, the moment I put the envelope in my pocket I felt different. He then said that I needed my good life back. I wouldn't be able to do the job if I looked and felt like a bum. But I had to remain a bum until I found another place to live and moved out of Janet's apartment.

"Why? What does the apartment have to do with it?"

When I moved in, I was a bum who slept rough, he said. I had to move out as the same person, or Janet would suspect something. That was what I should always avoid: suspicion. I had to be like a chameleon: always blend in, always change color according to the environment, and keep that color as long as I stayed in that environment.

"Don't change anything, Baldy. Not even your daily routine. Even so, if she's smart, she'll notice that you've changed inside. So avoid talking to her."

"Okay."

"Don't get a haircut, either. Don't shave. Let everything grow. We'll go later to a hairdresser and get you a trendy look."

He would get me an apartment in Manhattan. He had a lot of clients who had leases on rent-controlled apartments that they didn't need anymore but weren't stupid enough to give up, so they sublet them.

Once I had moved into the new apartment, he would give me

real money to buy stuff again: clothes, music, etc. He remembered how important music was to me.

"By the way, how many records did you leave behind, Baldy?"

"Almost one and a half thousand."

"Shit! Buy only CDs now. They are much smaller. If you have to move, throw away the plastic cases and take only the discs and the artwork with you. This way you can pack hundreds of CDs in only one bag. You can always buy new plastic cases later."

He then asked about my long-term plans. I told him everything, omitting only the part about leaving the country. If he was willing to give me a job, he was probably expecting a long-term commitment.

"Very smart. When you get the birth certificate, I can help you with the Social Security number. I know a few people."

The offshore part was also smart, he said, though I should be very careful with that. But that would be a topic for much later. I was impressed. Mad Dog had offshore dealings.

* * *

It was already past three in the afternoon, and the restaurant was emptying. Mad Dog said that he preferred crowded places, and suggested that we move to a coffee shop a few blocks away. We went separate ways. I got there first, found a table, and sat down. I opened the envelope under the table and counted the money. Yes, $2,000! I took out $500 and put the bills in my wallet.

Mad Dog arrived, and we ordered coffee and cake. He then started explaining his theory of crime to me. There was no perfect crime, but there were a few things you could do to tilt the odds in your favor. As a rule of thumb, the more difficult and dangerous the crime, the higher the reward. Bank robbery paid better than ATM robbery, for example. And faking fifty-dollar bills was more profitable than faking five-dollar bills. Therefore, criminals normally committed crimes as difficult and risky as their skills and resources allowed, in order to get the highest possible return. The police also aimed for the highest possible return on law enforcement. They assigned their cops to cases matching their skill sets.

The secret, according to Mad Dog, was to set up a structure much more complex than required by the level of crime you committed. You lowered your returns but increased your chances of not getting caught. You did a one-thousand-dollar job using the infrastructure needed for a ten-thousand-dollar job. Like doing ATM robbery with a crew that could rob a bank. Or printing fake five-dollar bills instead of fifty-dollar bills. The cop investigating one-thousand-dollar jobs didn't have the skills and resources to catch you. The one who did was too busy dealing with the real ten-thousand-dollar jobs to bother with you.

"You just disappear from the radar screen, Baldy."

"If it's that easy, why isn't everyone doing it?"

"People are greedy, Baldy. To operate this way you need modesty, patience, and brains. That's in short supply in our industry."

"So you never got caught?"

"No. No criminal record in almost ten years in the business. What about that? And I want to keep it that way. So, if you want to work with me, I expect modesty, patience, and brains from you." He paused for a short while. "If you get caught, you'll pay not only for the new crimes you'll commit as a dealer, but for the others in California, too."

"You don't need to remind me of that."

"I hope not!"

That was sounding more and more like a job interview to me. He had checked my skills, my attitude, and my long-term plans. Now he was telling me about the corporate culture. Should I also behave like in a job interview and start brownnosing him?

"So, you discovered the perfect crime, Mad Dog."

"There's no perfect crime. Never forget that. You can have bad luck and be discovered by accident. Shit happens all the time. You can find yourself in the wrong place at the wrong time, and that's it."

"I can confirm that!"

"And then there's snitching, Baldy. People talk. Especially when the cops offer them a deal."

"And how do you solve that?"

"If you don't tell people anything, they won't know what to tell the cops, right? The name of the game is compartmentalization. If you need to know, you'll be told."

To be a good criminal you had to think and behave like a spy. You had to set up many cells operating independently from each other, ideally not even knowing about the existence of each other. If one cell was discovered, the others would survive. And so would you. Compartmentalization kept you safe.

I had to learn everything about intelligence services and undercover agents. Especially legends. A good spy didn't get detected because he had what in the spy trade was called a legend, a made-up story about his life. A spy was like an actor playing a role.

"I have to become a spy?" I asked, smiling.

He noticed my disbelief. "Listen, Baldy, for the last time: if you want to work with me, you'll have to do it my way. Are you in or out?"

"Of course I'm in!"

We would go to a bookstore afterwards, where he would show me a dozen good books that I should read in the following days. I should write their names down but not buy anything. It would be suspicious if I arrived home with many books and stayed inside reading them. Janet would wonder what had happened.

I should continue with my routine, leaving the house in the morning and coming back in the afternoon. But instead of going to Brooklyn, I should come to lower Manhattan and hang out in bookstores. I should lose my tail on every trip to Manhattan and back. Losing tails should become second nature to me. It was possible to spend a couple of hours reading inside a bookstore without calling attention. I should then move to the next one. I should never visit the same bookstore two days in a row.

"Besides reading, you should treat yourself to a good lunch, go to the movies, and so on. But don't buy stuff. Don't take anything home. Continue cooking the same cheap food for dinner every evening. Don't change your life. As long as you live in that apartment, you're a bum. Now let's go."

When we got to the bookstore, Mad Dog showed me twelve books, half of them spy novels, the other half handbooks on how to become a spy. I never knew that kind of book existed.

"Isn't it too much, Mad Dog?"

"It'll keep you busy. When we meet next week, I expect you to have read at least half of them."

When we were outside again, I asked, "When and where are we meeting next time?"

"Right here inside this bookstore. Saturday at noon."

"What if something happens? How can I contact you?"

"You can't. Be here. You have no excuse not to show up."

"What about the pager?"

"You can keep it for the week, but hide it well. If for some reason I can't make it on Saturday, I'll call the pager."

"Is that how we'll communicate in the future? You can call me, but I can never call you?"

"No! But we have to set up safe communications channels first. I'll work on that. Be patient. And don't do anything stupid. Remember: patience, modesty, and brains. Take care, man."

He started walking away, but then stopped and came back. "One last question. Do you still doubt it, Baldy?"

"Doubt what?"

"Fate!"

"I don't get it."

"That's homework. Just think about fate. Bye."

Mad Dog had always loved to hear the story about my first meeting with RW. He laughed every time as if it was the first. Whenever someone new came to RW's apartment to hang out with us, sooner or later the usual question came, "How did you guys meet?" Mad Dog always said, "Tell him the fate story, Baldy." He called it the fate story because it ended with the line, "Before that day I had never believed in fate, but now I'm not sure anymore." It was only a joke, of course, like RW's shooting theory. Stuff you said to make other guys laugh. I didn't believe in fate.

What was Mad Dog trying to tell me? Well, I had one week to think about that. I headed home, really happy. First job I ever got without a résumé.

[2/4]

The next day I started my new routine. What a nice change. Sitting inside a cozy and warm bookstore reading spy handbooks and spy novels did beat the hell out of walking down mean streets deep in Brooklyn, not only freezing but risking my ass.

The books I had to read were really cool. That was Mad Dog's world. Everything started to make sense to me: the yes-or-no story, the pager story, the talk about tails, cells, legends. A lot of sense, actually. Mad Dog wasn't mad, he was a genius.

With each day that passed I got a bit more relaxed. The tension of the previous weeks was decreasing slowly but surely. That was good. One unintended consequence of that relaxation was that I started having trouble concentrating. Every now and then my thoughts would wander to my family back home.

The fur coats were to blame; they were all over town. Manhattan in April and November always made me remember home because of the tanned, middle-aged Latin American women walking around in their fur coats.

Latin America was no place for fur coats. With the exceptions of the southern countries and the Andean mountain areas, winters were pretty mild down there. If you wanted to wear a fur coat, you had to fly to America or Europe. New York City was a popular destination. It was closer to home and offered endless shopping opportunities.

Most rich Latin American women avoided coming in the winter, when it would be appropriate, because it would be unbearably cold. But autumn and spring were cold enough to wear fur coats. Mom had three. Most of her friends also had more than one. They kept the coats stored in a refrigerated warehouse. Once a year, in April or November, they picked up their coats from the warehouse and brought them to New York. Some people walked their dogs. Mom and her friends walked their fur coats in Manhattan.

Mom preferred November over April because it was more practical. She could do both her personal and her Christmas shopping. A lot of her friends thought the same. The size of their travel group varied from year to year. Sometimes only three or four women came. Sometimes up to a dozen.

Mom and Aunt Maria came every year, always for two weeks, and always on November third or fourth. As good Catholics, they had to attend mass for our dead relatives on November second, All Souls' Day. They always left immediately afterwards. First praise the Lord, then go shopping.

Their husbands, Dad included, loved those trips. They finally had unlimited time for their mistresses. The price was steep; the trips were followed by outrageously high credit-card bills. But what was the point of being rich if you didn't spend the money?

When I was attending Columbia University in the eighties, those fur coats drove me nuts. I had to meet Mom each time she came. There was no way around it. But she never wanted to meet me somewhere indoors. No, we had to go out, go shopping, do this and that, always outdoors. And most of the time she brought her entourage along. Nice weather, fifty degrees Fahrenheit, and there I was: walking around Manhattan wearing a light jacket surrounded by my mother and her friends wearing fur coats. Ridiculous!

With time I started to consider it part of nature. Summer ended. Leaves started falling. The first birds started flying south. Tanned, fur-coated women started showing up all over Manhattan. A few weeks later they also flew south, together with the last birds. Then it got really cold. Thanksgiving came, and winter followed. Time for the second wave of fur coats, worn by pale-faced, English-speaking women. They disappeared at the beginning of spring. A few weeks later we had the third wave. The tanned, fur-coated women were back. So were the birds. That was nature, with its cycles.

The interesting thing was that no one I knew noticed those three different waves of fur coats. I started to use that knowledge to my advantage. I had a great time betting with friends.

"See that woman over there, the one wearing the fur coat? Wanna bet twenty dollars she's Latin American?"

"How can you know? She's so far away."

"Wanna bet or not?"

"Sure."

We went to her, and I addressed her in Spanish. I never lost a bet. The woman was always surprised. "How could you guess?"

After I left New York in 1988, I only came back in the summer or winter, so I hadn't seen the Latin American fur coats in three years. Moving from one bookstore to another and seeing those women walking their fur coats gave me the creeps. It was a very weird feeling to know that Mom was in New York City at that very moment.

I was sure that she had come. She wouldn't cancel her trip for anything in the world. Granted, she had probably been shocked to hear about my troubles in California. It ruined the family reputation. What an awful thing to happen less than three weeks before her scheduled departure. But staying home wouldn't change anything, and it would ruin Dad's extramarital vacations. I could almost hear Dad, always a pragmatic person, telling her, "You should go, honey. Giving up your trip won't make things better."

Mom's hunting ground in New York was Midtown and Uptown. She wouldn't be caught dead in lower Manhattan. Only middle class people went there, she told me many times, to buy fakes in Chinatown. Mom and her friends could afford the real thing. So there was no danger of running into her on my way to the next bookstore. That was good because I would be in deep trouble if she recognized me and tried to make contact. She was probably being followed by the Feds. Better said, being tailed, to use my brand new spy jargon.

I had to grin every time I imagined the scene. Five or six tanned, middle-aged women wearing fur coats, followed by the same number of pale-faced federal agents wearing black suits and ties under their gray raincoats. That was the stuff of comedy movies.

But even if it were safe, I really didn't want to meet Mom. What could I tell her? Like everyone else, she believed that I had become a drug dealer and a murderer. I couldn't prove that it wasn't true. But the truth wasn't much better, either: I was now training to become a real drug dealer, and my boss was a black man. She couldn't handle that.

* * *

It was a strange feeling to know that life went on as usual for Mom and everyone else I knew back home while I was in New York City fighting for survival. Science fiction movies sometimes used the concept of parallel dimensions. For the first time in my life it didn't seem so far-fetched to me. It did feel like we were living in two completely different dimensions, even though we were sharing the same space and time.

In about one week Mom would fly home. Then she would give her traditional winter-opening party, which was always on the first Saturday in December. That party was the biggest hit in town. Everyone who was anyone came. After that she held her biweekly winter salon evening. Very big cultural happenings.

Mom was very into art and culture, and she wasn't alone in this. Most rich people back home shared her passion, meaning that pretty much everyone we knew was into it. Art and culture were cool and made you feel good, especially when you had the power to determine who was a good artist and who wasn't.

In the Middle Ages the oldest son inherited the title and the land, while his younger brothers had no choice but to become either priests or soldiers. The daughters were married off to rich men or had to become nuns. Back home it was still pretty much like that. It had nothing to do with being the oldest son, though. We had come a long way. If you could handle money well, then you would take care of parts of the family business together with your other money-savvy brothers. If you couldn't manage a busi-ness, then you became a successful artist. It didn't really matter what: painter, sculptor, musician, writer, architect.

By the way, we had come a long way on the female side, too. Your sister couldn't run a business, but besides marrying a rich guy, she could also become an artist. The only thing we didn't like was when two artists married each other. That could screw up the gene pool.

Most wealthy families had at least one artist, male or female. And because we were a closed group, they were all very successful. We just patronized each other's relatives. The important thing was, we kept the power. Because after money, art and culture were the next things you had to have under your control. So you bought someone's daughter's paintings, and he bought your cousin's sculptures.

We did all purchases exclusively at the four art galleries owned by someone belonging to our circle. Since we were the only ones with the money to buy art, all other art galleries opened by outsid-ers eventually went broke for lack of customers. Ninety percent of the work those four galleries carried came from our artists. As Dad taught me, whoever controlled the point of sale controlled the market.

Of course our artists had a hard time coping with the burden of the family name. Poor guys. They were really very talented, but many people outside our circle said that they only made it because they belonged to rich and powerful families. All that mean criticism was very hard, but the kids were tough, and they didn't let that disturb their work.

If you were rich and powerful and lucky enough not to have anyone in the family who made art, you compensated by support-ing it. Mom was totally devoted to it. She was into painting. She loved her salon evenings, when she invited old favorites as well as new talents to talk about art. Mom loved to discover and support new talent. Normally they were just back from Europe, especially France, where all the young heirs and heiresses went to further develop their innate talents.

While Mom thrived on it, Dad only played along. For him it was convenient because young artists weren't very expensive, and he didn't have to spend much money buying their work. When they became established, which our people made sure they did, the early work Dad had bought for a reasonable price gained value. Since he had already bought so much of the guy in the early stage, he didn't have to buy anymore when his prices were inflated. As an investment adviser would say, Dad concentrated his art investments in the emerging markets.

In my childhood I found those salon evenings very boring. But later, in my early teenage years, I learned to enjoy them. It was fun to watch the same movie being played by different actors over and over again. I saw it all, from expressionists to minimalists.

Those evenings had the same social function as the support group meetings they had in America: they made everybody feel good. The artists were pretty happy to finally show that they were really good and deserved all the attention they were getting. Our people were also very happy because it proved that we weren't soulless capitalists. We also enjoyed the spiritual side of life, the beauty of human creativity, especially when the money we spent to show it circulated among ourselves.

But probably the happiest of them all were the artist's parents. It was a relief to know that your lazy offspring, the guy who couldn't calculate a compounded rate of interest, who didn't know what a share or an option was, had finally found an occupation that would bring him money and status. And the most important thing: it kept him out of the family business, which he would probably damage if he got involved.

* * *

Sometimes Mom would find a really talented artist, most of the time a poor or middle class guy who had the talent and the strength to keep working until he made it. Those were cool evenings. It was normally after the opening night for his first exhibition at one of the four art galleries belonging to our people. It was great to watch the guy, very excited for being among the rich and powerful for the first time in his life. You could see it in his eyes: satisfaction, pride, and happiness.

Yes, he had gone through a lot of hardship: poor education, no family name to help him. He had to be really good to compete against the rich families' offspring. It took a lot of talent, dedication, and hard work. In short, the vision thing that Dad and Americans so much loved.

The rich families were also very excited. When you had to

put up with mediocrity most of the time, it was really soothing to meet real talent for a change. Besides that, those poor and truly talented artists had two very important functions.

First, they proved that our group did support talent, regardless of social class. Talent was talent, and all that crap that we only bought each other's stuff was bullshit. We would buy more from outsiders if there were more good ones around. It was not our fault that the best artists belonged to our group. And this led to the second and more important reason: legitimization. If we really recognized talent, regardless of social class, it meant that our people were really good. This gave us a great cover: as long as we supported a real artist here and there, our artistic relatives were able to claim that they were talented and made it despite, not because of, their family name.

There was a time when I considered becoming another talentless artist. I was about twelve years old and starting to realize what role I was supposed to play later in life. I didn't like what I saw. It would be better to become an artist than to get involved in the family business. I really didn't want to work with Dad and my older brothers. They would only boss me around like they always did. I would always be the little kid to them. Worse, as the youngest of four sons, I would only get unimportant companies to run.

It was only after I changed school in 1979 and was offered the chance to study and work in America that I gave up the idea. Twelve years later, having followed Dad's flawed plan and lost everything, I had to ask myself why I hadn't just stayed home and become another talentless artist.

[2/5]

Those recollections were disturbing my concentration. I wasn't reading fast enough. On Monday evening, the third day into my new routine, something happened that brought me back to reality. I was cooking dinner in the kitchen when my roommate asked me, "What's happening, John? Happy again?"

I didn't understand the question and asked back, "What do you mean?"

Her answer was disturbing. "You seem different."

How could she tell? I had kept my routine. I hadn't bought anything. I was cooking the same cheap food as before. "Different? How?"

"You're whistling. Never heard you whistle before."

Damn, I hadn't even noticed that I was whistling. I was letting the guard down. I had to think quickly. Why should John the bum be happy? What could have happened? What could have changed? But I couldn't come up with anything.

I tried to gain time. "How's that, Janet? Whistling means change? Never heard that one before."

"Your mood has changed. You were depressed Thursday evening, and you're happy now."

"So what?"

"Well, you told me about a dead friend, but I didn't buy that. It's a woman, right?"

She was observing me! I would never doubt Mad Dog's wisdom again. I asked myself what Mad Dog would do if he were me. The first thing I could think of was to deny everything and counterattack.

"Oh, checking out your chances, Janet? Planning to make a move on me?"

She immediately went back to her uptight modus. "Of course not!"

"Really? Why are you observing me, then?"

Her tone of voice became aggressive. "I'm not observing you. You were whistling! That was all. Couldn't not overhear that!"

"I whistle all the time. Why is it different now?"

She raised her voice. "You don't! It's the first time you've done it since you moved in!"

"Maybe it's the first time you heard me doing it. But I do it all the time, Janet."

She frowned and looked at me in a strange way, as if trying to find out what was wrong with me. That was really bad. Mad Dog had expressly warned me that I should never arouse suspicion. I had to try something else. Was it too late for a U-turn?

I smiled and said, "I'm only joking, Janet. Of course you're right; something really happened!"

She smiled, too. "I noticed that. That's why I asked. You don't have to tell me, though."

She was still on the defensive but seemed more relaxed now. "I have no secrets, Janet."

She smiled again. I remembered what I had read in the last

days. In situations like this you had to make people talk. If you knew what they were thinking, you could make up the right lie. I would try that.

"Why do you think it's a woman?"

"Come on, John. This emotional roller coaster of yours: today sadness, tomorrow bliss. It must be love!"

"Right! Love! What else could it be if not love? And what do you think? Have I got her or not?"

Seemed the right question to ask.

"Of course not! Or you wouldn't be here all alone, right?"

Obviously. "So why am I whistling, then?"

"Hope?"

That was a good one. That would do.

"Yes, Janet, you've got it. I think that I have a good chance."

She seemed satisfied. It looked like the suspicion was gone.

I decided to tease her. "But why do you think it's a woman and not a man?"

She giggled. "Come on, John, you aren't gay!"

"How can you know?"

"I'm a woman. I can tell."

I winked. "You can't be sure until you try, right?"

She laughed, a bit nervously. "Are you making a move on me?"

I smiled. "Not at all! I was told that I can get killed for that."

We both laughed, and I winked. "But you know where my room is."

She giggled again, very nervously. "Let's have dinner, John. I'm hungry."

We had a pleasant dinner together. I was relaxed again. It seemed that she had only been curious. But I wasn't happy with my handling of the situation. I had almost made her suspicious of me. That would never happen again, I promised myself. Never.

That evening I decided to change my routine. I would read my books in Brooklyn instead of lower Manhattan. There would be no fur coats there to distract me. Rich Latin American women never set foot in Brooklyn. The number of bookstores was not as high as in lower Manhattan, but there were countless cafes and restaurants. Now that I had money again, I could buy a book in the morning, read it in different cafes during the day, and throw it away before returning home, even if I hadn't finished it. The next day I could buy another copy and continue reading.

That was how I spent the following days. The absence of fur coats plus the memory of the close call with my roommate helped me to focus. I read five books in four days in Brooklyn, compared to only two books in three days in Manhattan.

* * *

On Saturday I went back to Manhattan to meet Mad Dog.

"So, Baldy, what about fate?"

I had completely forgotten my homework.

"Sorry, Mad Dog, I was too absorbed in my studies to think about fate. But look at the bright side. I read seven books."

He smiled. "We'll get back to fate later. Let's have lunch. We have a lot of work to do."

We went to a Chinese restaurant. We had no time for small talk, so after we ordered, Mad Dog got right down to business.

"So Baldy, what did you learn this week?"

"That you're a very smart dude, Mad Dog."

He laughed. "You've just started, and you're already brown-nosing me? Want a pay raise or what?"

I told him about my close call with my roommate. He listened, seeming very interested.

"Well, Baldy, for someone caught with his pants down you reacted very well."

"Thanks!"

"But don't you ever get caught with your pants down again!"

"I won't. I've learned my lesson."

"How's the lose-the-tail training going?"

"Very well. It's becoming second nature to me. I do it every time I take a train."

"Good. Now let's talk about your living situation."

He had found an apartment for me in the Village. It was neither big nor nice, he had heard, but it was furnished, and I would be living alone. It cost $2,500 a month. That was more than the market price, but I was paying for discretion; no questions asked. The apartment was unoccupied, and I should move in right away. I would have to pay only $1,000 for the second half of November. He gave me an envelope.

"Five thousand dollars. Three and a half thousand for rent until the end of the year. The rest to spend."

Inside the envelope there was also a piece of paper with

a phone number. The guy subletting the apartment was called Thomas. He was expecting my call that evening to arrange a meeting the following day to give me the keys and get his money. Thomas had been told that my name was Jeff.

"Is he one of your clients?"

"A friend of a client. The client vouches for the guy. As long as Thomas gets his money, he's happy. Cash, no receipt."

"Should I move in right away?"

"Of course. How are you going to handle this without arousing any suspicion? What are you going to tell your roommate?"

"That's what I was going to ask you, Mad Dog."

He grinned. "I asked first, Baldy. I was quicker."

Shit, he was testing me. I told him that since Janet thought that I was in love, I could build on that and say that I wanted to move in with the woman.

He shook his head, looking displeased. "That sucks. Totally suspicious stuff to say."

"Why?"

"Is that how life works? You meet a woman today, the next week you move in with her?"

"Well, I'm John the bum, right? I'm the drifter, the guy without a day job. Why wouldn't I do it?"

He laughed. "Oh, of course you would, if you got the chance! But no sane woman in the world would take you in so quickly. And Janet is smart enough to know that. She'll know that you're lying and will ask herself why."

I should tell Janet that I was leaving town for a few weeks. I should look angry, distressed, depressed, whatever emotion I could fake to make her think that my love story had gone terribly bad. It was a credible thing to do: I got my heart broken, and I took some time off. I should say I was coming back sometime in December.

"Why should I say that I'm coming back?"

"Come on, Baldy. Think!"

I couldn't come up with an answer.

"Rent, Baldy."

If I said that I was coming back, she would ask me for the December rent. I should tell her that I would pay rent when I got back. She wouldn't agree because it would be too risky for her. She couldn't trust a bum. She would probably say that she couldn't wait and would rent the room to another person in December.

Then I should tell her to do it right away and give me back what I had paid in advance for the second half of November.

"Give me a break, Mad Dog. She'd never do it!"

"Exactly!"

"So why should I ask?"

"So that you can get pissed off, man. This creates a bad vibe between the two of you. If you ever meet her again, you have a good reason not to talk to her. She works in a bar somewhere around here, right? You told me that."

He was thinking about the future, about a possible, if not very probable, casual meeting. That was clever.

"Do you always do this, Mad Dog? Cover the most insignificant detail?"

"Keeps me alive. It's like playing chess. You should always keep an eye on all pieces. I can see you don't play chess."

"No. Should I start?"

"Definitely."

"I have to learn how to be a spy. I have to learn how to play chess. Anything else?"

"Acting lessons?"

I almost choked on my food. "You're kidding, right?"

"All you're going to do from now on is acting. If you become a good actor, you'll do fine. If your acting sucks, you're doomed. And so am I."

"And which role will I be playing, by the way? You haven't told me yet."

He smiled. "Coach. You'll become a coach for business people."

"Like a football coach?"

"No. A psychological coach."

"Like a shrink?"

"Kind of. A shrink only listens to your shit. A coach helps you find a solution. You'll be the first PSMT."

"PM what?"

"PSMT. A personal self-motivation trainer. The perfect American profession. Some people have personal fitness trainers. Why not a personal self-motivation trainer? Mind fitness, man. It's trendy. It's cool. It's very New York City."

It sounded insane. "You probably have it all figured out. Please explain."

[2/6]

First he told me about his operation. Getting stuff to sell was easy. The city was awash in drugs. Getting customers to buy was very easy as well. It was also easy to get dealers willing to sell to those dopeheads. If you avoided the streets and had other people selling the drugs for you, then you could make a living without getting caught.

Mad Dog had already explained to me in our first meeting his theory of compartmentalized cells. Each of his cells consisted of about ten drug dealers controlled by what he called a cell master. Only the cell master knew him personally, though the dealers knew they worked for a guy called Mad Dog. Only for that reason was I able to find him. He had a few cells operating in Brooklyn and Queens. Those cells sold to dopeheads who had the guts to buy stuff on the street.

That wasn't an option for his rich clients. They didn't want to meet street dealers. They lived in nice apartment buildings with doormen. That ruled out embarrassing visits. If you solved the problem of delivering the merchandise without embarrassing that kind of customer, the sky was the limit. At that moment he was doing it himself, but not in a very efficient manner. He met the clients for lunch or dinner. As they ate and talked, Mad Dog gave them the cocaine, and they gave him the money.

"Come on, Mad Dog! Just like that? In the middle of a restaurant? And nobody notices it?"

"I gave you money twice during lunch. Did anyone notice?"

I smiled. He was right.

His problem was that he could only do two clients a day, one for lunch and one for dinner. That would mean ten clients a week if he could fill all his slots. But most clients preferred lunch to dinner. He was averaging six a week, about twenty-five a month. He had no more capacity for growth. That was where I came in.

"You could do ten clients a day, Baldy! Fifty a week! Two hundred a month!" His eyes were shining.

I laughed. "Ten a day? I can't eat that much!"

"You won't do lunch, man. You're going to deliver the stuff directly to the clients inside their offices!"

When I heard that, I panicked. I was counting on meeting people outside. Streets, parks, maybe a movie theater. Places where

I could get rid of the stuff easily and run away if something bad happened. Anonymity was the best cover. I told him that.

"You're wrong, Baldy. Completely wrong. In life nobody bothers you if you look like you belong at the place you just happen to be. Belonging is the secret, not anonymity. "

* * *

The idea had already been in a very developed stage when I showed up. He had spent the last days perfecting it. He finally had the missing piece: the legend. I needed a fictitious occupation that would justify my visit to the clients' offices without attracting much attention. It had to be something that wouldn't cause embarrassing questions. I couldn't say that I was in a business like advertisement or accounting, for example. Someone could ask which company I worked for, and that could be dangerous. If I mentioned a real one, there was always the possibility that the guy knew someone who worked there. If I mentioned a company that nobody had ever heard of, that would be suspicious, too. And there was no place for suspicion in his plan.

Personal self-motivation trainer was the perfect legend. Only the clients and I would know what I was there for. Most of the clients were too busy to get away from their desks for very long, so they could justify having a person come to see them in their offices once a month for coaching. As a freelance coach I wouldn't be working for any company. Therefore, there would be no problems with company-related questions. PSMT wasn't a real profession, so no questions about education, degrees, or previous work experience.

In the improbable case that someone else showed interest in my work and wanted to hire me as a real coach, I would say that I was very busy and couldn't take on any new clients. If the client was asked about the coaching by some of his co-workers, he would say how great it was, and that everybody should try it. Who would have anything against a guy who was trying to improve himself? Bosses would love him, colleagues would envy him, and subordinates would respect him.

"That's what this country is all about, Baldy: self-improvement. Tomorrow will be better than today. The American dream."

I called his attention to the fact that it was strange that someone would need another person to help him self-motivate himself.

The word "self" implied no outside help, after all.

"Not at all, Baldy. If you have a guy who can help you to get where you want to go quicker, you hire him. This is America. Time is money. And don't forget that you'll see them only once a month. The guys will have the rest of the time to self-motivate themselves. It's perfectly okay."

I would dress up like an executive, walk past doormen, receptionists, and secretaries right into the client's office, close the door, deliver the stuff, get the cash, sit there for forty-five minutes, do small talk, and leave. On a given day I would book clients with offices very close to each other. Fifteen minutes would be enough to move from client to client. Between eight in the morning and seven in the evening I could easily cover ten clients.

"That's seven and a half hours of work, two and a half hours of exercise outdoors walking from office to office, and one hour lunch break. Nice workload, right?"

"What about pay?"

He smiled. "How much did you make robbing that woman?"

"Seven hundred."

"What about at least three times that per day? Tax free?"

Yes, that was real money! I would deliver standard packages of cocaine, each one costing $1,000. One quarter of the money was for me, another quarter for him, the rest was for suppliers and other operational costs.

"One thousand dollars' worth of cocaine! Isn't that too much for one person?"

"Not really. For the average dopehead it'll be enough for a month. Never forget this: they're paying extra for safe delivery."

He would transfer most of his clients to me. He had already talked to all of them, and the overwhelming majority liked the idea. He would keep the three who had opposed the idea until they changed their minds. When I finally reached full capacity, I would be handling fifty clients per week.

"That's fifty thousand dollars a month for you, Baldy. More than enough for a good life, right?"

I was excited. Excluding big-ticket items like vacations and cars, in my life I had never spent more than $10,000 in a given month. And I had always lived with style. I would be able to have my good life back and still save at least $40,000 each month, half a million in one year. That was a great job, definitely worth the risk. He noticed my good mood and smiled.

"It'll take time until you're that far, though. Now with only twenty-odd clients you'll be making about five thousand a month. But that's enough for rent and a comfortable life, right?"

"Yes, that's great, Mad Dog! Best news I've had in weeks! I'll repay the money you advanced me as soon as possible."

He grinned. "Consider it a sign-on bonus."

I then understood how valuable I was to him.

"Thanks a lot! How long do you think it'll take until we have fifty clients per week?"

"I hope less than one year."

Great. I could save a million in less than three years.

"What happens then? Will you hire a second PSMT?"

"I don't know yet. Haven't planned that far ahead. For the moment you'll be a one-man cell. I might increase the cell. Or I might create another one completely independent from yours. Time will tell."

"Time will tell, but you won't tell, right?"

He laughed really loud. "Right, man! You're starting to get it!" Then he became very serious and looked me in the eyes. It was a scary look. "Listen to me, Baldy. I'm trusting you with my best clients. It took me a long time to get them. Don't fuck up!"

"I'll do my best, Mad Dog!"

"You can do your best and still fuck up!"

"I won't fuck up!"

He was silent for a long time. The look got even scarier.

"Don't fuck up, Baldy, or I'll kill you!"

I froze.

"It's not personal. I like you. But business is business. You should know two things. One, I won't take a bullet for you. Two, I won't let you fuck up my business."

"I understand."

"Another warning, actually number three: sell the stuff, don't use it. Never do cocaine. Never! Cocaine is shit!"

"Never done it, never will."

"That's what everyone says when they start dealing. Then they see their clients doing it, want to try 'just this one time,' and get addicted." He looked me in the eyes again. "I can always tell when someone is doing it, Baldy. Don't start. If you do, you're out. Got it?"

"Yes."

"If you want to get high, smoke a joint. I'll always add a package of grass for your personal use. But do it only after work. Don't go to work high, or you're out. I can ask a few clients to keep an eye on you."

"I understand, boss."

"So, just for the record, what are the three things you should know?"

He sounded exactly like Dad, who always made me repeat his threats.

"You won't take a bullet for me. You won't let me fuck up your business. I'm not to do cocaine."

He laughed. "Good! Never forget that, and we'll be the best business partners. Now let's get out of here and have coffee somewhere else."

* * *

It was a great relief to leave the restaurant. Over coffee and cake he explained how the operation would proceed.

I should move apartments on Monday. The following weeks I would be busy working on my legend. I should do extensive research on the subject of self-motivation. Read everything I could get on coaching, self-help, positive thinking, the power of the mind, dreams. I needed to master the field's specific vocabulary in case people other than the clients engaged me in conversation. Fortunately, bookstores were full of self-help literature.

The money that I would have left after paying rent I should use to buy nice casual clothes, a small stereo with a CD player, and some CDs. "I know that music will lift your spirits, Baldy. You should be happy again."

We would meet again in ten days, when we would first go to a hairdresser and afterwards buy clothing. Mad Dog had a pretty good idea of how a PSMT should look. He was also already looking for a person to give me acting lessons.

I didn't like the idea much. "Are you sure acting classes are necessary?"

"Definitely. Your acting skills will make or break this operation."

He was expecting to spend about $2,000 on the PSMT look and $3,000 on acting lessons. Adding the $7,000 he had already given me, my sign-on bonus would total $12,000.

"I'm investing twelve thousand dollars in you before you even make a trade."

"I'm truly thankful for your help. And trust me, I won't let you down. When do I start dealing?"

"December tenth. It's a Tuesday. You have an appointment at ten in the morning."

My first trade would be with a very good client of his, a guy called Joe. There would be a second trade two days later with a client called Peter. Those two guys had helped him develop the idea of the delivery service, and had volunteered to be the first customers. Mad Dog would call them after my visits to get their feedback.

"They'll be watching me?"

"Not you, but their environment. How people around them react to you and the whole PSMT idea."

Based on their feedback we would fine-tune my performance. We were meeting one last time on Saturday, December fourteenth, to work on that. The week after that I would start dealing for real. He was already setting up appointments.

The week before Christmas was a great time to start, he said. First, clients needed extra stuff for the holidays. Second, offices would be bustling with activity, everybody trying to get things done before the end of the year; reports, bookkeeping, inventory. Third, there were all those Christmas parties to attend. And last but not least, Christmas shopping had to get done in between all that. For all those reasons nobody would have much time to bother with me.

He placed two pagers on the table. "Now, show me what you've learned. Why two pagers?"

I was asking myself the same question. "Can they transmit text messages or only phone numbers?"

"Only numbers. We don't need more than that."

I had learned that when spies used two devices to communicate, each device transmitted only a part of the message. To decipher the entire message you needed both devices and the code. Someone getting hold of only one device wouldn't have a chance. And even if someone got both devices, he still had to figure out the message using a code unknown to him.

If the only message those pagers could transmit was a number, what could the code be? Would I have to add both numbers, or subtract one from the other, to get the real phone number to call back? Or maybe take a few numbers from one, like the first, third, fifth, and a few from the other, like the second, fourth, sixth?

"I'm waiting, Baldy."

I sighed and told him what I was thinking.

"Not bad, man! You've got the theory right. That's what we want people to think in case they get your pagers. To them, it's a red herring, leading them nowhere. To us, the two pagers solve our main problem: identification. You'll know that's me calling, and I'll know that you have the pagers. Both pagers receive the same phone number, one pager right after the other. This way you know it's me and not someone else calling the wrong pager number. If only one pager rings, it's not me!"

"I get that. But how can you know that I, and not someone else, have the pagers?"

"I call twice. The second call thirty minutes after the first one. To you the first call is just a warning that I want to talk to you. It has practical reasons. I can't know where you'll be when I call the first time, right? You could be taking a shower or riding the subway. You need time to finish whatever you're doing and go looking for a phone. But even if you are close to a phone, never call back the first time. Wait for the second call thirty minutes later."

"That's ingenious, man! If someone calls back right away, you'll know that it's not me. Someone else has the pagers."

"Right! That's our secret code, Baldy. The same applies to you when you call my pagers."

He placed a piece of paper on the table with two pager numbers written on it. When I was about to put it in my pocket, he grabbed my hand.

"No records. You have to learn the numbers by heart. Never write them down. Leave the paper on the table and memorize the numbers now."

After I did that he said that we were done for the day. We would meet again on Tuesday, November twenty-sixth, in a coffee shop not far from my new apartment in the Village. We'd then get the PSMT look.

"Be there at ten in the morning. Before I go, tell me my pager numbers again."

I did. He was satisfied. "I'll page you as soon as I get the acting teacher. Always keep those pagers close to you. Now call that guy Thomas. He's waiting. Remember, you're Jeff to him. Bye."

* * *

I sat there for a long time, mentally going through the whole thing we had discussed. We covered a lot of territory in those few hours. It seemed that we had the perfect plan. That gave me cold feet. In the previous weeks I had learned that things didn't always work according to plans. What about Dad's insurance policy? What about the ATM robbery?

Then I remembered that I was supposed to become a self-motivation trainer. I started telling myself that it would work. I would become the best PSMT in the world. I would make one million dollars and get out of America in less than three years. I left the coffee shop and went looking for a pay phone to call Thomas, all the way repeating to myself, "One million dollars in less than three years!"

[2/7]

My new apartment was a furnished studio; one single room plus bathroom. The furniture was crap, but at least it was my own place. No roommate to bug me.

Janet reacted exactly like Mad Dog had predicted. She was home when I returned to the apartment Sunday afternoon after receiving the keys to my new place. I told her right away that I was getting out of town for a few weeks. She demanded the December rent in advance. I refused to pay. She told me that she would rent the room to someone else in December, and I demanded my money back. The second half of November was paid for. She said it was my decision to leave early. We argued. I left the apartment as soon as I could pack my few belongings.

I felt great in my new apartment. Five weeks had already passed since the shooting in California, and I was still alive and kicking. No Colombians and no Feds had found me. And the chances of that happening were diminishing with each day that passed.

My situation had improved considerably. I wasn't on the run anymore, hiding inside a warehouse in Mafia-controlled territory. No more walking the mean streets of Brooklyn talking to drug dealers. I had real money and a safe place to hide. For the first time in five weeks I could see light at the end of the tunnel. I would make it. The caveman would not only survive, he would get his good life back.

I decided to stay home in the next days reading and listening to music, going out only to buy groceries and to exercise. I planned to go jogging every morning. Monday was dedicated to shopping: clothing, music, food, and books. It was great to be able to spend money again. I bought a small stereo, about fifty CDs, casual clothes, warm clothing for jogging, and twenty books: ten spy books and ten books on coaching-related stuff.

Tuesday morning I was reading a spy handbook in bed after breakfast when the first pager started beeping. Shortly after that the second one beeped, too. Both showed the same number. It was Mad Dog. What did he want so soon after our last meeting? There was a pay phone not very far from my apartment, so I didn't have to hurry.

* * *

Half an hour later the pagers beeped again. I called the number.

"Mad Dog?"

"What's up, Baldy?"

"Not much. Enjoying my new home."

"How many CDs have you bought?"

"About fifty."

"That's my man! Listen, I found you an acting teacher."

I sighed, and he laughed. "That was deep, man."

"Sorry, it's just that…"

He interrupted. "I know. You don't like acting. It's dangerous, right? You could get in touch with your feelings."

There he went again. "No, Mad Dog. It's just that I have enough on my plate right now. I have almost twenty books to read."

"Reading can be boring. Acting classes will bring spice to your life. I found the perfect guy for you. You'll love him!"

"How's that?"

"You know, most acting teachers work with your emotional memories, especially the painful ones; what people call feelings. But both of us know that you have none, right?" He laughed. I rolled my eyes. "We needed another method, so I found a guy who'll teach you how to act without bothering with the inner-self stuff. How about that?"

"Sounds great..."

He became angry. "Okay, Baldy, since I'm not getting any appreciation for my efforts, I'll play the boss card. I'm the boss, remember?"

He sounded just like Dad. "Yes, Mad Dog. You're the boss."

"Okay. Then here are your orders: you'll see this guy five afternoons a week, Tuesday to Saturday, from three to seven."

Shit, four hours a day. "For how long, boss?"

"Three whole weeks, until Saturday, December seventh."

Oh, man!

"In case you haven't figured it out yet, it's a total of fifteen classes. Sixty hours of training. Private classes, by the way. He guaranteed me that you'll be ready when he's finished."

"And how much will this cost?"

"Five thousand dollars."

He had planned to spend $3,000 on acting classes.

"You're over budget!"

"I know. But the guy is supposed to be really good."

"Are you sure you want to invest this kind of money?"

"Yes. As I said, your acting skills will make or break this operation."

I wasn't convinced. "If you say so..."

"If you say so, if you say so," he repeated in a mocking voice. I thought that he was trying to be funny. I was wrong. "Listen, man," he said in a very angry voice. "Stop playing the spoiled kid. Get real! If you screw up acting, you lose your fucking job before you even start. Got it, Baldy? If you screw up, you're fucking out!"

He was really angry. I had never heard him speaking in that tone of voice. That brought me back to reality pretty quickly.

"I won't! I've told you that I won't fuck up!"

"So stop behaving like a prick!"

I had to change the charged atmosphere. I couldn't lose that job. "I assume that classes start today? How do I get to the guy?"

"His nickname is Red. Comes from Conrad. Shitty name, isn't it? I'd change it too if I were him. He lives in the Village. Not very far from you."

He gave me the guy's address and phone number.

"What's the legend here, Mad Dog? Who am I to this guy? Why do I need acting classes?"

"That's much better now. You're talking like a grown-up. Very important questions."

He had found the teacher through one of his clients. Red had very good references. Calling as Steven Young, Mad Dog told Red on the phone that both of us worked for a top-secret government agency. Mad Dog was in charge of staff training. I, Mike Bell, had a desk job, but was training to become an undercover agent. Mike was very uptight and needed extra help. Maybe acting lessons could help? The agency we worked for dealt with money laundering, and needed to infiltrate big corporations.

"No shit! And the guy believed this crap?"

"Who knows? Maybe he did. Maybe he only pretended to. Who cares? He needs the money. I paid upfront. Cash, no receipt. A messenger delivered the money yesterday. The cool thing about this crazy legend is that you don't have to explain shit to him, because it's all supposed to be top secret."

He laughed, and I had to laugh, too. He was mad, but he could solve problems in a very elegant way, I had to admit.

"So Baldy, or I'd better say Mike, be there today at three and work your ass off. I'll get updates on your progress. By the way, we have to bring next week's meeting forward from Tuesday to Monday. We need a lot of time to get the PSMT look. We don't want you to miss classes in the afternoon, right?"

"For nothing in this world!"

"See you next Monday at ten. Take care, Mike. And enjoy classes!"

I could hear him laughing before he hung up. I sighed. Sixty hours of acting classes. That would be hell.

* * *

To my surprise I actually enjoyed acting classes. Red told me that I wouldn't learn to play characters created by authors. Instead, I would learn to create believable characters myself. Be both playwright and actor at the same time.

He had devised a course in two parts. In part one, covering the first two weeks, I would create a different character every two days, totaling five roles. Two would be blue-collar characters: janitor and plumber. Three would be white-collar: stockbroker, computer specialist, and bookkeeper.

In part two I would spend the third and last week developing one single character, this one much deeper and detailed compared to the first five. I would learn to impersonate a psychologist.

"That's what you wanted, right? Steven told me that you're already doing a lot of background research on it. He mentioned a test you have to take at your agency. He didn't give me many details, though. He was very secretive about the whole business."

I had to remember all I could about those six roles: the people I had met in real life and the fictional ones I had seen on TV or read about in books. The more details I could come up with, the more realistic the characters would be.

That Tuesday we started with the janitor, and spent the whole afternoon composing the character. On Wednesday we were ready. It wasn't perfect, but not bad for my first time. I created a Latin American immigrant. I could do the accent well. Red asked me where I had picked up the accent. I told him that I had lived in Miami for a while.

Thursday and Friday we did the plumber. It was bad. I tried to do a New York Italian accent but it sucked. Red told me that I learned a great lesson with that character. "You build upon what you have, Mike. Don't try things you know nothing about, like Italian accents."

Saturday we started the stockbroker, to be concluded the following Tuesday. The first five days just flew by. I was always too tired to read anything after classes, so I went to the movies instead. There was always a spy movie showing somewhere.

[2/8]

On Monday I met Mad Dog for the PSMT look. He was very happy and relaxed.

"Baldy! I've heard you're making great progress."

"Thanks."

"I've also heard that you're enjoying it. Could this be true?"

"Yeah, it's true. If you want to hear it, you were right."

He gave me a big smile. "What was that? Can you say it again?"

"You were right, and I was wrong!"

"Thank you! Nice to hear that. Ready for the PSMT look?"

First he took me to a hairdresser. I hadn't shaved or had a haircut in weeks. I thought that the guy would have a lot of work to do, but he didn't cut or shave much. He taught me how to wear a ponytail to look stylish, and trimmed my beard a little. I couldn't see much difference afterwards, but both he and Mad Dog were very happy with the results.

At the hairdresser's we were joined by Helen, an image consultant. Mad Dog introduced me as Kenny. "Nice to meet you, Kenny. Nice haircut! Now let's get the right clothes for you." She was very beautiful and had a great body. I wondered what kind of relationship she had with Mad Dog.

They took me to a few shops, where I had to try a lot of outfits until they could agree on a single piece. Mad Dog had a very nice leather briefcase with him, and every outfit had to complement that briefcase. I assumed that it was the special briefcase he had told me about, which I would need to transport the drugs and the money. It had a false bottom.

It took about six hours to get all the stuff we needed. He bought me five suits, ten shirts, two belts, and three pairs of leather shoes. We didn't even have lunch, only grabbed a falafel on the way from one shop to the next. The total bill was $4,500. Adding the hairdresser and the fee he paid to the style consultant, he spent more than $5,000 that Monday. Once again, way over budget.

* * *

It was almost seven in the evening when we finished and the woman left. Mad Dog and I went to have dinner together at his favorite Italian restaurant in Little Italy. It was small and packed. He seemed to know the people well, because they gave us a table very quickly.

"Connections, Baldy. Connections are everything in life."

"Dad used to tell me that all the time. What's your connection to Helen? Are you a client?"

He smiled. "I knew it! You were undressing her with your eyes. And she seemed to enjoy it! Client's recommendation, Baldy. Met her personally for the first time today. Only talked on the phone before. But forget about her. She's a witness. I know you must be horny, but wait until your legend is perfect. Anyone you talk to during this transition time could be dangerous. If you're desperate, go see a hooker."

The waitress who came to take our orders heard this last sentence and gave me a funny look. Mad Dog told me that the house specialty was spaghetti with pesto. They also had the best tiramisu in town. He ordered that for both of us.

"Do you like the PSMT look, Baldy?"

"Yeah, it's cool. Expensive, though. Adding the acting classes, you're at least five thousand over budget."

"Right. But it's worth it. Last week I was able to get five new clients. More will come."

"Where from?"

"Always from the same source, friends of existing clients. Now that they know I have free capacity and a great new delivery service, they're spreading the word."

"Isn't it dangerous? If the word reaches the wrong guy..."

"Of course it is! I've told you already, there's no perfect crime. We do what we can to set up a safe operation, but it can come crumbling down very quickly if some asshole talks too much."

"So why do you let them talk?"

"How are we supposed to get new clients? Place an ad in the paper? This is the safest way, Baldy. The clients only recommend people they know well. If you get caught, they'll get caught, too. We're all together in this shit. Dealers and clients. It's like we have a collective security agreement. Everyone has an interest in keeping the operation safe."

"But interest alone doesn't guarantee safety, does it?"

"No. But it goes a long way. The ones who can really fuck us are the people very close to the clients, like ex-wives for example, who know about the scheme and want to use this knowledge to frame them."

"I assume that dopeheads have bad marriages. So it's a matter of time until an ex-wife spills the beans, right?"

"Can't help it, man. You've got to trust fate. If it's supposed to happen, it will happen. There is nothing you can do about it."

Fate! There he went again. I thought this was the right time to finally tell him. "I don't believe in fate. I don't think there is someone controlling this shit. It's all random."

He smiled. "You're mixing things up. Fate doesn't mean any-one controlling anything."

"Really? What does it mean, then?"

"It means that there are a few things that you're supposed

to experience in life. Sooner or later these things will happen to you."

I shook my head. "It's all random, man. One thing leading to the other. Shit happens. You react to it. More shit happens. Afterwards we try to give a meaning to it because we can't accept that it's all random, all quantum physics."

He laughed. "All quantum physics? What about the shooting in Texas?"

"What about it? Do you believe that when I was born it was already decided that twenty-five years later I'd be inside that restaurant on that date?"

"Of course not! Your life isn't planned that way. You have free will. You can choose your destiny."

"You just made a U-turn, man! You're contradicting yourself. If you can choose, then there's no fate."

"Fate and choice go hand in hand. Fate keeps presenting you with opportunities to make choices."

Man, that reminded me of the Communist study group in college. Those endless discussions leading nowhere. At least one could argue economics on a scientific level. Esoteric stuff was impossible to discuss. I tried my best.

"You could use that definition for life too, you know? Shit happens all the time, giving you opportunities to make choices."

"But it's not random, Baldy. That's where fate comes in."

As much as I didn't want to hear that, I had to. That guy aggravating me with the fate crap had saved my life. He had given me a job that would be the way out of my desperate situation. He had already invested almost $20,000 in me before I could even prove that I could handle the job. I was very thankful for everything and very afraid to lose that chance. If that esoteric stuff was important to Mad Dog, I had to bite the bullet, listen to it for as long as necessary, and try to change the subject at the first opportunity.

"What about the shooting in Texas, Baldy? You haven't answered it yet."

"In my opinion I was in the wrong place at the wrong time. A random choice I made took me there. Now please explain to me why I'm wrong. Why was I supposed to be in that joint at that date and time?"

"Not that specific joint."

"I don't get it."

"I believe that you were supposed to have an experience like that in your lifetime. That joint just offered you the opportunity. You took it."

"How could I know about the opportunity? I can't see the future. And if I could, I'd never have gone to that place. I'm not crazy!"

"Of course you're not crazy! That's why this stuff doesn't happen on a conscious level. If your ego gets involved, it blocks everything. That's why you only felt it, on a very deep and unconscious level. The universe works through feelings and intuition."

When would he start talking about elves, dwarves, and fairies? "Okay, let's see if I got it right. I chose to be there because I was supposed to have that experience, right? What if I had arrived late and missed the guy? Would I then have fucked up my life?"

"No, because you'd have another opportunity later on. Who knows how many you had already been offered but refused?"

How could I argue with that? "I still think it was random. Sorry."

"Of course you do. It's easier that way!"

"Okay, could you please show me the briefcase? I'm very curious about the false bottom."

"Changing the subject? Are you so uncomfortable with this?"

I sighed. "Not uncomfortable. I just don't see the point of going on and on."

"The point is understanding life. It's not random at all, man. Why do you think you got Winston as a roommate?"

"The university decided to put us together. You'd have to ask Columbia about their decision. Someone had to share a room with Winston. That someone turned out to be me. A random choice, I suppose."

"Random? Winston? The guy who came to New York to find me? The guy who taught you how to search for me? Years later you used that knowledge and that training to track me down on your own. You built on that, didn't you? We're sitting here together now because fate put Winston in your room!"

"You're only rationalizing past random decisions, Mad Dog. If I'd had another guy as a roommate, I could have made different friends in college, which could have led to different career choices, different places of employment, and so on. No MBA in

California, who knows? Then the setup would not have happened, and I wouldn't need to find you."

He nodded, smiling in a condescending way.

"My life could probably be completely different now if I hadn't met Winston. But how can I know? It would also be different if Dad hadn't sent me to the American school, or if no revolution had happened in Nicaragua. According to your logic, fate caused the Nicaraguan revolution in order to convince Dad to make me change schools and send me to America. Then fate made you leave Jamaica in order to make Winston come to New York to search for you. Then fate put Winston and me in that dorm room. That's absurd!"

He sighed. "You're not there yet! Let me show you the briefcase."

It was finally over.

The briefcase was really cool. Hidden inside the false bottom was a watch: a Rolex.

"It's for you, man. A PSMT can't wear a plastic watch."

"It must have cost a fortune!"

"It's fake, Baldy. If you want a real one, buy it yourself."

I had to think about Mom. "Chinatown?"

"Yeah, where else?"

"Mom would hate you for that."

"I know your mother hates all black people. Except Winston, of course, because he's only dark skinned."

"You're mixing things up. Dad upgraded Winston to dark skinned. To Mom he'll always be black. So will you."

"If she already hates my black ass so much, why would a fake Rolex make any difference?"

"She hates fake stuff. That's why she hates Chinatown. If she could, she'd have everyone there arrested. Buyers and sellers."

"Why does she care about fakes?"

"They destroy her upper-class status. What's the point of being rich and able to afford the real stuff if the poor can have a copy for a fraction of the price and no one can tell the difference?"

"You know what, Baldy? No offense meant, but you have fucked-up parents."

"No offense taken, man. You're completely right!"

***

The waiter brought our food. We ate and talked about the occasion when I took RW home. Mad Dog had always enjoyed the story, especially the part when RW was upgraded to dark-skinned guy. We tried to imagine Mom's face if I had taken both RW and Mad Dog home.

When we got dessert, he went back to business.

"So, Baldy, you're all set now. You have the PSMT look and the briefcase. You're working on your acting skills. Only one thing is missing, right?"

"Two! The drugs and the addresses."

"You'll get that in two weeks. Talking about your new name!"

"I haven't chosen one yet."

"But I have!" He was grinning. That was a scary sign.

"Why can't I do it myself? What if I don't like your choice?"

"Because it's not a matter of taste but of having the right name. It's not easy, you know? It can't be a real name like Paul or John, because someday you'll get that birth certificate with another name. How will you explain the name change?"

"I hadn't thought about that."

"See? We have to think very long term here. A lot of small details to consider. If you can't change the name, you need a nickname. Something like Baldy. Actually, Baldy would be perfect, but we can't use it. Too many Colombians and Feds out there."

"A nickname? That's actually clever, man!"

"Thank you. It's nice when you show appreciation for my efforts."

"Yeah, brownnosing always works."

"But not any nickname will do. It must be something easy to remember and have a positive meaning, so people won't care what your real name is. Like Eagle, for example."

I froze. "Please tell me it's not Eagle!"

He smiled. "Much better than that!"

I stopped eating. I didn't want to choke on my tiramisu.

"Mad Dog, if I were into that esoteric stuff of yours, I'd say that I have the intuition that I won't like it."

He laughed. "You'll love it! It's very close to Baldy, actually. In life the answer is sometimes closer than you think."

I braced myself for the worst. He smiled and said it slowly, "Birdy!" I hated it.

"Great, isn't it, Baldy? It's short, easy to remember, and

sounds like bird, which is a surname. You could be a John Bird, who became Birdy."

"Come on! I'm not a bird!"

"You'll teach people how to fly, how to reach for the stars! You'll make birds out of people! Isn't that a great image?"

Unfortunately I couldn't share his enthusiasm. But I didn't want him to play the boss card again. I didn't want to be called a prick in person. It had been bad enough on the phone. I tried to hide my disgust.

"Okay, I think I only need time to get used to it. I didn't like Baldy in the beginning, either."

"With time you'll love it. By the way, what was Baldy supposed to mean again? Something about selling out, right?"

"It means 'bendido a los diabolicos Yankees.' It's Spanish for sold out to the diabolic Yankees."

"Cool. You've come a long way. Now you'll become a Yankee yourself. Why don't we find a meaning for the acronym? What could Birdy mean?"

"I think it's already good enough meaning a bird. What about the business cards?"

"Oh, I had almost forgotten them."

He gave me a pack with 250 business cards. They looked nice and had a very clean design. The first line had only the word Birdy in bold type. Beneath it, the words personal self-motivation trainer. At the bottom, a Manhattan phone number. In case someone called, the people answering the phone would take a message and page me. For that he gave me a third pager. This one was alphanumeric and could transmit text and numbers. If I didn't understand a message, I should call back the same number. My password was "Birdy Twenty-two."

At around nine we were finished. I put the briefcase, business cards, and the new pager in my shopping bags, and we left the restaurant together.

"We meet again in two weeks, Baldy, on the day before your first deal. You have only two more weeks to become Birdy the PSMT. Go to work!"

* * *

I went home, unpacked the stuff, put on one of the outfits, and looked in the mirror. It was a strange feeling. All the pieces were there: the ponytail, the beard, the outfit, the briefcase, the business cards, the work pager, and the name. The whole idea was so brilliant that it was almost insane.

The following two weeks passed very quickly. Acting lessons consumed all my time and energy. I was working on my characters almost round the clock and got better every day. Both the stockbroker and the bookkeeper came out really well, finance being one of my favorite subjects. The computer specialist could have been better if I had known more about computers. It showed again that I needed a lot of information to build the characters. Therefore, I intensified my readings and observations for the coach role. The only option I had to observe psychologists and coaches in action was on the screen. I bought a videocassette recorder and some films to watch at home.

When Red sent me off, he told me that he was impressed by how much I had learned in such a short time. My motivation had continually increased; the last week especially had been very intense. I could really impersonate a coach, he said, as if I had been born to play that role. I was very happy to hear that, even though I couldn't be sure if he was telling the truth or only trying to justify his fees. He was an actor, after all.

[2/9]

When I met Mad Dog on Monday, the day before my first trade, I was nervous. Besides the occasional joint, I had never bought, carried, or stored any drugs before. We met in a Japanese restaurant not far from Washington Square. He came with a backpack, which he placed under the table. He ordered sushi. I went for sashimi.

He told me that there were a few books inside the backpack. Some of them were hollow, like cases. They had the packages of cocaine inside. He had another backpack, of exactly the same model, also full of books, some of them also hollow. We would meet every Saturday to exchange backpacks. I would bring mine with his share of the week's revenue hidden inside the hollow books. He would bring his with more dope for the following week.

He had brought me fifty packages and would bring me another fifty the following Saturday. It was much more than I would need in the next days, but I had to have many weeks' worth on supply at any time in case we weren't able to meet in a given week. Sometimes he had to disappear on short notice.

The packages were vacuum-sealed and I should never open them. The clients could buy any number of packages they wanted, but never fractions of a package. I should start the workday with twenty packages in case some clients needed more than one.

The clients should get only one appointment per month. If a client had to cancel an appointment for whatever reason, I should never offer a replacement appointment very quickly. I should say that I was booked out for the next two weeks even if I had absolutely nothing to do. I found the rule intriguing and asked why.

To educate them, was the answer. If they had to wait two weeks, they could run out of cocaine before we met again. That was a dopehead's worst nightmare. They would never cancel an appointment again unless they had a very good reason. Rescheduling too many appointments would ruin my productivity. We wanted fifty appointments every week.

Another educational measure was keeping address and appointment books. If I got caught with written notes, I would bring down everyone with me. The clients should see that I had the address book. They should be scared of getting caught if I got arrested. That would make them think twice before they told someone about our scheme.

"People like to talk, Baldy. To tell war stories. They should talk. That's how we'll get new clients. But they should talk only to other dopeheads they know and trust."

"How should I deal with queries? What's the procedure?"

If someone called, I should first ask which client gave him my name. I should then get in touch with the client who recommended me and check the new guy. Only after I was completely sure that the new guy was safe should I give him an appointment.

"Is it always a guy? No women?"

"That's interesting, isn't it? We have only two female clients at the moment. By the way..."

"Don't fuck them."

He laughed. "Right! How did you guess?"

"You don't want me to fuck anyone."

"No woman related to the business: no female clients, no secretaries, and no co-workers. The rest of the world you can fuck as you wish."

"Thanks. Very generous."

"You won't socialize with the female clients except during the forty-five minutes you're inside their offices. If they invite you to a social function like a Christmas party, it's okay to go if the client really insists. But better to avoid it if you can."

"Listen, I can understand why I shouldn't get involved with secretaries or co-workers. They think that I'm a real coach. They don't know that I'm a drug dealer. I could talk too much and get in trouble. But the clients know exactly who I am. And I know who they are. It would be a safe relationship as far as I'm concerned."

"Theoretically, yes. But sex can lead to feelings, and feelings can be hurt. What if you want to break up and the woman doesn't? What if she blackmails you?"

"If she brings me down, she'll go down as well. Isn't that deterrent enough?"

"Only when people are behaving rationally. Broken hearts are anything but rational. The desire for revenge can make people blind to potential self-harm. Got it?"

I sighed. "Yes, I got it. Tell me more about these two women. Are they good looking?"

"Both of them are very good looking. Marilyn might be a dyke. Or she doesn't like dark-skinned guys. I don't know."

I had to laugh.

"She never made a pass at me. Could happen to you. Catherine definitely likes men. She could try something."

"Talking about your own experience?"

He nodded.

"Thanks for warning me. But why so few female clients?"

"I believe that women like drugs as much as men do. It seems that what they don't like is buying the stuff. Probably because it's so risky, you know? Women are much smarter than men. Why should they do it themselves if they can get someone else to do it for them?"

"What about socializing with the male clients? Is it allowed?"

"Not only allowed, but also recommended."

"Why?"

"All work and no play makes Jack a dull boy. Remember that movie?"

"The Shining? Yes, I remember. It was creepy. Are you afraid that I'll start killing people with an axe like the guy in the movie?"

"I hope not! But you need a social life. You don't have any real friends left, do you?"

"Not really."

"So hang out with the male clients. The best network one can have. They're rich, powerful, and know pretty much everyone who matters in this town."

"And the rules? Besides not fucking them, which I don't intend to do?"

"Only one: if other people are present, you're Birdy the real PSMT, never Birdy the drug dealer."

"Is that all?"

"Yeah. But until you're ready to play Birdy the real PSMT very well, you should avoid meeting the clients' friends. If someone suspects you, both you and your client will be in deep trouble. Then you'll fuck up the business. You know the rest."

I nodded, rolling my eyes.

He didn't like it. "You don't seem to understand how dangerous this shit is." He started giving me safety instructions. I had to watch my back all the time. I should always assume that I was being followed. I should lose my tail three times a day: in the morning going to work, after lunch break, and when returning home. Never walk the shortest route to the next client. Always watch for suspicious activity around me.

"Remember, Baldy, there are lots of cops and drug dealers out there to get you. And if they get you, they might get me as well."

That irritated me. "You told me that they'd never find me!"

"Man, I'm not talking about your Baldy past. I'm talking about your Birdy present."

That irritated me even more. Weren't we supposed to have the perfect cover?

"But nobody knows about Birdy! Why should I worry?"

He started talking in a very aggressive way. "Listen, Baldy, there's an army of cops out there hunting drug dealers everywhere in this town. You got frisked in Brooklyn, remember? Those guys are still out there! Got it?"

"Yes, I get it! But what about the drug dealers? The Colombians are in California. Why should they care that I'm dealing in New York?"

He sighed and became even more aggressive. "I'm not talking

about dealers in California, but in New York City. You're dealing inside someone else's territory, and you can get fucking killed for that."

I didn't like his tone of voice. Just like Dad.

"Whose territory?"

"I don't know who owns what here. Manhattan is basically in the hand of Latino gangs. You know, Colombians, Puerto Ricans, Cubans, the whole brown scum."

That was offensive.

He noticed my disgust. "Sorry, it's not personal. Manhattan streets are mean streets, and Latino dealers are mean motherfuckers. We fear them, we don't cross them, but we definitely don't like them."

"But our clients would never buy anything from a street dealer, right? It's not like we're stealing these dealers' customers. Why should they care?"

He rolled his eyes. "I forget that you're a beginner."

Now he was patronizing me. "Yeah, so teach me."

"Basically, drug dealing is about three things: territory, foot soldiers, and reputation. If you lose one of them, you lose all of them. And then maybe even your life. If you let a motherfucker deal inside your territory, it ruins your reputation. The enemy won't respect you anymore. Your supplier won't respect you anymore. Even your own people won't respect you anymore. If your supplier and your foot soldiers desert you, then you lose your territory, too. Do you get it or not?"

"Yes, I'm not stupid."

"No, you aren't. If you were, I wouldn't have hired you. Never forget that you're invading someone else's territory and can get killed for that. And that the cops are out there to get you."

"I won't. I'm just frustrated. I hoped that it would stop."

"What would stop?"

"The paranoia. The fear of Feds and Colombians. Always watching my back."

"It never stops. Sorry, man, that's the price of doing business. You'll have to get used to it."

He gave me a sheet of paper with the names, office phone numbers, and addresses of my first two clients typed on it. He then briefed me on the two guys, Joe and Peter, and their secretaries.

"Secretaries are very important, Baldy. Always be nice to

them. Bring them small presents, flirt with them, pretend you love them, but…"

"Don't fuck them!"

"Right, I think you got the principle."

"Why are secretaries so important?"

"They are like the police. If they don't like you, they can make your life miserable. Be nice to them. Whenever you get a new client, try to get as much information as possible about their secretaries before your first delivery."

He waved to the waiter for the bill.

"So Baldy-Birdy, you're all set. Take your dope home and hide it well. It's worth fifty thousand dollars."

"I think I need a few professional tips on hiding dope."

"You don't have to be a professional. If the police come for you suspecting that you're a dealer, they'll have the drug-sniffing dogs and will tear apart the whole place. You can't hide drugs from them, so don't waste your time trying. Just hide it in a place where a nosy person won't find it by accident."

"Example?"

"A hole in the mattress?"

"I thought that would be too obvious."

"It is! But no one will find your drugs there by accident. If someone starts checking your mattress for stuff, you're in trouble already. So think twice before letting someone inside your walls."

"Meaning I should let no one in?"

"Ideally, yes. When you have more money, you should get another apartment for yourself and keep this one just for socializing. Until then, try to fuck the women in their own apartments. It's safer that way."

"Is that how you do it? You have a love nest?"

He smiled and winked. I took it for a yes. Then he put money on the table for the bill and stood up.

"I've gotta go, Baldy. See you next Saturday. Good luck tomorrow. And don't shit your pants walking home with the cocaine. Nobody will notice."

I paid, put the backpack on, and left. It was heavy. In the first minutes I didn't feel relaxed at all walking home with fifty thousand dollars' worth of cocaine on my back. But after a while I noticed lots of other people walking around with what seemed to be heavy backpacks. Just like me. Mad Dog was right once again.

[2/10]

I got home and hid the stuff in the bathroom, at the bottom of the dirty laundry basket. Then I copied the clients' contact information to my address book. Mad Dog had put some grass in the backpack. That came in handy; I really needed a joint to relax. The last time I had smoked marijuana was in Stanford.

I slept very well. The next day I woke up early, had a big breakfast, got dressed, and went to see Joe. I was scared to death.

Joe was an advertisement executive on Madison Avenue. He had a very good looking secretary named Nancy. She was in her late thirties and had been working with Joe for almost ten years.

"Morning. I'm here for Mr. Joe Williams. I'm his personal self-motivation trainer."

She gave me a beautiful smile. "Oh, sure. You must be Birdy?"

"And you must be Nancy. Joe told me a lot about you. He said that you're his guardian angel!"

She looked flattered. I wondered if he slept with her.

"Really? Oh, don't believe him. Joe is such a sweet guy! Never says a bad word about anyone. I'm not an angel!"

I smiled. Sure she wasn't.

She smiled back. "He's waiting for you. Let me tell him you're here."

She called him. "Hi, Joe! Birdy's here for you."

From the way she talked to him, I would bet that they were lovers. Did she know what I was really doing there?

"You can go in now, Birdy."

"Thank you, Nancy."

"By the way, please lock the door. You know, coaching is a very private matter. Joe can get very emotional, and he doesn't want people to see him distressed."

Joe had thought about everything.

"I will. See you later, Nancy."

* * *

"Birdy! Nice to finally meet you! Please sit down."

Joe was exactly like Mad Dog had described him: vertically and horizontally big, meaning very tall and very fat. I wondered how his heart could handle his cocaine addiction. He also had a big mouth and never stopped talking.

He bragged about how he and Mad Dog alone had developed the idea of the special delivery service. Apparently he wasn't aware that there was another guy involved, Peter, who I would meet in two days. Once again Mad Dog had compartmentalized information.

Joe told me about all the possible legends they had considered and discarded; how simple and brilliant the coaching idea was now that it existed, but how tough it had been to come up with; how many hours it took to create the name PSMT. One could tell that Joe was in advertisement. I was glad when the forty-five minutes were over and I could leave.

Nancy beamed a very sexy smile and said, "You look tired! It must be very exhausting."

"Yeah, it demands a lot of concentration. Joe told me I should make my next appointment directly with you."

She smiled once again. Was she teasing me?

"Tuesday is normally a quiet day. What about Tuesday, January seventh?"

I looked at my empty 1992 appointment book. "The seventh is fine. I have time. Same time as today?"

"Yes, ten o'clock. It was nice meeting you, Birdy. It's kind of early to say this, but since we're not meeting until next year, Merry Christmas and Happy New Year!"

"Same to you, Nancy! Enjoy the holidays!"

That was it. I had made my first drug deal and had earned $250 in forty-five minutes. I took the subway home, losing my tail, changed into my jogging clothes, and went running to relax. No need to call Mad Dog. He would call Joe directly. After jogging I spent the afternoon reading. That evening I treated myself to a very nice dinner and went to the movies afterwards.

The following day was cold but sunny. I dressed warmly and took the train to Coney Island, the first time I'd gone back there since my ATM fiasco. True to that saying, "criminals always return to the scene of the crime," I couldn't avoid walking to the spot at the end of Coney Island Avenue where I made the woman stop the car and tried to kill her with the toy gun. Less than two months had passed, and I could remember every detail. But the feeling of desperation was gone.

I spent a couple of hours on the empty beach. When I couldn't bear the cold anymore, I went to the diner at the subway station and had lunch. As with each time in the past, I wondered how many more years that place would survive before being replaced by a fast-food franchise.

***

On Thursday I went to see Peter, a hotshot investment banker whose office was in the World Trade Center. Dad had taken me a few times to the public observation area at the top of the south tower, but I had never been inside any office there. Peter's office was located almost at the top of the north tower. I had been warned that his secretary, Mrs. Jones, was very bitchy and I should be very careful. But first I had to pass the receptionist.

"Good morning. My name is Birdy. I have an appointment with Peter Johnson at eleven."

"Just a second." She called someone and announced me. "Mr. Bird for Mr. Johnson." I thought about correcting her, but the call was over very quickly. She pointed to the left. "Please go this way, Mr. Bird."

Peter's room had an anteroom bigger than my apartment. The secretary, Mrs. Jones, had a huge desk. I wondered how big Peter's room and desk would be. Before I could say anything, she asked me in a disapproving voice, "You're the personal self-motivation trainer, right?"

"Yes, ma'am."

"Please take a seat. Mr. Johnson will be with you shortly."

The leather sofa looked expensive and was extremely comfortable. I wondered if Peter was really busy or if Mrs. Jones was only giving me the treatment she thought I deserved. It didn't really matter. Mad Dog had told me to take any punishment with dignity. Never complain and never frown. It didn't matter when I got to see the client. Important was when I left.

I should always leave at a quarter to the hour and move to my next appointment. No exceptions to this rule, even if I had no appointments afterwards. If the guy left me waiting for more than forty-five minutes, I should excuse myself, tell the secretary that my next client was waiting, and leave without making a follow-up appointment. When the client called later begging for a new appointment, he should be given one in two weeks at the earliest. This would teach a lesson to the person who made me wait. If it was the client himself, he would have only himself to blame; if the secretary, she would feel the client's wrath.

After ten minutes the secretary's phone rang. I could hear her saying, "Yes, he's here. I'll send him in." Peter certainly knew the bitch well and suspected that she was making me wait. She didn't look pleased and spoke without looking at me.

"Mr. Johnson will see you now."

"Thank you very much, Mrs. Jones," I said in a friendly and polite voice.

Peter was very different from Joe, also tall but very thin. The first thing he said to me was to lock the door and take a seat. It was a huge room, and Peter had a huge desk; everything was even bigger than I had imagined. And what a great view!

He seemed anxious. His eyes shone when I gave him the package.

"You don't mind if I do a line, do you?"

"Please, go ahead."

I had seen people doing cocaine at parties, and had heard that many people did it at work. That was the first time I saw someone actually doing it at his desk. After a few seconds his mood changed. He asked if I could sell him a second package. There would be a lot of parties in the following days, and he needed extra dope. He gave me the money and started to talk.

Unlike Joe, he never mentioned Mad Dog or the PSMT idea. He talked about the building. His dad had worked for the company that built it, so he knew a lot. He explained to me the principle of the so-called tube-frame design. The elevator shafts were like massive tubes at the core of the building. The facade was made of steel columns spaced closely together. That was the reason why the windows were so narrow. The outside steel frame was like a second tube, reinforcing the first tube at the core. For this reason some people called the tube-frame design "tube in tube." This made the structure so strong that the building didn't need many columns cluttering the floor plan. That was interesting to learn. But he went on for a quarter of an hour, giving me more information about the building than I cared to know. Then he moved on to baseball.

Mad Dog had warned me that Peter was a die-hard Mets fan. I knew the basics of the game, but I didn't follow the season because I didn't like baseball. I had gone to the library to check old sports magazines, just in case. The Mets had finished fifth in the National League East in 1991. Seemed good to me. Not to Peter.

As he complained about the season, boring me to death, I had to remember RW. He hated baseball more than I did. "Almost as bad as cricket," he always said. "The only positive thing about it is that it doesn't take as long." In his opinion baseball must have evolved from cricket, "if you could call that evolution."

At eleven forty I had to interrupt Peter and ask him to make an appointment directly with his secretary. I was afraid that the bitch would make me wait forever.

"I hate her too, Birdy. I wish I could fire her. But she's been with the company for more than thirty years, and she's very competent. Being nice is not a requirement in our line of business. We're investment bankers. We screw people for a living!"

He laughed at his own joke and called Mrs. Jones. After an appointment was made for January, I left his office.

"See you next month, Mrs. Jones. Enjoy the holidays."

"Thank you," she said, without looking up.

Maybe she should do some cocaine to lighten up, I thought.

* * *

I met Mad Dog on Saturday for a very short meeting in a coffee shop. I noticed that he looked tired and tense. I asked if there were any problems. He answered only, "Yes." When I asked what the matter was, he said that it wasn't worth mentioning. As he had already told me, the whole business revolved around only three things: territory, foot soldiers, and reputation. It was always one of the three.

We only had time for an espresso. He had brought me his backpack with fifty more packages of cocaine. I had brought him mine with his share of the deal, $2,250. I had earned $750.

"Any feedback from the clients, boss?"

"Yes. You did well. Both Joe and Peter were very satisfied. No need to change anything."

I was expecting more enthusiasm, but I didn't say anything, afraid of aggravating him. He gave me the list for the following week's deliveries. Twenty-seven names. There was also background information on the clients and their secretaries. Altogether five typed pages.

When he stood up to leave, he said, "Baldy, I'm really glad I found you. The business would be much easier if there were more guys like you out there." Though I was sorry for his troubles, that comment made me happy. He then said, "Take care and see you next Saturday. And remember: watch your back, man! Mean motherfuckers out there!"

That made me nervous. I spent extra time losing my tail on the way home. I hid the dope in the bathroom and went for a walk. But I couldn't calm down. The first two trades with Joe and Peter had gone well, but they had been single trades. The following week I would have to do five or six deliveries per day. Five days operating inside enemy territory.

I would have only fifteen minutes to move from one appointment to the next, so Mad Dog made appointments in geographic clusters: Wall Street on Monday and Tuesday; Madison Avenue on Wednesday; Tribeca on Thursday; Midtown on Friday. Would the cops or the Latino dealers notice me moving from building to building? Would they find my briefcase suspicious? Would they come after me?

To stop thinking about the enemy, I spent the rest of Saturday and the whole Sunday learning the information about the clients and their secretaries by heart. I had to go to the library again for information on football and politics. The football season was ending, and many clients would surely talk about the Super Bowl in January. There were quite a few political junkies on my list, and they could talk about the upcoming primaries for the 1992 presidential elections.

I was so busy that I forgot my fears for the rest of the weekend. Sunday evening I went to bed early, and had a nightmare about the shooting in Texas. In my nightmare the shooter was a Latino dealer and he was yelling, "How dare you invade my territory? Manhattan belongs to me! You're ruining my reputation! Die, you brown scum!"

I woke up at around two in the morning, bathed in sweat. My mouth was dry. I drank water, put on clean pajamas, and changed the bed linens. I feared falling asleep again and having the same nightmare. But if I stayed awake, I would be too tired the next day. I remembered that I had marijuana. It was very late, though. What if I overslept the next day? I set up a second alarm clock just in case, smoked a joint, and felt asleep shortly afterwards.

The next day I woke up feeling tired but relaxed. My first appointment was at nine.

* * *

That Monday, December sixteenth, 1991, I officially started my new career as drug dealer. The caveman was exactly two months old. Coincidence, of course, but Mad Dog would probably see meaning in it.

Everything went smoothly. Yes, the whole plan was sound, and the weeks of preparations paid off. There I went, from office to office, from delivery to delivery, in and out in forty-five minutes. I could pass receptionists and secretaries without problems. No questions, no suspicions.

"Larry is waiting for you..." "Mr. Silverstein will see you soon..." "Please take a seat. Mr. Roberts is on a phone call right now, could take a few minutes..." "Jim is finishing a meeting, said you should wait in his office..."

The clients were all nice. No wonder; I was like Santa Claus bringing them Christmas presents. More than half bought two packages; one even bought three; a lot of unexpected extra revenue. I sold forty-five packages of cocaine that week. Adding the three packages that I had sold to Joe and Peter, the total for December was forty-eight. My income was $12,000. It really felt like Christmas.

After one of my deliveries, right after the secretary and I had made the next appointment and I was about to leave, she told me, "You must be very good at your work. Bill sounded so different on the phone right now! Before you came, he was very anxious and bitchy. Now he sounds like another guy. He hasn't been this happy and relaxed in days. What did you do to him?"

I couldn't say that her boss had no more cocaine left when I came, and that was why he was in such a bad mood. He had done a line in front of me. When I left, he was high and happy. I winked and said, "Coaching works! Happy Christmas!"

That was the moment when I realized how really brilliant the PSMT idea was. The clients had a great excuse for feeling good, happy, and self-motivated right after I left their offices. They were high on cocaine, but whoever saw them would probably say with enthusiasm, "This self-motivation training is really doing you good, man!"

I had the impression that being a drug dealer would be lots of fun. I met a lot of very interesting people that week, and would meet many more in the future. They were very happy to see me. I had what they wanted, and they were thankful for that. The funny thing was that they didn't want me to think that they were drug addicts. No, they all had a very cool relationship with the cocaine. It enhanced their quality of life; it opened up their minds; it provided new perspectives; it let them explore other sides of their personalities.

To convince me that they weren't dopeheads but creative, intelligent, charming, and cool, they talked. About everything. I just sat there and listened. I had always been fascinated by the human mind. That job would give me the opportunity to observe it deeply.

[2/11]

I met Mad Dog for lunch on Saturday, December twenty-first, to exchange backpacks and Christmas presents. I had the following three weeks off, a hard-won vacation. I was planning to start my library research. The birth certificate was my next goal.

Mad Dog chose a Jamaican restaurant in midtown. To my surprise he was already there when I came. That was unusual. When he saw me, he smiled. He looked happy. It seemed that he had solved the problems that were bothering him the last time we met.

When I got to the table, he stood up and gave me a hug. "Baldy! You did great! I've heard back from a lot of clients. Everyone was very satisfied with the delivery service."

I had that impression, too.

"I told you that I wouldn't screw up."

"Yeah, I'm proud of you!"

The waiter came. Mad Dog suggested that we both have the house specialty, and I agreed. Not only because it was a Jamaican restaurant. He seemed to know a lot about food in general, having done lunch with clients almost daily for so many years.

"How many packages did you sell?"

"Forty-five this week."

He whistled. "Kids are going to party hard, ain't they, Baldy?"

"Looks like that. Your share is thirty-three thousand seven hundred fifty dollars."

"I brought you seventy packages of cocaine this time."

"I won't have place for dirty laundry anymore inside the basket. It will be full of cocaine."

He laughed. "You're hiding it there? What about the mattress?"

"Haven't figured out yet how to make the hole I need without destroying the thing."

"There are books about this stuff. Haven't I told you?"

"Nope."

"Sorry. I wanted to, but you already had so much to do. I decided to tell you later, but I forgot."

He gave me the titles of a few books. I wrote them down.

"You won't be selling this much in January. New Year's resolution kind of thing. 'Less drugs this year.' It doesn't last long, though. And I have eight new clients for you. What about that?"

Now it was my turn to whistle. That was great news. He gave me a sheet of paper with the names.

"Existing clients called me directly and gave me these names. Friends of theirs. I told them that in the future they should call the number on your business card and leave a message. You call them back. You gave them the cards, right?"

"Of course, boss. Following all agreed upon procedures."

"Good man! Please get in touch with everyone on this list and ask them about working environment and secretaries."

"I also got two pager messages regarding potential new clients. I haven't called them back yet. If we can get them, we'll have thirty-nine clients in January. You almost doubled your client base in one month!"

"I told you that the demand was there. The only thing missing was the delivery service. I'm sure that you'll get a few more calls in the next weeks. You could start the next delivery cycle with fifty clients."

"That would be great! What about the few who didn't want to be coached? Will you continue to do lunch with them?"

"I have to. They are afraid of direct delivery to their desks. The PSMT idea is too wild for their companies, they say. But there are only three left. I can handle that."

"What are you doing with all the free time you've got now?"

"It's great to have more free time, but I kind of miss them. Very entertaining folks, aren't they?"

We both laughed. "Yes, they talk a lot. I just sit there and listen."

"Like a real coach, Baldy! In a way, you're their therapist, you know? They'll tell things they don't tell anyone else."

"That wasn't my impression. They talked about everything but themselves. Very smart and interesting stuff, but nothing really personal."

"It was the same with me in the beginning. They have to get used to you first. And trust you. Then it'll come. Now they're only testing the waters."

"Any complaints about me?"

"Not really. Catherine asked about you. Did she make a move?"

"Man, Mad Dog, forty-five minutes of flirting! It was hard to resist. She's hot, man!"

"Very hot. In her third marriage now."

"No shit! That young?"

"Why does it surprise you? She's kind of average, you know? With the exception of Jeff Moore, the short guy in Tribeca, re-member?"

"Yes. What about him?"

"I believe that he's the only one who's still in his first mar-riage. All others are either divorced or already in their second, third, fourth, or even fifth marriages."

"Fifth marriage? Give me a break! Who?"

"Mark Taylor, for example."

"The old fart?"

"Yeah. He likes young blondes. Anyway, back to Catherine. Second husband caught her in bed with an Italian guy and almost killed both of them. She has a thing for Latin lovers, I suppose. Watch out, man! Husbands can be dangerous."

"Is that true? Or are you only trying to scare me?"

He laughed. "Both, Baldy! Don't go down that road. It's not worth it. It could ruin our business. Forget Catherine. It's only a pussy, man. Only a pussy. There are many more out there."

I had heard that from RW years before. Almost the same words. Was that a Jamaican thing?

"Anyway, Baldy, I told her that you're definitely gay but still in the closet. No use trying to seduce you."

"Thanks, man."

"But she'll try again. I'm sure. Resist, Baldy! Resist!"

"I will."

"The new people should get appointments in the same two

weeks as the existing clients. So you'll work only two weeks a month and can take the other two weeks off until you have about one hundred clients."

"Thanks, Mad Dog. That's a good idea. I need time off to research the birth certificate."

"I can help you with that. I might have some free time at the beginning of the year."

I wasn't sure if I wanted his help, but I couldn't tell him that. "Yeah, thanks."

The waiter brought our food, interrupting the conversation. Mad Dog took the opportunity to give me a short lecture on Jamaican cuisine. He told me about the restaurants he was planning to go to once he got to Jamaica after Christmas. We stuffed ourselves like there was no tomorrow.

* * *

When we finished eating, the conversation drifted back to the PSMT operation.

"So, how does it feel, Baldy? To be a real drug dealer?"

"Good. It feels very good. It's different than what I had expected, though."

"How?"

"I trained hard to convince people that I'm a real PSMT."

"And as far as I know, you did very well."

"Yeah, but I never trained for what happened after I got inside and closed the door."

"What's so hard about that?"

"The listening part. I didn't train for that. It's fun but very tiring, you know?"

"Tell me about that! But you'll get used to it."

"And I have kind of a guilty feeling."

He gave me a surprised look. "For breaking the law? I thought the caveman didn't give a shit about the law."

"Not that. You never feel guilty about sustaining people's addiction?"

"No, because if it wasn't me, it would be someone else. At least I try to sell them clean stuff. There are people out there selling garbage." He looked me in the eyes. I felt uncomfortable. "There is no place for guilt in this business, Baldy. Drop it!"

"I will. But it's sad, isn't it? The clients have families, careers, money, lovers, status, all things other people strive to get. And they're ruining everything with their addiction, aren't they?"

He sighed. "That's the traditional way to look at the situation. After almost ten years in the business, I see it from a very different angle."

"Which is?"

"In my opinion, cocaine is only one of their many addictions."

"Really? What else do they take? Ecstasy?"

"I'm not talking about drugs."

"You mean alcohol?"

"No intoxicating substance. I'm talking about other kinds of addiction."

"Don't get it, man."

"The career, the money, the sex, the status: aren't they all addictions? These people are searching for kicks, Baldy. Cocaine is just another road they take when they realize that the other stuff doesn't work anymore. They have a big void inside of them. Something is missing. They try to fill this void with career, status, money, sex, drugs, you name it. But nothing works for long."

Oh, man! He was not only into new-age crap, he was also into psychoanalyzing people. "That's a very practical way to look at things. It does minimize our responsibility, doesn't it?"

He didn't like my comment and gave me an angry look. "I'm not trying to minimize anything! We are dealers and we sustain people's addiction. Period. But so does everyone else. We sell our clients cocaine. Other people sell them expensive cars, apartments, clothing, sex, hope. Everyone is catering to the same need: fill that big void that can't really be filled."

That was a funny concept.

"You see no difference between drugs and expensive cars?"

"No."

"Cocaine can kill you. It ruins your life. You told me so!"

He sighed. "Yes, that's true. But the other stuff fucks you too, you know? It only takes longer. In the long run, it all comes down to different kinds of addictions and different kinds of drugs. But we're all dealers, Baldy. Many of our clients are also very successful dealers. The companies they work for are also sustaining other people's addictions. Filling the void."

Did he really believe that crap?

"And this void you're talking about, can it never be filled?"

"Not with the stuff everybody sells, Baldy. Just a replacement for the real thing."

"Which is?"

"You haven't figured it out yet? Come on! You're smart!"

I didn't have a clue. "I don't know, Mad Dog. Some unfulfilled childhood dream?"

"It probably has to do with childhood, yes. But not dreams."

"What then?"

"In my opinion? Love."

I had an urge to laugh but luckily could suppress it. Couldn't avoid smiling, though. Not even in my wildest dreams would I have imagined hearing that kind of stuff from him. Mad Dog, the drug dealer hardened by years in the trade, talking about love!

He didn't like my reaction. "What's so funny, Baldy? I know that smile of yours, and I don't like it."

"Sorry, I just found it funny to hear you talk about love."

"You think I'm not able to feel love?"

"Of course you are! It's not that."

"What then?"

"Talking about it."

"Not everyone is as uptight as you are, Birdy boy."

"Do you talk to your other dealers about love, too?"

"Why shouldn't I?"

"I can't imagine the conversation. That's all."

"Really? What do you know about my other dealers? You just bumped into one of them when you were searching for me. You never really talked to him."

He was very serious now. Not angry but kind of disgusted.

I tried to smooth things out. "Man, it's okay! Take it easy, Mad Dog. I didn't want to offend. It's just..."

"Just what?"

"The first time Winston and I found you, I was taken to that apartment, and I saw all those Jamaican guys armed to their teeth. I couldn't imagine them talking about love."

"Because they were black, right?"

I thought, "Come on, you're not going to play the race card now, are you?"

"Black guys are dangerous animals, right? No feelings. No soul. It's buried very deep inside of you, Baldy!"

"What's buried deep?"

"Your racism. You're just like your mom!"

Now I was offended. "Beg your pardon? I wouldn't be sitting here with you if I were like my mom!"

"You didn't have a choice, did you?"

That hurt. "Man, we have known each other for how many years now? You know that I'm not a racist. Winston is my best friend!"

"Maybe because he's rich and well educated? A dark-skinned guy, as your father would say? Me? I'm saving your brown ass, so I must be okay as well. But the rest? The other black guys out there selling dope on the street are all scum, right?"

I was deeply annoyed to hear that. He had known me long enough and well enough to know that I wasn't a racist.

"You have a chip on your shoulder, Mad Dog. It has nothing to do with their color but their occupation. I don't know much about dealers, but don't forget that only two months ago I had five drug dealers and an undercover cop inside my living room. None of them were black. Then the shooting. I doubt that those dealers sat down later on and talked about love."

"Those three guys weren't dealers but professional killers. Never forget that. Not all drug dealers are killers."

"But not angels, either."

"Are you an angel, Baldy?"

"No! Of course not!"

"But you think that you're better than my other guys, right? Not violent. Not mean. Just a well-educated, polite, and sensitive drug dealer."

"Not better. Just not that hardened."

He laughed, a mix of sarcasm and anger. "Not hardened? Really? You tried to kill a woman because she was annoying you! How much harder can someone get, Baldy? She was no menace to you. She was preaching about Jesus and you pulled the trigger."

That caught me off guard. "I was out of my mind! I never intended to!"

"Intentions don't change anything. Murder is murder."

"Of course it does. It wasn't premeditated. It just happened. That's what they call extenuating circumstances."

"Bullshit! There are no extenuating circumstances! It makes no difference if it's premeditated or not. Take Jerry Carter, for example. A guy I knew. He started beating someone up, and the guy had a heart attack and died. They gave Jerry life without parole."

"You think he didn't deserve it?"

"According to your line of argumentation, no. He never intended to kill the guy."

"People can get hurt and die when they get viciously beaten up, can't they? Jerry knew that death was a possible outcome before he started roughing the other guy up."

"So that makes Jerry a mean motherfucker?"

"Yes!"

"At least he had a good reason to beat the guy up. What about that guy inside the movie theater restroom? You almost killed him, didn't you? For what? Whistling?"

He gave me a mean smile. I swallowed hard.

"So you're now going to throw the whole shit back at me? I was under a lot of stress. It wasn't me who did those things. It was the caveman inside of me."

"We all have cavemen inside of us! But only you have the right to act like one, right?"

"Man, this was supposed to be a Christmas celebration."

"It is, Baldy! Maybe I'm giving you the best Christmas present ever by making you aware of what's going on inside of you."

"Maybe. But I'm very disappointed to hear that you think I'm a racist. I thought that you knew me better."

"This conversation is not about me knowing you, but about you knowing yourself."

The waiter came to take the empty plates. We sat there in silence, waiting for dessert. After we got it, he started again.

"I like you, Baldy. Don't get me wrong. If I thought you were a racist bastard, I'd never have let you find me. You're not racist on a conscious level. But there's a lot of stuff buried down there. A lot of shit from your mom."

That reassured me a bit. "I can't be blamed for my upbringing."

"No, you can't. But you can do something about it."

"Like what?"

"Therapy?"

I had to laugh. "Come on, man! Therapy?"

"It has helped me a lot."

What? Mad Dog in therapy? The conversation was really

getting weird.

"You do therapy? No shit!"

"Black men aren't supposed to?"

"Please, don't start again! How long have you been doing it?"

"Since the summer of 1989. Two and a half years already. I owe you that, Baldy."

"Me? What do I have to do with it?"

"You helped me see a few things."

"In 1989? I was in Miami!"

"No, much earlier. It just took me some time to understand."

"Mad Dog, why are you telling me all this?"

He grinned. "Okay, let's get to the point. Let me ask you something. Why are you getting into the business?"

"For the money, of course!"

"That's what everyone says. Make money quickly and retire to some island. By the way, which island are you planning to go to when you have saved enough to retire?"

That was a tricky question. Was he suspecting that I wouldn't stay around for long and trying to make me admit it? And what would happen then? He had already invested so much money in the operation, and he needed me. How could I tell him that I was planning to leave in three years at the latest? I didn't know what to say.

"Come on, Baldy, do you really believe that I don't know? That you plan to save as much money as you can and then leave?"

"Why would you think so?"

He laughed. "Don't be so uptight, man! I know that you don't plan to stay around for long. But it doesn't really matter. Do you know why?"

I didn't say anything. It was definitely a trap.

"Because you'll stay around for years, Baldy! Regardless of your intentions. Nobody ever leaves this business unless they get shot or arrested. Drug dealing is like Hotel California."

"You mean, you can check out anytime, but you can never leave?"

"Worse. You can leave any time, but you don't want to. That's the fucking problem."

"I'm in for the long term, Mad Dog."

He laughed. "Yes, that's true. but you don't know that yet! You still believe that you'll get out soon. When, Baldy? And where to?"

I remained silent.

"Listen, man, you don't have to worry. I know that you won't leave. That's why I'll help you get all the stuff you need in order to leave. I'll help you get the birth certificate, the driver's license, the passport, the bank accounts, the offshore structure, everything that you need. And when you're all set, you won't leave."

"Of course I won't leave!"

"Of course? It's obvious to me but not to you. Stop lying to me, will you?"

I sighed. "Okay, man, I confess."

"That's much better. Destination and time frame?"

"A place where no Feds or Colombians will find me."

"And does that place have a name?"

"Hong Kong."

He had a laugh attack. Everybody looked at our table. His laugh was so contagious that other people started laughing, too. It was like the whole restaurant was laughing at me. Very upsetting.

"No shit! Hong Kong? So you can mingle, right? Nobody will notice your brown ass among the Chinamen! Perfect cover, man! Haven't you learned anything from your readings?"

That annoyed me. "I came up with that destination before I started my readings. I just want to get as far away as possible. It doesn't have to be Hong Kong. It can be Australia or New Zealand, for example."

"It doesn't really matter since you'll never leave. Time frame?"

"When I have a million. Could be done in three years."

"Interesting! Most people think five years."

"Was that your case?"

"More or less."

"Destination?"

"Jamaica, like most of my guys."

"And why are you still here?"

He smiled. A really happy smile. "Thanks, Baldy! Finally! That's what I want to talk to you about, man. The reasons why people don't leave the business."

"Which are?"

"The same reasons why they join the business!"

"The money? You get addicted to the easy life?"

"No, it has nothing to do with money, man. Wake up!"

That was irritating. He was contradicting himself. "You just said so! You said that people don't leave for the same reasons they join. And they join because of the money!"

"They think they do."

"You are talking in riddles now."

"Think, Baldy, think!"

Shit, just like at school. "The void? Is drug dealing also a form of addiction? Are you trying to say that we're like our clients?"

"Much more complicated than that."

"Then explain. Give me an example. Why haven't you left the business, for example? Why did you join if not for the money?"

"Let's go somewhere else for coffee, and I'll tell you. We've been here long enough already."

[2/12]

We paid and walked to a coffee shop nearby. Each had his backpack on. Same model, same color, and same size. Nobody seemed to notice or care. It was really incredible.

After we got coffee and cake, he started. When he was a kid he wanted to grow up and become like his dad, someone who fought the bad guys and did the right thing. When his dad got shot...

He paused. I saw his eyes getting misty, but he didn't cry. I felt like teasing him about letting his feelings flow, but I didn't dare.

He continued, fast-forwarding the story. After both parents died, his life changed radically, but not his plans for the future. Mad Dog didn't lose his desire to go into law enforcement. It even got stronger. He would find the bastards who had killed his dad and would kill them all. His dad was doing undercover work when he was killed, Mad Dog had learned. So he decided to become an undercover agent as well. When he came to America, he spent his free time learning about the trade. He read all the library books he could get ahold of and saw all the movies on TV. His aunt never gave him much money, so he couldn't afford to go to the movies.

I asked if he could have become a spy in America, being a naturalized citizen. Or was he planning to go back to Jamaica? That could have been a problem, but he never got to find out. In high school he realized that he couldn't work for the government. He had what his teachers called a problem with authority. Since he didn't want to have a boss, he decided to become a drug dealer instead. The whole spy thing could be applied to drug dealing.

No difference.

I had to question that. In my eyes there was one big difference: he had changed sides. If he had gone into law enforcement, he would be the good guy fighting the bad guys. Instead, he became a bad guy himself. He smiled and said that with time he realized that there were no good or bad guys. Some people had a license to be bad, others didn't. That was all. Only the guys without license were persecuted. The rest ran free fucking other people for a living.

License to be bad was a new concept to me. I told him so, and he smiled. We should not pass judgment on our clients, he said, but Rudy Wilson, for example, had a license to be bad. Did I know that the company Rudy worked for was what people called a corporate raider? Of course I did. A very successful one, by the way. He asked, and what did corporate raiders do? They bought companies for cheap, ripped off their most valuable assets, destroyed a lot of jobs, loaded the companies with debt, and dumped them on the stock market. They were bad guys screwing a lot of innocent people for profit.

I told him that he was talking like a Communist. Then I remembered Dad. Was it really buried deep inside me? Was I a black hater like Mom and a Commie hater like Dad, and just didn't know it? Was Mad Dog right?

He shook his head. I should say that to the people who had lost their jobs and had their lives destroyed in one of those transactions. Companies like Rudy's had a license to be bad, and they used it. Everybody admired how much money they made. Nobody seemed to care about the destruction they left behind. And that was only one example.

I nodded as if I agreed. I didn't want to argue the other side. It would only get us off topic. I was very interested in his story and wanted him to go on.

His adoptive father, Malcolm, got laid off in 1981 at the beginning of the long and mean Reagan recession. He couldn't find another job that paid as well as the one he lost. He had to take a shitty job, and his wife had to go to work to make ends meet. Malcolm got bitter and started drinking. He spent his evenings with a bottle, watching television and bitching and moaning about the bad guys. Corporate raiders got a lot of media coverage those days. Whenever his adoptive father saw one of them on TV, he cursed the guy. He had lost his job because of a guy like that one on television, he believed. He then invented the expression license to be bad, the only useful thing Mad Dog ever learned from him.

Malcolm started beating up his wife and kids, especially Mad Dog, the adopted one. One day Mad Dog hit back, and Malcolm threw him out of his apartment. Homeless at seventeen, he had found shelter with an older Jamaican friend, Charlie, who had also left home and was dealing drugs. Mad Dog decided to start his own drug-dealing business and to apply to the drug business everything he knew about living undercover and creating legends. He would do it for a few years, save a lot of money, and then go back to Jamaica. Like everyone else, make big and leave. He even set a date: his twenty-fifth birthday, in January 1990.

And then I came along. He had to admit that in the beginning he thought that I was a sissy, but not because I was rich. Winston was also rich, but he was no pussy like me. I shouldn't be offended, he said. He just wanted to tell how it was. He had changed his mind since then. But for a long time he had that image of me.

In one of our many evenings together in RW's apartment in Harlem, he had heard me talking about my identity problem: how living in two different cultures had screwed me up; how I didn't know who I really was. When I finished talking that evening, he asked me what I was going to do about it. Why didn't I go see a therapist, for example? I was rich and had a lot of free time. It could help. "Like today, Baldy, you laughed and told me that you didn't need any fucking therapy!" He concluded that, like most people, I liked to whine about my problems, not willing to do anything about them. "Do you remember that evening, Baldy?"

I shook my head. No recollection. Mad Dog wasn't even supposed to be there, he said. The woman he was seeing at the time had gotten sick and canceled their date. He decided spontaneously to check on RW, not knowing that I was there. Maybe fate put the two of us together in that room for that conversation. I sighed and thought, there he goes again with his fate crap. He smiled, said, "Very deep," and continued to tell his story.

In the following years, whenever he had to create a new legend for himself, to pretend to be who he wasn't, he thought, "Baldy, you're such a pussy! Getting fucked up with only two identities while I have dozens!"

I was wondering what all that had to do with me. He noticed

my impatience and told me that we were almost there.

He dated a lot of women in his life. They were all the same, he said; always wanting to get serious in a relationship, having kids and stuff. But he was a drug dealer. He didn't want to have a serious relationship, let alone a family. If he got arrested or killed, his wife and children would suffer. He didn't want his kids to experience what he had gone though. That was completely out of the question. Whenever a woman started talking about commitment, he answered, "Maybe someday, honey, after I quit the business. But not now." When the woman asked when he would quit, he answered that he didn't know. Sooner or later the woman left him, tired of no commitment. He then moved on to the next relationship. "Only pussies, Baldy. Only pussies." I knew that already.

Then came the year 1989. His last year in the business, according to his plan. He had stashed enough money in Jamaica to live well for the rest of his life. He met a woman he really liked. I noticed he didn't say love. Was he afraid that I was going to laugh again? Her name was Marcia. They got along really well, and eventually she started talking about marriage, kids, and so on. He told her what he had told all other women before her. He couldn't do it. He was a drug dealer. It was too dangerous. She then asked him, like all others before, why not start a new life? Why not quit and go back to Jamaica?

"That was in the summer of 1989, Baldy. A few months before my deadline. Do you know what I said?" I shook my head. He paused for a moment, trying to control his feelings. "I told her that I couldn't quit any time soon." Then Marcia told him that she knew exactly what his problem was. He claimed that he couldn't have a serious relationship because he was a drug dealer. But it was the other way round; he had become a drug dealer in order not to have any serious relationships. He was just fucking hiding from life. She left him.

"Fucking hiding from life! The chip came down, Baldy!" Marcia was right. He finally understood that what had unconsciously attracted him to an undercover life was the lack of bonds that came with it. Spy or drug dealer, you could have no long-term relationships. Friends? You expected to lose them sooner or later. Lover? She would never be upgraded to wife. Children? They would never be born.

When he started dealing, he thought that the lack of bonds would be the price to pay. Unpleasant but inevitable. Little did he know that it had been his real, unconscious reason to become a dealer. He saw the obvious: as a child he had lost his dad, his mom, his best friend Winston, his sisters, and his grandparents. Everyone he loved was taken away from him. After that he shut out the outside world. Deep in his soul he was afraid of losing even more people. His choice was to not have anyone to lose anymore.

It became clear to him that he wasn't going to leave the business. He was trapped. That was when he decided to go into therapy. He needed help. Like me, he was fucked up because of his childhood experiences. But, unlike me, he would be a real man and deal with it. I found that offensive. "Don't take everything personally, man! Want more coffee?"

I nodded. He stood up to get it. I was really offended by his low opinion of me. When he came back, I asked if the therapy had been of any help. When he said it had, I asked why he was still around. After all, if he knew why he had joined the business, then he knew what was keeping him in it, right? Using his own words, I asked why he wouldn't be a real man and deal with it. Why wouldn't he leave the business for good?

He said that he could feel my anger. That upset me even more. I was getting it wrong, though. He was there to help me. I asked, how could he help me if he couldn't help himself? He was just playing the do-as-I-say-not-as-I-do game.

He replied that advice could be sound, even if the person giving it was not yet ready to follow it, and told me the story of a former client called Walter, now living in Washington D.C. Walter's marriage was going down the drain and his wife had suggested that they go see a marriage counselor together. He refused. His lawyer told him to go, in case it came to a divorce. Then Walter could claim that he had tried to save the marriage until the very end. That would be good for his image and might get him a more favorable divorce settlement.

That advice convinced Walter to try counseling. He didn't want to give his future ex-wife a penny more than he had to. But his prejudice against therapy was stronger than his desire to save money. At the beginning of the first session he asked the therapist if she was married. The answer was yes, she was now in her third marriage. Walter then asked the therapist, if she wasn't able to save her own marriages, how in hell was she going to help him save his? And he walked away.

I said that it made a lot of sense to me. Mad Dog replied that it made no sense at all. A person who went through two divorces knew a lot about relationships breaking down. She could understand the issues, having had them all. She could give sound advice, even if she wasn't able to follow it herself. Walter was just prejudiced. And his lawyer was right. Walter got stuck with a very bad divorce settlement.

I thought, "Man, how much longer will this conversation last?" And what was the point, really? Okay, he had told me his life story. That was nice. It showed that he trusted me. He had never told me anything personal before. Everything I knew I had heard from RW. But he had confessed that during all those years we spent hanging out together, he had a very low opinion of me. That hurt. I had always had the impression that he liked me.

"Are you wondering why I'm telling you all this shit, Baldy?"

"Actually, I am."

"You're joining the business to hide! Just like I did!"

"Hide from what?"

"From your identity problem! What else? It's the dream life for you, man. You can pile up so many identities that you'll never have to figure out who the fuck you really are."

"It makes no sense to me, Mad Dog."

"How many identities have you got already? Let's see..." He started counting on his fingers. "To your family you're Pablo; to Winston and me, Baldy; to the Brooklyn drug dealers, Winston Twenty-two; to your clients, Birdy, the drug dealer; to the clients' co-workers, Birdy the PSMT; to your former roommate, John the bum; to Red, the acting teacher, you are Mike; to Thomas, your landlord, you're Jeff; to Helen, the style consultant, Kenny. That's nine, right?"

"So what?"

"Nine identities in two months! And that's only the beginning. The number of identities will keep growing. And you'll love it! You'll go on a splurge, man. You'll get addicted to it. Left alone, it'll take you years to realize that you're only hiding behind your fucking legends."

"But you won't leave me alone, I suppose?"

"Of course I will! I'll never bring up this conversation again unless you come to me and ask. I know that you'll forget about it as soon as you leave this place. You have much more interesting stuff to do than think about this shit, right?"

Who was he to pass judgment on me? "There's one thing I don't understand, Mad Dog. If you think that I'm doing something bad, why are you helping me? Why don't you stop me?"

"Because I don't have the right to stop you. You have to do what you have to do. It's your fate, man. You have to go through this shit. Like I did."

I closed my eyes, and heard him sighing.

"I know, you don't believe in fate, right?"

"No."

When I opened my eyes, he was smiling.

"When I heard about your troubles in California, I thought that you had finally gone into hiding from your identity problem. Drug dealing was perfect for that. I found it weird that we had both chosen the same path. When I heard that you were looking for me here in New York, I got goosebumps."

"Why?"

"We had made similar choices, taken similar roads, and now those roads were about to cross. I suspected that you'd ask me for a job. Once a dealer, always a dealer. The Hotel California thing. When you told me that you weren't a dealer yet, I hesitated. Why not stop him now?"

"Fate told you not to?"

He didn't like the irony. "I realized that I didn't have the right to stop you. It was your destiny. You had to go through it. The only help I could give you was having this conversation. The rest you have to do yourself."

I sighed. What could I say? "Well, I appreciate it, Mad Dog."

He smiled, not really convinced.

"Really, Mad Dog! No kidding. I just need some time to digest the whole thing. But thanks. And Merry Christmas, by the way!"

"Merry Christmas, Baldy!"

I gave him my present: a CD with seventies Turkish psychedelic rock. Besides Marley and rap, he also liked sixties and seventies music, especially psychedelic rock.

He was impressed. "You and Winston are two fucking music maniacs! Where do you guys get this kind of stuff? I didn't even know that Turks made rock music. I thought they only did the belly-dance thing."

"Fate brought me to these CDs!"

He laughed. Then he gave me his presents: a CD and an envelope. I opened the CD first. I couldn't recognize the band. He told me it was a new rapper, a guy called Tupac. His very first record, released only three or four weeks before.

"He's better than all other rappers. You'll love him."

"Thanks. Can't wait to get home and listen to it."

I opened the envelope and found a horoscope inside for a person named Caveman, birthdate October sixteenth, 1991. That was the date of the shooting in Texas.

"You were reborn that day, Baldy. That's when we'll celebrate your birthday next year."

A horoscope! Well, it would make interesting reading.

"Thanks, man. I'll read it carefully. Maybe I can figure out when fate will strike next!"

"It doesn't work that way, Baldy."

"I was only joking!"

"I know. But I had to say it for the record." He looked at his watch. "Time to go. By the way, you'll start your library research soon, right?"

"Yeah, beginning of January."

"I've looked at a few death notices in the last days, and I noticed that not all show the birthplace."

"Shit, I didn't know that!"

"Caught with your pants down again. Try to figure out how you'll get that information. Otherwise you'll be wasting your time in the library."

I sighed. "Yes, I will."

"I have an idea, but I have to make a few phone calls first. Take care. And Happy New Year, by the way!"

"Happy New Year, Mad Dog! Enjoy Jamaica!"

I walked home; in my backpack lots of cocaine and a horoscope. I didn't know which of the two made me feel more uncomfortable.

[3]

[3/1]

Christmas Eve I spent alone in my apartment, not in the mood to go out, thinking about the good life that I had lost forever. Here I was in New York City putting up with awful December weather and working as a drug dealer to sustain other people's addiction instead of enjoying a carefree life.

Christmas Day was sunny but very cold. If I had been home, I would have spent the day on the beach. It was a family tradition to invite friends and extended family to our beach house on Christmas Day. I thought about dressing warmly and going to Coney Island, but decided not to. Better forget the old traditions. The past was dead and buried.

I couldn't stop thinking about what Mad Dog had told me regarding my inability to deal with my identity problem. A few things he said made sense, but there was also a lot of bullshit. That was typical of him. You had to separate the wheat from the chaff. But I was getting good at it. Leaving the esoteric stuff aside, the real-life advice he gave me was good and worth following.

Of course I would leave the business as soon as I could. It wouldn't take more than three years. Christmas 1994 I would spend in my new country, whichever country that turned out to be. I would meet my deadline. Until then I would enjoy life. I had always been good at it. The few weeks I lived in poverty were enough. Never again.

New Year's Eve I also stayed home. I spent the first of January building a safe hiding place for the cocaine, the thing that would make my new life possible. I had never built anything with my own hands before, so it was a big challenge. I bought all the tools and materials I needed for the task in the last week of 1991. Instead of using the mattress, I decided to hide the dope inside the drywall.

Drywall was a curious thing. Back home we always built walls with bricks and mortar. Americans built interior walls using wood frames covered with gypsum boards, what they called drywall. Sometimes they also built exterior walls that way. To exterior drywall they added insulation, but interior drywall was usually left hollow. What a perfect place to hide stuff!

I had one drywall separating the bathroom from the rest of the apartment. The bathroom side was covered with tiles. The other side was painted. I decided to cut a hole on the painted side, hide the cocaine inside the wall, close the hole with a lid, and use a framed poster to cover everything. Eventually, when I got enough reserves hidden inside, I would seal the lid and apply a coat of paint to the whole wall. If needed, I could take off the lid without problems, damaging only the paint job.

According to my research, drywalls were built with vertical studs placed every twenty-four inches center to center. I knocked on my wall and could confirm that the space between studs was about that. I chose to make a square hole sixteen by sixteen inches in size. I bought four patching panels and paid the guy at the hardware store to cut each panel down to the size I needed. I brought home four perfectly square lids, just in case I broke one by accident. I didn't trust my manual skills.

Using the lid as a template, I drew a square on the wall. With the drywall knife I made a cut big enough to insert the drywall saw. Sawing in a straight line was tougher than I had expected. To prevent the lid from falling inside the wall, I used four metal stoppers. To the lid's backside I attached four flat magnets. Wonderful; the lid fit, held in place by the magnets and the stoppers.

Using cling film I made two bricks of cocaine, each brick containing fifty packages. I fixed two screw hooks to the studs inside the wall. Then I took a piece of thin nylon rope and attached one end to one screw hook and the other to one of the bricks, and let the brick fall slowly into the wall. I did the same with the second brick and closed the lid.

After inserting two screw hooks one foot above the lid, I hung the framed poster and took a step back to contemplate my piece of art. Mad Dog would be proud of me. It had taken me the whole afternoon, but I had a very good hiding place.

What I didn't have was an answer to his question: how to find out where the children had been born if that information wasn't available in the death notices. I had to postpone researching the death notices to the second half of January. Maybe Mad Dog would have the answer by then.

* * *

On Friday morning, January third, he paged me. I called back, and he invited me for lunch. He told me to bring my backpack, he had more stuff for me. We met in an Afghan restaurant.

Like in all restaurants we had been together before, waiters knew him well. They called him Jason. Jason Walker was the name he used to make reservations. To the clients he did lunch with he was Christopher Allen. Most called him Chris.

We had a very pleasant time together, nothing compared to our meeting before Christmas. From the restaurant we moved to a coffee shop, later to another one. There was no new-wave shit this time. No talk about fate or feelings. He told me about his short trip to Jamaica during the holidays. He didn't get in touch with RW because it wasn't safe yet. We celebrated how successful customer acquisition had been. Meanwhile the customer base had more than doubled to fifty-three people.

Mad Dog then told me how to solve my birth certificate problem. He convinced me that I actually needed two birth certificates. I shouldn't experience losing my identity ever again. Once was enough. I needed a reserve identity in case the new one I was going to build with so much effort and cost was discovered and I had to drop it. Therefore, there would be two of me: Mr. A and Mr. B. Both identities would own the offshore companies and control their bank accounts. Regardless of who left the country, Mr. A or Mr. B, I would always get to my money. That was ingenious; why hadn't I thought about it myself? His analytical and planning capabilities were awesome. And his attention to detail was really impressive.

There was no way to know the odds of getting a birth certificate from a vital records office. We should be very conservative and expect a success rate of no more than twenty percent. If I needed two birth certificates, I should write at least ten letters. Why twenty percent and not ten or thirty? "Can't tell, Baldy. Just a gut feeling." I decided not to question that.

Mad Dog wanted a birth certificate to create an emergency identity kit for himself. He proposed that we share the costs. Since I would be doing most of the research and as such covering most of the non-monetary operational costs, I would get the first two birth certificates. In case we got more, one would be for him and the rest to sell and equally share the revenues. A fair and generous proposition.

Buying certificates on the black market would be quicker but not recommended. The going rate was between $3,000 and $5,000, but neither of us could really tell the difference between a real one and a forgery. And we couldn't know how many copies of the same certificate were in circulation. It was too dangerous to share the new identity with other criminals. It would be much harder and more time consuming, but we had to find the certificates ourselves. Like all criminal enterprises, this operation required modesty, patience, and brains.

It would cost us a lot of money. One major cost would be getting the information about the birthplaces. It couldn't be done without inside help, and that help was expensive. We also needed help with the return addresses since vital record offices didn't accept P.O. boxes. Finally, we had to pay people to help us get Social Security numbers and driver's licenses.

Mad Dog's idea to find the birthplaces was brilliant: school records. Every kid had to show a birth certificate to enroll at first grade. He found a Jamaican guy working for the New York City Department of Education who had access to all student records, past and present. The guy would check the birthplaces for us; the price was fifty dollars per name. Also here we should expect a success rate of no more than twenty percent, just to be on the safe side. Accordingly, fifty names would bring us ten out-of-state births. The resulting ten letters would deliver two birth certificates. But we needed at least three. It was better to find one hundred names. Twenty letters would bring us four birth certificates, two for me, one for him, and a spare to sell. Hopefully more.

A lot of people moved to New York from neighboring states. They traveled back to visit their relatives now and then, usually for Thanksgiving, Christmas, or in the summer holidays. Many traveled by car and got involved in crashes. Sometimes whole families lost their lives. We should focus on those car crashes. Death notices involving several members of a single family were much easier to spot on a newspaper page. A few of the kids killed in those accidents could have been born in another state before their family moved to New York. That choice also narrowed the scope of the search: two and a half months in the summer, one week in November, and three weeks at the turn of the year. Altogether one hundred days per year.

Mad Dog was born in 1965 and I in 1966. We could easily pretend to be two or three years younger or older than we really were, so we should search for kids born between 1963 and 1968. The age at which kids started school varied, but it was safe to say that at seven all were already attending elementary school. We should therefore research newspapers for the years 1970 to 1975. For kids born in 1963, it would cover deaths between the ages of seven and twelve; for kids born in 1964, between six and eleven; and so on until it covered deaths between the ages of two and seven for kids born in 1968. We had to ignore all deaths before the age of seven because we couldn't have those names checked. We would research borough-specific papers, starting with Brooklyn and Queens.

He gave me a real driver's license, stolen from a guy who had long hair and beard but didn't look much like me. It was the best ID Mad Dog could buy in such a short time. It was good enough since nobody really examined picture IDs, he said. Many old newspapers were stored on microfilms. I might need a library card to see them, and I needed a picture ID to get that card. As always, he had thought about every detail.

[3/2]

I enjoyed my last three free days, Saturday to Monday, and on Tuesday, January seventh, I was back at work. My first appointment was with Joe at ten. Nancy looked gorgeous. The moment she gave me her sexy smile, Mad Dog popped up inside my head, telling me, "Don't fuck her!" Yeah, brainwashing worked. Sine was a number, you wrote résumés to get job interviews, and you didn't fuck the secretaries.

Once again Joe bragged about how clever the PSMT idea was. He missed doing lunch with Chris, meaning Mad Dog, but the delivery service was much more practical and time saving. He gave me the name of two potential new clients, and I did the required background check on the guys. When I was finished, I asked him point blank, "Does Nancy know?" I had the impression that he was taken aback by the question, even though his vacillation lasted only a few milliseconds.

"Of course not! Why would you think so?"

"Just a hunch."

"Hunch? Oh, shit! I should have guessed that Chris would choose a new-age guy to take his place!"

That was interesting information: I wasn't the only one who found Mad Dog's new-age crap annoying. I was about to make a mean comment on esoteric stuff when I remembered that Mad Dog was still in contact with Joe. That could get me in trouble. There was one thing that I had learned in my previous life that applied to this one as well: always make your boss look good, and never say anything bad about him.

"You don't believe in intuition, Joe?"

"Humbug!"

"What about fate?"

"Give me a break, Birdy! I've already had too many arguments with Chris about fate. I'm not going to start with you!"

Yeah, I wasn't the only one! I liked Joe much more after that. I had two other clients that morning. The afternoon was free, and I went to the movies. On Wednesday I had four appointments, on Thursday five, and on Friday two. With the exception of Peter, all were first-timers. Like Joe, Peter was more relaxed this time, though still boring. All others were polite and superficial. Two of the new secretaries were very hot, just like Nancy. Man, some guys had it all.

Altogether, the fourteen clients in that week bought twenty-two packages, an average of 1.57 packages per client. Almost as high as in December. That was a surprise. Mad Dog had said that December had been an exception, and sales would go down in January.

* * *

When we met on Saturday, he was very pleased to hear about the high average. The clients were probably buying cocaine for their friends. Maybe even reselling for profit in order to lower their addiction costs.

It made no difference if the guys introduced new clients to us or kept those for themselves, he said. Both increased our revenues. One day I would reach full capacity: 200 clients per month. If we managed to sell an average of 1.5 packages per client, we would have the equivalent of 300 clients buying one package each. That meant $300,000 monthly sales. My share would be $75,000.

In my second workweek I saw thirty-nine clients. Twenty-seven I had already met in December; twelve were first-timers. Also this time I could notice the difference in conversation. Many second-timers started to talk about themselves. Catherine talked about her marriage, how bad things were and how lonely she was feeling. I was falling for her. She was my type of woman, and my will to resist was decreasing proportionally to the growing intensity of her flirting. To get her out of my head, I thought the whole time about Mad Dog's threat. "Don't fuck up my business, or I'll kill you!" That helped. But I had to come up with a better solution, or I might not survive my next appointment. Amazing what kind of problems one could have in life.

That week I sold fifty-nine packages and got thirteen recommendations for new customers. I met Mad Dog again on Saturday, this time for Mexican food. He was delighted to hear that January's final average was 1.53. The long-term average with his lunchtime clients had been 1.2. Some clients were definitely buying to resell.

I should announce a new pricing structure in February. The first package would cost $1,000, the second $800, and the third and all subsequent ones only $600. My cut would remain the same: $250 per package. The discount would come from his share. Lower prices would make dealing more profitable to the clients, giving them an incentive to buy more.

* * *

I spent an afternoon calling all libraries in Manhattan, and made a list of the ones that had the newspapers I needed. I didn't want to go to the same library every day. On Monday I started searching for death notices; two weeks of very hard work, taking only the weekends off at Mad Dog's insistence. "You need a rest. All work and no play makes Jack a dull boy!"

Mad Dog came three times to help. It was nice to have someone to talk to during lunch break, which we had to keep short. Public libraries had short opening hours, normally from ten in the morning to five in the afternoon. We finished one borough newspaper for Brooklyn, but found only forty-seven names.

Contrary to our expectations, quite a few death notices included birthplaces. Among them, kids born in New York were the majority, but we still found five born out of state. That made me happy. We could write for those birth certificates immediately, I said. But Mad Dog, always the analytical mind, cautioned me. "These are the names everyone is looking for, right? The low hanging fruit. What if they have already been taken?"

He knew a guy who worked for the Social Security Administration. That guy would help us get our Social Security numbers later. Mad Dog would ask him to check if those five names had been issued Social Security numbers after their deaths, meaning that someone else was already using them for criminal purposes. That was a very clever security precaution. But it left us with only forty-two names.

Over the weekend, to get over my frustration, I did more manual work in my apartment. I needed more holes in the drywall. The first one was full. I had 300 packages of cocaine hidden inside; my emergency reserve. I needed an additional hole for short-term storage, and another for my savings and Mad Dog's money. The second hole would be hidden behind another poster. The third one would be closer to the floor, hidden behind a short bookcase. I needed one for my books, which I had piled on the floor.

Saturday morning I went shopping and bought the short bookcase, the second framed poster, and the material that I needed for the paint job. First I made the two holes in the wall and built the lids. After that I sealed the lid hiding the reserve dope and painted the wall. Then I assembled the bookcase. It was evening when I finished. I was tired but very happy. That Saturday was February first. I had started February exactly like January: making holes in the drywall. What a coincidence. If he knew about it, Mad Dog would surely find an esoteric explanation for that.

At the beginning of the year I had set myself a monthly budget of $5,000. Half of it was for rent, $1,000 was for eating out on workdays, Monday to Friday. Ten dollars bought me a snack for lunch, like a falafel, a soup, or a sandwich, plus a soft drink; forty dollars a nice dinner. The remaining $1,500 was for everything else: eating out on weekends, grocery shopping, subway tokens, clothing, music, movies, etc.

I made $20,250 in January and spent less than $5,000. Adding the money that I had left from December, I had savings in the amount of $20,000 now hidden inside the drywall.

[3/3]

On Monday, February third, I started dealing again, and had twenty-one clients that week. Everybody loved the new prices. I sold thirty-two packages, an average of 1.62. Mad Dog would love to hear that. We had an appointment on Saturday, in a Korean restaurant. He came late and looked distressed.

"What's happening, Mad Dog?"

"They killed Chepe Gordo!"

Gordo was Spanish for fat. Chepe was a nickname for José. A Latino dealer was dead. So what?

"Who the hell is Chepe Gordo?"

He gave me a sarcastic smile. "A guy we both work for."

"I thought I had joined a Jamaican gang, not a Latino one."

"You did. But we still work for him. You went to business school. Almost got an MBA. You might be familiar with the concept of a supply chain?"

His tone of voice was angry. If he was in such a bad mood, our conversation would certainly end badly. I didn't want that. "Yes, I do. But I'm not familiar with the drug-dealing industry. Maybe you could explain it to me? If I understand it, in the future I might be able to grasp the meaning of someone like Chepe Gordo getting killed. It probably has deep implications, but I don't have a clue. Why don't you begin with territory, foot soldiers, and reputation?"

He gave me another sarcastic smile and became silent. It looked like he was pondering if it was a good idea to tell me what I wanted to know. The waiter came, and we ordered.

"Okay, Baldy, you're probably right. I can't expect you to understand what kind of shit we might be getting into in the next weeks if you lack the most basic knowledge."

In his opinion, the key to understanding the drug-dealing business was to recognize that it had two dimensions: a horizontal and a vertical one. On the horizontal level one person alone owned a given territory exclusively. East Fifty-fifth Street in Crown Heights, for example, where I met the guy who later led me to him: that territory was owned by that guy, and he made sure that no other drug dealer trespassed. It was the same all over New York City. Every single street was exclusively owned by a member of one of the many ethnic gangs: here the Jamaicans, there the Dominicans, over there the Mexicans, and so forth. Nobody shared territory.

Mad Dog had operations in Brooklyn and Queens. Each of his cells had about ten to twelve foot soldiers, managed by a cell master. He had one extra layer of management between him and the cell masters: every three to four cells were managed by what he called a handler. He had two handlers in Brooklyn and one in Queens. I did mental calculations. That meant ten to twelve cells and more than one hundred foot soldiers. I was impressed. It was a small army.

His operation was the opposite of a lean and mean operation. It had too many layers of management. Most dealers with an operation of similar size dealt directly with their foot soldiers. His bloated management structure cost him a lot of money, but it kept him safe.

His direct suppliers were also Jamaicans; two cousins, Charlie and Vincent. He had been working with Charlie, the one in Brooklyn, from the very start. Vincent in Queens came a few years later with his cousin's introduction. The Jamaican connection ended at that layer in the supply chain. Above that, it was all Latinos and Italians.

His Jamaican suppliers bought their stuff from two different Latino dealers, both Colombians. That much he knew. How many layers there were above them, no one could really tell. The drugs moved from South America to the streets of New York along very sophisticated supply chains. I should imagine retailers buying from wholesalers, wholesalers from importers, importers from exporters, exporters from producers.

Both our supply chains were in the hands of Colombians, but it was a known fact that five Italian Mafia families ruled New York City. Somewhere along the supply chain the Italians and the Colombians worked together. If the Italians controlled the Latinos or the Latinos controlled the Italians, he didn't know or care. Inside the supply chain it was impossible to know exactly what happened too many layers above or below you. That was why he could be part of two different and competing supply chains. But only his Jamaican suppliers, Charlie and Vincent, knew about it, and they didn't care. The Jamaican bond was stronger than anything else.

On the vertical level a lot of people owned East Fifty-fifth Street in Brooklyn: the foot soldier I met; his cell master; the cell master's handler; Mad Dog; Charlie, his Jamaican supplier for Brooklyn; the Latino retailer supplying Charlie; the wholesaler; the importer; the exporter; the producer. And somewhere along the supply chain Italian Mafia guys. So many dangerous people owned that single street that it made it a pretty safe territory. Only a lunatic would dare to invade it.

"Unfortunately, there are lots of lunatics out there, Baldy."

There were a lot of latecomers to the business. They had no territory and were willing to go to war to get it. One example was the Rodriguez family, the Mexicans who had set me up in California. They had built their own supply chain bypassing the main Colombian exporters and bringing their cocaine directly from Peru and Bolivia to Mexico, and from there to California. Now they wanted to move to the East coast. They had already established a bridgehead in Atlantic City. New York City was next.

That information made me feel uncomfortable. "So the Rodriguez family killed this guy Chepe Gordo?"

"I don't know it yet, Baldy."

It could have been an inside job. There was no loyalty in the business. People got betrayed all the time, most of the time by other people inside the same supply chain wanting to move up. Inside problems tended to get sorted out quickly. The supply chain was like a living thing. It liked peace and order and tended to rearrange itself whenever peace was broken or order disturbed. Every dead guy was replaced quickly. Since Chepe Gordo was so many layers above us in the Queens supply chain, if it had been an inside job, it wouldn't matter to us.

On the other hand, if it had been the work of a lunatic wanting to take over Chepe Gordo's territory, then the whole Queens supply chain would be under attack. Even Mad Dog and his people would be affected. Until he found out what we were dealing with, he had to lie low and be ready to fight. He was going to disappear for a few days or even weeks, depending on how bad things got. But I had enough dope to go on for a very long time.

"Does this happen very often, Mad Dog?"

"Inside jobs happen all the time. Invasions every few years."

"Why don't you give up the streets and concentrate on the PSMT business? It's much more profitable and safe, isn't it?"

He gave me a sad smile. "You don't understand how things are connected, Baldy. Maybe you should think about it and tell me next time we meet."

There he went, patronizing me. I hated when he did that. "I'll certainly not figure it out by myself. Since you'll have to explain it to me anyway, why don't you do it now?"

He sighed. "The street operation is a necessary cover for the PSMT operation. I need territory, foot soldiers, and reputation.

If I retire from the streets, I'll become like you: a nobody."

I didn't like the comment but didn't complain, afraid to aggravate him. The situation was serious. He was tense. "But it's much safer this way, isn't it? Being a nobody?"

"It's only safe because you have me above you and not some other motherfucker. You're still part of the supply chain and work for the Colombians and the Italians!"

"But they don't know about it!"

"Because I've never told them, man! Wake up!"

I should imagine he got killed and I decided to continue the PSMT thing on my own. I would need a new supplier. The guy I would eventually find would probably be delighted to hear about the PSMT operation and gladly agree to supply me. But not having foot soldiers to back me up, I would be completely dependent on him. He could decrease my pay or take away half of my clients and give them to someone else. I had no bargaining power whatsoever. "Being a nobody is shit, Baldy!"

But much worse would be the increased risk. The operation wouldn't be secret anymore. People liked to talk, especially when they could brag about how cool and smart they were. And the PSMT idea was too good not to brag about. Very soon a lot of people around my new supplier, including many foot soldiers, would know about me: the guy delivering dope to New York's elite disguised as a personal self-motivating trainer. That information was very valuable to the police and prosecutors. Most of the time they arrested only the small fry: foot soldiers and poor dopeheads. They would love to get a rich Park Avenue guy for a change.

Foot soldiers got arrested all the time. A guy facing a long prison term would be willing to tell the cops everything about the PSMT operation in order to get a reduced sentence. In Mad Dog's opinion I would get arrested in less than six months.

No one in our two supply chains knew about the PSMT operation. Even Charlie and Vincent thought that Mad Dog was selling the cocaine in Brooklyn and Queens. The street operation was a necessary cover for the PSMT operation. We needed foot soldiers risking their lives on the streets for a fraction of the money we made so that both of us could safely sit in that Korean restaurant enjoying a great meal and having a nice chat. "You owe your nice job to those black guys, Baldy. To every single one of them. Even though they are uneducated, ruthless, and hardened by years in the business. You owe them! Never forget that!"

Mad Dog the preacher attacked again. I swallowed hard but didn't let him notice that I was annoyed. Better change the subject. There was something that I had wanted to ask him for a long time but had never had the guts to. Now it seemed the right opportunity.

"Have you ever killed people, Mad Dog?"

He smiled. He didn't seem to mind the question. "You mean directly or indirectly?"

"What?"

"You want to know if I did it myself or if I had other people do it for me?"

"Both, I guess."

"I'm not sure about directly. I was ambushed once with some of my guys, and we shot back. There were dead on both sides, but I couldn't tell who killed whom."

"And indirectly?"

"Lots of times. You have to get to them before they get to you, Baldy. Attack is the best defense. But I leave it to the professionals. I can't shoot very well."

"And how do you feel about it?"

He smiled again, this time mischievously. Something was coming. "Great! What about you? How do you feel about it?"

He was probably expecting me to say that I felt bad about it, which I did. But I wouldn't give him a reason to call me a pussy. "I can live with it. I can understand why you have to do it."

He laughed. "No, Baldy, that wasn't my question. My question was, how do you feel about the people that you have killed indirectly?" His mischievous smile still on his face, he winked. "Talking about your dad, Baldy. He does it for the family, right? So you do it indirectly, too!"

Speaking in a tone of voice like he was rubbing dirt on my face, he reminded me that I had talked many times about Dad's fear that the Reds would someday take away everything he had, and maybe even kill him. He could understand Dad because he was in the same situation. The only difference was his enemies' colors: brown and black instead of red. And his territory was much smaller, too. Dad owned a fucking country, he said, and laughed. I had also talked about the political situation in the sixties, seventies, and eighties: the street protests, the political repression, the torture and killings of Communists. Dad had actually run the country behind the scenes, and our dictators basically did what Dad told them to do.

"When the military killed people, they were doing it for your dad. Your dad killed those people indirectly. And so did you!"

I didn't say anything. He stood up. "Take care and keep your ears to the ground, Baldy."

"When will I see you again?"

"Who knows? Buy the local papers. There you'll find everything you need to know about the war, if there is one. Stop reading those business papers you like so much. Forget the stock market. Now your life depends on what happens on the streets of New York. Bye."

He left. And it was about time. I was about to explode, really aggravated by his preaching. He was so full of shit. Not only esoteric, but also left-wing. I wondered who would hate him more, Mom or Dad?

[3/4]

I went home and added the seventy packages to the fifty-seven that I had in short-term storage. That was more than enough for the remaining forty-five clients in February. In the second half of the month I would do library research. If Mad Dog didn't show up before the end of February, I would have to use my reserve stash, ruining the paint job that I had done only one week before. So much work for nothing.

That thought didn't improve my mood. On top of that there was the Catherine problem. Our next appointment was on Tuesday morning. I was falling for her in a big way. How to stop her? Better said, how to stop me? She was my fourth client at twelve o'clock. I wondered why she chose that time. I once told her that I normally did lunch between one and two. Was she planning to invite me for lunch after the appointment? She seemed to have a battle plan. What about mine?

The only idea I could come up with was to do to Catherine what I had done to Joe: annoy her with new-wave crap. If that didn't work, I could escalate. I'd had my share of uncomfortable conversations with Mad Dog. I could use some of the stuff on her that he had used on me. The idea made me feel better.

On Sunday I bought a local paper, but there was no information on Chepe Gordo's murder. Same thing on Monday. Maybe there would be no war, I hoped, and Mad Dog would be back soon. Tuesday morning I left home with the conviction that I would stop that flirting for good.

* * *

When I entered Catherine's office and saw her, I started having second thoughts. I was really attracted to that woman. What was the problem with a good love affair? Why should I listen to Mad Dog?

But I had prepared for that reaction. "Think about Nancy," I told myself. If I were to get in trouble, Nancy was a much better option. She wasn't a client. She wouldn't be able to harm the business if things ended badly.

Catherine didn't waste time. "Do you have time for lunch after our appointment? They opened a great new deli across the street."

I was expecting that. "Sorry, Catherine. I have another appointment right after this one."

That upset her. "You said that you always do lunch between one and two!"

"Normally yes, but today is an exception. A client desperately needed an appointment, and I had to sacrifice my lunch break."

I was prepared. I took a brown paper bag from my briefcase and showed it to her.

"Today I'll have to eat a sandwich on the road."

She smiled. "Well, so you won't have a proper meal all day. Let me treat you to a nice dinner, then. When do you finish work?"

She was not letting go. But I was prepared for that, too.

"Sorry, I'd love to, but I'm meeting the boss for dinner this evening. Chris and I have a few issues to discuss."

She frowned. That was the window of opportunity I was waiting for.

"You know, Catherine, it wasn't supposed to happen today. That's how fate works."

The look on her face!

"Please don't give me that crap. I don't believe in fate."

Which made her even more attractive. "Why not?"

"It's all random, Birdy. Shit happens. That's all."

"You mean all quantum physics?"

"Yeah, exactly."

Oh, man, what was I doing? Not only a great body but also a soul mate. She was the right woman for me.

"Why does the concept of fate make you so uncomfortable?"

"Because it's all bullshit. I've told Chris a lot of times."

It seemed that Mad Dog bugged everyone with his fate crap.

"And what did Chris say?"

"A lot of stuff that didn't make sense. Like you're gay, for example."

Bang! I never thought she would mention it. Even more surprising was how she kept her eyes on the ball and didn't let anything disturb her plans. We were back to the subject of sex.

"You have a problem with gays, Catherine?"

"Not at all. I have many gay and lesbian friends. That's why I can tell that you aren't gay. Hundred percent hetero."

"If that was true, I'd have made a move on you long ago. You're a very attractive woman."

She smiled. "I believe that you're afraid of making a move. You're scared."

"Of what?"

"I don't know. You tell me."

Shit, I had lost control of the conversation. She had turned the tables on me and was psychoanalyzing me. I was supposed to be doing that to her.

"It's good that you mentioned fear, Catherine. That's the subject I wanted to discuss with you today."

She smiled again. "Your fear of women? Don't worry, Birdy, I think I can help you with that." After a short pause, she added, "Actually, I'd love to help you with that!"

She was smiling lasciviously. I hesitated. What was I doing? Why shouldn't I have her? The flesh was weak after all. I was Catholic. Only Protestants had a problem with lust. Then a voice inside my head told me to think about Nancy. But it didn't work. Nancy was just a thought. Nothing compared to that real woman in flesh and bones in front of me. And so much flesh...

She was still smiling, a victor's smile. She knew that I was cracking. Think about Mad Dog, I told myself. I closed my eyes. I could see him saying, "Don't fuck her, Baldy! You'll fuck up my business! I'll kill you for that!" That helped. I could focus again.

If the fate crap wasn't working, I had to use heavier weapons. I opened my eyes. She was still smiling, waiting for my surrender.

"No, Catherine. I mean your fear of getting to know yourself well. You're using your sexuality to escape from yourself. Sleeping around is not the solution."

She frowned. She wasn't expecting a rejection. "Who do you think you are to psychoanalyze me? You're only a drug dealer! You have no fucking right to say this stuff to me!"

Oh, man, she said fucking. She had never used an expletive before. And her tone of voice showed that she was really pissed. Her anger was scary. Maybe even scarier than her flirting.

"Sorry, Catherine, I didn't want to be rude. Yes, I'm only a drug dealer. But being a dealer I know a lot about addiction. Sex can be an addiction, too."

She smiled lasciviously. "Yes, a wonderful addiction!"

Shit, there she went again. I couldn't resist that smile. I had to make her angry again. I needed even heavier weapons. I remembered my conversation with Mad Dog about addiction and the void. Maybe I should try that. It could be overkill, though, like dropping an atomic bomb. But I had to take the risk because I couldn't come up with anything else.

"But it won't fill the void, Catherine."

"Which void, Birdy? Are you talking sexual metaphors?"

I couldn't believe my ears. She really didn't let go.

"No metaphors here. Though there is a connection between the void and love."

"Which void, Birdy?"

I sighed. I was going to drop the bomb now. This was the point of no return. Goodbye flesh.

"The big void that people try to fill with sex and drugs is caused by the absence of love."

Shit, it sounded really corny. Mad Dog would have done it much better. But it was too late now.

She frowned and stood up. "Are you saying that nobody loves or ever loved me? I don't have any fucking void, Birdy! Get the fuck out of my office! Now!"

"Catherine, we still have half an hour left. What will your secretary think?"

"Get out!" she screamed.

Had someone outside heard her? I stood up and left quickly

before she started screaming even louder. When I got outside, the secretary was already on the phone with Catherine. I waited for the call to end.

"So, Birdy, it seems that the boss has another migraine."

"Does it happen often?"

"Yes. Let's make the March appointment. Do you have time on Thursday, March twelfth?"

That meeting ruined my day. I had two other clients that afternoon. They were both very nice and talked about really interesting stuff, but all I could think about was Catherine's wrath. And Mad Dog's.

[3/5]

Late in the afternoon that Tuesday, riding the subway to lose my tail, I saw a newspaper headline: "Drug War in Queens." Shit, I had forgotten to buy the paper that morning. If there was a war going on, I should watch my back. I spent the next twenty minutes losing my tail. When I was completely sure that no one was following me, I bought a newspaper and walked home.

Five dealers had already been killed, but it wasn't clear yet who was fighting whom. No mention of dead Jamaicans; that was good news. On Wednesday the death toll went up to nine Latino dealers. Thursday and Friday brought the body count up to thirteen. We had the worst case scenario: competing Latino drug families were fighting for a slice of Queens.

Despite the war and the Catherine situation, I had a very successful drug-dealing workweek, my last in February. I sold seventy-five packages, bringing February's average to 1.65. I would end the month with more than $40,000 in savings. But that didn't make me happy. What if something happened to Mad Dog? We had created the mother of all drug-dealing operations, but now it could end at any second. And I had no control over the situation whatsoever.

Instead of sitting at home worrying about the war, I decided to go to the library on Saturday. There was a lot of work to do. All work and no play might make Jack a dull boy, but being dull was the least of my problems. I had sixteen days until my next shift. I would take no day off until I had the hundred names.

In the previous weeks I had developed a sick addiction to

statistics. I was keeping tabs on all possible metrics, even though I knew that past performance was no guarantee of future results. But I needed to feel in control. I wasn't going to start leaving things to fate. That was Mad Dog's way, not mine.

In January Mad Dog and I had searched 600 newspapers and found forty-two death notices, not counting the five that already had information on birthplaces. We weren't sure about those being safe. Therefore, I didn't want to use them to calculate my averages. Leaving out those five, it took 14.3 issues and roughly two hours to find one death notice. Extrapolating those figures, if I needed another fifty-eight death notices, then I had to research 830 back issues, and it would take 117 hours. Even if I shortened my lunch break to fifteen minutes, I had only 6.75 hours per day. Altogether 108 hours. There was a gap of nine hours. I had to do the job quicker this time.

At ten in the morning on Saturday I arrived at the public library. I worked like a maniac, but I had only three death notices when I left at five. I bought the newspaper on my way home. The drug war was getting hotter, but I couldn't tell how bad things really were for Mad Dog, and consequently for me. I smoked a joint and went to bed early.

The next few days went like that. Research. Dinner. Update on the drug war. Joint. Bed. My performance started to improve. Four death notices on Sunday; five on Monday; three on Tuesday; and six on Wednesday. On top of that, two death notices with birthplaces.

The Wednesday paper had alarming news. The Rodriguez family, the Mexicans who had set me up in California, were behind the war, fighting for territory in Queens that belonged to a Colombian crime family called Menezes. The Colombians were fighting back and attacking the Mexicans in Atlantic City. That was really bad news.

But nothing compared to what appeared in the Thursday paper. During the day I found seven death notices, bringing the total to twenty-eight, almost half of what I needed. And it took only six days to find them. I still had ten more days to research. I would find fifty-eight names. I was feeling so good that I went to the movies after dinner. I got home at around ten and checked the paper for news on the drug war.

There was a double page dedicated to it. I froze when I saw a picture of me with the caption, "Pablo aka Baldy aka the Ghost." My hands started to shake and my heart to beat fast, like someone had pressed a button and made my body behave strangely.

The police suspected that I was involved in the war. I had gone underground since the killings in Stanford in October 1991. There was reason to believe that I had moved to the East Coast to run the family's Atlantic City operations. Since nobody had seen me since October, people had started calling me Pablo the Ghost. The Menezes family under attack in Queens had put a $500,000 bounty on my head. The paper reminded readers that another Colombian family, the Gonzalez in California, had already done the same in October. Meanwhile, that bounty had gone up to $250,000. My head was now worth three quarters of a million to the person who killed me.

I had to stop reading. I needed fresh air. I stood up, opened the window, and stood in front of it with my eyes closed, deeply breathing the cold air. My head was about to explode. Man, now the complete New York underworld knew that I was in town, plus the police and the Feds. Had everything been in vain? My flight, the search for Mad Dog, the training to become a PSMT? After all I had gone through, would I have to hit the road again?

It was a very cold February evening, and soon I started to freeze. I closed the window and went back to bed. My heart was still pounding. Would my heart fail before the Colombians had their chance to kill me?

I smoked a joint to relax. It took longer than usual, but I calmed down and fell asleep. But fears never slept and I had a very nasty nightmare. I was back inside the fast-food restaurant in Texas, again under machine-gun fire, but this time the shooter was Mom. I was dressed only in my dirty underwear, trying to dodge the bullets, while Mom was shooting and screaming, "Shame on you, Pablo! To die wearing dirty underwear!"

I woke up at three thirty in the morning, bathed in sweat. The sheets were completely wet, and my mouth was very dry. It was the second nightmare in two months. The first one in December happened right before I started dealing. In that one a Latino drug dealer had been the shooter. What the hell was Mom doing in my nightmare now?

I drank water, put clean pajamas on, and changed the bed linens. I had work to do the following day in the library, so I set up two alarm clocks, smoked another joint, and fell asleep again. The nightmare came back, but I was too drugged to wake up, which was even worse. I kept dreaming the same shit the whole night. It only stopped when the alarm clocks rang at eight. Never again I would smoke a joint to fall asleep after having a nightmare.

* * *

Over breakfast I thought that maybe I'd better flee. But that would be a very stupid thing to do. I had the best chance to fix my life if I stayed in New York and carried on with the PSMT operation. Nowhere else could I get the money that I needed to start over as quickly and as easily. I looked very different now. Nobody would recognize me. I had to take the risk. After all, I was the caveman, and the caveman had no fears.

I went to the library and worked very hard that Friday. The research helped me forget the drug war and everything else. I found nine death notices that day, my record. Compared to the previous evening, the paper didn't have bad news. The war was now spreading to Brooklyn but nowhere near Mad Dog's territory.

I stayed up late watching movies on my VCR, and went to bed after midnight hoping that I would sleep through if I were tired enough. This time I didn't smoke a joint, but neither fatigue nor abstinence helped much. Very soon Mom was back with her machine guns. At one thirty I woke up. Not only were my pajamas and bed linens completely soaked, but also the mattress, like I had pissed in bed. Man, I never knew you could sweat that much in sleep. I had to turn the mattress over.

At around two thirty I was sleeping and once again under machine-gun fire. I woke up two more times that night. Since I didn't have any clean bed linens left, I had to use towels to cover the mattress. Things were getting out of hand. I needed sleeping pills, but I couldn't buy them without a prescription.

I found six death notices on Saturday, plus three with birth-places. Only fifteen more and I would be finished. After work I bought bed linens, pajamas, and two additional alarm clocks. The paper had good news that evening. The Mexicans were losing the war. The five Italian Mafia families had decided to join forces against them since the war was ruining everybody's business. That news made my day. It would be over soon. Things would go back to normal and the nightmares would stop.

Yeah, right! Saturday night was really bad. At five in the morning, after waking up for the fourth time, I set my four alarm clocks for noon. I badly needed to sleep. Sunday afternoon I went to the library for three hours only, and found two death notices. Afterwards I went home, packed my dirty laundry, and went to a coin laundry. I used five machines simultaneously to wash everything, and read the paper while waiting. The Mexicans seemed to be retreating from New York City. They were even losing part of their Atlantic City territory. There was nothing about dead Jamaicans. Good news.

Sunday night was relatively better. I only woke up twice. Me and my metrics: now I was keeping tabs on nightmares. That was sick. On Monday I found seven good death notices and another three with birthplaces. Only eight more to go. That night I woke up only once. Things were improving.

On Tuesday I found four death notices and had only one nightmare. On Wednesday I found the last two death notices I needed. Finished in record time. Fear could really help you focus. I left the library at three in the afternoon. Altogether I had one hundred names to give to Mad Dog's contact at the Department of Education, and another eight for the Social Security guy.

I slept well Wednesday night. For the first time I didn't have a nightmare. Was it over or just a pause? After all, the war was still going on. The Mexicans had retreated from New York, but were holding their ground in Atlantic City. No more news on Pablo the Ghost. No news from Mad Dog, either. He had been gone for three weeks already. I could only hope that he was alive and well. On Thursday I opened my reserve stash. What I had left in short-term storage wouldn't be enough for the next weeks.

* * *

I used my last free days to research my medical condition. Things were improving, but there was no guarantee that the nightmares would really go away. And even if they did, that they wouldn't come back anytime in the future. As always with symptoms, the kind of nightmares I was having and my physical reaction to them could mean a lot of different things.

The one that seemed most plausible was post-traumatic stress disorder. A lot of soldiers returned from Vietnam with that. Left untreated it could lead to drug abuse and alcoholism, relationship problems, and even self-destructive acts and suicide attempts. The shooter in Texas was a Vietnam veteran. Would that be my future? One day freaking out and shooting everyone around me?

The solution was psychotherapy, the last thing I wanted to do. No way. I shouldn't blow the problem out of proportion, I thought. The shootings in California and Texas were still very fresh in my mind. I should do nothing and just wait. Time healed all wounds. There was no real need for therapy.

The moment I made that decision, Mad Dog popped up inside my head, "You'll do anything to avoid therapy, won't you?" Was that also part of the post-traumatic stress disorder? I answered, "Mind your own business and come back. I need you as a friend and supplier, not as a psychologist." It was a silly thing to do, but I felt better afterwards. Though I did have nightmares Saturday night.

[3/6]

I had eighty-five clients in my two workweeks in March, thirty-seven in the first and forty-eight in the second. It was nice to have so many clients and make so much money, but I had underestimated how tiring the job could be. Ten clients a day were a lot; it meant seven and a half hours of conversation. The clients did most of the talking, but I still had to pay attention, follow their thoughts, make a comment here and there, and laugh at their jokes. At the end of the day I was exhausted.

I saw Joe on Tuesday. For the first time he wasn't in a good mood.

"Birdy, have you heard from Chris? I'm worried about him."

I wondered why. Was it because he liked him, or because he feared losing his supplier? I couldn't possibly ask.

"Don't worry, Joe. Chris is big enough to take care of himself. He's just keeping a low profile. It'll be over soon."

"Nasty war, isn't it? Much worse than the last one."

"When was the last one?"

"You don't remember? How long have you been working with Chris?"

"One year."

"Really? He told me he'd known you for ages."

He looked at me in the same way my former roommate had

done when I told her that I whistled all the time.

"I've known Chris for ages, but I lived many years on the West Coast. I got some problems there and moved back to New York last year. Since then we've been working together."

That was basically the truth, just a little bit twisted. I had learned that mixing true facts with fiction gave you much more convincing lies than using fiction only.

Joe seemed to believe me. "I see. The last war was about three years ago, December 1988 and January 1989. Chris disappeared in those two months."

I had already left New York at that time. I didn't remember reading anything about that war, but as Mad Dog had said, maybe I read the wrong kind of newspaper.

"You've been a client for that long, Joe?"

"Chris and I go back a long way. First met in 1985."

Like me! "That's why he trusts you so much."

He smiled, looking flattered. I thought, that's a treasure of information sitting right in front of you. If I made him talk, maybe I could learn things that Mad Dog would never tell me.

"Tell me more about the last war, Joe."

He explained who fought whom for which territory, how vicious everything was, and how it ended. The Mexicans had started that one, too. That was how they got their foothold in Atlantic City.

"And what happened to Chris during the war?"

"I wish I knew. He never told me anything about it when he returned. Said that he had gained territory but lost some men."

"Did he get hurt?"

"Not physically. But probably got some trauma, I guess, because in the summer he asked me if I could recommend him a therapist."

So maybe Mad Dog had post-traumatic disorder like me. And he had told me that he went into therapy to find out why he hadn't left the business. Was he compartmentalizing information? Telling Joe and me only what each one of us needed to know?

"Oh, you found him his therapist, Joe? Chris likes the guy so much that he keeps telling me to go into therapy myself."

"I can only recommend. I've been doing therapy for five years now. It's great!"

Shit, him too.

"If you want, I can find you a good one, Birdy."

"Thanks, Joe. I'll keep that in mind. When did you and Chris start doing lunch together?"

He smiled. "Shortly after we met. Chris's idea. He told me it would be safer that way. I thought, no way. Too suspicious."

Mad Dog convinced him to try it once. He was surprised: nobody noticed. He tried it a few times. When it became clear to Joe that the lunchtime operation was safe, he started recommending Mad Dog to friends, and so the number of clients grew along the years.

"But I was the first one, Birdy. The prototype."

Was he? I should ask Peter.

"Fate brought you and Chris together!"

He gave me the don't-give-me-the-fate-crap look. I smiled. Then something occurred to me. If he had been there from the beginning, maybe he knew Catherine?

"You introduced all other clients to Chris?"

"Basically, yes. Then they introduced some of their own friends. But all threads lead back to me."

"What about Catherine?"

"Catherine Anderson?"

"Yes."

He gave me a funny look. "Is there a problem with Catherine?"

"No, I just wanted to know if you know her."

"Very well. Her brother and I went to college together. I introduced her to Chris a few years ago."

What now? Should I involve him or not? He noticed that I was hesitating.

"What's the problem, Birdy? You didn't..."

"Fuck her? No, of course not!"

Stupid thing to say. It just slipped out of my mouth.

He found it funny and laughed. "I was going to ask you something completely different. But I see the problem. You're having lusty thoughts, aren't you?"

I didn't know what to say.

He noticed my embarrassment and laughed again. This time really loud. "Don't worry, Birdy. Most guys do. She's really hot, isn't she? But she's married, you know?"

"Of course."

"And it's not good to mix business with pleasure."

Was he speaking from personal experience? Did he get in bed with Nancy? Should I tell him that Catherine made the first move? Would he believe me? Maybe I should go for the twisted lie again.

"I won't deny that I was very attracted to her and..."

He interrupted me. "You were or you are?"

"It doesn't matter, Joe. You're right regarding mixing business with pleasure: it doesn't work. So to avoid the temptation I tried to have a serious conversation with her, but I think that I screwed up in a big way."

"In what sense?"

"Wrong topic?"

He gave me the same look I got from Mad Dog when he thought that I had said something stupid. "Which topic, Birdy?"

And he talked in the same tone of voice, like a teacher reprimanding a student. Had one picked it up from the other? Worse, it worked. I really felt like a student caught red handed.

"The void inside of us that makes us do the stuff we do."

He closed his eyes and sighed. "Man! You talked about 'the void'?" He stressed the word void in a very strange way. "Shit, Birdy, you don't talk to people about 'the void'! Only their therapists do."

He didn't sound angry; rather upset. It seemed that only imagining the scene was already hurtful.

I tried to apologize. "I admit it was a clumsy thing to do, but..."

He interrupted me again. "Clumsy? It was rude, Birdy. Plain rude!"

"I know. I blew it."

"How did she react?"

"She interrupted the meeting and threw me out of her office."

He closed his eyes again and shook his head. Then he looked at me, kind of sad. "You're in deep trouble, man. Catherine is very polite and sweet. She must have been very distressed to do this."

"I guess she was."

He was silent for a few seconds, which meant an eternity for a guy who never kept his mouth shut.

"And why are you telling me all this, Birdy?"

"I need help, man. Chris is not here. You're the second in

command."

He laughed. "Second in command?"

"Well, kind of, aren't you? You created the PSMT operation with him, right? Only the two of you."

That boosted his pride. He gave me a broad smile. "Yes, the most brilliant idea since chewing gum! It's a pity it has to remain secret."

"So, where else can I go for advice and help?"

He thought for another eternity of ten seconds, then smiled.

"All right. What do you want the second in command to do for you?"

"I don't know. Advice? Intervention? Peace offer?"

"I see. I'll give her a call. When are you seeing her again?"

"Thursday next week. At least I have an appointment. I don't know if she'll see me."

"I think she will. She needs the dope like everyone else."

"Yes, and if we're to continue meeting every month, we should fix the situation, right? The bad vibe must end."

"You don't like conflict, do you? Let me guess. Overbearing mother?"

"I don't understand your question, Joe."

He smiled in a patronizing way. "Sorry, never mind. I'll try to call Catherine in the next days. Give me a call on Friday."

"Thank you very much."

I remembered Peter. Did Joe know him?

"What about Peter? Did you introduce him to Chris, too?"

He laughed. "Got in some kind of trouble there as well?"

"No, just curious."

"Peter who?"

"Peter Johnson. Investment banker. World Trade Center."

"Never heard of him."

For the rest of the meeting we did small talk. I was relieved that Joe was willing to help, but I was also upset about his comment on my mother. What a hypocrite. One moment he tells me that I shouldn't stick my nose into other people's personal problems. Right afterwards he does exactly that to me.

Worse, how could he know that Mom was really overbearing? Was he just trying to be funny, or could people in therapy read other people's problems? Was that the reason why Mad Dog told me that I was a closet racist and that it was buried so deep that I didn't even notice?

On my way out Nancy was all smiles, but even that couldn't improve my mood. Actually, it made things worse. So much flesh...

***

Peter was out of town and booked for the following week, together with all other clients who knew Mad Dog personally. So all my meetings that week were easy. Most of the new clients had heard about the war, but since I was there delivering their dope, they didn't think it concerned them.

Friday at noon I called Joe.

"You screwed up big time, Birdy. She'll fire you next week."

"She'll what?"

"Fire you. She'll ask Chris to take her back. If he doesn't, I'm supposed to buy stuff for her."

Shit, I had lost one of Mad Dog's clients. What would he say?

"Is there really nothing you can do, Joe?"

"Listen, Birdy, maybe it's better this way. Unhappy clients can be hell. Sometimes you're much better off without them."

"You're probably right, but this is not my call to make. Catherine is Chris's long-term client. He might not like it."

"Catherine is only a client, Birdy. There are thousands others out there. Just get another one to replace her."

Only one among thousands; like pussies? Joe too? Did he learn that from Mad Dog?

"By the way, this phone call never happened, okay, Birdy? Don't tell Catherine next week that I talked to you, or she'll be mad at me. Promise me this."

"No word to Catherine. Thanks, Joe."

***

Actually, Joe was right. We would start April with more than one hundred clients, four times more than what Mad Dog had when I found him. Why should I care about losing Catherine? Only one client, with thousands more out there. Besides that, she was mad at me but not at Mad Dog. She still wanted to continue her business relationship with him. Therefore, she had no interest in revenge and wouldn't do anything stupid that could harm our operation. So I had followed his orders. To say it in his own words, I hadn't fucked her, and I hadn't fucked up his business.

My ordeal was over. Now things could only get better with no more Catherine to tempt me, the drug war ending, and my nightmares gone. I had only one more week of work and afterwards three weeks off. This time it would be a real vacation.

[3/7]

The following week went very well. The new clients didn't give a damn about the war. Only the clients who personally knew Mad Dog were worried. A few had tried to contact him, but he didn't call back. I tried to make them talk about Mad Dog. Most did. I heard a lot of anecdotes but nothing relevant. It seemed that nobody knew Mad Dog really well.

Thursday came. I was mentally prepared for my last meeting with Catherine. I had the advantage that I knew what was going to happen. My priority was not to make things worse than they already were. I decided not to argue, to take it like a man, and leave, regardless of what she said or did.

Our meeting was short. After I got in and took a seat, she said, "I want three packages today."

No greetings. No smile. I gave the stuff to her, and she gave me the money. She stared at me, probably expecting me to say something. I remained silent.

"This will keep me going for three months. Chris will be back before that. You're fired! I'll go back to Chris."

I nodded but said nothing. I could feel her anger.

"You're such an asshole. Don't even have the guts to defend yourself. Get out of here!"

The secretary didn't seem surprised to see me leaving so early. She had probably been told that I would be fired. Under the circumstances, it was actually a very good outcome. Everything was over without many tears. Mad Dog would be able to fix things up, if he wanted to. To me, that chapter was closed.

* * *

I saw Peter on Friday, March thirteenth, my last day of work that month. If he was worried, he didn't show it. I tried to talk about the drug war, but he changed the subject to the Democratic Party primaries. He was upset because the governor of a redneck state deep in the South, a guy called Clinton, was winning everything. Peter was afraid that Clinton would beat Bush in the November election.

Dad's sweet revenge part two, I thought. Dad hated Bush so much that he wished for a Democrat to win the election. Not that it really mattered, Dad told me. Our country's transition from military dictatorship to democracy had showed him that it made no difference which political system you had. There was always a way to control the country. Carlos was completely right: democracy was business as usual without the political prisoners. Money ruled in all systems.

America wasn't different, Dad believed. Elections cost a fortune in America. There must be very rich people paying to get their minions elected, just like he did back home. The French queen Marie Antoinette had once said, "Let people eat cake," Dad told me. The American elite let people eat the cultural wars. So it didn't really matter who won the American presidential elections. The same guys who were now behind Bush would later be behind that redneck guy. But it would give Dad great pleasure to see Bush go. Revenge was a dish better served cold.

What an evolution in Dad's political thinking! He had gone from cold warrior using brutal military force to crash all opposition, to sophisticated political operator using the media to channel the opposition's energy towards futile fights. And Carlos was behind it. I had never thought that possible. That was definitely Darwin's law of evolution at work: survival of the fittest. Either you adapted or you died.

I considered telling Peter all that just to see how he would react, but decided not to. A typical political junky, he couldn't see the forest for the trees. Let him eat primaries, I thought. I listened politely for about fifteen minutes, then I tried to change the subject to Mad Dog.

"How long have you known Chris?"

"Long time. Why do you ask?"

"Curiosity?"

"I'm not going to talk to you about my relationship with Chris. Why don't you ask him directly?"

So uptight. "Sure, I'll ask him."

And there we were, back to the redneck and the primaries. The following Tuesday Michigan and Illinois would vote. Polls showed the redneck winning both states. Peter went on and on and on. Well, it was Friday the thirteenth. It couldn't be helped.

* * *

I sold 132 packages in March, an average of 1.55. I got recommendations for another twenty-one clients, bringing our total to 106 in April. I still had 220 packages of cocaine, more than enough for the April clients. But there would be no dope for May.

I had three weeks off and I enjoyed every single day. On Saturday there was a very long newspaper article about the war that had just ended, listing all the dead and arrested. Mad Dog was not among them. The status quo had been restored. The same Italian Mafia families and their Latino partners ruled New York as before. The police had not missed the opportunity to clean up and had arrested a lot of people, but there were enough guys out there waiting to take their places. The supply chains would repair themselves and go back to business as usual.

In those three weeks I watched a lot of movies and went to a few rock concerts. I also had a lot of lunch and dinner appointments with clients I liked and wanted to get to know better.

I started asking around for a second apartment, something bigger and better than what I had. Not a single-room studio, but a real apartment with living room, kitchen, bathroom, and at least one bedroom. Ideally two, so I could have a home office with a place for a computer. Now I had no space in my studio apartment and had to buy a laptop. With the money I could have bought a PC with a big monitor plus printer, but at least I could work at home. I only needed to go to the copy shop to print files.

Mad Dog would be back soon, and he needed a lot of stuff from me: the names for the guy at the Department of Education, the new clients' names and background information, and my sales report. I used to give him that stuff handwritten. But whenever Mad Dog gave me written information, it was always printed. I was going to do the same.

I didn't save files to the laptop's hard drive. I used floppy disks instead, which I hid inside the wall. After giving Mad Dog the printout, I would destroy the disks because I read somewhere that experts could recover deleted files from hard or floppy disks. If the police got me, they would find my handwritten address and appointment books. But they didn't need to know more than that.

***

In my second vacation week I got a message on my work pager. "Back in NYC. Lunch next week. Chris A." That A definitely stood for Anderson, Mad Dog's lunchtime legend. He had never before used the work pager to communicate with me. Maybe it was the safest way to send a sign of life at that moment. To use pay phones he had to go to public spaces. It was probably still too dangerous for that.

That message cheered me up. Things were going back to normal. On Friday I got another message. "Tuesday noon. Drag queen phone. Chris A." I imagined the face that the person taking the message made when Mad Dog said "drag queen phone." I had a lunch appointment with a client that day, but I managed to move it to Thursday.

[3/8]

On Tuesday shortly before noon I was standing by the pay phone across the street from Washington Square. It rang at twelve sharp. Mad Dog was never late.

"Baldy-Birdy! What's up, man?"

I was really happy to hear his voice. "I'm fine. Worried about you."

"I'm great! Hungry. Crave some Ethiopian food?"

"Same restaurant as the last time?"

"Yes. See you there in ten minutes."

I was shocked to see him. He had lost weight and had bags under his eyes. "You look like shit, Mad Dog! You need a vacation!"

"Taking one as soon as things are running smoothly again. You need more dope, don't you?"

"Still have two hundred twenty packages. Enough for April."

"I brought you a very heavy backpack today. One hundred packages."

"And I brought your money: one hundred thirty three thousand seven hundred dollars."

He whistled.

"And two name lists. One hundred names for the Department of Education guy and eight names for the Social Security guy."

He whistled again and smiled. "You've been busy, Baldy!"

"It helped me forget the war."

"I have bad news on those five names. Four of them have been issued Social Security numbers in the last years. We're not the only ones searching those newspapers, are we?"

The waiter came, and we ordered.

"Now give me the full report, Baldy. What happened while I was away?"

Omitting only the nightmares, I told him everything, leaving Catherine to the end.

"I'm really sorry, Mad Dog. The whole situation was more than I could handle. But I avoided the worst. I didn't fuck her, and I didn't fuck up the business. She's still around, isn't she?"

"Yeah, I got about ten messages from her on my old lunchtime pager."

"Are you mad at me?"

He laughed, that disarming Jamaican laughter that I loved so much. "The good thing about these wars is that they help you put things into perspective. Considering what could have possibly gone wrong, I have to be thankful for coming back and finding the PSMT operation undamaged and running smoothly."

I was relieved.

He smiled. "Which doesn't mean that what you did was okay. You were really unprofessional dealing with Catherine."

He didn't miss an opportunity to tease me.

I changed the subject. "How was the war?"

"Do you really want to know? You should add a few dead bodies to your long list."

He had definitely missed teasing me. I changed the subject again. "Have you ever heard of post-traumatic stress disorder?"

"Of course."

"Do you have it? After so many wars?"

"Probably. I've been through a lot of shit." He then gave me his mischievous smile. "But nothing compared to two shootings in two days."

He wasn't giving up. "You really missed teasing me, didn't you, Mad Dog?"

"Yeah, a lot." Then, tongue in cheek, "Couldn't forget you with all that press coverage!"

Shit, he had read it!

"Pablo aka the Ghost. How did it feel, Baldy?"

I wasn't going to tell him about my nightmares. "I wonder how they came up with that bullshit."

"I'm talking about your feelings."

"It's very scary to know that everyone thinks I'm here."

"The second time, right?"

"Second time what?"

"That you read an article about you. First time was in Texas?"

Shit, he remembered everything that I ever told him.

"When you freaked out and changed directions? Went south to meet death?"

I nodded, wondering what he was up to.

"I was afraid you'd have the same reaction again and come to Queens looking for a shooting."

I couldn't resist hitting back and making fun of the fate crap.

"You're forgetting fate. I was supposed to have that experience only once. I've got that behind me." I smiled as I said that.

He gave me the fuck-you look. "What happened when you read that article, Baldy?"

"I thought those journalists were out of their minds. Then I feared for my life. I'd be stupid if I didn't, right?"

"Remember what I said about fate giving us opportunities?"

How could I forget that humbug?

"That article could have been one of those."

"Opportunity for what, Mad Dog?"

"To start processing all the information inside of you."

Oh, man, it would be one of those long days.

"Maybe I'll get third time lucky."

"You definitely will," he said with sarcasm in his voice.

We finished our meals in silence. I tried to hide my anger. Man, was he just bluffing, or could he guess what had happened? The nightmares and stuff? And if yes, how? The therapy thing? Anyway, I should be careful with what I told him. It was always used against me at some point.

* * *

We went to a coffee shop for coffee and brownies. He wanted to tell me about the next steps in our birth certificate operation. I was glad to move to operational topics. We normally had much better conversations on those.

After we got the names back from the Department of Education guy, we needed to write to the vital records offices. P.O. boxes weren't accepted as return addresses. He knew a janitor in the housing projects in Alphabet City. The guy had set up extra mailboxes in various buildings. He rented out those mailboxes to people needing fake physical addresses. Alphabet City was a shitty neighborhood, but people in other states didn't know it. It had a Manhattan zip code, and that was more than enough.

That janitor wanted $100 monthly rent for each name, and $200 for each letter that arrived. I asked if it wasn't dangerous. If the price for a birth certificate was between $3,000 and $5,000, that janitor could get much more than $200 for each letter. What if he sold it to someone else? The janitor didn't know much about birth certificates, answered Mad Dog. Besides that, he didn't have the contacts to sell them. And he would be risking his life if he betrayed us.

The Social Security guy had checked those few names for free, but he wanted $1,000 for each number he helped us get. They would be real numbers, everything legal. We would have to apply in person like everyone else. The price was for not asking questions. "As you well know, Baldy, people must pay a premium for special treatment."

He also had a guy at the Department of Motor vehicles, who charged the same: $1,000 per appointment. We would have to take the test and everything, like any other applicant. The guy would make sure that everything went off without surprises.

In America you applied for a passport at the post office and got it a few weeks later delivered by post. We didn't need any extra help there. Only a physical address to get the passport.

He advised me to get fake glasses for identity B. I should wear them with my hair hanging loose. He recommended a really nerdy frame. He was going to get one of those for himself, and we could go shopping together the next time we met. That would be in four days.

"I want to set you up before I leave for Jamaica. I'll take at least two weeks off. Bring the backpack on Saturday." He stood up. "Now I'm going to take care of the Catherine problem."

* * *

I enjoyed my last vacation days. Friday evening I met people for the first time as a real PSMT at a client's birthday party. Great apartment in the Upper East Side. It was a small crowd; about the right amount of people for my first time. I held my ground well. I even got one guy interested in real coaching. That was amazing. We exchanged business cards. I told him that I was booked out but would call as soon as I had an opening.

On Saturday I met Mad Dog in a Lebanese restaurant to eat kibbeh. He looked much better after getting some sleep.

"How were things with Catherine?"

"Everything's fine. She doesn't send you her greetings, though."

He had good news. The Department of Education guy had returned fifteen names. And the Social Security guy had found two additional names that we could use. Adding the one name he had already cleared, altogether we could write eighteen letters.

Mad Dog brought me a list with the eighteen names and their respective addresses in Alphabet City. My next assignment was to go to the library and search the addresses of each vital records office on my list and write the letters. It would take two to three weeks to get the birth certificates. When making appointments for May, I should reserve two mornings to apply for the Social Security numbers. We would do the driver's licenses in June.

"Then we do the passports, the bank account here in America, and finally the offshore companies and their bank accounts on the islands. Soon you'll be all set and ready to leave."

He gave me that smile that I so much hated. Better to change the subject.

"I'm looking for a new apartment. Have started asking around."

He gave me a condescending smile, clearly showing me that he knew I was changing the subject.

"Why don't we go get those glasses, Baldy?"

[3/9]

April flew by. Springtime was in the air, and the Latin American fur coats were all over Manhattan. The PSMT operation was running smoothly, and money was coming in like crazy.

I had forty-three clients in the first workweek, forty-six in the second, and seventeen in the third, totaling 106. I sold 165 packages of cocaine to them, averaging 1.56. At the end of the month I had $100,000 in savings. I saw Mad Dog on Saturday to exchange backpacks. It was a short meeting because he was taking a plane to Jamaica that evening.

My number of outings as a real PSMT started to increase. I went to three parties in April; everything went well. I had mastered my legend to the smallest detail. I met a lot of very interesting women and had a few one-night stands. I kept meeting people who wanted to hire me as a real PSMT. That was really weird.

In my third workweek Mad Dog came back from Jamaica but didn't have time to meet me. We talked briefly on the phone, and he told me that he had heard from the janitor that five letters had already arrived.

I had the last week of April off and really enjoyed it, knowing that those weeks off work were going to end soon. I already had 122 appointments booked for May. In June I would probably reach 150. To serve any additional clients I would get after that, I would need a fourth workweek. Then I would have a full-time job. Probably in July.

* * *

I met Mad Dog on Saturday, May second, and we went to a Turkish restaurant. He looked good, and seemed to be rested and happy. A total of eight birth certificates had arrived. He had all names checked by the Social Security guy, who found out that one of the birth certificates was damaged goods. That name had been issued a Social Security number a few years before. But seven clean birth certificates were still a lot: two for me, one for him, and four leftovers to sell. He had found someone willing to pay $5,000 for each of the four clean certificates and $2,000 for the damaged-goods one. That meant $22,000 in revenues.

The Department of Education guy got $5,000. The Social Security guy and the driver's license guy would get $3,000 each. The janitor had already gotten $3,400, but we still needed him. We needed three mailboxes for our Social Security cards. Rent and three additional letters would cost us $900. Altogether the operation costs would add up to $15,300. That meant a profit of $6,700; $3,350 each.

I chose the name Michael Edwards for my main identity and Anthony Harris for the emergency one. Mad Dog took Daniel Miller. He gave me the two birth certificates.

We went to a coffee shop, where he told me about his vacations. I told him about my socializing as a real PSMT. He was also surprised to hear that there was demand for a real PSMT.

"Crazy shit, isn't it, Baldy? By the way, it's good that you're socializing and getting laid again. No danger of a second Catherine disaster."

"Let's change the subject. Tell me about Peter."

"Right, Peter! He said that you've been asking questions. Spying behind my back?"

"Not at all! Just trying to check some facts. Joe says that he was the first lunchtime client. I wondered if Peter would say the same. Who was the first one? Joe or Peter?"

None of them. Joe had been a client since 1985. Peter came in 1986. The first lunchtime client had been Walter in 1984, the guy who refused marriage counseling because the therapist was twice divorced. I became tense when I heard him mentioning Walter's story.

"Don't worry, Baldy. I'm not starting that conversation again. I'm only answering your question. Walter was the very first one."

"And Joe the second?"

"Third. Please don't tell him that. It would hurt his feelings."

* * *

Mad Dog set up the first appointment with the Social Security guy, Jackson, in the first week of May. I was very nervous, but things went well. Michael Edwards, my new me, applied for his Social Security number easily. One week later I was back as Anthony Harris. Jackson almost didn't recognize me in my nerdy look. That was good. Mad Dog also applied for his number in that same week.

I met a lot of clients for dinner and went to many parties in May. Especially fun was a client's party both Mad Dog and I attended. For these occasions Mad Dog's legend was Chris Allen, self-employed massage therapist practicing by house call only. Both of us met people interested in hiring us and left the party with their business cards. He said that he was proud of me. Those cards were the ultimate proof that I had mastered my legend to perfection.

Joe took us for dinner at the end of the month to celebrate the operation's success. He told us how everybody around him got so excited because he had a PSMT. He had heard a few times,

"You too? A friend of mine also has a PSMT. Is that the same guy? Could you give me his number? I'd like to try." The news about me was spreading around quickly.

Joe wasn't happy with the unexpected side effects. What a pain it was when people started discussing self-motivation theories with him. He didn't have a clue and hated the subject. Could I recommend good literature to him?

Between dinner and dessert he went to the restroom to do a line. Mad Dog looked at me, seeming to read my mind, and said, "He's always been like that. Enjoy the silence while it lasts."

Joe came back and restarted the conversation as if he had never left the table. Now high, he started looking at the funny side of things. We could be starting a new trend without knowing it. Supply always followed demand. If there was demand for real PSMTs, sooner or later they would start showing up all over Manhattan. This was America, and one shouldn't underestimate the power of trends in the country.

In his crazy scenario, PSMTs would multiply at an unbelievable rate. Eventually there would be the first article in a lifestyle magazine about the new trend in town. "NYC Going Crazy for PSMTs!" Next step would be invading the West Coast. Every hotshot Hollywood actor and producer would get a PSMT. Sooner or later there would be a film about one.

After both coasts were conquered, the PSMT wave would sweep the rest of the country. Someday there would be the first PSMT convention, and the AAPSMT, the American Association of Personal Self-Motivation Trainers, would be founded.

Joe, Mad Dog, and I could have started a whole new industry, and we wouldn't make a penny out of it. We should have registered the trademark and gone for franchising. The business idea of the decade.

* * *

We had a lot of fun that evening. Joe took a cab home. Mad Dog and I walked to the subway station. He was very quiet.

"Enjoying the silence, Mad Dog?"

"No, reflecting on what Joe said."

"Crazy shit, wasn't it?"

"Maybe we should register the trademark..."

"What? You don't think this shit is possible, do you?"

He wasn't listening. "Create a company and register the trademark…"

"Are you serious?"

"Black & Brown, Incorporated. What about that?"

It sounded like a rhetorical question, so I didn't answer.

"Slogan: Bringing color into white people's lives!"

I had to laugh.

"You know, Baldy, this could work!"

"Why would it be better than what we already have? Counseling will never be as profitable as dealing."

"Scalability, Baldy! A franchise covering the whole country! Joe is a clever motherfucker!"

"Shouldn't he be part of the business, then? Black, Brown, & Fat, Incorporated?"

"I love the guy, but you know that I don't do business with drug addicts."

"You aren't serious about this, are you?"

"Not really, Baldy. But who knows? America is crazy enough. It could happen. Take care."

He boarded the northbound train. I waited for the southbound one.

[3/10]

On June first I got the keys to my new apartment. It was not very far from the first one and had two bedrooms, living room, bathroom, and kitchen. The furniture was nice. My landlord was a guy called Eric, a client's cousin. Rent was $5,000. It was really overpriced, but that happened when you were a drug dealer. People thought they could rip you off. As Mad Dog would say, I was paying for discretion and no questions asked. Rent doubled my monthly expenses to $10,000. But I was making five times that.

The second bedroom was a mix of guest room and home office. It had a sofa bed, a big desk, and bookshelves. I decided to hide my stash there, inside the drywall with the lid hidden behind a short bookcase. I built everything pretty quickly this time.

Mad Dog strongly advised me against giving up the old apartment. If the police were on my trail, I might not be able to return to my new apartment and get the stuff I needed to leave the country. I should hide the second passport and enough cash in the old apartment.

In the first week of June I got both driver's licenses. For my main identity I used my new address; for the reserve identity, the Alphabet City address. That way nobody would be able to connect Michael Edwards to Anthony Harris.

Mad Dog knew a Jamaican guy working at a branch office of a big bank on West Fifty-seventh in Manhattan. I knew the street very well; it was Mom's hunting ground. She always stayed at the Plaza, only one block away. I opened a checking account and deposited $10,000.

* * *

I had 145 clients in June, three full workweeks. Joe was booked for the first Tuesday. Now that I had a new apartment and could perfectly play my role as a real PSMT, maybe the time had come to try my luck with Nancy. Mad Dog had warned me not to, but he didn't need to know. The danger was Joe finding out and making a big fuss about it. It was better if he knew from the beginning. As they said at weddings, speak now or forever hold your peace.

"Joe, can I ask you something?"

"Go on."

"Is Nancy single?"

The look on his face!

"Come on, Birdy, you're not going to do it again, are you?"

"Do what?"

"Get in trouble mixing work with pleasure. Have you already forgotten the mess with Catherine?"

"I never had anything with Catherine. I resisted the temptation to the very end."

"Right! And what an end that was. Got fired."

The desperation in his voice!

"Yes. But Nancy can't fire me because I don't work for her. Is she single?"

"Of course not! A woman like Nancy? Give me a break."

"Married?"

"Chris has forbidden you to get involved with the women!"

"Did he tell you so?"

"Of course! All women are off limits to you!"

"No, Joe. Off limits are only the female clients and the male clients' women. This doesn't apply to Nancy." Now I would give him the checkmate. "Could it be that I'm invading your territory here? If so, please tell me."

Got him! If he said yes, he would be confessing. If he said no, I would have a free hand.

"What are you insinuating, Birdy? That I fuck Nancy?"

"Not insinuating anything. Just asking. Because if you are, I won't make a move."

Would he confess?

"Why don't you try Catherine? Now that she's not a client anymore, Chris wouldn't mind."

Clever move! But he wasn't getting away that easily.

"I like Nancy better."

He sighed. Was he going to confess now?

"It's too dangerous. She might find out that you're a dealer, and then I'm fucked. They have no tolerance for drugs in this company. I forbid you to get involved with my secretary!"

That was a very clever way to settle the matter without admitting anything. But since Nancy was not worth that kind of trouble, I had to accept defeat.

"Okay, Joe. Take it easy. I'll stay away."

He looked relieved.

"Do you think you could set me up with Catherine?"

"You kidding me? After what happened?"

"You just said so. I should forget Nancy and go for Catherine."

He gave me the fuck-you look. Then he said, tongue in cheek, "Why don't you ask Chris for help? He's seeing her once a month."

"I will. I have this feeling that fate brought Catherine and me together. It was supposed to happen, you know?"

He sighed. "Of course. Go for it, then."

I had annoyed him too much already. It was time to change the subject. "Listen, I've been thinking about what you said when we had dinner. The franchising idea is really great!"

His eyes lit up. "Isn't it? I'd love to do the ad campaign for the whole thing!"

He talked about the idea for the rest of the meeting. I couldn't avoid flirting with Nancy on my way out. So much flesh…

***

I met Mad Dog on Saturday, this time in an Argentinian steak house. First thing he asked me about was Nancy. Joe had called and asked Mad Dog to tell me not to make a move on her. Either Joe was really scared of getting caught or jealous. Or both.

"I told you already: no secretaries!"

"I was just teasing him. I think he's having an affair with her."

"That's none of your business!"

"It's strange that he won't admit it, isn't it? It's not like I'll use it against him. I know about his drug addiction. What could be worse?"

"Feelings, Baldy. Maybe he deeply loves her, and she doesn't love him back. He's probably jealous and possessive."

"Why doesn't he admit it?"

"Look who's talking. What about your feelings?"

I changed the subject to the offshore operation. That was supposed to be the subject of our conversation that Saturday.

Dad had taught me the basics. He always used top-notch law firms to set up his companies, and only opened accounts at offshore branches of his Swiss banks. His offshore structures were very safe. But I had no access to Dad's legal team. I would have to use the services of offshore company formation agents.

Mad Dog warned me that there were a lot of dodgy people working in the field. Things could go terribly wrong, and he personally knew a few guys who had lost money offshore. He gave me homework: to think about the whole process and identify what could go wrong and how to avoid it. That was the kind of homework that interested me. I couldn't afford to lose my money. I went to the library to research.

You needed an agent on the island to provide the company with the required registered address. The agent also filed all legal papers with the registrar of companies and paid the annual fees. When you ordered the company, you told the agent the directors' and shareholders' names. The agent set up the company and nominated the directors. Then he filed the names of all directors and shareholders with the registrar.

After that the agent sent you certified copies of the certificate of incorporation, the memorandum and the articles of association, the resolutions appointing the directors and allocating the shares, and a list of all directors and shareholders. You needed most of those documents to open the company's bank accounts.

What could go wrong? I could see only one possibility: if the registered agent didn't pay the annual fee to the registrar and pocketed the money instead, the company would cease to exist, and I would never be told. If the bank found out, the account would be closed. Who would keep the money? Either the bank or the local government. I couldn't find that information. Anyway, one would need a lot of lawyers to get it back.

"Not bad, Baldy. I know one case just like that. But this is only the small-time criminal pocketing annual fees. It can get worse than that." I was overlooking a step right at the beginning. The agent set up the company first, nominated the directors afterwards, and only then filed the director and shareholder names with the registrar. What if he filed someone else's name instead of mine and gave me a fake copy of the filing with my name on it? That someone would be the legal owner and director. I would have no legal claim on the company, and I wouldn't suspect anything.

I couldn't double-check the agent's work. I couldn't write to the registrar and ask who the owners and directors were because all company information was kept secret. That was the whole point of going offshore. Normally the same agent opened the company's bank account. Usually the company directors managed the account. Whenever there was a change of directors, you only needed to show the bank the proper documentation and the company's new directors had instant access to the account. A registered agent could change directors any time. He only needed to fake some signatures.

Theoretically I could pay an agent to set up a company and open its bank account, get back all the documentation, wire a lot of money to that account, get copies of the bank statements, feel happy and safe, and never even imagine that I had no legal claim on the company and the money.

Mad Dog had once mentioned Jerry Carter, who got life without parole for unintentionally killing a guy. The guy had a heart attack while Jerry was beating him up. This time he told me the whole story.

Jerry had a small drug-dealing operation. He set up an offshore company on the British Virgin Islands using a company formation agent in upstate New York. The same agent opened the bank account.

In a few years Jerry wired about a million dollars to the BVI.

He got a copy of the bank statements every month, forwarded to him by the agent. One day his mother in Jamaica got sick, and he needed money to pay for her treatment. He called the bank to arrange a wire transfer to Jamaica, but nobody at the bank knew who Jerry was. He wasn't authorized to manage that bank account, and therefore the person he was talking to ended the phone call, claiming bank secrecy laws.

Jerry didn't know what to do. Not only he had lost his savings, his mother was going to die. He drove all the way to Albany to surprise the agent, who never got the chance to explain anything. As soon as Jerry started beating him up, he had a heart attack and dropped dead. Jerry fled, but people in the neighboring offices heard the noise and saw him driving away. They wrote down the car's license plate number. When Jerry arrived home in Brooklyn, the police were already waiting for him.

He was charged with manslaughter. He tried to explain his situation. The dead guy had stolen his money, and his mother was going to die if Jerry didn't get it back. When the cops found out where the money had come from, Jerry got charged with drug dealing and money laundering as well. So Jerry Carter got life without parole, and both the guy in Albany and Jerry's mother died. But the people responsible for the scheme were still walking around free. Probably still ripping people off in the same way. Mad Dog called them offshore thieves.

Very rich people like Dad could buy the legal protection they needed. Big criminals were respected and feared. No one would mess with their money. The offshore thieves preyed on small guys. Small guys with legal and legitimate offshore operations could theoretically go to court to get their money back, though it was not an easy lawsuit to win. Small criminals like Jerry Carter, Mad Dog, and me, couldn't. And the offshore thieves knew that.

The only solution was to spread the wealth around. Mad Dog suggested that I create companies in three different jurisdictions: the BVI, the Bahamas, and the Cayman Islands. Each company should open bank accounts in the other two jurisdictions, never on the same island where it was incorporated. For example, the BVI company would have accounts on the Bahamas and the Cayman Islands.

I would need nine different company formation agents; three to set up the companies and six to open the accounts. The compartmentalization thing. Even if a registered agent stole my company, he wouldn't know which banks the company used.

There was still one potential danger. Someone working at the bank would know the company's registered address and could theoretically contact the registered agent and try to convince him to join forces and together steal my money. That was why I needed so many accounts. It could happen once, maybe twice, but it couldn't happen six times. There was safety in numbers.

I asked where I would find nine different agents. He answered that there were dozens out there, just like pussies. I had to laugh. It seemed that the saying applied to pretty much everything. He had already selected nine good ones for me that he had done business with before. I asked how he had solved his problem regarding the two shareholders needed to set up an offshore company in most jurisdictions. Did he also have an identity B?

He nodded. In the early eighties one of his foot soldiers, a guy called Joshua, was killed. Joshua had a lot of Mad Dog's dope and money in his room, and shared an apartment with other criminals. Afraid that one of Joshua's friends could get to the stuff before he did, Mad Dog broke in, searched the room, and found the drugs and the money. He also found a plastic bag containing the guy's birth certificate and driver's license, as well as some old pictures. He took everything with him.

Joshua had no papers on him when he was shot. He had run away from home many years before and had no more contact with his family. All his friends were criminals. No one came to claim the body, and the police never found out who he was. He was buried as an indigent. About one year later, when Mad Dog started to plan his offshore strategy, he decided to use Joshua's identity.

"In case you are wondering, Winston advised me on going offshore."

"When was that?"

"The year after he found me."

"He never said anything! All this stuff going on behind my back?"

"If you need to know, you'll be told. First rule of spying, Baldy. Now back to business."

He gave me a printed list with the nine agents and what each was supposed to do for me. I needed a copy of both passports, so I would have to wait until they were delivered at the end of the month. I also needed to rent three P.O. boxes to use as company addresses. All bank statements should go directly there. The registered agents should send their annual bills to those P.O. boxes as well.

I asked him how I would wire the money offshore. I couldn't use my own bank for that. He said that wire transfers would be the topic of another conversation. I went home really impressed. He was so street smart.

I had a date that evening with Emily, one of the secretaries, a very attractive redhead. We had dinner together, and afterwards I brought her to my new apartment. We spent the night and the whole Sunday together. Who needed Nancy?

* * *

On the following Monday I applied for the passports at two different post offices. At the end of the month Mad Dog brought me the passport for identity B that had been delivered to the address in Alphabet City. I was finally ready to set up the companies and open the bank accounts.

In July I had 173 clients to see in four workweeks. In the first three weeks I was completely booked out. In the last one I had only twenty-three clients. Mad Dog and I met to exchange backpacks at the end of every workweek. My July average was 1.57. I ended the month with a quarter of a million in savings.

In July I got so many recommendations for new clients in August that I had to let down a few people. I had reached full capacity. From about twenty-five when Mad Dog was doing lunch with them when I found him to 200 in August: an eight-fold increase in only ten months.

In the last meeting in July, I asked, "What now, Mad Dog? Are you hiring a new PSMT?"

"Don't know yet, Baldy."

"You probably know but won't tell, right?"

He laughed. "No. Just haven't found another Birdy yet. Can't do with just any guy, as you know."

"Maybe it's time to ask for a raise."

"You'll get a raise soon. We're going to increase revenues. Indirectly, you'll get more money. That's the same, right?"

"Are you going to raise prices?"

"There are other ways."

"Like what?"

"We're averaging 1.5 packages a month. What about raising that to 1.8 or even higher?"

"How are we going to do that?"

"We won't do anything. The clients will. That's why we introduced the new prices a few months ago, remember?"

"We'll recruit them as dealers?"

"Indirectly, yes. When they recommend someone, tell them that you have no free capacity. If they want to help their friends out, they should buy more from you, taking advantage of the lower prices for bulk purchases, and resell the cocaine to their friends."

"And they'll do it?"

"A few, yes. Wait and see."

* * *

That day Mad Dog taught me how to transfer my money offshore. I was going to use what he called informal bankers. You gave them cash, and they wired money from their own offshore accounts to yours. It was done in their offices right in front of you. The guy's bank confirmed the transaction by fax. I should keep a copy of the fax until I got the monthly statement from the bank showing the deposit. I could make transfers in any multiple of ten thousand dollars. The commission was paid on top of the transferred amount.

For each transfer I had to call the guys twice. The first time a few days in advance to make the appointment; the second time the day before the transfer to be told exactly where to go. Since all they needed were phones and fax machines, they changed offices frequently. Today here, tomorrow there.

I knew that kind of operators back home. They dealt in foreign currency. You gave them cash in the local currency, and they transferred the amount in dollars from their bank accounts in the United States to yours. That was how the upper middle class got their money out. Rich people like Dad had better ways.

Those illegal foreign-currency operators back home could get away with it because our government wasn't really interested in catching the operators' clients. Upper middle class people were the government's most loyal supporters. I had expected that the U.S. government wouldn't tolerate that.

"It doesn't, Baldy. That's why it's so dangerous. And being

dangerous, so fucking expensive. The bankers charge twenty percent."

"Twenty? That's a lot!"

"Price of doing business. Take it or leave it."

"Do you trust them?"

"As far as you can trust anyone in our line of business."

Mad Dog gave me the names and phone numbers of three
different guys. I should use one guy for each company and its two
bank accounts. The compartmentalization thing again. Each of
them knew Mad Dog by a different legend. The same would apply to me.

[3/11]

On the following Wednesday I did my first wire transfer. I
was told to go to a shabby office building downtown. The office
was at the end of a corridor on the fifth floor. There was a camera
above the door, which was locked. I had to ring the bell.

Two very big, armed Latino guys came to meet me at the
door. Once inside, they frisked me and controlled my backpack. A
third armed guy observed everything from a safe distance. There
were cameras on the ceiling. When the two security guards were
sure that I wasn't armed, one of them took me to see José, the
guy I had the appointment with.

It looked like the average office: a very big desk with a computer, a printer, a few phones, and three fax machines. Again,
cameras on the ceiling. Sitting behind the desk was a short Latino
guy. Surprisingly, the guy was nice and polite.

"Hi, I'm José. Nice to meet you, Andrew. Did Brian send
you?"

Andrew Hernandez was my legend with him. Mad Dog's was
Brian King. Mad Dog had told José and the two other informal
banking guys that I was a messenger for him.

"Yes, two transfers. Twenty thousand each."

I gave him a sheet of paper with the details for both accounts
and the money; $48,000 including commission.

"Brian's got a new company?"

"I don't know. I'm just the messenger."

He nodded, still looking at the sheet of paper. "At least it's
my first time with this company. I don't save anything on the

computer, but I have a good memory. Never seen this one before."

He counted the money quickly and put it inside a drawer, then wrote the information on his computer, printed out two sheets, and read them carefully. After that he signed both and faxed them using two of the fax machines. When the faxes went through, José called the banks.

"It's done, Andrew. The confirmation faxes will arrive in a few minutes. Would you mind waiting in another room? I have to see other clients."

I stood up and left the room. The security guard who had brought me there was waiting outside. He took me to a room with a few chairs in it, where another client was waiting. No security guard inside, only cameras. I avoided making eye contact with the other client; so did he. After five minutes the same security guard came for the other client. I sat there alone for another few minutes. The door opened again, and the security guard told me to come with him. He brought me back to José, who gave me copies of the two faxes.

"You're all set, Andrew. Will I see you again, or was this a one-time job?"

"Can't say. I do as I'm told."

He laughed. "Don't we all? Keeps us alive, doesn't it? Take care!"

"Take care, José!"

And I was out of there. It was really scary. And I would be doing that three times a month.

* * *

When I met Mad Dog the following Saturday, he told me it was good that José had believed that I was only the messenger. He would respect me more.

"Why do they fear you? Do they know about your business? I thought that it was a big secret."

"It is, Baldy. But I always come with two bodyguards. Very mean motherfuckers."

"Do they let them in?"

"Of course not! They must stay outside. But it's enough to make everyone inside very nervous. I don't have to wait in the other room for the faxes, for example. I stay inside José's room all the time."

"Premium treatment? I want that, too!"

He winked and smiled. "You're starting to understand the principle of reputation, territory, and foot soldiers, Baldy."

"But they see only the foot soldiers."

"They're smart enough to figure out the rest."

* * *

The other two transactions went very well, too. All informal bankers operated in a similar way: security guards armed to their teeth, cameras, waiting rooms, and a friendly and professional guy doing the transaction. I wondered if there was such a thing as professional standards for the informal banking sector. Maybe they had their own association providing training courses? This was America, after all. You never knew.

In August I sold 305 packages of cocaine to my 200 clients, averaging 1.53. I managed to transfer $120,000 offshore. I still had $175,000 hidden inside the drywall in my old apartment.

Now working full-time, I would sell at least 300 packages per month. I had exactly that amount as an emergency reserve in my old apartment, hidden inside the first hole in the wall. Mad Dog thought that it wasn't enough. I needed at least six weeks of emergency supply; 450 packages.

Those extra 150 packages I hid inside the second hole, together with my emergency identity kit: passport, fake glasses, birth certificate, driver's license, Social Security card, $20,000 in traveler's checks, and $10,000 cash. I sealed the lid and painted the wall. It was my third time, and I was getting really good at it.

Only the third hole, behind the short bookcase, was still open. I was keeping my reserve cash there. I tried to spend at least one night in the apartment every week. Therefore, I kept clothes, music, books, and food there. I decided to use that apartment to bring Sweet Jamaica back to life. I remembered with fondness the old days when RW, Mad Dog, and I spent the evening listening to Marley, smoking joints, and talking.

There was only one problem: I didn't have a separate bedroom for Mad Dog to spend the night, and neither of us wanted to share the bed. Mad Dog couldn't go home at the end of the evening. He never set foot outside when he was high. He needed to be one hundred percent alert and ready to react to any possible threat.

My new apartment wasn't very far, so I decided to let him sleep in Sweet Jamaica until he got sober. I wasn't afraid of walking home stoned.

* * *

Our first Sweet Jamaica evening was on a Saturday. Mad Dog was really impressed with the drywall solution. Not only with the idea, but also with the execution. He took off both posters, examined the walls carefully, and couldn't find where exactly the lids were. He smiled and said, "Good job, Baldy. I should give you a medal!" That was nice to hear. He was a specialist in that kind of stuff. I showed him the third hole behind the short bookcase. That impressed him, too. He rolled a joint and asked me to put on a Marley CD. Like in the old days.

We sat on the floor side by side, our back to the drywall, and talked, passing the joint back and forth.

"Four hundred and fifty packages of cocaine behind us, Mad Dog. Almost half a million dollars hidden in there. A very expensive wall to lean against, isn't it?"

"Only if sold to our clients. The street value is half that."

"What? We're charging them double?"

"No, man, we're charging them the street price. What's really expensive is the delivery system. Forgot that?"

"A quarter of a million is still a lot of money. Your money, by the way. Now you know where it is if anything happens to me."

"Nothing will happen to you as long as you don't do anything stupid. I've been around for ten years already. And I have a lot of enemies out there."

The CD started playing the "Chances Are" song. Mad Dog sang along. "Although my days are filled with sorrow, I see here, a bright tomorrow..." I loved the song, too.

Then he asked me to put on "Redemption Song." He smiled and said, "It's the therapy song, Baldy!" I didn't get what he meant. I had to get up and change the CD; that song was on the Uprising album.

We listened in silence. When the lines he had been waiting for finally came, he looked at me and sang along, "Emancipate yourselves from mental slavery, none but ourselves can free our minds..." When the song was over, he said, "That's what you need therapy for, Baldy-Birdy."

And so the evening went: joints, Marley, and reminiscences. I went home at one in the morning, completely stoned. He stayed there for the night.

[3/12]

In August I got everything on my list that I needed to start a new life abroad. Now I only had to figure out where to go and to save enough money. I already had $300,000. If sales went up the way Mad Dog had predicted, I could have my million before the end of 1993, one year ahead of schedule.

Life was good. Real friends I had only one, Mad Dog. We had lunch together every Saturday, and were going to have Sweet Jamaica evenings every now and then in the future. I had 200 amazing clients, to whom I was a drug dealer, and dozens of acquaintances, to whom I was a real PSMT. I was still dating Emily and had started dating Ann, another secretary. Here and there I had one-night stands with women I met at parties. I was invited to a few every week.

I was having more fun as Birdy than I ever had as Baldy. I also loved New York City even more than I had in my college years. Especially the garbage.

I had another passion besides the fur coats: New York City's garbage, which I could appreciate all year round. Contrary to the fur coats, I had to keep that fascination to myself. Every time I tried to tell people about it, they thought that I was crazy. "I've heard all kinds of remarks about this city. But it's the first time I've heard someone saying he enjoys the garbage. Are you crazy or something?"

It was difficult to explain. It was a fact that people didn't like garbage, though they produced lots of it. After all, garbage smelled bad and made the neighborhood look nasty. I couldn't say that I liked the smell or the view. What I liked was the fact that in New York you saw garbage in all neighborhoods.

I had first noticed it when I was a very small kid. I was awed. Dad thought that it was weird. "What's so interesting, Pablo? You've never seen garbage before? It's disgusting. They should clean it up. We don't have this much garbage back home." That was the interesting thing. We didn't have it back home. Why did they have it here? What was different about New York?

Every city in the world produced garbage, which was collected in different degrees of efficiency so that you had the clean cities and the dirty ones. But in every single city, whether clean or dirty, you had what one could call levels of cleanliness. You could tell where you were based on the amount of garbage you saw. Some areas, normally where the rich lived, were very clean. The poor lived in the dirty neighborhoods. The middle class areas were something in between.

This was true all over the world, with only one exception: New York City. Here you could see garbage everywhere, even on Fifth Avenue, Wall Street, or Broadway. That was the reason for my fascination.

Yes, Dad, I had seen garbage before in our city's bad neighborhoods, but not in front of a five-star hotel. Not in front of an expensive store. Not in an area where people like us spent time. How could you tell where you were, whether in a good or bad neighborhood, if you didn't have the garbage to help you?

With time my initial fascination developed into true appreciation. "It's cool, it's democratic, garbage all over," I used to say, trying to convince people of the beauty of it. But most people didn't enjoy the garbage's philosophical or political sides. I never found anyone who shared my enthusiasm. Even RW found it strange.

The question was, if the garbage wasn't appreciated, why was it still there? Not because the city's administration decided that it should treat all streets equally instead of concentrating the biggest amount of resources on cleaning the nice areas and leaving the bad ones to rot. And it wasn't because New Yorkers had anarchist souls or egalitarian beliefs, and littered the nice areas on purpose as a protest against the discrimination of the bad areas.

Why then? That was the big mystery. It was as if the city refused to be cleaned. As if New York's garbage had a life of its own. As if it was a wild animal. No one could tame it. The garbage was actually subversive.

I had always enjoyed traveling around the world, but I rejoiced every time I came back to this beautifully dirty island. It was fascinating to walk around Wall Street and see garbage lying on the sidewalk, when you knew that billions of dollars were traded every second in that narrow street.

After I became a drug dealer, my year-old appreciation for New York's garbage developed into love. True love. After all, the garbage and I had many things in common. Nobody liked or wanted garbage, but it was there, sticking its finger up at everyone. Just like me. I wasn't supposed to be walking around Manhattan streets, totally free. If the Feds or the Colombians could get their hands on me, I would be dead or behind bars.

But they couldn't. I was like the garbage: uninvited, unwanted, uncontrolled, and unaccounted for. I was totally outside the system. I didn't legally exist, and made a living selling a product that wasn't supposed to be sold so that people could support an addiction they wouldn't admit they had. It was like I lived in a parallel world, in another dimension, like in a cheap science-fiction movie. It was a surreal situation.

No, surreal was not the right word. Because I was real, the cocaine was real, the addiction was real, and the money was real. Also real was the great feeling that everything that was going on wasn't supposed to be happening. Maybe subversive was a better term.

Yes, my existence was now subversive. Just like the garbage.

[4]

[4/1]

It happened in the second week of September. Joe was my third delivery that morning. I entered the building and got on the elevator, thinking about Nancy. Should I make a move on her? The elevator door closed. I noticed that there was another guy inside, but kept daydreaming as the elevator started moving. That was when he asked, "Do I know you? From Columbia, maybe?" I looked at him and froze. Somehow he looked familiar. Probably Columbia, but I couldn't tell.

"Sorry, it must be a mistake. I never attended college."

He looked me in the eyes. "Really? I could swear we've met."

I was saved by the elevator bell.

"I don't think so. I'm getting off here. Take care."

My heart started beating fast, and my hands started shaking. Why couldn't I keep my body under control when stuff like that happened?

Nancy noticed that something was wrong. "You okay, Birdy? Look kind of distressed today."

"I'm fine, Nancy. It's just a bad day."

"You work too hard. You should relax now and then. Go to the movies, for example."

The way she was smiling at me made me even more nervous. Maybe it was the state of shock I was in. It just slipped out of my mouth, "Only if you come along, Nancy."

I instantly regretted my mistake. Stupid thing to say.

"I'd love to!"

What now? "We'll talk after my meeting."

She gave the most gorgeous, sexy smile ever. "See you later!"

* * *

Joe also noticed that I was distressed. I told him about my close encounter inside the elevator.

"This double life is shit, isn't it, Birdy? I'm getting into trouble because of it, too."

"How come?"

"My boss has heard about my coaching. He knows two other clients of yours. Can you believe it? Such a big city."

"So what?"

"He thinks that if everyone in New York is doing it, then it might be a good thing. He keeps asking questions."

"And what do you say?"

"Well, I read the books you recommended, so now I can talk about it endlessly."

"What's the problem, then?"

"The more I talk, the more interested he gets."

"Oh, shit. What a day!"

"Right, what a day! He was here earlier. Bumped into my office and made me talk about self-motivation for almost an hour."

I could feel his pain. "Shit, Joe."

"Tell me about it! I'll do a line now. Want some?"

"No, thanks."

After he did his line his mood changed, and he started talking about self-motivation and other forms of new-age crap. Sitting there listening to him helped me calm down a bit. When I got out, Nancy was all smiles. She had a few movie suggestions for the next days. No way was I going out with Nancy. Mad Dog would kill me. I told her that I had a lot of appointments in the next evenings. She took it like a woman but didn't let me go until we had exchanged private phone numbers.

After work I met a few people in a restaurant. Client's birthday, wonderful evening. I met a very hot woman, and she gave me her phone number. Very promising. I got home late. I prepared my briefcase for the next morning, set up two alarm clocks, smoked a joint, and went to bed at around midnight.

* * *

I had the worst nightmare ever, very long and very detailed. I was again inside the elevator on my way to see Joe. The other guy was also there, but he looked different now. He had a beard and a ponytail and was carrying a leather briefcase. Just like me.

He asked, "You a PSMT, too?"

I just stood there with my mouth open. What did he say? A PSMT, too? It couldn't be real. Maybe I didn't hear him right. I had been daydreaming about Nancy. I must have misunderstood him. I was the only PSMT in the world. It was a legend. My legend!

"Pardon me?"

"My name is Johnny. I'm a personal self-motivation trainer, a PSMT. What about you? You look like one, with your beard and ponytail."

I didn't know what to say. I tried to change the subject.

"Sorry, but I'm not feeling well. I have a headache."

"You should ask one of the secretaries for a painkiller. These ladies are very nice. And very hot, too." He winked and smiled. "Too bad that we're not allowed to fuck them."

"Why not?"

"Our professional code of conduct!"

The elevator bell saved me.

"I'm getting off here. I'll ask for the painkiller. Thanks for the tip."

I remembered that Joe had predicted that we would start a trend, and eventually real PSMTs would start showing up all over town. But that was supposed to be a joke. Dinner talk. It couldn't be real. There must be a better explanation. Mad Dog! Yes, it had to be Mad Dog. Who else? That guy was dealing. Mad Dog had recruited another dealer and hadn't told me about it. He and his compartmentalizing shit. Almost scared me to death. I relaxed and went to see Joe. I asked him if he knew who that guy was supplying.

"Johnny, you said? He's not a dealer. He trains a buddy of mine in the accounting department on the tenth floor."

"What do you mean he's not a dealer?"

"He's not! My buddy doesn't do drugs. Johnny is the real thing. He does self-motivation training. There are a lot of guys offering the service. It seems that PSMTs are the hottest thing in New York City these days. Everybody has one."

Then someone knocked on the door. Joe asked me to unlock and open it. Nancy was outside, all sexy smiles.

"Someone here to see you, Birdy."

She stepped aside, and Mom walked into the room holding two machine guns, one in each hand, just like the shooter in Texas had done. Joe screamed, scared to death. Mom yelled at him, "Shut up! This doesn't concern you!" Then she pointed both machine guns at me and started shooting and screaming, "How can you die wearing dirty underwear, Pablo?" I then noticed that I had nothing on but my dirty underwear. Mom kept shooting and screaming. "Your dirty underwear is so disgusting, Pablo! What a shame!"

That was when I woke up, bathed in sweat. It was four in the morning. I drank water, took a shower, and went to the kitchen to make coffee. I didn't dare to go back to bed. I had never had such a complicated and vivid nightmare before.

* * *

Wednesday was a very long day. I was tired, having slept only four hours that night. I had a dinner party that evening, but I didn't feel like going. I came home right after work and cooked dinner. After that I tried to watch a movie on my VCR. I was so tired that I fell asleep on the couch, sometime around nine.

The nightmare came back. I was once again inside Joe's office and Mom was shooting at me with her two machine guns. I woke up at ten, all wet, and so was the couch.

I couldn't stay awake the whole night. I considered smoking a joint, but I had tried it during the drug war and it hadn't helped much. Instead, I brought the television and the VCR to my bedroom to watch movies until I fell asleep again, which happened at around midnight.

Mom was waiting for me. This time I was inside the elevator. When it stopped and the door opened, she was standing outside, holding her machine guns. She started shooting and screaming, and I woke up.

It was one in the morning. Same shit as always. I was thirsty and all wet. I really should go see a doctor about that sweating, I thought. I fell asleep again at around two. The next nightmare was longer and more complex. I was back inside Joe's office. This time Joe was having sex with Nancy on his desk. Johnny, the PSMT guy, was standing by the door.

Nancy was screaming, "Birdy, you weren't man enough to fuck me, so I had to do it with Joe! Shame on you!"

Joe was screaming, "She's mine and only mine, Birdy! Don't you dare touch her!"

Johnny was screaming, "He's a drug dealer! I'm the real PSMT! I don't fuck the secretaries!"

Mom kept shooting and screaming, "How could you do this to me, Pablo? To die wearing dirty underwear?"

Then Catherine got inside the room and started screaming, "Birdy is afraid of women! Birdy is afraid of women! Shame on you, Birdy!"

To which Mom replied, "He's a shame to the whole family!"

I woke up at three in the morning. The usual drill: water, clean pajamas, clean bed linens. That night I woke up two more times, so naturally I was dead tired in the morning. Consequently,

Thursday was a very long day. I had to cancel a date I had that evening.

Thursday night was as bad as the night before. Nightmares, nightmares, nightmares. Friday was an even longer day with an even worse night.

I looked very bad when I left home on Saturday to meet Mad Dog for lunch. I had very dark bags under my eyes. He was going to notice it. Maybe I should go for the twisted lie. Admit that I was having sleep problems but not tell the real reason.

[4/2]

He didn't smile when he saw me. "So it's true!"

"What's true, Mad Dog?"

"That you look like shit. It's worse than I thought."

He knew already! The bastard was really spying on me. That made me angry. "Who told you?"

He frowned, maybe reacting to my aggressive tone of voice. "Don't shoot the messenger, Baldy! What's the problem? You aren't doing drugs, are you?"

"Of course not! I'm having sleep problems."

"Why?"

"Wish I knew."

"Sleeplessness?"

"Nightmares. I think I have post-traumatic stress disorder."

"I bet you have. How long has this shit being going on?"

"This time, since Tuesday."

Stupid thing to say. He didn't know anything about the other nightmares. Too late now.

He frowned again. "This time? What do you mean, Baldy? Why don't you give me the whole story?"

I was too tired to put up a fight. I told him about the very first nightmare in December, the series of nightmares during the drug war in February, and the new series since Tuesday night. I explained how the typical night went: having a nightmare, waking up thirsty and wet, putting on clean pajamas, changing the bed linens, drinking water, falling asleep, having another nightmare, waking up again. My emotional state triggered the nightmares. In December I was scared to start my dealing career. In February it was the article in the newspaper about Pablo the Ghost. Now it was the guy recognizing me inside the elevator.

The waiter came, but Mad Dog sent him away. We weren't ready to order yet. He asked what exactly happened in the nightmares. I told him that there were many variations, but basically it was about someone shooting me.

"Like in Texas?"

"Basically, yes."

"Inside that fast-food joint?"

"Used to be. But since Tuesday I get shot inside Joe's office."

He nodded and asked me the question I was dreading to hear.

"And who's shooting, Baldy? That lunatic?"

"No, it was never him. The first time in December it was a Latino drug dealer because I was invading his territory. You had scared me so much, remember? I should watch my back because Manhattan streets were so mean."

"Yes. And who else has shot you?"

I hesitated. It was really embarrassing to talk about that.

"The quicker you tell everything, the better you'll feel, Baldy. Believe me."

"All right, all right. It's always Mom."

He looked at me, surprised. "Your mom? Why?"

"Because of the fucking dirty underwear! What else?"

He made a funny face, and I realized my big mistake: I had never told him the dirty-underwear story. Me and my big mouth! I avoided his eyes, but I could feel them piercing me.

"I'm waiting, Baldy."

"Listen, Mad Dog, this is private, okay?"

"It stops being private when it makes you sick and you can't perform your duties. Tell me the whole fucking story. Every detail."

"You'll laugh and make fun of me."

"Not today. Promise. The situation is too serious for that. You can bet that someday I'll tease you. But not today. Go ahead."

I told him the whole story, always looking down. I was expecting a laugh attack after I finished, but he stayed silent. I thought he might be grinning. I looked up and saw him observing me, very seriously.

"Scary shit, Baldy. This is fucking weird. At the very moment you were going to die you thought about your mom and your dirty underwear?"

His reaction was even scarier. If he wasn't laughing, maybe

I was really in trouble.

"I was under stress. It was the second shooting in two days."

"Who are you trying to convince? Me or you?"

I sighed. "Do you think I'm completely fucked up, Mad Dog? Please be sincere."

"What I find completely fucked up is your refusal to face the facts and do something about this shit. You need therapy! When will you finally accept this?"

"You've been trying to get me into therapy since we met in November."

"Had you started back then, you'd be in much better shape now."

Maybe he was right. "What do you suggest?"

"You have to deal with the nightmares first. Get this shit under control and start sleeping again. You probably need a post-traumatic stress disorder specialist for that. Two shootings in two fucking days! After that you can start digging into the deeper shit with another therapist."

"Which deeper shit?"

"Mom, dad, siblings, childhood, identity, everything."

I sighed. He smiled for the first time. "That was deep! Why don't we order now? While we wait for the food, I'll make a few phone calls from the pay phone outside. You need to see a doctor today."

He called the waiter, ordered for both of us since I didn't have a clue about Mongolian food, and went outside to use the pay phone. He was back in fifteen minutes. He had made an appointment with a psychiatrist that afternoon at five; Dr. Andrew Barnes, a client's recommendation. I asked how much I was allowed to tell Dr. Barnes. Mad Dog said that I shouldn't give him any real facts. I should say that I was traveling in Colombia and landed by accident inside drug-dealer territory, where I survived two shootings in two days, both times as an innocent bystander.

The waiter brought our food and we ate mostly in silence, only talking shop now and then. Sales were going up. The average for the first workweek in September was 1.7. But that didn't cheer us up. We didn't go for coffee afterwards.

* * *

At five I was at the doctor's office. Dr. Barnes prescribed me

sleeping pills and anti-anxiety medication in case I had anxiety attacks during the day. But that alone wouldn't be enough. I needed
therapy for my post-traumatic stress disorder. Ten weekly sessions
were about average, he said. He called a few therapists he knew.
One had a free slot Mondays in the early evening.

The sleeping pills were wonderful. That Saturday I slept the
whole night for the first time in days. Sunday at noon Mad Dog
paged me. I called him back. He wanted to hear how I was doing,
and that worried me. If he was scared, that meant I was really
in trouble. I told him about my therapy appointment Monday
evening. He said that I should keep the legend that I had used
with Dr. Barnes. With that therapist I should focus on the post-
traumatic stress disorder only. I complained about the therapy
length. He said that ten sessions were nothing. I should be glad
if I could solve my problem in such a short time.

"Baldy, man, it's good to hear you in your I-don't-want-no-
fucking-therapy mood! You must be feeling much better now. See
you on Saturday. Take care."

* * *

I was very nervous about my first therapy session. Dr. James
Clark seemed to be a nice guy. I asked how much a session cost.
I didn't have health insurance and would pay cash. He said $250
per session would do. I agreed, not knowing if it was expensive
or not. He smiled. I had the impression that if I had haggled, I
could have gotten a better price. Too late.

Dr. Clark was a Vietnam veteran, like most of his patients.
I spent the whole session explaining my trauma. I gave him the
twisted lie: I had gotten lost in drug-dealer territory in Colombia.
Someone stole my luggage, which explained the dirty underwear.
The first shooting happened inside my hotel room. The second
inside a restaurant. It was a good story. The rest of the stuff was
true: my fear of getting shot by a Colombian killer, my dirty-
underwear paranoia, Mom popping up inside my head at the
very moment I was going to die, and so on.

Dr. Clark told me not to underestimate what I had gone
through. Many of his patients hadn't been as close to action in
Vietnam as I had, and still had developed post-traumatic stress
disorder. Those soldiers knew they were going to see combat when
they arrived in Vietnam and had trained for it. I had been caught

by surprise. Twice.

I didn't know what to think. Should I feel reassured? Apparently there was no way I could have avoided the post-traumatic stress disorder. Or should I be scared? Vietnam had been scary shit, I had heard. How could I have a worse trauma than many Vietnam vets?

Dr. Clark confirmed that ten sessions were about average, but it was still too early to tell. I left with mixed feelings. Therapy was not as bad as I had feared, but it was theoretically open ended.

That evening Nancy called, wanting to know if I had time for her that week. Oh, man, I had completely forgotten about her. What now? I was in deep trouble already. I didn't need to dig deeper. On the other hand, maybe Nancy could help me recover quicker. I could see her as part of my treatment.

I told her that I'd love to see her but under one condition: Joe should never know about it. I had the impression that he would be jealous. She giggled and said, "Oh, but that was such a long time ago!"

Yeah, I had been right about Joe and Nancy. Mad Dog would certainly praise that as intuition. Intuition my ass. It was only good observation and analytical skills. We agreed to have dinner on Friday.

The rest of the week was uneventful. The sleeping pills were great. I slept through every evening. I was counting the days until Friday.

[4/3]

We had a wonderful dinner. Nancy told me that she'd had an affair with Joe in the mid-eighties. He had wanted to leave his wife for her, but she refused. She didn't like him that much. Besides that, she didn't want any serious relationship at the time. She had just gotten out of a very bad marriage.

She invited me over to her apartment. The sex was wonderful, and it was late when I finally fell asleep. I tried hard not to. I had forgotten my sleeping pills and was afraid that I could have a nightmare and wake up bathed in sweat. That would scare her. Luckily I didn't have a nightmare, but I had a dream with Joe. He was crying, telling me, "Why did you do this to me, Birdy? You don't love her like I do. Why didn't you go to Catherine? She's the slut. Not my Nancy!"

I woke up at around noon; Nancy was already up. I could hear music in another room. I remembered the dream and made a mental note to discuss it with Dr. Clark. I had guilty feelings, and that wasn't good. I had to smile. I was becoming just like my clients, who were always telling me stuff like, "Oh, I have to discuss that with my therapist."

As always on Saturdays, I had to do lunch with Mad Dog, but I didn't have my backpack with me so I had to go home first to get it. Mad Dog was very punctual, and he expected the same of me, so there was no time for a romantic breakfast in bed. Nancy protested, saying that I had told her that I never worked on weekends. I said that I was so booked out that I had to see some clients outside business hours.

I promised to come back later and stay for the rest of the weekend. We could leave for work together Monday morning. She didn't like the idea. To leave the house early in the morning accompanied by a man was like marriage. She wasn't looking for that kind of relationship. I should go home Sunday evening.

I met Mad Dog for spaghetti with pesto in his favorite Italian restaurant. I was feeling great.

"Therapy is doing you good, Baldy! Tell me about it."

I told him about Dr. Clark and my first session. It would get even better when I got the second therapist, he said. I protested. Two therapists. Two sessions every week. That looked like overkill to me. I had wasted too much time already, he replied. I would be done with Dr. Clark by the end of the year. In 1993 I would have one therapist only. I never knew what I really needed, he continued, and I always fought hard against his suggestions, only to admit later that he had been right all along. I had resisted act-ing classes as well. Had I already forgotten that?

He asked if we could meet in Sweet Jamaica in the evening. I told him that I was booked up until Sunday evening.

"What's going on, Baldy? Got a serious relationship?"

"Me? Never! I had to cancel a lot of appointments last week. Now I have to catch up."

"Baldy the slut!"

"Womanizer. You say slut only to women."

"A male slut then."

"Womanizer."

He laughed. "That's bullshit, Baldy, and you know it. Slut is fucking negative compared to womanizer. Why should you get a better deal just because you're a man?"

"I didn't know you were a feminist."

"I'm not."

"Why do you care if women get a raw deal or not?"

"I don't. I get upset about you. Your self-image is screwed. It doesn't match your real self. You still don't know who the fuck you are."

Oh, man, he wasn't going to start psychoanalyzing me now, was he? I didn't have time for that. I had a hot woman waiting for me.

"Yes, I admit that I have a serious identity problem. But now I have a therapist, and soon I'll have two. I'll work on that."

He gave me the fuck-you look. "Speaking of women, Catherine sends her greetings."

"How's she doing? Could you finally calm her down?"

"Sure. She's ready to give you a second chance."

Yes, Catherine! "I'm all booked up. But if she's willing to meet me privately, any time. She has my page number."

He gave me a patronizing smile and shook his head. "She's way out of your league, Baldy."

"Why don't you let me find out for myself?"

"There are some experiences not worth having."

I smiled and said, tongue in cheek, "I thought you didn't have the right to stop me from meeting fate."

"You don't believe in fate, Baldy."

"No. But for Catherine I'd consider converting!"

* * *

On Monday I saw Dr. Barnes, the psychiatrist, before going to see Dr. Clark, the therapist. How deep I had fallen! Dr. Barnes told me to slowly reduce the medication dose. That week only half a sleeping pill each night. The following week only a quarter. If the nightmares didn't return, I could stop taking the pills. In case the nightmares came back, I should go back to a pill every night and contact him as soon as possible.

The second session with Dr. Clark was very intense. I got the impression that I would be able to overcome the problem, or at least learn how to control my reactions during an anxiety attack.

In my last workweek in September I transferred $120,000 offshore. It was the same scary shit as in the previous month. Those security guards gave me the creeps. After that September transfer I had almost a quarter of a million hidden offshore, and $100,000 still in America.

My life went back to normal. I had a social life again. I had no intention of dating only one woman, regardless of how hot she was, though I would consider making an exception for Catherine. I couldn't stop thinking about her after all those months. If she was ready to take me back, maybe she had forgiven me. I should definitely make a move.

I wasn't that afraid of Mad Dog anymore. Business was going well. In September I sold a total of 340 packages, averaging 1.70. We would definitely reach an average of 1.8 or even higher. That would mean $90,000 income for me, and around $225,000 for him. Every month. The operation was making both of us rich very quickly. He needed me as much as I needed him.

I spent my second weekend with Nancy, Friday evening to Sunday afternoon, this time in my apartment. I met Mad Dog quickly for a coffee Saturday afternoon, exchanged backpacks, and went back to her. Before she left on Sunday, Nancy told me that she had enjoyed spending two whole weekends with me, but had no intention of seeing me that much. One night a week was exactly what we needed. Too much time together ruined the sex, she said. I could live with that. Maybe she was even right. At any rate, I would have more time for the other women.

Mad Dog paged me Sunday evening, and when I called him back, he told me that he had found the second therapist. I would have sessions Thursday evenings. The first one was scheduled for October first, with a Dr. Paul Nelson. It would cost me $500 per session. I had to protest. That was double Dr. Clark's price, and Dr. Clark was already overcharging me. Mad Dog said that if Dr. Clark knew that I was a drug dealer, he would probably charge more. I complained that I would spend $3,000 a month on therapy. He told me to stop whining; I could afford it. It had been very hard to get an evening slot for me. Dr. Nelson was really good, and I could trust him.

And so October started with therapy. I repeated to Dr. Nelson everything that I had told Dr. Clark. Dr. Nelson was very interested in Mom and the dirty underwear part of the story. Who wouldn't be? You didn't need to be a psychotherapist to know that it was sick.

* * *

On Saturday I met Mad Dog in Sweet Jamaica. He looked happy. We sat on the floor, smoking and listening to the music. He was leaning against the wall and I was sitting in front of him.

"So, Baldy, do you have anything planned for Friday, October sixteenth?"

"Maybe. Frank Davis, one of the new clients you've never met, invited me to a dinner party. But I'm not sure if it's on that Friday or the following one."

"I knew it! You forgot."

"Forgot what?"

"Your birthday."

"My birthday was in March."

"Not Pablo's. Your new you."

"Michael Edwards? It's in May."

"Talking about the caveman!"

I had tried really hard to forget that date.

"I gave you a horoscope for Christmas."

I never read it.

"And I told you that we'd celebrate your birthday this year, remember? I'm throwing you a big party. It was supposed to be a surprise party, but it's better to tell you now and reserve the date. If I wait too long, you might be tied up that day and not able to come. So many women, so little time."

I smiled but said nothing.

"So it'll be a half-surprise party. You now know about it, but you won't know where it will happen or who's coming."

"Who's coming?"

"Some people you know and some you don't."

"Clients?"

"Many clients, yes. But I won't say more. Just cancel whatever appointment you have and keep that evening free."

He rolled another joint.

"May I ask you something personal, Baldy?"

"Sure."

"Why this fixation with older women now?"

"What?"

"Older women. Like Joe's secretary. What's her name?"

Shit, had he found out? "Nancy?"

"Yeah. Joe told me that she's about as old as Catherine, meaning almost fifteen years older than you."

"So what? They're both hot. I wouldn't trade Catherine for two twenty-year-olds."

He frowned. "I'm talking about life experience. Fifteen years are a lot, man. They are way ahead of you."

"You mean their biological clocks are ticking? Catherine is already married and wants no kids. She told me that. And Nancy doesn't want even marriage, let alone kids."

He looked surprised. "How do you know that?"

I had to pay attention! "If Nancy wanted a husband, she'd have one by now. She's so hot! Guys would leave their families for her."

"Talking about Joe? What do you know, Baldy?"

I really had to watch my mouth. "I don't know anything because Joe doesn't talk. But I bet he has a thing for her, or he wouldn't have complained to you."

"Maybe. But we're changing the subject. Why older women now?"

"I don't care about age. For your information, I'm dating three women about my age right now..." I couldn't tell him that two of them were secretaries. It wasn't wise to mention Nancy, either. "...and one much younger, too. Why shouldn't I date someone older? It has a practical side, you know? They are only looking for love affairs, no serious relationships. Unlike women our age."

He laughed. "Why has this become an issue now? You never had any problem getting rid of women, right?"

I nodded.

"When did this start, Baldy? This attraction for older women? After the shooting? Back in the eighties you always dated girls your age. Other students."

"I was surrounded by them."

"There were also professors and older graduate students. You never went after them."

I had to laugh. "You don't fuck your professors, Mad Dog!"

"Maybe not. But you can still be attracted to them."

"I don't understand the point of this conversation. Why do you care about my sex life?"

"I don't think it's about sex. It's about something else. Is there any connection to your mother?"

"Oedipus complex? Me fucking my mom? Give me a break!"

I stood up to change the CD while Mad Dog started rolling another joint. I put on the Catch a Fire CD and pressed the repeat button. I was so high that I wasn't sure if I would be able to change CDs again later on. And Sweet Jamaica needed music.

I was also hungry and thirsty. I had trouble walking the few steps to the pantry. I got back with packs of junk food and two cans of soft drinks; we never mixed marijuana with alcohol. After we ate, Mad Dog lit the joint, took a drag, and passed it to me. I took a drag and my head almost exploded. One drag too many.

"Baldy, I find the dirty underwear story really scary."

So did I, but what could I do? And what did that have to do with the older women? He was probably as high as I was.

"Dr. Nelson says that this fixation with clean underwear is a sign of Mom's repressed sexuality. Or something like that."

I passed the joint back.

"Baldy, I'm talking about the out-of-body experience you're supposed to have shortly before you die. People say that you see your whole life flashing before your eyes. How could you miss it because of fucking underwear? What a waste!"

I had to lay down on the floor. My head was spinning.

"What's a waste?"

"It's fucking rare, you know?"

"What's rare?"

"To have an out-of-body experience and survive to tell the story. To watch the movie."

"I didn't see any movie!"

"That's the point! You're entitled to this, you know? It's kind of a birthright, and your mom stole it from you, man. Fucking mean thing to do."

"I have to discuss that with both my therapists."

He laughed.

I closed my eyes. "Listen, Mad Dog, I can't go home today. You keep the bed. I'll stay right here on the floor."

"All right."

"Mad Dog?"

"What?"

"Don't worry. I won't climb into your bed later on to fuck

you. You're too young for me."

I could hear him laughing before I fell asleep. When I woke up the next day, Mad Dog was already gone.

[4/4]

On Monday I had an appointment with Dr. Clark. I asked him about the out-of-body experience. It was related to the trauma, so it was his area of expertise. I would talk about the Oedipus stuff with Dr. Nelson. So there I was, compartmentalizing therapy.

Dr. Clark didn't find my experience strange. Everyone reacted differently in a situation like that. He had never had any patient who had an out-of-body experience, but he knew that some people had it.

The question was what caused it. I should forget the esoteric bullshit. There were scientific explanations. It could be psychological. Some people had so-called fantasy prone personalities. Or it could be neurological, caused by a brain malfunction. I should be happy that I didn't have any of those problems. I was better off without the out-of-body stuff.

I had an appointment with Joe the next day. When Nancy gave me that sexy smile of hers, I thought, what a pity that she wanted to meet only once a week.

"Watch out, Birdy. Joe is in a very bad mood today. Been like that for days already."

"Has he found out?"

"What?"

"About us?"

She laughed. "How could he? Relax! Nothing to do with us. I think it's about Mathew, the big boss. But I don't know the details. Good luck!"

* * *

Joe did look very distressed. I had never seen him like that.

"What happened, Joe?"

"I'm in deep shit, man. I screwed up a very important campaign, and we lost a major client."

"Shit happens, right?"

"Not in this company. They don't like failure."

"Are they going to fire you?"

"I don't know. But I don't want to wait and see. I need your help, Birdy!"

"Whatever I can do, Joe."

I really meant that. I had a very bad conscience about sleeping with Nancy. I couldn't forget my dream. "Why did you do that to me, Birdy? You don't love her like I do..." I felt very sorry for him.

"You must coach my boss. For real. No drug dealing."

No way. I didn't feel that sorry. "You know so many therapists, Joe. You can surely recommend him to a top-notch guy."

He shook his head. "Mathew wants to be coached by you, Birdy."

"Why me?"

"Because he finds the idea of having a PSMT cool."

"Tell him that I'm booked out."

"I've done it already. He wants me to convince you to make an exception for him. It's my chance, Birdy! I need a little brown-nosing. Getting Mathew coaching sessions with you would help me a lot. He really wants this!"

If I were in a similar situation, I would ask, too. What did Joe have to lose? Nothing. I would be the one stuck with Mathew.

"Joe, I've never coached anyone. If Mathew finds out that I'm a phony coach, I'll lose my cover. And you'll lose yours, too. That would be much worse, wouldn't it? You told me that your company has no tolerance for drug use."

He sighed and lowered his head. He looked very sad. I started pitying him again.

"Birdy, man, he'll never realize that you're a phony coach. How could he? He has never seen a shrink in his whole life! Will you help me?"

"It's too risky!"

He didn't like my objection. I could feel his anger now.

"You guys owe me! Both Chris and you! I helped you guys set up this shit!"

"Of course we owe you, Joe. And I'd love to pay you back. If I could coach, I would gladly do it."

He tried to control his anger. "Come on, Birdy! There are courses, you know? Tell Mathew that you can only start in January. Then you'll have three months to learn. Chris told me that you took acting classes. Why not coaching classes? There's a very good coaching academy here in Manhattan. I called them. They have a five-weekend program. Ten eight-hour days. The next course starts on the twenty-fourth."

Five weekends! Eighty hours! That would ruin my social life.

"I work on weekends too, Joe."

He got really angry and raised his voice. "It's only five fucking weekends! Nothing compared with what's at stake here! The recession might be over, but the jobs aren't there yet. I can't lose mine. I have a family. Plus an ex-wife and children from that marriage. I have to pay alimony and child support. You have to help me! You guys owe me!"

"What about money, Joe? Have you told Mathew that my coaching session costs one thousand dollars?"

He laughed angrily. "Are you out of your mind? I have one of the best shrinks in town, and he charges me four hundred!"

That was the proof that Dr. Nelson was overcharging me.

"I told Mathew that you charge five hundred. It's a lot, but he has to consider that you come to see us. This saves time, and time is money. But you can't charge more than that!"

"So Chris will lose five hundred dollars every time I see your boss!"

He banged his fist on the table and started screaming. "You guys are making a killing! Much more than two hundred thousand dollars revenue a month! And you can't afford to lose five hundred dollars?"

I lowered my head. I couldn't look him in the eyes. He was right about that. We were making a killing. I decided to play a double game: pretend that I agreed with him and behind his back convince Mad Dog to refuse. I probably didn't need to argue my case much. Mad Dog would never do anything that could potentially harm our operation.

I looked him in the eyes and smiled. "You're right, Joe. It could work. We should give it a try. We owe you this!"

He smiled. He looked really happy. "Thanks, man! I knew that you wouldn't let me down!"

I felt ashamed. He was really a nice guy. And there I was, lying and plotting against him. And sleeping with the woman he loved so much.

"But as you know, it's not my decision to make. Chris is the boss. I have to talk to him first."

He smiled again. He looked relieved. Poor guy.

"I'll do it myself, Birdy. I'm meeting him for dinner this evening. Seven o'clock. I'll tell him that you agreed. Thanks, man!"

That hit me hard. Caught in my own web of lies! I had to call Mad Dog before they met.

"Birdy, I knew that you'd agree, so I told Mathew that next month he can come by to meet you personally at half past the hour. When you make the next appointment with Nancy, please ask her to coordinate with Mathew's secretary."

"Okay, Joe."

"Mind if I do a line now?"

"Go ahead."

After he got high, he started talking about his boss Mathew and didn't stop until the meeting was over.

On my way out Nancy told me, "Now you're the one looking afflicted. Was it so bad?"

"Yes, I could really use some company tonight."

"Sorry, Birdy. I have a birthday party this evening. But I'm sure that there are a lot of girls out there who'd die to spend the night with you. Give them a chance!"

I smiled and nodded. She checked Joe's appointments.

"What about Tuesday, November third? Ten o'clock as always?"

I told her about Joe's request. She phoned Mathew's secretary.

"He can only do nine thirty. Can you come at nine?"

"Sure. See you on Friday, Nancy."

"Can't wait!"

* * *

I couldn't reach Mad Dog during lunch break. I started calling the clients I had in the afternoon, asking if I could move our appointment to another day. Timothy agreed. I was meeting him at four. But I couldn't reach Mad Dog between four and five, either.

I was finished with my last client at a quarter to seven; it was too late to try again. Mad Dog was certainly already on his way to meet Joe. I went home really pissed off. That was what I got for feeling sorry for other people and promising to do stuff I didn't want to.

I tried to get a last-minute date but wasn't successful and went out to eat alone. I didn't enjoy my meal. I knew that somewhere out there Joe was talking to Mad Dog at that very moment. My only hope was that Mad Dog would see the danger and refuse to do it.

I didn't hear from Mad Dog in the next two days. That was unusual. He always paged me back when he had missed a call. Maybe he was having one of his reputation-territory-foot-soldier problems. That would mean that he never got to see Joe, and I still had time to convince him. That thought gave me hope.

** * **

Thursday evening I had my second therapy session with Dr. Nelson. I asked him about the Oedipus complex. I was now dating older women. Was I looking for a replacement for Mom?

"Aren't we all, Scott?"

Scott Campbell was my legend with him. To both Dr. Clark and Dr. Barnes I was Donald Baker.

"What do you mean, Dr. Nelson?"

"We tend to pick partners who are like our parents. Any woman you feel attracted to will have something of your mother in her personality."

"So you're saying that it's okay to date older women? I'm not unconsciously trying to sleep with Mom?"

"Are you?"

"Give me a break, Dr. Nelson! Mom is so uptight and so obnoxious! Totally unattractive. I can't imagine why any man would want to have sex with her."

"Your father? At least once?"

I laughed. He had a good sense of humor.

"Dad did have sex with her, more than once. Six children! But I wonder if he ever enjoyed it."

"I see. But let's leave your parents' sex life out of it. At least for now. Yours is more relevant. Tell me more."

I told him about my affairs. Among the women I was dating, the one I liked most was Nancy. But the one I really wanted to have was Catherine. Both were older than me. A friend of mine thought that my attraction to older women was something new and kind of weird. I had to admit that it was a new development. I had never dated older women before. But I didn't think it was weird. Why should age matter?

"You're right, Scott. Age is not a problem in itself. What could be a sign of a problem is the quantity. Why so many women?"

I had to laugh. "Come on, Dr. Nelson! What's wrong with fooling around?"

"Absolutely nothing. But what's wrong with having a serious and meaningful relationship with only one woman?"

"That's not how our brains are wired, Dr. Nelson. The evolution thing. Men are supposed to spread their seed around because they have so much of the stuff. Women are wired differently. They need long-term commitments because of the children."

"I don't dispute evolution, Scott. Though in America you should be careful who you say this to." He laughed, but I wasn't sure if he was joking or not. "But we can't dispute the fact that human beings have a deeply-rooted need for intimacy and companionship. That's why there are so many couples out there. If relationships weren't good, people wouldn't have them, would they? It's probably also wired into their brains. The evolution thing?"

"So you're telling me that I should stop fooling around and settle for a steady relationship?"

"I'm not telling you to do anything. I'm only asking you why this doesn't seem to be an option at the moment."

"It never has been, Dr. Nelson."

He looked surprised. "You've never had a real relationship?"

"Nope."

"Why?"

"Dad always told me to have as much fun as possible before I settle down and get married. That's what he did."

"And did he stop fooling around after he got married?"

I could see that he was trying to corner me. But I wouldn't give him the pleasure. "No, Dr. Nelson. He continued fooling around afterwards. He's always having affairs, which drives Mom crazy. Very bad marriage. Now you'll tell me that Dad isn't the right person to give me advice on relationships. Then you'll say that I'm just hiding behind a hollow excuse. Right?"

He smiled and gave me a puzzled look. "What's going on, Scott? We're not in a court of law here. You don't have to be on the defensive. Relax! And please stop second-guessing me."

"You were going to tell me that, weren't you?"

He gave me a look that I couldn't identify, something between stop being a prick and you're such a strange person.

"Back to your father's advice about having fun. Are serious

relationships not fun?”

“No, most of the time not.”

“How can you know if you never had one?”

“I’ve never seen a happy marriage.”

“How many marriages have you seen? Some marriages are good. Some are bad. You can’t generalize.”

“Are you married? Or are you talking theory?”

“Yes. My second marriage. First one was hell. Second one is great. Ten years and still happy. We can’t generalize, Scott. Some marriages are bad. Some are good. Some are somewhere in between. Can we agree on that?”

I nodded.

“But that’s not the issue, Scott. The issue here isn’t marriage, but relationships between two adults. It doesn’t have to end in marriage. Marriage is only one of the possible outcomes.”

“The most common outcome is breakup, isn’t it?”

“Yes, pretty common. Why should that be a problem?”

“Why start something that is going to end anyway?”

“Because between the beginning and the end there is the middle. And that middle can be very gratifying and last a very long time.”

“I can live without that.”

“Can you? Or do you hope you can?”

“Why hope?”

“I think that you might be cracking, Scott. Some part of you, deep inside, might be longing to finally have a real relationship, to finally fall deeply in love. You’re like a volcano about to erupt.”

I had to laugh. “How can you know that? The intuition thing?”

“You don’t believe in intuition?”

Man, I was paying him to aggravate me. And paying much more than the going rate, which was even more upsetting.

“Dr. Nelson, is that what therapy is all about? You pay a guy to get on your nerves?”

He laughed. “Yes, that’s the whole point. It’s good that you are angry. It means I’m doing my job well.”

“I’m not angry! I just don’t believe this shit. Intuition, fate, out-of-body experiences: it’s all bullshit. I believe only in science, Dr. Nelson. Facts!”

He smiled maliciously; just like Mad Dog did sometimes.

“Is it okay if I aggravate you with some crude facts?”

I nodded, wondering what he was up to.

First, it was a fact that human beings longed for love, affection, and companionship, he said. I was a perfectly average human being, so that applied to me as well. Second, I had suffered a serious psychological shock and developed post-traumatic stress disorder. I didn't have my emotions under control, and was even in treatment for nightmares and anxiety attacks. There was a lot of deep subconscious stuff coming up. Third, my attraction for older women was a recent development, something that came up after the shock.

"So, Scott, if you add it all up, what's the conclusion? An educated guess based on facts and not intuition?"

"No clue."

"In my opinion, the logical conclusion is that you're soon to have your very first relationship. But you are so scared that you built a safety net, just in case."

"Which safety net?"

"Age, Scott. You hope that the age difference will offer you an escape route. If things get really serious, the biological clock will come to your rescue."

That was nonsense! "You call that logical?"

"That's how the mind works, Scott. You have your conscious self, what we call the ego, and your unconscious self. The ego is in control. When the unconscious self wants to do something that the ego doesn't approve of, it has to fool the ego. That's where the sudden attraction to older women comes in. Looks safe, so ego lowers the guard. An ingenious move. But watch out, Scott! Your unconscious self might be taking you for a ride."

"How come?"

"There is no safety net. It's an illusion. The age difference might not save you."

"Come on, Dr. Nelson. Are you telling me that Catherine will want to marry me? She's already married. She's only looking for an affair."

"Why this fixation with marriage, Scott? You can have an intense, meaningful, and long relationship without marriage."

"She'll never leave her husband for me."

"That's what you're hoping for. What if she does?"

I had never considered that possibility.

"You're saying that I should stay away from Catherine?"

"It's not my job to tell you what to do. My job is to help you get to know yourself better."

"You seem to know me better than I do. I could use some advice here. Should I stay away, Dr. Nelson?"

"See the pattern, Scott? You're always planning your moves like life is a chess game. You never listen to your heart. Why?"

"I like to be in control!"

"How much control do you think you have over events?"

"I don't know. But at least I can control the choices that I make. That's a good start."

"You seem to like this Catherine a lot. You won't resist her much longer. And even if you do, another Catherine will come along. It's bound to happen, Scott. Sooner or later."

"I don't believe in fate!"

"Who's talking about fate? You're looking for love so intensely that you'll eventually find it. It's all about the laws of probability. Probability is math, and math is a science. But time is up. See you next Thursday."

* * *

I left Dr. Nelson's office very confused. One thing was clear: he dug much deeper than Dr. Clark. I should ask him about the out-of-body stuff, too. Just in case.

The next day I had a date with Nancy. We went out for dinner and saw a movie afterwards. I brought her to my apartment, and we had a wonderful time together.

I couldn't avoid thinking about my conversation with Dr. Nelson. I liked Nancy, but I definitely wasn't looking for a relationship. She wasn't, either. Both of us felt comfortable with our arrangement. It was good that way. Why would it be different with Catherine? Dr. Nelson didn't have a clue.

We had brunch, and she left shortly after three. I ran to meet Mad Dog in a coffee shop, hoping that he wouldn't show up.

[4/5]

He came on time, as always.

"Sorry that I couldn't call you back, Baldy. There were some problems."

Saved! I was relieved. "It's okay, Mad Dog. We can talk now. I just wanted to warn you about Joe before you met him. You guys were supposed to have dinner on Tuesday."

"We had a wonderful dinner. Interesting development, right?"

Shit, they had met! But he couldn't have agreed.

"You're not doing this, are you?"

He looked surprised. "Joe told me that you loved the idea! Did he lie to me?"

I couldn't say that I lied hoping that he would do the dirty work for me. "I find the idea shit, but I recognize that we owe him."

"We owe him a lot, Baldy."

"Only for this reason did I agree. I wasn't sure if you would. It surprises me. It seems very dangerous to me."

"Dangerous? It's perfect! It'll bring an extra layer of protection to our operation. Legitimacy. If we can prove that we have one real coaching client, then people will assume that all others are real, right? Just like your artists back home. You told me about them, remember? Now I can appreciate the beauty of it. You brown people are really smart!"

Me and my big mouth! Again paying the price for talking too much. I could see the parallels, of course. It was a smart thing to do. But I'd be the one doing it. And I didn't want to.

"So you agreed?"

"Of course I did! I was surprised that you agreed so easily, though. Almost couldn't believe when Joe told me. That's not you. You normally put up a fight. Five weekends coaching academy!"

"You wouldn't have agreed if I had put up a fight?"

He smiled. "Maybe. Why? Regrets?"

Of course I regretted everything. "No, just worried."

"You don't need to worry, Baldy. You'll make a great coach. I can already see you asking your clients, 'And how do you feel about it?' You have to look them in the eyes when you say that."

He started laughing, and I couldn't resist laughing, too, though I wished I hadn't. It gave him the impression that I was for it. I wasn't.

"But isn't it a lot of work to satisfy only this one guy? More hours than for acting classes! It's a very low return on investment!"

"That's exactly what I thought! We're on the same wavelength, Baldy."

Maybe we still could stop it.

"That's why we should take more than one real client, Baldy.

Say one every week? Four a month?”

Very bad idea. “What for?”

“To improve your legend. It’s only four additional appointments every month. You can handle that. By the way, your share remains the same. You won’t lose any money.”

I asked myself why he was doing that. “Wait a minute, Mad Dog! You aren’t thinking about that crazy franchising idea, are you? Black & Brown, Incorporated? What did you and Joe talk about on Tuesday?”

He laughed. “Baldy, man, I always try to turn problems into opportunities. If we have to save Joe’s ass, we might as well do a pilot project and test a crazy idea.”

“You just said it: it’s a crazy idea. But you’re the boss. If you want to waste money on this, it’s your problem. Now let’s talk about the operational side. I see a lot of complications.”

He looked amazed. “I’m impressed! You’re taking it like a man. No fights, no protests. Therapy is really doing you good!”

I answered tongue in cheek, “And how do you feel about it?”

He had a laugh attack, and so did I. Everybody in the coffee shop started looking at us. Mad Dog suggested that we go to another one.

* * *

Once there we agreed on the operational details. I was going to coaching academy for five weekends in a row. We couldn’t exchange backpacks at lunchtime in those five weekends, so we’d have to do it in the evening. I wasn’t going to sacrifice Friday or Saturday evening. Two evenings were taken for therapy. We had to meet for dinner either on Tuesdays, Wednesdays, or Sundays.

Mad Dog had already enrolled me at the coaching academy using my new identity, Michael Edwards. It was good to have a diploma in that name, he said. It would make my legend stronger. The coaching course would end the weekend before Thanksgiving. I could take the Thanksgiving week off. I should go through all the business cards I was given by people wanting to hire me as a real coach, and choose the three other clients I needed.

He then told me about my upcoming birthday party. He had booked a nice restaurant in the Village, which seated 200 people, exclusively for us. He had invited only one hundred guests, so there would be open space for a cocktail party before dinner and for dancing afterwards. He had engaged a band.

I should arrive between seven and seven thirty. Guests would start arriving at eight. We would start with the cocktail party. Dinner would be served at ten. The birthday cake would be cut at midnight. Afterwards we would dance. At six in the morning there would be breakfast for those still around.

I had been to a lot of parties like that, but no one had ever thrown me one. Not even my parents, who were much richer than Mad Dog. I wondered how much it would cost. If I needed proof that he liked me and appreciated my work, this was it.

Before he left, he couldn't resist teasing me. "You'll be introduced to a lot of hot women. But I'm afraid you might not like them. Not old enough for you."

***

The following workweek I was very busy. I saw Dr. Clark Monday evening. My fifth session. I had an informal banking appointment on Tuesday. In the evening I met Mad Dog in Sweet Jamaica. We had a few very pleasant hours together, then I went home at midnight. He slept in the apartment.

I had a date with Nancy on Wednesday, and it was great, as always. It made me wonder how good it would be with Catherine. Why should I let Dr. Nelson scare me? Catherine was just looking for an affair. It would be over in a few months. Maybe I should give her a call.

[4/6]

Friday I was very excited about my birthday party, checking my pager after every meeting to find out about the location. The message finally arrived at around four in the afternoon. I happened to know the place. It was really cool and really expensive. Mad Dog was just like RW: he had style.

I got there at a quarter past seven. There were security guards outside, two huge guys dressed in dark suits. They reminded me of the guys guarding the informal banking offices. There was also a very beautiful young woman holding a guest list in her hand. When I told her my name, she smiled and said, "Happy birthday, Birdy! Chris is waiting for you."

The restaurant was bustling with last-minute activity. I could hear the band doing a sound check. A lot of people were running around, most of them dressed in white: waiters and busboys. The few guys dressed all in black and conspicuously standing around doing nothing were definitely security.

I saw Mad Dog talking to the musicians and walked towards him. When he saw me, he smiled and came in my direction.

"Birdy, man, happy birthday!"

He gave me a hug.

"Thanks, Mad Dog."

"Chris, please. No Mad Dog in here. Don't forget it."

"Sorry, Chris. Thanks a lot, man. This is a great party. Best birthday present I ever got!"

"The party hasn't started yet. How can you say that?"

"I can see it's going to be great."

He gave me a bright smile. "Your intuition is telling you this?"

Man, he never missed an opportunity to bug me. Even on my birthday. "No, just an educated guess. The location is wonderful, the place is famous for its great food, the band sounds good, and knowing you, I can be sure that only cool people were invited. In short: all the ingredients for a great party!"

He smiled again. "So you have to add up all that stuff to come to your educated guess? It's much quicker with intuition, you know? Gut feeling?"

What could I say? "I'll work on that with Dr. Nelson."

He gave me a condescending look. "Let me give you your birthday present."

He took a finely wrapped rectangular package from his breast pocket and gave it to me. What could that be? Another horoscope? It was a Rolex wristwatch; a real one, no fake, exactly like the one the killers had taken from me in Stanford. That model had cost more than $20,000.

"It's the same model, isn't it, Birdy?"

"Yes! How did you remember?"

He winked. "Never noticed that I have a very good memory? Now put this on and give me back the fake. What will your mother think of you? Wearing Chinatown fakes!"

I had to laugh. Yeah, what would Mom think of what had happened to me in the last year?

"Thanks, Chris! I know how much this watch costs. And I can guess how much this party is costing you, too. Very generous!"

"You deserve it, Birdy. You've already sold more than two thousand packages of cocaine! Black & Brown, Incorporated is making a killing! Let's toast to that."

He waved to a waiter. The guy came over and Mad Dog ordered champagne. While we waited, I noticed that the security guys were observing us.

"Are those your guys or a security company?"

"Security company. My people would feel out of place here."

* * *

The waiter arrived with a bottle of champagne and a few glasses. He put the tray on a table nearby, opened the bottle, poured each of us a glass, and left. Mad Dog raised his glass.

"To the caveman!"

"To Black & Brown, Incorporated!"

We drank and chatted. At ten to eight Joe arrived carrying a present. He looked very happy, and he definitely owed that happiness to me. I had saved his ass. And the price would be high: eighty hours of stupid coaching academy, followed by monthly coaching sessions with his weird boss. I thought, "We're even now, Joe. I don't owe you shit anymore."

"Birdy! Happy birthday, man!"

He put the present on the table and hugged me really tight. At that moment I understood what the expression bear hug meant. He then hugged Mad Dog the same way.

"Great party you organized here, Chris!"

"Our Birdy deserves it, doesn't he, Joe? He's the best personal self-motivation trainer in the world!"

Mad Dog poured Joe a glass of champagne and refilled our glasses. We toasted.

"To you, Joe! Without whom none of this would have happened. We really owe you!"

Joe was moved to hear that. "Thanks, Chris! But now I owe you guys, too! Mathew was so glad for my help in getting him a slot with Birdy that he forgave me for screwing up. We had a long talk yesterday and put everything behind us. I'm starting with a clean slate!"

* * *

We talked for a few minutes. At five to eight Mad Dog and

I moved to the entrance. It was time to greet the guests. Joe went to do a line in the bathroom. Mad Dog showed me a very long table to the left side of the door, then he waved to a girl I hadn't seen yet. She was very good looking and had a great body. Mad Dog made the introductions.

Her name was Susan, and her job at the party was to take care of the presents. While Mad Dog and I greeted the guests, Susan would discretely pick the presents I received and bring them to the table. The party service company would deliver the gifts sometime in the following week. I should call them to make an appointment.

Susan went to the spot where we had been chatting before to get Joe's present, which was still laying on the table. Mad Dog noticed me watching her.

"She's hot, isn't she? Twenty-two. Student. Philosophy major. She does part-time work for the party service company, like the girl outside. There are a few more inside. These are the women you should be dating, Birdy."

I laughed. "I wouldn't mind taking one of them home with me."

He looked at me, a little annoyed. "You know what I mean, don't you?"

The arrival of the first guests saved me from having that conversation. We spent more than half an hour greeting the guests and receiving presents. The restaurant filled pretty quickly. At twenty to nine Mad Dog sent Susan outside to check the guest list. I watched her.

Mad Dog bugged me again. "Go for it, Baldy!"

I didn't reply. Susan was back soon. Twelve people hadn't shown up yet. Mad Dog decided not to wait anymore.

"Okay, Birdy, let's party now! Whoever is late will have to look for us."

We moved around the crowd, at first together, but eventually we got separated. At around nine forty-five I was talking to a client and his wife when I heard a female voice saying behind me, "Sorry to crash your party, Birdy!"

I turned around, and it was Catherine. I was so happy to see her! She looked divine in a black cocktail dress. My heart started beating fast. I never knew that I liked her that much.

"Happy birthday, Birdy!" She hugged me and kissed me on

the cheek. What a wonderful perfume! She then gave me an envelope. "Your birthday present!" I put it in my breast pocket. She smiled. "Are you okay, Birdy? You haven't said anything yet. Are you mad that I came?"

Only then did I realize that the whole time I had only stared at her without saying anything.

"Sorry, Catherine. Of course I'm not mad at you! It's great that you came. I would have invited you, but it's a surprise party, you know? How did you find out?"

"Joe tipped me about it."

"God bless Joe!"

"There he is," Catherine said, pointing in his direction. "Talking to Chris."

I wondered if Joe was explaining to Mad Dog what the hell Catherine was doing there.

"Do you think Chris will kick me out, Birdy?"

"Never. Chris is a gentleman. He'll wait until the party is over. Only then he'll tell the security guards to beat Joe up. And probably me as well."

She giggled. "You're always so funny! I've missed you, Birdy. Why won't you come back? Chris says that you refuse to. I can't believe it!"

"It's true, Catherine. I don't want to be your dealer anymore."

She gave me a teasing smile. "What do you want to be, Birdy?"

"Your lover?"

Her smile became even more provocative. "You could be both, you know?"

"I'd rather not mix business with pleasure."

She came closer and whispered, "I'm all for pleasure!"

My heart was beating really fast now. Yes, Catherine! Finally!

"I've got to go now, Birdy!"

"Why? You just arrived!"

"I have to meet my husband for dinner in half an hour."

Shit! "When will we see each other again, Catherine?"

"I gave you a present. It's all in there. Goodbye, Birdy!"

She hugged me again, this time tighter and longer. Then she gave me an even more provocative smile, turned around, and walked away. I stood there, watching her leaving, and wondered for the first time if Dr. Nelson could be right. Was I cracking? Definitely confused. My heart was pounding. Inside my head I heard,

"Is this love, is this love, is this love that I'm feeling?" I thought, "Am I going crazy?" But it wasn't inside my head. The band was really playing "Is This Love," one of my favorite Marley songs.

It couldn't be a coincidence. I looked in the direction of the stage and saw Mad Dog there. He had requested the band to play the song. He walked in my direction, smiling and moving his lips to the song. He was going to tease me.

But Joe arrived first, with a bright smile on his face.

"That was my second present, Birdy. Inviting Catherine here. Like it?"

"Loved it, Joe! Thanks, man. I really appreciated that. Was Chris mad at you? I could see you guys talking."

"Not mad but concerned. He worries about you and Catherine. I wonder why."

"So do I. It's none of his business, is it?"

"Of course not. But you know..."

Mad Dog arrived, still smiling, and Joe stopped talking. I got ready for the scorn. But he said nothing about Catherine. Instead, he told me that it was time to announce dinner.

[4/7]

Dinner was delicious. Two very attractive young women, who were very interested in my coaching activities, sat at our table. First the girls from the party service and now those two. Mad Dog had certainly staged the whole thing. That couldn't be a coincidence.

After dinner another very beautiful girl from the party service brought the cake. It was big, with two small figurines on the top, like a wedding cake. But instead of the traditional bride and groom, it had a man dressed only in his underwear and a woman pointing two machine guns at him.

Bastard! How could he make a joke of that? And on my birthday. It was an inside joke, of course. Only the two of us got it. The guests thought that the man was wearing diapers, so symbolizing my youth. They had been told that I was turning twenty-six that evening. Many guests, especially the clients, were older than me. Then some of the guests noticed the machine guns and thought that my girlfriend had caught me with my pants down and was threatening me. Everyone found that version very amusing. There were lots of laughs. The one laughing the loudest was Mad Dog.

Later he told me, "I didn't laugh or tease you when you told me. But I promised that I would do it someday, remember?"

After cake Mad Dog told the crowd that the dance floor was open. It got filled quickly. I took the chance and went to the restroom; I had to check Catherine's present. I got inside a stall, locked the door, opened the envelope with care, and found a card inside. She had very neat handwriting. "One candlelight dinner in a hotel suite overlooking Manhattan's skyline. On a weekday of your choice from six to ten. Catherine." Yes!

I knew that her husband was in finance and did business with the Japanese. He worked late because New York City was thirteen hours behind Tokyo. When his business partners started working at eight in the morning in Japan, it was seven in the evening in New York. He needed at least three hours to take care of the daily business, and never left the office before ten in the evening. Catherine was a corporate lawyer and worked nine to five. Due to their work schedules they could only spend time together on weekends.

Her husband wanted to move to San Francisco because California was sixteen hours behind Japan. When the Japanese started working in the morning, it would be only four in the afternoon in California. He would be able to work until seven and have the evening free. Catherine didn't want to move. She loved New York. Besides that, the secret of a good marriage was not seeing each other too much, she told me once.

That was what "weekday of your choice from six to ten" meant. It was the time she had to fool around. I would call her on Monday and arrange our date for Tuesday evening, if possible. I had a client at five and another at six, but I could move their appointments to another day.

I left the stall happy, grinning like a fool, and met Joe outside. He also looked happy. Probably had done another line. When I got back to the dance floor, Mad Dog was dancing with one of the most beautiful women at the party.

* * *

A waiter came and told me that a guest had just arrived, and I went to greet him. It was one of the clients, who apologized for being late. He had spent the evening entertaining business guests from Europe, covering for a colleague who got sick at the last minute. He gave me a present and went to the dance floor to greet Mad Dog. Susan came to pick it up. Of all the women at the party, she was the one I liked most. After Catherine. But Catherine was gone.

I asked Susan to dance, but she said that she wasn't supposed to. Management was very strict on that. Besides that, she had to finish packing the presents in moving boxes before her shift was over at two in the morning. But we could talk while she packed. We started to chat, but were interrupted by a guest who wanted to say goodbye. Then another one. I checked the time. It was one in the morning. Time for the non-dancers to start leaving, I guessed.

It was lots of fun talking to Susan even though we were interrupted all the time by so many guests saying goodbye. I hardly noticed time passing. Soon it was two in the morning. Half of the guests were gone. Now only the hard-core partygoers were left. They would probably stay for breakfast. That was when Mad Dog came in, holding hands with the woman he had been dancing with.

"Time to go, Birdy. Great party!"

"Yes, great party! Thank you, Chris."

He came closer and whispered, "Take Susan home, Baldy. It's your birthday!"

"I'll think about it."

"Don't think. Just do it!" He then turned to Susan. "This young man here is always thinking, thinking, thinking. He'll never tell you that he likes you!"

What was he doing?

She smiled and answered, "That's exactly what I thought!"

Mad Dog laughed. "See, Birdy? Why don't you take Susan home and continue your party there?"

That was really embarrassing. I was planning to pick her up, but that was my decision to make. He had no business telling me how to live my life.

"Please, Chris, stop it!"

Mad Dog turned to Susan again. "See? He's a lost case. You have to do it yourself, Susan!"

He hugged both of us and left. Susan looked at me and smiled. A really nice smile. "Will you take me home or not? My shift is over already!"

I liked her direct way. We took a cab home and had a wonderful night. When I woke up the next day at around noon, she was still there. The afternoon was even better than the night. She was a very cool woman. We talked about everything, even philosophy. She told me about a course she was taking on a philosopher called Kierkegaard. I had never heard of him before, but I found even that very interesting.

At around four she got ready to leave. She kissed me goodbye and asked the question asked after every one-night stand. "When will we see each other again?" I didn't want to give her the usual answer, "I'll call you." She was too nice for that kind of bullshit. I was about to start an affair with Catherine in a few days and I wouldn't have time for Susan.

"Listen, Susan, I like you a lot. You're cool. So I'll be frank with you. I'm in the middle of a very complicated relationship right now. I don't know how long it will last. I have to deal with it first. Until then it's better that we don't meet."

I was expecting her to be disappointed. She smiled nicely instead.

"I understand. I'm in a similar situation, you know? I've been dating a guy for two years, but it's very bad right now. We'll probably break up soon."

She looked sad. I tried to cheer her up. "Maybe we'll bump into each other on Washington Square someday, after we have sorted out our affairs."

She smiled, gave me a last kiss, and said, "Yeah, you're right, let's leave it to fate."

The instant she left I regretted not getting her phone number. What if my affair with Catherine didn't last?

[4/8]

Sunday I had brunch with Nancy in her apartment and stayed until midnight. It was our sixth date, but it was still as good as the first time. I decided to keep seeing her despite Catherine. Catherine didn't have time on weekends anyway.

On Monday, between two appointments, I called Catherine, who seemed as excited about the whole thing as I was. Tuesday evening at six was perfect, she said, and told me the name of the hotel where she would make the reservation. I should ask for the room number at the reception desk.

On Tuesday, at five to six, I was standing outside the hotel suite. I had never been so nervous about a date before. My heart was beating fast. My hands were sweating. It was almost as intense as an anxiety attack. But the feeling was good.

I knocked. She opened the door slightly.

"Close your eyes and come in, Birdy."

I did what she said, and heard the door being closed behind me. When she spoke again, she was in front of me.

"Open your eyes!"

Wow! She was wearing the sexiest underwear I had ever seen. What a body!

"Happy birthday, Birdy!"

I could see a table set in the background, the candles lit. She smiled and said, "It's sushi. Won't get cold."

And off to bed we went. It was divine; better than anything I had ever experienced. Not only the sex: the way she talked, the way she smiled, the way she laughed, the way she called me "baby." Everything was special. Could Dr. Nelson be right? Was I about to fall in love? Or had I fallen already? How could I know for sure?

I felt in heaven and hardly noticed time passing. Suddenly she said, "Oh, my God! It's ten to ten!" Then she got up and started getting dressed. Shit, it was over.

"Can't you stay any longer?"

"Sorry, baby. Husband is waiting."

"When do we meet again?"

"What about Thursday?"

"I have therapy, but I can cancel it."

"Please don't! Therapy is important. What about Friday?"

That was too far away. "What about tomorrow and Friday?"

She smiled. "Yeah, why not? But tomorrow I can only meet at seven."

That was good. I would have to cancel only one appointment.

"Seven is great!"

"All right. I'll book another night here when I leave."

"Okay, but Friday you come to my place."

"No way, baby. We're lovers. We meet in hotel suites. See you tomorrow!"

I didn't have time to protest. She smiled, gave me an air kiss, and left. I wasn't supposed to leave with her. We were not to be seen together. I waited about ten minutes and went home.

* * *

Wednesday was a very long day. All I could think about was the evening with Catherine. But I had to see nine clients before that, including Peter. If he weren't one of Mad Dog's oldest clients, I would have dumped him already. He was a bore, and his secretary was a bitch. She always left me waiting until Peter called asking for me, every single time since I started in December. And the shit Peter talked about! I couldn't take it anymore.

Actually, why should I? I couldn't fire him, but he could fire me, just like Catherine had done. Why hadn't I thought about that before? I would annoy him so much that he would ask Mad Dog to take him back.

He was right in the middle of a diatribe against Clinton when I interrupted him.

"There's no difference, Peter. Bush or Clinton, it's the same. Nothing changes."

"What are you talking about? The Supreme Court is at stake! The president appoints the judges!"

"So what?"

"We don't need more liberal judges!"

"The judges only matter in the cultural wars, Peter. And the cultural wars don't matter at all. Not to people like you and me."

He gave me a funny look, like I was from another planet. I started talking about Carlos's theories and methods.

He listened impatiently, and after a while he interrupted me.

"You sound like a fucking liberal."

He had never used the F word before. That was a good sign. I was annoying him.

"Liberal? No! Liberals are damn softies. Peace and love and shit. I believe in power, Peter! Especially in the power of money. Money buys the cultural wars so that the rednecks won't fight for their rights."

"They don't need to fight because they already have all the rights they need. America is the most democratic and free country in the world."

"Money buys that, too: the illusion that you're free, that everyone is equal. But some people are more equal than others."

He became aggressive. "Don't give me this liberal bullshit!"

Then I had a brilliant idea: why not add new-age crap to that conversation?

"Sorry. Fate brought me to you, Peter. To question your beliefs."

The face he made! Yes, I was doing fine.

"Take the opportunity that fate is presenting you and ride with it, Peter."

His face was red now. "I thought that Chris was bad, but you're much worse. At least Chris's fate stuff is funny."

"Fate is never funny, Peter. Fate is a motherfucker."

He looked at his watch. I did the same. It was three thirty.

"Listen, Birdy, I have a very important meeting after this, and I need time to get ready. Do you mind leaving early today?"

Yes, the liberal and fate mix was working!

"Not at all! We'll continue next month. By then Clinton will be elected, and you'll see that nothing has really changed."

He gave me the fuck-you look. I left. Mrs. Jones was surprised to see me. I could identify a spark in her eyes, as if she knew that Peter had thrown me out. It could only mean that the end was near.

* * *

I was finished with my last client at a quarter to six. At seven I was knocking on the hotel suite's door. The second evening went like the first: it was like being in heaven. I had never felt so good with a woman before. Very worrying was the emptiness that I felt after she left. That was also a completely new feeling to me. I had to wait two days until Friday to see her again. That was an eternity. Worse, after meeting her on Friday I would only see her again on Tuesday. Four days!

On Thursday I told Dr. Nelson about my affair with Catherine. I almost had a laugh attack when he asked me, "How do you feel about it, Scott?" I remembered Mad Dog's joke. Yes, that was really therapy in a nutshell, wasn't it? How do you feel about it? We talked the whole session about my feelings for Catherine.

Friday was another very long day. A client's secretary, Sharon, whom I had been flirting with for months without success, was surprisingly all smiles. Had she broken up with her boyfriend? But it was too late for her. I wasn't interested anymore.

The evening with Catherine was wonderful. Once again. The only thing that bugged me was her refusal to come to my apartment. I didn't want to meet her only in hotel suites. But I couldn't make her change her mind. She left at ten. Alone, I felt the same emptiness as in the previous times, as if life was meaningless without her. Should I worry? No, time would take care of that, I told myself. A few more dates and I wouldn't mind anymore. It would be just like it was with Nancy.

* * *

The first day of coaching academy on Saturday was awful. I didn't want to be there. The other students and the teachers were nice, but it felt like a waste of time. All I needed to do was to ask Mathew and the other guys, "And how do you feel about it?"

Saturday evening Nancy came to my apartment. I was glad to see her, but I felt somehow guilty for betraying Catherine. I had never had that feeling before in my whole life. Nancy noticed that I was different and asked what my problem was. I didn't want to tell her about Catherine. I said that the coaching academy was bugging me, but I couldn't fool her for long.

"It's a woman, isn't it, Birdy?"

"Are you women trained to detect this kind of stuff?"

"Some people call it intuition."

I told her about my affair with Catherine and about the awkward feeling I had that I was betraying her.

Nancy laughed. "She's married, for God's sake! She's the one betraying her husband!"

I didn't find it funny.

"Wait a minute, Birdy! You're not in love, are you?"

"No!"

"Don't do it! It never ends well!"

I nodded.

"And don't dump me because of her! I saw you first!"

"Never!"

"Promise me that!"

She also made me promise that we would meet every Saturday. As a kind of inoculation, she said. If I started dating only Catherine, I would be in trouble. I thought that she was exaggerating, but I really liked Nancy. It would be an easy promise to keep.

* * *

I met Mad Dog Sunday evening to exchange backpacks. He

asked about meeting in Sweet Jamaica sometime in the next week. I told him that I didn't have any free evenings.

He smiled. "Susan?"

I shook my head.

"Catherine?"

I nodded and braced myself for his sermon. Nothing came. Puzzling.

"No Sweet Jamaica until coaching academy is over? Shit!"

I smiled and said, tongue in cheek, "It wasn't my idea, you know? I still think that it's a very low return on investment."

"Right now, yes. It looks like that. But we can never know..."

I interrupted him and completed his sentence. "What fate has in store for us, do we?"

He looked at me, baffled. "How did you know that I was going to say that?"

Yeah, how? Educated guess, of course. He was Mad Dog, after all, and he believed in the fate crap. What else would he say?

"Intuition, Mad Dog! Intuition!"

He laughed. "Are you trying to fuck with me?"

"Yeah, and how do you feel about it?"

We both had a laugh attack. The whole restaurant looked at us. We finished our meal quickly and left the place.

[4/9]

In my last workweek in October I had three appointments with my informal bankers: on Monday, Wednesday, and Friday. I transferred $120,000 to the islands. After those transfers I had $360,000 offshore and about $30,000 in America. That was forty percent of my one-million-dollar goal.

In October I sold 355 packages, averaging 1.78. A record. If I could keep that average, I would save at least $70,000 every month, needing only another nine months to reach my million. I would be able to quit in the summer of 1993.

That thought didn't cheer me up, though, as I lay alone in bed in my apartment Friday evening. Catherine couldn't see me that evening. Her husband had a very important business dinner that they had to attend as a couple. Some big-shot Japanese business partner had come over accompanied by his wife, and the Japs needed special attention. Or so she said. I couldn't know if it was true or not.

Emily called me Wednesday morning asking if I had time on Friday. I lied and said that I didn't, even though I already knew that Catherine wouldn't be available. Emily didn't like it. I had the feeling that she wouldn't be calling again, but I didn't care. She was really nice, but I only cared about Catherine now. I didn't feel like seeing Nancy on Saturday, either. I called her Friday evening at around nine to cancel our date. She wasn't home, so I left a message on her answering machine and went to bed.

At around eleven the phone woke me up. It was Nancy.

"I'm worried about you, Birdy! You're really falling for her!"

"And if so?"

"You'll dump me! You promised that you wouldn't."

"Listen, Nancy, you can have any guy you want."

She giggled. "I know. But at the moment I want you. Don't dump me, Birdy. I want to be there when she leaves you."

"What?"

"I find guys with broken hearts really sexy, you know?"

"You're betting that she'll dump me?"

"Yes, that's where the smart money is, Birdy."

"Listen, I want to go back to bed."

"We can talk again tomorrow. I'm coming at seven. Be there, or I will tell Joe about us."

"You'll what?"

She laughed. "Just kidding. But be there. Good night."

After that bad joke I was completely awake. I got up and went to the kitchen. While I prepared something to eat, I kept asking myself what had happened to the caveman. Only one year before I had been on the run, fighting for my life. I stole; I robbed; I assaulted; I searched for Mad Dog in the mean streets of Brooklyn; I got frisked by the police; I started a career as a drug dealer. A mean motherfucker, as Mad Dog would say.

I was now doing two therapies simultaneously and worrying the whole day about a woman. Worrying so much that I didn't want to see the others. Womanizing wasn't fun anymore. What a pussy the caveman had become!

* * *

Coaching academy on Saturday was terrible; I was happy when it was over. I went back home to get ready for Nancy. She came at seven, and we went out for dinner. We talked a lot about love affairs, relationships, breakups, and stuff. I asked if we could be only friends. She gave me that sexy smile of hers and said, "No way, Birdy!"

On Sunday coaching academy wasn't much better, but at least I had my second weekend behind me. Only three more to go. Mad Dog didn't show up for dinner, but he paged me later. I called him back, and he apologized. Reputation-territory-foot-soldier stuff had come up.

On Monday I started my first workweek in November. I had Dr. Clark that evening, session number eight. On Tuesday I saw Joe at nine. His boss Mathew joined us at nine thirty. A very strange guy. He needed help from a real therapist, I thought, not a fake PSMT. What if I screwed him up even more? Well, it had never been my decision to coach him. He had fought hard to get me. What was that saying again? He got what he wished for.

The evening with Catherine was bad. I would have one whole week off at the end of the month, and I wanted to travel somewhere with her. She didn't like the idea at all. We didn't have to leave town to have sex, she said. I told her it wasn't about sex but spending time together. Taking long walks and talking.

She laughed when she heard that. "Holding hands? Like two lovebirds?"

"Yeah, exactly. What's wrong with that?"

"We're lovers, baby! I'm married, remember? I don't want people to see us together. We meet in hotel rooms only."

"Maybe it's time to face the facts, Catherine. You don't seem to enjoy your marriage. Why pretend it's important?"

"My marriage is my business, okay? It doesn't concern you."

"Of course it does! It's the reason why I can't see you more often. You're always hurrying home."

"Listen, we see each other three times a week. That's a lot!"

"I could handle more!"

"Why do you want more time with me if you don't use it? Stop talking and come over here!"

That settled the argument for the evening. The next day I tried to start it again, but she wouldn't let me. Would we now argue every time we met? She had enough arguments with her husband already, she said. She didn't need that with her lover.

* * *

Thursday evening I talked to Dr. Nelson about my frustration. Catherine had a shitty marriage. Why would she hang on to it?

"Isn't it funny, Scott? You got exactly what you ordered: a married woman who won't leave her husband for you. That was your safety net. But now you want her to do just that!"

Holy shit, he was right; I wanted that! "Any advice?"

"Follow your heart!"

"It seems that my heart wants a woman almost fifteen years older to leave her husband for me. There's no future in that."

"The first part was your heart talking. The part about the future was your ego."

"So what? The ego can be right now and then, can't it?"

"The ego is always right, Scott. Always! That's the problem. You asked for advice. I'd say follow your heart."

That made me angry. "So that if the heart gets broken, you can fix it, right? More therapy sessions? More money?"

He laughed loud and long, like he was having a mini laugh attack. "Exactly! Fuck them up and then fix them later! That's the most important thing in this profession. Now that you're going to become a coach, never forget that. Never! It keeps the money coming in."

I wasn't sure if he was joking or not.

"By the way, time's up, Scott. See you next week."

I went home very confused. Things were really getting out of hand. I was seeing Catherine the next day. What should I do?

* * *

I did nothing. In the afternoon I got a message from her on my work pager cancelling our date that evening. I tried to reach her at the office, but her secretary said that she had left for the day. Migraine. That evening I didn't want to be alone in my apartment. At first I thought about calling Nancy but dropped the idea. I really felt like going to Sweet Jamaica. We hadn't been there in ages. After work I paged Mad Dog, and he called me back. "Great idea! I'll be there at nine."

The moment Mad Dog saw me, he noticed that something was wrong. After we smoked the first joint, he tried to bring up the subject.

"So, Baldy, how's it going with Catherine?"

"I don't want to talk about it."

"I see… I won't say that I told you so."

That was very considerate of him. Unusual. "Thanks, man."

"But I told you so!"

I had to laugh. Considerate my ass! But I really didn't want to talk about that. I changed the subject.

"You miss Jamaica? Going there for Christmas?"

"No way! Someone has been looking for me."

"Who?"

"Winston, I suppose. The only other maniac who has this thing about searching for me is sitting right here. It must be him. I haven't called him since you showed up. We used to talk about once a month."

"He's probably looking for me as well."

"Could be. But it would be dangerous. Is he thinking that after only one year everybody has already forgotten you? The Feds never forget you. Neither do those Colombians. Brown scum!"

"Has he tried to find you here, too?"

"Not yet. But if it's him, that's his next move, I suppose."

He rolled the second joint. "He has absolutely no chance. You can't find me if I don't want you to."

"So what are you doing for the Christmas vacation?"

"Visit my money. Cayman or Bahamas. Haven't decided yet. Do you want to come along?"

"Not really. I'd have to go through immigration. Too many officers in uniform. I could get an anxiety attack. I'm not there yet, man."

We smoked pot and talked about the old times with Winston. At around midnight I left. I had coaching academy the next day.

* * *

That weekend was like the previous one; two days of boring coaching academy and Saturday night with Nancy. In the following workweek I saw Dr. Clark Monday evening, Catherine on Tuesday and Wednesday, Dr. Nelson on Thursday, and Catherine again on Friday.

Friday was a very bad day. Catherine told me that we couldn't continue meeting three times a week. First, it would kill our love affair. Second, she had a social life, too. She had to see her friends. It hurt to hear that, because I wanted exactly the opposite: to see her more often. I told her so.

"Come on, baby! That will destroy everything. We have such a great affair! Why jeopardize that?"

I hesitated. Should I tell her or not? Dr. Nelson had told me to follow my heart, but I had never said it before.

"I love you, Catherine!"

I saw the surprise on her face. She tried to smile, but it didn't work out. She looked rather sad, like she was lost in bad memories.

"Listen, baby, you're confused! These things happen sometimes. It's just a phase, you know? Don't mix affairs with love! It doesn't end well."

That hurt. I was hoping to hear that she loved me, too.

"I don't want it to end, Catherine!"

"Neither do I. It's such a good affair!"

"I want more than an affair!"

She sighed. "Remember your birthday? I asked you what you wanted to be if not my dealer. You answered, my lover."

"But now I want more!"

"There isn't more, baby. I'm a married woman."

"You could leave him!"

She laughed. "For you? You're twenty-six, for God's sake. I'll turn forty next year!"

"So what?"

She shook her head. "No way!"

She started getting dressed. I told her that it was early, but she said that it was better that way. I should use the weekend to cool down. It was just a phase I was going through, she insisted. It would pass. I was only infatuated with her. It couldn't be love.

I felt like crying, but I could control myself. I wasn't going to cry because of a woman! I went home, smoked a joint, went to bed, and dreamed of Catherine the whole night. She kept telling me, "It's just a phase you're going through, baby. It will pass."

[4/10]

I didn't feel like going to coaching academy on Saturday, but staying home wouldn't help me much. I needed to get Catherine off my mind. After coaching academy I went home to meet Nancy. She immediately noticed my mood.

"Do you want to talk, Birdy?"

"Not really. Let's go to the movies."

The movie helped me forget my troubles for two hours. Dinner was nice, too. There was a good club not far from the restaurant where we danced until one in the morning. I was only killing time, afraid of going home with her. I didn't feel like having sex.

She noticed my mood. When we got home, she told me that she was too tired for sex. I found it a very sweet gesture. She was really a friend.

Coaching academy on Sunday was a bit better than on Saturday. We covered a lot of practical stuff that I would need in my future coaching activities. In the evening I met Mad Dog in a Vietnamese restaurant to exchange backpacks. He probably noticed my mood because he didn't tease me.

On Monday I had my last session with Dr. Clark. I was happy that it was over, but I felt sad that I would never see him again. I had come to respect him a lot. He was a good man doing the right thing: fixing people up and helping them get over the shit they had gone through. He said that we could never really know if someone was cured or not. Post-traumatic stress disorder was a very mean thing. But at least I had the tools to keep my anxiety attacks under control. If the nightmares started again, I should call him. He would always find a slot for me.

I now had one more free evening for Catherine. When I told her that on Tuesday, she didn't like it at all. I hadn't really listened, she said angrily. She had told me on Friday that three times a week were already too much. Now I was suggesting four?

"How can you become a coach if you don't listen to people?"

That made me angry. "I never wanted to be a coach, I was forced to! And yes, I can listen very well. When I was selling you dope, you told me more than once that your marriage was bad and that you were lonely. Each time we meet in this hotel room you tell me how much you enjoy my company. Why do you refuse to see me more often if you like me that much?"

"Listen to us, baby! We're having a fight like a married couple. Come here! We could use our time better."

"You do enjoy it, don't you?"

"A lot! Come here!"

"So why don't you want to spend more time with me if you like it so much? I have the Thanksgiving week free. We could go somewhere together."

She frowned. "I can't. I'll be in California with my husband."

That was news to me. "The whole week?"

"Yes. Monday is a national holiday in Japan. Thursday is Thanksgiving. We'll just take the whole week off."

"What will you do the whole week in California? You hate California! You told me that. I do listen!"

She sighed and looked at me in silence for a few seconds. I had the impression that she was pondering if she should tell me something or not. All of a sudden she looked sad. It seemed that she had made up her mind and knew that I wouldn't like what I was about to hear. I braced myself for the worst.

"I'll have to learn to like California, baby. We're going there to look for an apartment to buy in San Francisco."

That hit me hard. "You're not..." I couldn't finish the sentence.

"Yes, baby, we're moving to California. In January."

It felt like someone had punched me in the stomach.

"It's my third marriage, you know? I want to save it, at least try to. We agreed to see a marriage counselor in California."

I exploded. "You want to save your fucking marriage? Really? We're having an affair right now!"

She smiled sadly. "Yes, I know this is awkward. But I really like you! I wanted to have this very last affair before we moved west. That's why I crashed your birthday party."

That hit me even harder. "You already knew you were moving before you started this?"

"Yes."

My eyes got misty. I didn't want her to see me crying, so I covered my face with my hands. She came over to caress me and I pushed her way.

She protested. "Hey! Don't be rude! It's not my fault! It was an affair between two consenting adults. You just ruined it!"

I stood up and got dressed in silence.

"Come on, baby, you're not going to end it this way, are you?"

I didn't answer.

"We have more than a month until Christmas. Let's enjoy it!"

I looked her in the face to tell her to go to hell, but I just couldn't say it. I really loved that woman. Instead, I turned around and just walked away. The last thing I heard before I slammed the door was, "Come on, baby, don't be silly!"

Once outside the suite I started crying. I tried hard to hold my tears back, but they didn't stop flowing. I didn't want people to see me crying, so I took the stairs instead of the elevator. The suite was on the sixteenth floor. By the time I got to the lobby, I had calmed down. Exercise was good. I decided to walk home.

On the way home I had time to think. That was what I got for following my therapist's advice. I would never fall for that crap again. I had always suspected that love was really overrated. Now I knew it. Not worth it. Never again.

I got home past midnight, smoked a joint, and went to bed. The next morning I saw that Catherine had left three messages on my answering machine the previous evening while I was walking home. I should call, she said. We needed to talk.

I didn't call her back. What was there to talk about? She only wanted an affair. But I could have that with Nancy or any other woman. I didn't need Catherine for that. I was angry with her and even angrier with myself. Why didn't I see it coming? Why didn't I listen to Mad Dog?

On Wednesday I got two messages from Catherine on my work pager. I called the message service company and told them not to page me regarding any message from Catherine anymore. When I got home in the evening, I found two messages on my answering machine. Same as before: call me; we need to talk.

While I was eating, the phone rang. That made me angry. I unplugged both phone and answering machine and finished my meal. Catherine knew where I lived. Would she try to come by? Since I didn't want to see her, I decided to spend the next nights in Sweet Jamaica. I packed the things I needed, including enough packages of cocaine for the rest of the week, and left.

* * *

Thursday evening I had Dr. Nelson. The first thing I told him was, "Be warned: if you ask me how I feel about anything today, I'll punch you in the face."

He looked at me half surprised, half satisfied. Then he smiled. That irritated me.

"What's so funny? Never seen an angry guy before?"

He didn't answer; just sat there, looking at me and smiling.

"Lost your tongue?"

"There are a lot of things I could say, Scott."

"Why don't you?"

"Can't take the risk. You might punch me in the face. I need my front teeth, you know? I've lost them once."

"Are you teasing me?"

"No. I'm not a fool to tease you. I can feel your anger. I guess I know what happened."

"I don't want to talk about it!"

"Me neither, because I would have to ask about your feelings, and I could lose my front teeth. You're my last client today. Why don't we go for a beer?"

"I thought that a therapist wasn't supposed to socialize with his patients."

He smiled. "We're not supposed to get in bed with them. A beer is okay."

"Do you do this often? Go drink with your patients?"

"No. But I'd feel more relaxed talking to you if there were other people around us. If you start beating me up, I can get help."

"That's not it. You have other intentions, don't you, Dr. Nelson? You're planning to fill me up with booze and make me talk."

He laughed. "You're smart, Scott! You'll make a great coach."

"I'll go for a beer with you, but I won't talk about it."

"It's all right. We can talk about your parents' sex life instead. What about that?"

I sighed.

"That was deep, Scott."

"Shit! You too?"

"Me what?"

"I have a friend who says the same thing when I sigh. It's annoying!"

"Sorry. Do you want to go for a beer or not?"

Well, why not? There was a table-dance bar not far from his office. I always walked past it on my way to therapy.

"You know what? Let's go to that seedy bar down the road. Drink beer and watch the girls dance."

He laughed. "You kidding me? My wife would kill me!"

"She doesn't have to know, does she?"

He hesitated. I told him, tongue in cheek, "Follow your heart, Dr. Nelson. Fuck the ego!"

"Yeah, let's go! But let me call my wife first so that she won't worry. Could you please wait outside?"

"Don't tell her about the pole dancing."

The call took almost five minutes. I was already thinking that he would cancel when he came out with a big smile on his face.

"It's been years since I've been to a table-dance bar!"

I couldn't miss the opportunity. "And how do you feel about it, Dr. Nelson?"

He didn't answer. Only laughed, looking really happy, like a kid about to do something forbidden.

* * *

On the way there I got more depressed. Whenever I believed that I had hit bottom and couldn't fall any deeper, I always managed to dig further. Having a beer with my therapist! That was pathetic.

At first we just sat there and watched the girls dance. Then Dr. Nelson started talking and didn't stop. First he told me lots of therapist jokes. Then he talked about his youth in the sixties, telling me crazy stories literally involving sex and drugs. Like going to Woodstock but not remembering much, having been stoned all the time. Acid trip. Dropping out of college for two years to live in a commune in California. Dr. Nelson, a hippie. Hard to believe.

He did it because of a woman. When she broke up with him, he decided to come back to New York and finish his degree. In the early seventies he got involved with a married woman. Her husband caught them in bed and beat up Dr. Nelson really bad. He lost his front teeth and had to get implants. That was why he got nervous when I threatened to punch him in the face. I felt ashamed and apologized.

We left shortly before midnight. I accompanied him to the subway station.

"So, Scott, why did I tell you all these stories?"

"To cheer me up?"

"Yes, but there were other reasons. Can't you guess?"

"To show that a shrink also has a human side?"

He laughed. "Yes, in case you weren't sure yet! Do you believe now?"

I felt ashamed again. "Sorry..."

"It's okay. You're close, actually. What makes us human, Scott? Our experiences! The things we do and how we feel about them. Not our thoughts!"

"There you go again with feelings, Dr. Nelson!"

"Yes, because that's all there is, Scott. That's what we remember later; that's what really matters!"

"I don't like the feelings I'm having now."

"I'd be surprised if you did. A broken heart is a terrible thing. But it helps you to grow and become a better human being."

"I'd rather pass."

"We all would. But we can't know in advance that it's going to end like this, can we? It's a risk we have to take."

"I'm not sure it's worth it."

"It is! And that's what I want to tell you today. There are two reactions to what you're going through right now. The first one is to say 'never again.' A terrible decision to make. I hope you don't go that road."

To me it sounded like a pretty good choice.

"What's the alternative, Dr. Nelson?"

"To hope that you'll get lucky next time and to try again!"

Yeah, right! "I have to talk to my therapist about this. But time is up, Dr. Nelson. Good night!"

He laughed. "Can I give you a hug?"

"Not sure. First a beer, then a hug. You definitely want to fuck me!"

He laughed again and hugged me.

"Now go home and lick your wounds, Scott. The more you cry, the quicker you'll get over it."

I sighed.

"That was deep!"

Before I could say anything, he turned around and quickly walked down the stairs to the subway, laughing out loud.

[4/11]

Friday, November twentieth, was my last workday before my vacation, and my very last client was Peter at five. Great, I could dump all my negative energy on him!

"Congratulations, Peter! Clinton won!"

He gave me the fuck-you look. "Birdy, I'm not going to talk politics with you anymore."

How was I going to get rid of him without politics? I couldn't let him off the hook that easily.

"Afraid to see the light and vote Democrat next time?"

He gave me another fuck-you look and changed the subject.

"Guess who will play for the Mets next year."

Yes, the Mets! He loved them, didn't he? There were other ways to annoy him. If not politics...

"Who cares? Baseball is such a boring game! I always fall asleep in front of the TV."

He looked at me, surprised and offended. "I thought you liked baseball!"

"Hate it!" I told him RW's opinion about baseball, hoping that it would annoy him. It didn't. I then told him RW's shooting theory. He laughed and said that he didn't know that I could be so funny. Shit, it wasn't working. He wasn't supposed to have a good time. I had to annoy him.

But how? I remembered Catherine and the void.

"Do you do therapy, Peter?"

He laughed. "Who needs fucking therapy, Birdy?"

What a prick! I got angry, and not only at him. I realized that I knew that answer well. I used to say that myself. Was that how Mad Dog had felt when I told him that? Had it annoyed him as much as it annoyed me now?

"You'd rather use cocaine, right?"

He didn't like my comment and gave me the fuck-you look for the third time that afternoon.

"And make you rich with my habit. Lucky you!"

"Cocaine won't solve your problem."

"I don't have any problems, Birdy."

"I think you do. You're trying to fill the void. But it can't be filled with drugs, you know?"

He laughed sarcastically. "Are you on drugs, Birdy? That would explain your weird behavior."

"Changing the subject? Afraid of talking about the void?"

"Which void?"

Yeah, cornered! Now I would drop it. I looked him in the eyes, smiled, and said, "The void you have inside of you because you never knew love."

He looked at me with a funny face, but I couldn't identify which emotion it was. Fear? Sadness? Anyway, I had hit him. Or so I thought. All of a sudden he burst out into a very annoying and creepy laughter.

"What's so funny, Peter?"

"You..." He had to pause to laugh. "...a drug dealer..." Another pause and more laughter. "...talking about love!"

I got really angry. "What's so funny? You don't think drug dealers can feel love?"

He shook his head and tried to answer, still laughing. "Not feeling..." Laughter. "...talking about it." More laughter. When he could control himself, he added, "I can imagine you and Chris sitting at a table. One counting the money, the other making the cocaine packages. All the time talking about love. That's hilarious!"

He laughed once again. I felt like beating him up. Then I remembered that I had basically said the same to Mad Dog. I badly needed to apologize. What a jerk I had been. I checked my watch. It was half past five. Still fifteen minutes left, but I couldn't stay there anymore.

"Time's up, Peter. I can only see you in two months, at the end of January. How many packages do you want?"

Still laughing, he showed me four fingers. I gave him the stuff. "That's three thousand dollars."

"So much?"

"Same price as always: one thousand for the first package, eight hundred for the second, and six hundred each for the rest. Adding it all up, three thousand. You can add, can't you?"

He gave me an obnoxious smile. "But there's forty-five minutes personal self-motivating coaching included in the price, isn't that right? You're leaving earlier. Shouldn't I get a discount?"

I had started the meeting trying to annoy him. Not only was I unsuccessful, he had managed to make me angry. Asshole! I stood up.

"Merry Christmas, Peter, and Happy New Year. Don't miss Clinton's inauguration: January twentieth."

That annoyed him a bit, but he tried not to show it.

"My greetings to Chris. Send him my 'love,' will you?"

He stressed the word love in a sarcastic way. Then he gave me the fuck-you look for the fourth time that afternoon. I left without answering. Mrs. Jones looked very pleased; two meetings in a row ending earlier than usual. I saw hope in her eyes. I made an appointment for January and left.

* * *

Saturday I had coaching academy. After that I returned to my apartment to wait for Nancy. I hadn't been there since Wednesday evening. There were no more messages because the answering machine was disconnected.

Nancy came at seven, and she was worried. She had tried to reach me many times. Why didn't I answer the phone? Why did I disconnect the answering machine? I had broken up with Catherine, hadn't I? Was it bad? How did I feel?

Yeah, how do you feel about it?

I told her about our breakup on Tuesday.

"The bitch wants to save her marriage."

She frowned. "Watch your language! She's not a bitch. Never say it again."

I shook my head in disgust. "Women's solidarity?"

"No! It's just misogynic language. No respect. Actually, this Catherine deserves a lot of respect."

I couldn't believe my ears. "Deserves what?"

"Respect. For trying to save her marriage. The odds are against her, you know? But she's willing to try. Giving everything up and moving to another state. I don't know if I could do it."

"Of course you couldn't! You're not delusional. As you said, the odds are against her. She'll come back in three months."

"Maybe. But if someone is delusional here, it's you, isn't it? She never lied to you. It was only an affair, and you knew it from the very beginning. It's your fault and your fault only."

Whatever. There was no point in talking about that. I suggested dinner and a movie, so we went out and had a few hours of fun. I asked her if she wanted to travel somewhere with me the following week, but she couldn't. She was flying to Indiana to spend Thanksgiving with her parents. I should take the trip alone. It would help me to recover. She suggested that I rent a car and drive up north. Maine had wonderful beaches, great for long walks. She had spent a lot of summer vacations there with her family when she was a kid.

We didn't have sex that night; she said that she'd wait until I came back from Maine. We would then spend the night together, and she would make me forget Catherine. I thought, now she will give me the only-one-pussy-thousand-others-out-there talk. But she didn't. It was definitely a guy thing.

* * *

Sunday was my last day at the coaching academy, and I got

my certificate. Now it was official: I could coach people. That evening I met Mad Dog to exchange backpacks. I told him about Peter and apologized for my past behavior.

"Thanks, man! Nice to hear that. It was really offensive. Now you know how it feels."

"Yes, I do. What should we do about Peter? I don't want to see him anymore."

"We can't dump him, Baldy. But look at the bright side."

"I don't see any."

"He's like a mirror, isn't he? Helping you see your real self?"

I protested. "Do you think I'm a jerk like Peter?"

"Didn't say that. But somehow he helps, doesn't he? That's how fate works, man. It gives you chances."

What had fate to do with that? Nothing.

"I'm driving up to Maine. Taking long walks on the beach. Looking forward to it."

He gave me a condescending smile. He knew I was changing the subject, and he hated when I did that.

"Don't catch a cold. You can't miss work in December."

* * *

I left New York Monday morning and arrived in Maine in the early evening. No clients, no women, no Mad Dog. Complete solitude for one week. It felt good that way. I took long walks on the beach, trying to forget what had happened.

Early Saturday morning I drove back home and arrived in my apartment late in the afternoon, looking forward to my date with Nancy that evening. She came with a bag. Flashing that sexy smile of hers, she told me that she was staying until Sunday evening. She said that I looked better but still sad. Just the way she liked it.

We had a great weekend together. I didn't think about Catherine once. I thought, yes, it's over. I have it behind me.

* * *

On Monday I was back at work. The following day I had Joe. When I got inside his office, the first thing he said was, "Birdy, what have you done to Catherine?" He sounded angry.

"Pardon me?"

"Catherine has called. She badly needs to talk to you. Why

don't you return her calls, man? I never thought you were the kind of guy who uses them and dumps them!"

"What? The bitch is playing victim now?"

"She's not a bitch! Catherine is a sweet girl. Gets involved with the wrong men, though. Birdy, you don't dump women like you did, you know? That's vulgar!"

"I didn't dump her, Joe."

"That's not what she told me."

"There's a lot of stuff she doesn't tell you. Did she mention that she's moving to California for good in January?"

"Old story. They were supposed to move last January, but Catherine got promoted and they had to stay one year longer."

So she already knew it on the very first day we met! Suddenly all the bad feelings that I had managed to suppress came back at once. Shit, I didn't have it behind me as I had naively thought.

"Why didn't you tell me that she was leaving?" I yelled at him.

"I thought that you knew," he yelled back. "I thought that was the reason why you were so desperate. You wanted to fuck her before she left town!"

My eyes got misty. I wasn't going to cry in front of Joe. I stood up and went to the window, turning my back on him.

"What's the problem, Birdy?"

I didn't answer.

"Oh, man! You didn't... Shit, Birdy, did you?"

I kept silent. He stood up and came to me.

"Did you fall in love with her?"

"I don't want to talk about it." My voice cracked when I said that. What would he think?

He put his arm on my shoulder. "I know what you're going through. Been there once, Birdy."

Oh, no! He was going to start telling me about Nancy!

"Give me a hug, Birdy!"

I didn't want to, so I didn't turn.

"Please..." Now it was his voice that was cracking. "Please, Birdy, give me a hug..."

He started crying, and I felt so sorry for him. I turned around, and we hugged. He started sobbing on my shoulder. Oh, man!

"Come on, Joe. It's all right. What about a line?"

"Not in the mood. But let me tell you something I haven't told anyone else. Besides my shrink, of course."

I sighed. "Yes, but please, let's sit down."

* * *

He told me about his affair with Nancy, crying all the time. How he still loved her, how he suffered when he imagined her with another guy. He begged me never to make a move on her. That would break his heart. I sat there, feeling like shit: embarrassed for listening to very private stuff; guilty for sleeping with Nancy behind his back; sad to see him suffering; and scared to realize how long it took to heal a broken heart. His sobbing was contagious. I tried hard, but couldn't avoid letting out a tear or two.

His time was up, but he wasn't finished yet. I couldn't leave him in that situation, so I called Nancy outside and asked her to call my next client and say that I couldn't come to our appointment. Maybe she could arrange another one at the end of the day? I gave her the client's name and phone number. She could hear that I was worried and asked if everything was okay. "Later," I told her, and hung up.

It took almost an hour to calm Joe down. When I left, he gave me a bear hug and told me, "Thanks, man, it was great talking to you. That coaching academy was really good, wasn't it? It turned you into a real coach!"

He needed some cheering up. "It was your idea, Joe. Shows how smart you are!"

He smiled for the first time that day. "Thanks, Birdy! By the way, please don't tell anyone about this conversation. Especially Nancy."

"Of course not. I'm very good at keeping secrets."

If that was what coaching was all about, I wasn't looking forward to it.

When I got outside, Nancy told me that the client couldn't see me that evening. I should call later to make another appointment.

"What happened, Birdy? Is Joe okay?"

"Everything is fine, Nancy. Just a bad day. Happens now and then. But I'm late. See you on Friday."

"Can't wait!"

I was glad to be out of there, but I couldn't get those issues off my mind. I felt guilty because of Nancy, and scared that I would never get Catherine out of my system, just like Joe with Nancy. Then there was my fear of coaching other people and screwing them up. I was happy I had Dr. Nelson Thursday evening.

* * *

"How can I help other people if I'm already so fucked up, Dr. Nelson?"

"Who can teach you more about sex, a whore or a virgin? It takes a fucked-up guy to understand another one."

"Are you fucked up, Dr. Nelson?"

He smiled. "Oh, yeah, Scott! And so is my therapist."

"What? You do therapy?"

"Of course! You have your own issues. You have the clients' issues. There's always stuff to talk about. When you start coaching for real, we might need to see each other twice a week. One day for you, one for your clients."

Shit. It would never end.

"Do you talk to your therapist about me?"

"Sometimes. And he probably talks to his about me."

I sighed.

"That was deep, Scott!"

"Right..."

"You'll be a great coach, Scott. Believe me. Just avoid the only mistake a coach can make."

"Which is?"

"To pass judgment on your clients and their problems. Whatever they tell you, no matter how silly or outrageous it sounds, is important. Or they wouldn't be talking about it. Don't judge, and you'll be fine."

* * *

I had three very intensive workweeks until Friday, December eighteenth: 153 clients, four office parties, seven dinner parties, Christmas shopping. No time for Sweet Jamaica. I sold 330 packages, averaging 2.30. I wired more money offshore, closing 1992 with half a million dollars abroad.

It would have been fun to celebrate Christmas with Mad Dog or Nancy, but both had plans. Mad Dog had his guys and Nancy her parents. I thought about renting a car and going to Maine again, since I had almost two weeks off.

Nancy came over Friday evening. On Saturday, after she left at around eleven, I went to have my Christmas lunch with Mad

Dog. He suggested the same Jamaican restaurant as in the previous year. That made me nervous. Would it be déjà vu all over again? Another conversation about leaving the business?

[5]

[5/1]

Mad Dog didn't show up, so I ate alone and went home. He didn't page me that afternoon. I paged him in the evening, but he didn't call back. What a terrible time to have reputation-territory-foot-soldier problems, I thought.

In the middle of the night the phone rang. It was three thirty.

"Baldy, this is an emergency!"

It had to be important. Mad Dog had never called me at home before. If he was taking the risk, then it meant big trouble.

"What happened, man?"

"I'm on my way to Sweet Jamaica. Meet me there. Now!"

"Okay!"

He hung up. I took a cold shower to wake up, got dressed, grabbed the backpack, and walked to Sweet Jamaica as quickly as possible. Mad Dog had a copy of the key, and he was already there when I arrived at about quarter past four. Standing outside the door I could hear Marley's song "Guiltiness" playing loudly. "They'll eat the bread of sorrow..."

I found him sitting at his favorite place, on the floor with his back to the drywall.

"What happened, Mad Dog?"

"They killed Charlie!"

Shit. "When?"

"Friday night."

I sat down on the floor in front of him, and saw that he had been crying. His eyes were very red, and his cheeks were wet with tears.

"He was like a brother to me... He gave me shelter when my adoptive parents threw me out... He helped me start in the business... We worked together for ten fucking years!"

"Who killed him? The Mexicans?"

"No. Inside job. A guy called Arturo Loco. Fucking brown scum. But he'll pay for it! He'll eat the bread of sorrow!"

"Are you taking him down?"

"I'd love to. But Vincent asked me to let him do it. They were cousins, after all."

"What happens now?"

"After this guy Loco is killed, another Latino motherfucker will take his place. I don't want to work directly with the brown scum. Charlie was my buffer. He's gone now."

He looked me in the eyes. "I'm quitting, Baldy!"

I froze. "You're what?"

"Quitting. I was going to quit in the summer anyway."

"What?"

"I'm ready, man. Could have done it long ago. But I promised to help you get your million. So I was waiting until the summer. That's when you'd have it, right?"

"Yes."

"Sorry, but I can't wait anymore. Things will get ugly in the next weeks. I don't want to go through this shit again. I'll take the opportunity and disappear. People will think that I was killed."

"What about me?"

"How much money have you got now?"

"Half a million."

He knocked on the drywall behind him.

"There's another four hundred fifty thousand in here if you charge full price. How many more packages do you still have?"

"Around sixty."

"All yours. How much money in the backpack?"

"Seventy thousand and a few hundred."

"You can keep that, too. And this..."

He opened his backpack and dropped the contents on the floor: bundles of hundred-dollar notes. He picked up five bundles.

"Five thousand is enough. I can't board a plane to Europe with too much cash. I could get arrested. You can keep the rest. Almost one hundred thousand."

Things were happening too quickly. I couldn't process the information. Mad Dog was quitting!

"So, Baldy, altogether more than six hundred thousand dollars. Now you have more than a million. You can quit as soon as you've sold the cocaine."

All I could do was nod. He pulled his gun from under his sweatshirt, took out the ammunition clip, and gave both to me.

"I can't board a plane with that, either."

I didn't feel comfortable holding the gun.

"Don't worry. This one is clean. Never shot anyone with it."

"It's not that. It's just that I don't like guns."

"Then get rid of it for me, will you?"

I nodded. Man, Mad Dog was quitting!

"What will happen to your dealers?"

"Don't worry. The supply chain will rearrange itself. It always does. People won't wait forever for me to show up."

"What? You didn't tell your guys that you're leaving?"

"Only Vincent knows. There will be a few killings in the next days. I want people to think that I was killed, too. They'll forget me quicker this way."

"What about our PSMT clients?"

"Tell them that I disappeared. You don't know what happened to me. You'll have to stop because you lost your supplier."

"Even Joe?"

"No exceptions."

I nodded.

"Don't worry about them, Baldy. Nobody will miss me."

"I will!"

"Thanks, man! I'll miss you, too. We had a great time together. Black & Brown! Why don't you come along after you've sold the rest of the cocaine?"

"What are you going to do?"

"Travel around the world. Unlike you, I've never traveled much. I've been only to Jamaica and the offshore Caribbean islands. That's it. Never been anywhere in America, either. I only know New York City. It's time to catch up, at least abroad. I don't know when I'll come back to America. It would be fun to travel together, Baldy. Are you joining me later?"

Why couldn't I say yes? It was my plan, wasn't it? Make a million, leave America, and start a new life somewhere. Maybe we could do that together. Mad Dog was now my best friend. But I didn't feel excited about it. I didn't feel ready yet. Why not? Had he been right about the Hotel California thing? Would I never leave? That was worrying. Frightening, actually.

But maybe I was only confused. Things were happening too quickly. "How long are you planning to travel? And where to?"

"The whole world, Baldy. First Europe. Then North Africa. I've always dreamed of riding a camel. Cool, right?"

I nodded.

"West Africa. From Africa to Asia. Cross the Pacific to South America. Then Central America and Mexico. I guess I'll be two years on the road."

"And then?"

"I hope that when I get to Jamaica, I'll have a plan for the rest of my life. What about you, man? Are you coming? We could meet in Europe sometime in the summer."

"If you're leaving, the game is over. I have to leave, too."

"You have to but you don't want to. Is that what you're saying? You'll do it against your will?" He sighed.

"That was deep," I said. But it wasn't funny. None of us laughed.

"Baldy, don't look for another supplier. You have your million. Quit while you're winning. Mean motherfuckers out there."

"Of course I'll quit. I'm not crazy enough to continue this shit on my own."

He was watching me, looking for a clue, not really convinced. I felt uncomfortable and tried to change the subject.

"What about therapy, Mad Dog? Are you done?"

"Yeah, kind of. It's never over, you know? But three and a half years are enough for now."

"I've only had three months…"

"You can continue it somewhere else later on. There are thousands of therapists out there."

"Like pussies?"

He laughed. "Yeah, like pussies."

"I like Dr. Nelson, though."

"I see…"

Shit, the way he was looking at me! "How much should I budget for the trip, Mad Dog?"

"Nothing. It's on me. You won't need to spend your million. What about that?"

That was really tempting. Why couldn't I just say yes? But I only nodded.

He looked at his watch. "Half past four. I'm leaving at six. There's still time for breakfast. I'm starving."

Man, Mad Dog was quitting! I still couldn't believe it. In ninety minutes he would be gone forever.

"Where are you going to now?"

"Newark. Boarding a flight to Atlanta at nine. From there to Brussels at four fifteen in the afternoon."

"You have no luggage? Only an empty backpack?"

"I'll buy a small suitcase and some clothing at the airport. It's less suspicious that way."

"Let me give you your Christmas present."

I had bought him two spy novels. He unwrapped the present and smiled.

"Thanks, man! If I can't sleep on the plane, at least I'll have something to read. As if you knew that I'd need this!"

I understood the hint but pretended I didn't.

"I had a present for you too, Baldy, but I had to leave it behind. It was a Marley CD box that came out a few weeks ago. It's called Songs of Freedom and has a few previously unreleased songs. Would you please buy it and pretend that I gave it to you?"

"Sure."

"Thanks. Now let's eat. I'm starving."

* * *

I fixed us breakfast. Mad Dog hadn't eaten in almost twenty-four hours, and it showed. He had no time to talk. I could hardly swallow my food. Man, Mad Dog was quitting! It was over!

When he finished, he started giving me tips for unwinding the operation. I should cancel the discounts and tell the clients that I was short on supply and could sell them only one package each, for full price.

The answering service was paid for until the end of the first quarter. Afterwards the number on my business card would be disconnected for lack of payment. I should throw the pager and the business cards away. I shouldn't tell anyone about my plans, and just disappear into the night one day, like he was about to do. I should take both passports with me. One never knew if I would ever need identity B.

The most important thing was to take care of the offshore companies and bank accounts before I left. They all needed a new address outside the United States, ideally in Europe. The Channel Islands were a good option. He had chosen Jersey for his companies and taken care of everything in the summer. He had been ready to move for months now. He gave me the name of a company renting mail boxes in Jersey.

I should leave America directly to the Caribbean Islands. Visit my money, as he liked to say. Go to the banks, change the company addresses personally, and get a few company credit cards to access my money. I should tell the agents to charge the annual fees to those credit cards.

I was amazed. He was about to leave, and he still could think straight and give me sound advice.

"How can you be so objective, Mad Dog? You're leaving, man! You've been a dealer for ten years. It's a major change. How do you feel about it?"

He laughed, but I wasn't joking this time.

"I really mean it! How do you feel?"

"Baldy, I don't know how I feel. Sad and angry because Charlie is dead; disappointed because you and I didn't have the time to finish this properly; excited because I'm starting a new life; curious about the world out there; guilty for leaving you behind; hopeful that you'll join me soon. How do you feel?"

"Overwhelmed. I can't believe this is happening."

He looked at his watch. "Quarter to six. I should get going. Black men can't get a cab easily in New York. Even black drivers won't stop for us."

"We could call one."

"It's okay. If I can't get anything by six, I'll take the subway and then the train. Give me a hug, man."

I had tried very hard not to cry, and until that moment I had been successful. But when he hugged me, I started crying on his shoulder. He did the same. It felt awkward.

I tried to stop it with a joke, "I wish Peter could see us now!"

We both laughed. He let go and looked at me, smiling, but tears were still rolling down his face.

"You're still so uptight, Baldy-Birdy! But somehow better than a year ago. There's hope for you!"

"Thanks, Mad Dog."

"Listen, Mad Dog has just died. Call me Douglas now."

Wow! After so many years! "I will. I have to get used to it, though."

"Can I call you Pablo from now on?"

"Yes, if you wish."

"Okay, Pablo, I'm leaving now. I'll get in touch soon. Take care. See you in Europe?"

"I hope so. Please call when you arrive in Europe tomorrow, will you?"

"Why? It will be in the middle of the night here."

"It doesn't matter. I'm not leaving town until I know that you're safe."

"Nothing will happen."

"Call anyway."

"Okay, I'll call as soon as I can. I promise."

He put on his backpack and walked to the door. Before he opened it, he looked at me with that mischievous smile of his.

"By the way, Pablo. You still haven't answered me after all this time. What about fate, man?"

"What about it, Mad... Sorry, I have to get used to Douglas. What about it, Douglas?"

"Do you still doubt it?"

What could I say? The truth? Why not give him a farewell present? A white lie wouldn't hurt, and it might make him happy.

"No, Douglas, I don't doubt it anymore. I haven't understood it completely yet, but there's definitely more shit out there than meets the eye."

He shook his head, still smiling. "I don't believe a word. But nice try, though. Take care!"

And he left.

I had the urge to listen to Marley's song "Chances Are." I put on the CD, pressed the repeat button for the song, and sat down at his favorite place on the floor, my back to the drywall.

Then I cried. "Chances are we're gonna leave now, sorry for the victim now..."

[5/2]

My only friend was gone. Never again would we meet in Sweet Jamaica to smoke joints and listen to Marley. The PSMT operation was finished. No more lunch together to exchange backpacks. And I didn't have a clue about what to do next.

I had my million now. Time to move on, according to my plan. But where should I go? I wasn't the same person who had come up with that plan. I had changed a lot since then. Were the Feds or the Colombians still looking for me? Was there really a reason to leave?

When I was set up in California, I had to run away. It was my only choice. New York City was the only possible destination because of Douglas. Working as a drug dealer was the only way to make enough money to leave. But was leaving America the only choice I had? And was the time right?

Douglas quit the business and left the country voluntarily. He didn't choose the exact time, but he was planning to do it very soon anyway. I wanted that luxury, too: to decide what was best for me and then do it when the time was right.

It took Douglas more than three years of therapy to get ready to leave the business. What if I needed that long as well? I didn't want to hide from the world for years, seeing only my therapist. As Birdy the PSMT I had a wonderful social life. I didn't want to lose it. Without the drugs my exposure to risk would be almost zero. Why not keep the legend after I stopped dealing? I was about to start coaching for real in January. I had four clients, but could have more if I wanted to. The demand was there. I had a lot of business cards from potential clients.

For the first time I saw real coaching as an opportunity and not as a problem. How bad could it really be? I was now used to listening to people talk about their lives. And $500 per session was a lot of money, double what I was making as a drug dealer. With a few more clients I'd be able to cover my high living costs and not touch my offshore savings.

That idea made me feel better. But then Douglas popped up inside my head. "You're dropping the drugs but not the legends. You're still fucking hiding from life." I sighed. He was right. What if I never left that make-believe world? As he had once said, I had to be a real man and do something about it: real therapy. If it had helped him, it could help me, too.

* * *

I went home. There was no message on my answering machine. No news was good news. I was very tired but didn't want to go to bed yet. Douglas would board the plane to Europe at four fifteen in the afternoon. I'd wait until then. I went to the kitchen to cook lunch. It was still very early, quarter to eleven, but I had eaten almost nothing for breakfast.

After eating I called Dr. Nelson. He had given me his private number for emergencies. I told him that I needed to have a very long conversation with him. One session wouldn't be enough. He never worked Tuesday mornings, and offered to see me in his office from nine to noon.

I watched two movies in the afternoon to kill time and keep me awake. At around five I called Atlanta airport to ask if the flight to Brussels had left on time. Yes, the bird had flown. I hadn't heard anything from Douglas, so unless he got arrested or killed, he would be on that plane. The plane would land at one in the morning New York time. I had at least eight hours until he called. I went to bed and quickly fell asleep.

* * *

At two thirty in the morning the phone woke me up.

"Pablo?"

"Mad Dog!"

"Mad Dog is dead."

"Sorry, Douglas. Where are you now?"

"At the airport. Just came through immigration and customs."

"Any problems?"

"Just the usual hassle you get for being dark-skinned."

"They've upgraded you already?"

He laughed. "Yeah! They even wanted to give me free health insurance!"

"It's good to hear you joking, Douglas. You sound much happier now."

"Yeah, I met this hot French woman on the plane. 'Françoise.' Cool name, right?" He tried to do a French accent when he said the name.

"Is she going to show you around?"

"Unfortunately she took a connection plane to Paris, but she's willing to show me Paris after Christmas. What about that? Never had a French girl!"

"Don't fuck her!"

He laughed. "Right! Sex leads to feelings, and hearts can be broken."

I ignored the comment. "Speaking of feelings, how do you feel now, Douglas?"

"Naked without my gun."

"You don't need it anymore. Nobody has a gun in Europe. You're safe now."

"Crazy, isn't it? How can you settle your scores without guns? Speaking of settling scores, when are you leaving for Maine?"

"I'm not going anymore."

"Why?"

"Not in the mood. Why?"

"Even better. I'm not sure if you can get New York papers

in Maine. Definitely not in Brussels."

"Why do you need the local papers? Homesick already?"

"To find out if Vincent has killed that motherfucker. He promised to do it before Christmas."

"Christmas present?"

"Yes!"

Shit, it was supposed to be a joke.

"Could you do me a great favor, Pablo? Could you buy the paper every day and check? If you're not leaving town, then I'll call again in two days."

"No problem."

"I have to go now. I didn't sleep the whole night talking to Françoise. I'm going to check into a nice hotel and catch up on lost sleep."

"If you sleep now, you'll turn day into night. Try to stay awake until the evening."

"Pablo, I haven't slept in three fucking days. I'm going to bed now. You go back to sleep, too."

"Yes, Mom. Thanks for calling. I'm really happy to know that you're safe. Enjoy your time in Brussels!"

"Definitely will. Buy the papers. I'll call Wednesday morning."

* * *

I went back to bed and slept until eight in the morning. After breakfast I called the car rental company and cancelled my reservation. Then I went to the coaching academy and had a very long talk with one of the advisors. There was a follow-up course to the one I had taken in the fall; also on weekends, but on Saturdays only. After that one I could take advanced courses.

I couldn't believe that I had voluntarily enrolled in and paid for the Saturday course. Amazing how priorities could change. In the afternoon I bought the newspaper. There was a short article on Charlie's death but nothing else.

Tuesday morning I went to see Dr. Nelson. I told him my whole story.

"Finally, Scott! It was about time! We can make real progress from now on."

I badly wanted progress. I didn't know in which direction my life was going, but I wanted to get there as quickly as possible. We agreed to have two sessions a week in 1993, Tuesdays and

Thursdays.

"By the way, what do you want me to call you now, Scott?"

"Please call me Pablo."

"Isn't Pablo Spanish for Paul? We have the same name. What a coincidence! Please call me Paul. No more Dr. Nelson."

"Aren't we getting too intimate?"

He laughed. "Still afraid that I'll try to fuck you? You're not my type."

* * *

I left his office very relieved. I had the feeling that I was doing the right thing, though I couldn't really tell why I felt that. Was that what Douglas called intuition?

I went to a CD shop and bought his Christmas present for me. I even had it wrapped as a gift. Then I went to the Italian restaurant he so much loved to have spaghetti with pesto, and tiramisu for dessert. It was strange to eat there alone. Even the waitress missed him and asked, "Where's Jason today?"

After lunch I bought a newspaper and went to a coffee shop. I got really happy when I saw a picture with the caption "Arturo Hernandez, aka El Loco, killed last night." Yes, that would make Douglas very happy. The paper also mentioned two other killings. One dead Colombian and one Jamaican. Luckily it wasn't Vincent. Was the dead Jamaican one of Douglas's guys?

He called on Wednesday, December twenty-third, early in the morning. He was happy to hear about his Christmas present.

"May that motherfucker burn in hell forever!"

"I bought the Marley CD box, Douglas. Thanks a lot. Several new songs. The 'Acoustic Medley' is awesome!"

"Yeah, I bought a box in Atlanta, too. And thanks for the books. Really good. Got to go, now. There's a woman I met."

"Douglas the slut."

"Womanizer, Pablo. Right? Isn't that what you call it?

I could imagine his smile on the other side of the line.

"Right! Happy Christmas, womanizer!"

"Happy Christmas, Pablo!"

* * *

Paul invited me to spend Christmas Eve with him and his wife, Betty. They had no children. Paul was a funny guy, but Betty was even funnier. We had a great evening together.

I was counting the days until Saturday, when Nancy was coming back from Indiana. I was dying to see her again. She was surprised when I called her Saturday afternoon. Was I feeling lonely in Maine? she asked. No, I was feeling lonely in New York and would love to see her. She couldn't. She was busy the whole weekend, finally seeing people she didn't get to see the whole year.

What about the following week? Did she have a free evening? No, other appointments. What about New Year's Eve? Or the weekend after that? She was leaving town Thursday morning and returning late Sunday night after visiting friends in Connecticut. Shit, no Nancy.

New Year's Eve I went to a great party in a loft in Tribeca. Ronny, one of my clients, was young, rich, and single; therefore, hot women, wild guys, and lots of drugs. Cocaine was everywhere. I left early with a very attractive woman. She took me to her place, and we had a great night. The next day I returned to my apartment at around noon. In the afternoon Douglas called to wish me a happy New Year. He was in Paris, and he would be staying there for a while because of Françoise.

"Are you in love, Douglas?"

"Not sure, Pablo. Time will tell."

"But you won't, right?"

He laughed. The Jamaican laughter. It was nice to hear it again.

"I've gotta go now. Take care, Pablo!"

[5/3]

On Monday, January fourth, I was back at work. I had basically the same routine as in 1992: five meetings in the morning, lunch break, and five meetings in the afternoon. Altogether 200 cocaine-addicted clients in a month. I had to go to my informal bankers three times a month to wire money offshore; Dr. Nelson every week, now in two evenings; Nancy every Saturday evening. But there would be no more lunch appointments with Douglas to exchange backpacks, and no more evenings in Sweet Jamaica. That part of my life was gone forever.

The only other change in my routine was real coaching. I felt uncomfortable with the idea of coaching Joe's boss. He was very strange, and I didn't know if I would be able to handle him properly. There was a lot at stake. If I screwed up, Joe would be in trouble, and I didn't need that extra dose of guilt. The three other real coaching clients I had chosen very well. I felt more relaxed about them.

Now with Douglas gone I had total control over the PSMT operation and could do whatever I wanted. But as much as I would have liked to get rid of Peter immediately, I decided to dump him only at the very end, when I had not a single package of cocaine left. If he called the cops and they came after me, there would be no evidence of my drug-dealing life. I didn't trust him.

The Monday clients didn't take the news about my supply problems well. Rationing was a nightmare for most of them. A guy who regularly bought three packages begged me to make an exception for him. He paid full price for all packages. That was good news. I wanted to sell my remaining stock by the end of February. If some clients kept reacting that way, I would make it.

* * *

Tuesday morning I saw Mathew. He was nervous.

"I don't know what to say, Birdy. Never done any coaching before."

"Just tell me about your motivation. Why coaching?"

He looked down. "I don't really know. Everybody is doing it. I thought I might try as well. Joe talks so much about how good you are!"

What an idiot, I thought. But I remembered Dr. Nelson. The only mistake I could make was to pass judgment. How hard it was not to judge!

"Listen, Mathew, everybody is doing a lot of stuff that you'd never think about doing. Like taking drugs, for example. So this can't be the only reason. There's something else. Why coaching?"

"Well, I always wanted to try therapy, but I'm afraid that people will think that I have problems. Self-motivating coaching is therapy-like, isn't it?"

"And if you like it, would you consider doing the real thing?"

"I don't know yet."

That was much better. What now? The secret was to make them talk. I only had to ask a question. But about what? Definitely not the void. I'd never make that mistake again. Maybe feelings?

"How does it feel to be the big boss, Mathew?"

He talked for forty-five minutes about it. How good it was to have power, how bad it was to be envied, and so forth. That was a good topic. I could dwell on that for a few more sessions.

"Time's up, Mathew. We'll continue next month."

He looked relieved and happy. "It was great talking to you, Birdy. Now I understand Joe."

"Thanks. See you in February."

When I left his room, I sighed in relief. Douglas popped up inside my head and said, "That was deep, man!" I had to smile. At least he wasn't telling me not to fuck the secretary, who was really hot. But she knew Nancy. I didn't want to get into that kind of trouble. I took the elevator down to Joe's floor. I hadn't seen Nancy in almost three weeks; she looked sexier than usual.

"Hi, Birdy! How was it with Mathew?"

That wasn't what I wanted to talk about.

"How I've missed you, Nancy! When do you have time for me?"

She blushed. "What about dinner tomorrow, Birdy?"

That meant I would have to go to Brooklyn after dinner and leave at around midnight. She didn't like sleeping in my apartment during the week, and never let me sleep in hers. The married couple thing.

"Great! I haven't been to your place for ages."

She smiled but said nothing. It wasn't her usual sexy smile, though. Something was definitely wrong.

"Talk to you later, Nancy. I have to see Joe now."

* * *

Joe looked very concerned.

"Birdy, have you heard from Chris?"

"Not since before Christmas. He never showed up for our Christmas lunch."

"I can't find him. He won't return my calls. Could something have happened? There seems to be some kind of war going on."

"Yes, and at least two Jamaicans guys have been killed. I'm worried. I only hope that he's just hiding, like last time."

"Right."

"But supply is low, so I have to ration. One package only until Chris returns."

That didn't affect him. Most of the time he bought only one.

"How was the session with Mathew?"

"Good. I think I'll be all right. But please tell me more about him. The more I know, the better."

He spent the rest of the meeting briefing me on Mathew. It was better than to speculate about Douglas's wellbeing.

When I got out, Nancy was on the phone. The way she was smiling was very suspicious. Who was she talking to? She noticed that I was observing her and blushed again. That worried me. I had known her for one year already and never seen her blush before. Now twice in one day. What was going on?

We made Joe's next appointment and agreed on a restaurant for our date.

"See you tomorrow, Nancy."

"Can't wait!"

It sounded like she could.

* * *

I went to the restaurant very happy, thinking, "Tonight is the night. Finally!"

"Listen, Birdy, there's something I have to tell you."

The tone of her voice was suspicious.

"What's happening, Nancy?"

She looked down. "I met a guy..."

"So what? I'm not jealous, and you know it."

She gave me an embarrassed smile and looked down again.

"You didn't fall in love, did you?"

Her eyes lit up. "Yes, Birdy! I think I met Mr. Right!"

I had to laugh. "I didn't know you believed in Mr. Right."

"I didn't! Until I met him. He's the one, Birdy!"

Was that a joke? Nancy and the one?

"It never ends well, Nancy. You told me so, remember? And you were right."

"It's different! Robert isn't married."

"So what? It never ends well, and you know it."

"I'm willing to try."

I sighed. "You're not going to dump me, are you? I saw you first!"

She lowered her eyes again. It looked like she was going to.

"How long has this been going on, Nancy?"

"I met him mid-December…"

"That was only a few weeks ago! You barely know this guy!"

"It was love at first sight, Birdy."

"I thought you didn't believe in love at first sight!"

"I didn't. But it seems that it does exist!"

"Nancy, remember what you told me when I was dating Catherine and didn't want to sleep with you anymore? About inoculation and stuff?"

"Yes, I do. But it's different now."

"I want to be there for you when it ends. I find girls with broken hearts very sexy!"

She laughed. "Come on, Birdy! Don't repeat the things that I told you."

"It worked with me!"

"It won't work with me, though. Let's stay friends!"

"I suggested that and you refused, remember? Friends alone wouldn't do it. And you were right. Please don't dump me, Nancy!"

"I'm not dumping you, Birdy. We'll stay good friends."

"My heart is still broken, you know? You promised that you'd fix it. You promised!"

She gave me the I'm-so-sorry smile. "I know, Birdy. I promised. And I did help a bit, didn't I? You're doing much better now."

"I'm not there yet!"

"You have your therapist. He can help you fix your heart."

"I can't have sex with my therapist."

She laughed. "You can have sex with any woman you want. We'll remain friends, Birdy."

"Without sex?"

"Yes."

"It won't work, Nancy. Every time I see you, I'll remember our good times in bed."

She gave me her sexy smile for the first time. "We had a great time together, didn't we? I'll never forget!"

Maybe I still had a chance. "And you'll give it up?"

"Come on, Birdy! You can have any woman."

"I know. But I want you."

"You don't love me."

"And you don't love me, either! Isn't that great? That's why it's so good!"

"But I love Robert!"

Oh, shit. "Are you sure, Nancy?"

"Yes. Please don't make it difficult for me. Let's stay friends."

I sighed. Really deeply. "Well, what can I say? You know where you can find me when you need company."

"Please wish me luck, Birdy. Please wish that I never have to come to you for company!"

It was lost. "Is it that serious, Nancy?"

She nodded.

"Well, then, what can I do but surrender? I wish you luck. You deserve it!"

"Thanks, Birdy! I haven't felt this way since I was sixteen!"

Nancy in love! Who could have thought!

"Does Joe know?"

"Of course not! Please never tell him."

"He still loves you. Do you know that?"

"Has he told you so?"

I was talking too much. "No, just a hunch."

"Yeah, I have that feeling, too. But there's nothing I can do about it."

Over dinner she told me everything about her Robert. Lawyer, forty-five, living in Connecticut, divorced, two small children. How they met, how well they got along. The usual story. Only that this was Nancy telling it. That was very unusual.

Nancy in love with Mr. Right. That surprised me more than Douglas quitting. What was left on my list of impossible things that would never happen? Mom liking blacks and me believing in fate?

I went home alone and in a very bad mood. No Nancy that evening. No more Nancy on any other evening in the future. No regular sex life anymore. All other women I used to date on the sideline had given up on me during the Catherine affair. That hadn't bothered me much because I still had Nancy. Now I had no one left.

* * *

There were more killings in Brooklyn that week. Douglas's Brooklyn supply chain was up in flames. A few Jamaicans got killed, but I never told Douglas about it. He never asked, either. He called in the second week of January, still in Paris with Fran-çoise. If Nancy could fall in love, maybe Douglas would marry

Françoise and have kids? Nothing was impossible anymore.

The three other real coaching clients in January went very well. Coaching academy was good. Focus and interest did make a difference. The only really unpleasant meeting I had was with Peter at the end of the month.

I hadn't seen him in two months, and wasn't looking forward to it. Now that I knew that I'd get rid of him very soon, I didn't need to bug him anymore. I decided to go back to my previous behavior: try to be nice and pretend that I enjoyed the conversation. He was probably expecting another annoying meeting. And being such an asshole, maybe even looking forward to it.

He looked very uptight when I came in, like a dog ready to attack. He was certainly waiting for a mean comment on Clinton's inauguration in the previous week.

"Happy New Year, Peter!"

"Happy New Year, Birdy."

"Peter, have you heard from Chris?"

"He's abroad on vacation." He didn't look concerned.

"I hope so."

"What do you mean, you hope?"

"I was supposed to have Christmas lunch with him before he left the country. He didn't show up. Haven't heard from him since."

"He disappears now and then. You should know this by now."

So arrogant. "There's some kind of war going on in Brooklyn. Many drug dealers already killed. Three of them Jamaicans."

He looked worried for the first time but tried not to show it.

"Why are you telling me this?"

"I'm afraid something could have happened to Chris."

"I'll try to contact him. He always calls me back."

Good luck! "Great. Then tell him that I'm short on supply. If he doesn't come back soon, I'll have to stop."

Now, that hit him. "What do you mean, stop?"

"Stop, Peter. Terminate the PSMT operation. I only have enough cocaine for the next month."

"You could get it somewhere else, couldn't you?"

"I work for Chris only."

"And it's your job to keep his clients satisfied until he's back! Get an alternate supplier until then."

Was that an order? "What if he doesn't come back?"

"He will."

"I hope you're right. But I'm rationing my stock. I can sell you only one package today."

He got angry. "You can't do it to me! I always buy two!"

"Not today."

He got angrier and raised his voice. "Who do you think you are, Birdy?"

"What do you suggest, Peter? A fire sale? I don't have much cocaine left to keep everyone happy."

"I told you to get another supplier."

"That's out of the question!"

"Well, if that's the case, you don't have to keep everyone happy. You only have to keep the special clients happy."

"People like you?"

"Yes! People like me, who helped you guys set this up. We have priority. It's your responsibility to keep us supplied until Chris comes back. If you can't increase supply, decrease demand. Get rid of some of the other clients."

"Chris alone can get rid of clients."

"He's not here. You just said that."

Maybe it would be better to cave in and pretend that he had won the argument. If he thought that his supply was safe, he would relax.

"Okay, I'll give you your two packages. Here."

He smiled and gave me the money: $1,800. I said nothing about full price. I wasn't going to fight him because of $200.

"Just relax, Birdy. Everything is fine. Chris will be back soon. He always comes back!"

"You're right. When he calls you back, tell him to call me."

"Of course."

"Should I leave now?"

"No way! You'll blow my cover if you keep leaving early."

I looked him in the eyes. "I don't think you enjoy the conversation."

He gave me the fuck-you look. "Not anymore. But you can't leave. Why don't you read the paper on the couch? I'll try to get some work done."

"Thanks, I will. Let's see what Clinton is up to."

I read the paper until my time was up. Mrs. Jones looked disappointed when I came out. Little did she know that pretty soon her wish to get rid of me would finally be granted. I made an appointment for the end of February, Friday the twenty-sixth, at two in the afternoon. The last appointment in my drug-dealing career.

When I got home that evening, there was a Paris postcard from Douglas waiting for me. I didn't know what I was missing, he said. "Get your brown ass over here as quickly as possible!" That made me sad. I wasn't going, and he would be disappointed when I told him that.

In January I sold 266 packages of cocaine for full price, averaging 1.33. I had only 253 packages left. I would be finished by the end of February. I transferred $350,000 to my offshore accounts in January, bringing my savings there to $850,000.

[5/4]

Douglas told me to disappear into the night without telling anyone, but I was staying in New York. I could bump into my former clients in the future, and I didn't want them asking me embarrassing questions. It was better to tell them that I was quitting, listen to their protests, and then disappear. But what if someone got angry and set me up? Many times I met clients directly after work still carrying my suitcase with cocaine and money; enough evidence to frame me. All it took was a phone call to the police.

So in February I avoided socializing with clients outside business hours. I didn't get many invitations anyway.

"You're quitting? What am I going to do now, Birdy?"

"What you used to do before we met. Go back to your previous dealer."

"You can't leave me, Birdy! I need you!"

"I'm not leaving. We'll keep in touch. What about dinner next month?"

Very few clients showed any interest in keeping in touch in the future. I was disappointed at first; I had thought that they liked my company. But it was probably safer that way. In the future, the less contact I had with that drug scene, the safer I'd be.

I only felt sorry for Joe. I felt very bad for lying to him, but that had been Douglas's wish. I had to respect it.

* * *

"What do you mean it's over, Birdy?"

"Chris is gone, man. Disappeared. I'm afraid he got killed."

"No way! We'd read about it on the paper, wouldn't we?" His voice was full of fear.

"Only if they found the body, Joe."

"Maybe things got very hot here, and he had to leave the country."

If only I could tell him the truth. "He would have called, wouldn't he?"

Joe became very sad. "Do you really think he was killed?"

I nodded, ashamed of myself.

He sighed. "What are you going to do now, Birdy?"

"Well, I'm quitting the drug-dealing business. But I'll keep coaching Mathew. Don't worry, Joe, I won't let you down on this."

"Mathew! I had totally forgotten about him."

"I haven't. I'm meeting him right after you. I'll tell him that we're done. You kind of graduated. After one year of coaching you've reached the point where you don't need it anymore. What about that for an excuse?"

"Yeah, it's good. Thanks for covering for me. But I have other worries right now."

Probably worried about where he was going to get his dope from now on. But I had thought about that. The only positive thing to come out of my conversation with Peter was to realize that I did have a very special client who needed to be taken care of: Joe. I gave him twelve packages. Enough cocaine for one year.

"A present, Joe: one year's supply. You now have enough time to find a safe and reliable supplier."

He smiled for the first time. "Thanks, Birdy! I don't have enough money on me right now. Can I pay you later?"

"I said it's a present. I don't want any money. I'm sure that Chris would have wanted it. You were his favorite client, Joe!"

His eyes got misty. Shit, he wasn't going to cry now, was he? I didn't need that.

"I can't believe it's over! I can't believe that Chris is dead!"

He started sobbing like a small kid. I waited. Paul Nelson had told me never to interrupt people when they were crying. It helped them to get the shit out of their system. It was tough to watch, though. It took him almost five minutes to calm down.

"Why don't you quit, Joe?"

He didn't answer.

"I know it's none of my business. It's your decision. That's why I'm giving you this much cocaine. You should do this out of conviction, not because you ran out of the stuff."

He started sobbing again. I waited.

"You're a really nice guy! You know that, Birdy?"

If he knew the truth about Douglas and Nancy, he wouldn't say that.

"Cocaine will kill you in the long run, Joe. Please stop."

"I'll think about it. I promise."

"Please hide the dope well. If you get caught with this amount, you'll be charged as a dealer."

"Really?"

I nodded. He said that he had a big safe at home and a small one in his office, hidden inside a drawer. He would bring the stuff home one package at a time.

"Mind if I leave early today, Joe?"

He looked sad. "We'll keep in touch, won't we, Birdy?"

"Of course! We can meet every month if you wish. Nothing will really change. Only the place we meet: a restaurant instead of your office. What about dinner sometime in March?"

We made an appointment and I stood up. He did the same, came over to me, and gave me a bear hug. Then he started sobbing again. I waited until he was finished.

"It's okay, big man. See you in a month."

But he just stood there, looking at me and blocking the way. I had to make him move.

"Please hide the cocaine in the safe before I leave. It's dangerous to leave it on the desk."

"Oh, yes. Thanks."

He went back to his desk, opened a drawer, got the safe, and put eleven packages inside, leaving one on the desk. When the safe was back inside the drawer and the last package had disappeared inside his pocket, I left.

* * *

Nancy greeted me with curiosity in her voice.

"Finished so early?"

"Finished forever!"

"What?"

"Joe's finished coaching. He doesn't need me anymore."

"So you won't come here anymore?"

She made a sad face, but I couldn't tell if she was really sad or only pretending. Maybe relieved?

"No. But now you have your Robert. You won't miss me."

"Come on, Birdy! We agreed to remain friends."

"Yes, we did. Call me anytime."

"What about Mathew?"

"I've just started with him. I'm going to see him now. And his secretary, by the way. Doris is very nice, as you know."

For a second I could see a jealous look on her face. But it was quickly gone.

"It's good to see you putting our affair behind you so quickly."

Was that sarcasm or disappointment?

"If you can't have the original, try the copy, Nancy."

* * *

The whole point of leaving early was to have more time to flirt with Doris while I waited for Mathew. I got there at twenty to eleven. We chatted for a while, exchanging the usual banalities. Then I took a seat to wait and flirt with her.

She ignored me the whole time. It didn't look like I had a chance. Maybe I should stop dating secretaries, I thought. Then Douglas popped up inside my head and said, "I've always told you not to fuck them! Thousands of other pussies out there!" I had to laugh. Doris gave me a disapproving look. I smiled and read the paper for the rest of the time.

The session with Mathew went well. He was surprised to hear that Joe was finished.

"It's not a lifetime thing, Mathew. It depends on the person. You can do it for one year or ten years."

"But how could Joe finish so quickly?"

"It's not a competition. Take it easy."

He then smiled. "Does it mean that you have a free slot now? I have a few friends who are very interested."

Good news. "Actually, I have more than one free slot at the moment. Take these cards." I had hired a new message service company and had a new phone number for my real coaching clients. "Please keep one for yourself because I have a new phone number now. The rest are for your friends. Tell them to call me. I still have a few slots, but they have to move fast."

"I will. I'll call right after we're finished today."

* * *

My three other coaching clients were also easy. My transition from drug dealer to real PSMT was going better than expected. Coaching academy was good, too. I was picking up the skills I needed very quickly. It was time to get more clients. Once again I went through all the business cards from people who had wanted to hire me as a coach in the past. I called them all, and twelve people were still interested. I gave them appointments in March. That brought the number of coaching clients to sixteen in a month, meaning $8,000 in revenues. A few more clients and I could cover all my living costs and leave my savings untouched.

With my social life frozen, I spent many evenings alone in Sweet Jamaica listening to Marley and smoking joints, thinking about my life and saying goodbye to the place. Douglas's gun I had already thrown into the Hudson River. Same for the two pagers we had used to communicate. The money was gone from that apartment, too. In February I transferred $150,000 offshore, reaching my million. The rest, about $80,000, I brought to my bigger apartment. The only thing I still had hidden in Sweet Jamaica was my emergency identity kit.

It was not wise to keep that in my bigger apartment. I decided to rent a safe deposit box at a bank. It didn't offer twenty-four-hour access, but it was a risk worth taking. It would be much cheaper than paying rent on Sweet Jamaica, which I would give up at the end of February. I would also give up the bigger apartment as soon as I could find another one. Eric, the guy renting the bigger apartment to me, probably knew or suspected that I was a drug dealer. I paid cash, and well above market rate. It would be not only cheaper, but also safer to live somewhere else.

[5/5]

My last workday as a drug dealer was Friday, February twenty-sixth. I had only five packages left. Two were for Peter and the rest for three other clients. From nine to twelve I saw those three clients on Wall Street. I then walked to a restaurant halfway to the World Trade Center, where Peter worked. His appointment was at two in the afternoon.

During lunch I could hear sirens outside. Whatever was going on was bad, because the sirens didn't stop. When the waiter brought me the check, he said that there had been an explosion at the World Trade Center. A bomb had gone off in the north tower. That was where Peter worked.

I walked the few blocks to the World Trade Center. It was pandemonium. Police, firefighters, and ambulances, just like after the shooting in Texas. The police had blocked access to the area, so I couldn't get close. The many cops made me nervous. I still had Peter's cocaine in my briefcase.

Suddenly fear started to overcome me. My heart started beating fast, and I had a difficult time breathing: all the symptoms of an anxiety attack. I had to get out of there, go home, and try to stop it, like Dr. Clark had taught me. If nothing worked, I would take an anti-anxiety pill. I walked as fast as I could to the subway.

When I got home I took a hot bath and did breathing exercises. It helped, but my heart was still beating quicker than usual when I finished, so I went out and jogged for almost an hour. I was still nervous when I finished, but at least the panic was gone.

At around six I turned on the TV for the news. The blast had happened in the garage. It was probably a terrorist attack, but no one knew yet who was behind it. A few people had died in the garage, but nobody else in the tower was hurt. They had to evacuate the whole tower, around 50,000 people.

The building would certainly be full of cops in the next days. No way was I going back there carrying cocaine for Peter. I had tried to bring him his cocaine but, as Douglas would say, fate had stopped me.

I was supposed to have quit the drug-dealing business by that time Friday evening. I had already burned all business cards and the address and appointment books. There was no reason to change my plan. I took those two last packages to the bathroom, opened them, and flushed the cocaine down the toilet. I then burned the packaging. I took a hammer and smashed the old work pager into small pieces. The last vestiges of drug dealing were gone.

All that activity made me feel better. At any rate my heart wasn't pounding anymore, and I could breathe easily again. Could it be that I had mastered an anxiety attack? I had to wait for the night to be really sure. Mom could still be out there, waiting for me with her machine guns. I cooked dinner and watched a movie on my VCR. At around ten I smoked a joint and went to bed.

* * *

I did have a nightmare that night, but it was different from the previous ones.

I was outside the World Trade Center, with cops and firefighters around me. Suddenly Peter came out of nowhere, screaming, "Where's my cocaine, Birdy? Where is it?"

I tried to make him shut up. "Be quiet! There are cops everywhere!"

Peter screamed to the cops, "Arrest him! He stole my cocaine!" One cop started frisking me. I was shitting my pants in fear. Peter screamed, "It's in the briefcase, officer! Inside the false bottom!"

The cop opened the false bottom. It was empty. "There's nothing here," he said.

Peter got mad. "Where's my cocaine, Birdy? Did you sniff it, asshole?"

I smiled and said, "No, I flushed it down the toilet! You're fucked, dopehead!"

Peter grabbed a gun from a policeman and cried, "I'm going to kill you, Birdy!" I ran for my life, with Peter right behind me. I could hear him screaming, "I'll kill you!" Then he started shooting. That was when I woke up, at two in the morning.

Shit, it had happened again. But I wasn't bathed in sweat this time. It wasn't Mom shooting. And I wasn't wearing my dirty underwear. That was somehow progress. Could it be that I just had an ordinary nightmare? I'd have to ask Paul about that.

The phone rang, scaring me to death. My first thought was, "That's Peter looking for his cocaine." But it wasn't possible. He didn't have the number. Catherine was the only client I ever gave it to, and she didn't know Peter. I picked it up.

"Pablo, man, sorry for waking you up."

"Douglas! It's all right. I was awake. Just had a nightmare."

"Because of the bomb? I heard about it at breakfast. That's why I'm calling. Peter works in the north tower, right?"

"Yes, and I was on my way to see him! Can you belive it? But I couldn't get through. The place was packed with police and firefighters. Why does this kind of shit always happen when I'm around, Douglas?"

"Fate?"

I sighed. He made no comment.

"Don't give me the fate crap now, Douglas! I just had a nightmare. And this afternoon I had an anxiety attack. Do you know what this means? I'm not cured yet. I need more therapy. It'll never end!"

"Listen, Pablo, I have nightmares myself now and then. It's normal. How's the business?"

"It's over, man. Today I had my last clients. Peter was supposed to be the very last one. I've sold everything. I'm clean now."

"Great! So when are you coming?"

That wasn't the conversation I wanted to have right after waking up from a nightmare. It wasn't the right time to tell him the truth. But would there ever be a good moment for that?

"Are you still there, Pablo?"

"Yeah, sorry. Listen, man, I have something to tell you. You won't like it."

"Yes..."

"I'm not coming. I'm staying right here until I finish my therapy. Otherwise I'll take this shit with me wherever I go. I'm sick and tired of it."

"You're not quitting the business, Pablo?"

"Of course I'm quitting drug dealing! Just told you so. I'll never deal again. But I'm not coming to Europe."

"You can do therapy here."

"Yes, but then I can't travel around, can I? If I have to be grounded somewhere, I'd rather be grounded here."

He sighed. "I can see your point. Well, if that's what you want..." He sounded very disappointed.

I tried to say something cheerful. "I have more news for you. I'll be a real coach, Douglas!"

"You what?"

"A real PSMT. Like with Joe's boss and the three other clients. I'm building on that. I already have sixteen clients booked for March. I take back what I said back then when I was forced to do it. It's not a crazy idea; it's a very clever idea. Five hundred dollars per session! What about that? "

He laughed. "Holy shit! That's ingenious! The best solution

ever! And you don't believe in fucking fate, Pablo."

"What does fate have to do with it?"

"Fate gave us an opportunity on a silver tray. When Joe told me about his troubles, I had this gut feeling that we should try it. Especially when you agreed so quickly."

"Give me a break, Douglas. You mean that you knew back then that I'd become a coach now?"

"Of course not! But I had the feeling that it was an opportunity, not a problem. Intuition, man. You probably felt it, too."

"Yeah, right!"

"Pablo, man, stop denying that you have intuition. It was your intuition that brought you to this solution! Or was it one of your educated guesses?"

I didn't want to start an argument. I was so glad that he wasn't mad at me.

"You're probably right. I'm so relieved now that I've finally told you. I was so afraid that you'd be mad. Thanks, Douglas!"

"I have to thank you, man! Now I'm finally free to enjoy my trip. I was so fucking afraid you'd do something stupid like finding a new supplier."

"Never! But you were right about the hiding thing. I know that I'm still hiding behind the PSMT legend. But I'll be a man and do something about it. I'll work on that with my therapist. I've told him everything about me. Now we're having sessions twice a week."

He whistled. "No shit! I'm proud of you, Pablo."

It was very nice to hear that.

"Listen, Joe was very sad to hear that you're dead. I felt sorry lying to him."

"You didn't lie, Pablo. That guy Chris is really dead. Joe never knew the real Douglas."

"You're right... How's Françoise?"

"No idea. It didn't work out. I'm in London now."

He told me about his adventures in Paris and what he was planning to do in London. It was three in the morning when he hung up. I put on one of my new Marley CDs and listened to the music until I fell asleep. No more nightmares that night. Yes, I had my post-traumatic stress disorder under control. On Monday I called Dr. Clark to thank him. I owed him that.

[5/6]

March was a pleasant month; no more drugs in my briefcase, no need to fear cops or drug dealers. I was only a coach with sixteen clients and a lot of free time. I could concentrate on my therapy, which was progressing slowly. Childhood and family stuff.

Mom and Dad married in 1952. Mom was very young, only seventeen, while Dad was twenty-eight. The first child came one year later. It was a boy, and he got Dad's name, Pedro. He would run our business empire. After him Mom had four other children, one every two years. Diego, the second son, was born in 1955. He would be Pedro Junior's right hand. After that, two girls; the first daughter, Manuela, in 1957, and the second, Juanita, in 1959. Then another son, Santiago, in 1961.

There was a five-year gap, and I was born in 1966. Mom was thirty-one and Dad forty-two. Unplanned pregnancy? Possible, but difficult to know for sure. If my parents had been serious about family planning, they would have stopped after Manuela. Two sons, an heir and a spare, plus a girl to round things up: mission accomplished.

Juanita was already one child too many. She never really belonged. Manuela bullied her all the time and made the boys do the same. No wonder Juanita married so early. It was her ticket out. Santiago didn't fare much better. He tried to be one of the boys but was never accepted by Pedro Junior and Diego, who by the way weren't interested in me, either. The age difference was too big. Manuela tolerated Santiago but was always mean to me.

Pedro Junior, Diego, and Manuela always treated me as if I wasn't part of the family. They used to tease me all the time, saying that I was adopted. Santiago played along. I could get along only with Juanita, but not for very long. I was twelve when she married.

From what Winston had told me, his childhood wasn't much better. No need to mention Douglas's. It was the same everywhere I looked. Mine was a dysfunctional family like all others.

"How long do you want to listen to this crap, Paul?"

"I think we've had enough."

"Great. What did you find out? What happened back then that screwed me up?"

He smiled. "Your childhood is pretty average."

"So I have been wasting time telling you irrelevant stuff?"

"It's not only about what you tell me, but how you tell it."

"There you go again."

"Why don't you get angry when you tell your story?"

"Why should I waste my time getting angry at stuff I can't change?"

"It's not a natural reaction to control your anger when talking about this kind of memories. You should be angry. Where's your anger, Pablo? Did you get angry as a child?"

"Probably. I don't remember."

"I doubt you did. Little Pablo learned to hide his anger, didn't he? Why? What was he afraid of?"

"Maybe afraid of being beaten up?"

"Could be. But there's no one here right now to beat you up. Why don't you get angry now?"

"I don't know."

"You should get angry. Buy voodoo dolls for each family member and pin needles on them!"

I laughed. "Come on, Paul! You don't believe this shit, do you?"

"That you'll hurt them? Of course not. But it's not about them. It's about you. Letting your feelings out. If voodoo is too much for you, then pin their pictures on the wall and throw darts at them. One picture for each family member, except Juanita."

"That's ridiculous!"

"That's your homework."

"I thought that therapists were supposed to help people control their anger."

"Only if it gets out of hand. Too little is as bad as too much. Two sides of the same coin. But time's up. Go home and get angry."

I didn't have any pictures of my family, so I bought a few magazines, cut out pictures of people who looked like my parents and siblings, and pinned them to my office's wall. Instead of darts I did the homework with my tongue, cursing and abusing them verbally for days. I could finally tell them everything that I had always wanted to. It felt good. Paul was a genius.

* * *

And so weeks and months of therapy passed. I worked on my anger, my fear of relationships, my need to hide, my identity problem, my this, and my that. Besides therapy, there was work, coaching school, and social life. I had one-night stands and short affairs here and there, but only one woman at a time. I wasn't in the mood for multiple affairs.

After weekend coaching academy ended in March, I took an advanced week-long course in the third week of April. I liked it so much that I took two others, in May and in June. I was slowly getting the hang of the whole coaching thing. The clients were happy, and I had the impression that I was helping them. I reached forty-seven clients in July. Thirteen of them, Mathew included, had sessions every two weeks. That added up to sixty sessions in a month, bringing me $30,000. More than enough. It was a light workload, with four clients a day in three workweeks, and a whole week off. I had a waiting list again.

The only former client I saw regularly was Joe, about once a month. I had no guilty feelings anymore. My affair with Nancy was over, and the guy who Joe had known as Chris was really dead. I could talk about the "late Chris" without any remorse. The only subject we never talked about was women. We made a deal: I wouldn't talk about Nancy, and he wouldn't mention Catherine.

Whenever I went to one of the restaurants Douglas had taken me to, waiters who had known him always asked, "Where's Jason?" Even the informal banking guys sent him their greetings each time we met. I was still making more money than I could spend, and I wanted to keep it safe offshore.

One day José asked, "Hey, Andrew, where's Brian, man?" I knew that the question would come sooner or later, and I needed a credible answer to keep me safe. All informal bankers thought that I was only a straw man for Douglas. That was good. Douglas had a reputation, and José and the other bankers would think twice before crossing him. I couldn't say that Douglas had left the business. But if he was still around, how was he wiring his money offshore? I came up with a pretty good lie.

"Brian's fine. He sends his greetings."

"I haven't seen him in months."

"To your own protection, José. Remember those bodyguards Brian brought along with him?"

"Scary motherfuckers! Never met them personally, but always saw them on the screen." He pointed to a monitor on his desk connected to the surveillance cameras inside and outside the office.

"One of them got arrested in January. Brian fears that he made a deal with the cops and told them about his movements. So he stopped going anywhere he had been with that guy. That includes all your offices. You have many, but it's no problem for the cops to have all addresses watched. They know exactly what to look for: a very tall black guy with bodyguards."

"But why didn't he tell me?"

"What were you going to do? Get new offices? Don't worry too much about it. He'll be back when he feels safe again."

"But how's he moving the money out now?"

"Come on, José! Do you think he tells me this shit? I'm still here doing my job, ain't I?"

"But much smaller amounts now."

"So that if I get caught, he won't lose much. I suspect that he has many others coming to you with small sums. Only they don't tell you that they are Brian's people. Any new clients lately?"

"We always have new clients. They come and go. But no transfers anymore to Brian's usual bank accounts. Has he opened new companies?"

"I don't want to know, José. Ignorance keeps me alive. That bodyguard I told you about? Two weeks after he was arrested someone cut his throat. Inside his cell."

"Oh, man, that hurts! I'd rather take a bullet. Let's change the subject. How much today?"

I told the same story to the two other bankers. They swallowed it as well. Douglas was gone, but his ghost was still protecting me.

* * *

In August I got a new apartment. One of my new clients was in real estate, and he got me a really cool place, much bigger than the old one, and for less money. I bought my own furniture and finally a good stereo. I also bought almost 1,500 CDs, replacing the records I had left behind in Stanford. I made a hole in the drywall to hide my cash savings and the marijuana Douglas had left me.

Douglas called from Italy sometime in October. He was in Rome but leaving for Morocco in a few days. The caveman's second birthday was coming soon, and he wasn't sure if he would be able to call from the desert. "Better early than never, Caveman. Happy birthday!"

Joe invited me for dinner to celebrate what he thought was my real birthday. October sixteenth was a Saturday in 1993. We went to the same restaurant as in the previous year. Joe was just out of rehab. He'd had serious heart problems in the summer, and had to quit cocaine for good. I was surprised to see how much weight he had lost. He looked healthier and happier. He was finally overcoming the fact that Nancy had quit her job in the early summer and moved to Connecticut to marry Mr. Right. That was what had caused his health problems; literally a broken heart.

I was invited to Nancy's wedding, but decided not to go. We talked on the phone a few times after we ended our relationship, but we really didn't have much to say to each other anymore. I didn't give her my new phone number and didn't ask for hers in Connecticut, either. So she was gone from my life.

I never saw Peter again, but once I bumped into Mrs. Jones early in the morning. She was probably on her way to work.

"Hi, Mrs. Jones! Remember me?"

She looked me in the eyes, clearly recognizing me, said, "No," and moved away. She and Peter really deserved each other.

[5/7]

One week after the caveman's second birthday I was invited to a party in a hotel. Client's birthday. After dinner I was watching the dance floor when I heard a voice behind me. "Happy birthday, Birdy!"

I turned around and found Susan, smiling at me. I felt so happy to see her, my heart started racing.

"Hi, Susan! Long time no see!"

"One year, right? Are you celebrating your birthday today?"

"No, it was last week. Today I'm only a guest."

"Oh, last week? I'd give you a kiss, but I'm not allowed to socialize with customers. Boss could be watching."

I hated her boss at that moment. I really wanted that kiss.

"How's life treating you, Susan?"

"Great! How about you? How did that relationship turn out?"

"Bad! But it's been over for a long time now. What about that boyfriend of yours?"

"He's gone, too. I'm single and much happier!"

The way she was smiling!

"When was that?"

"March."

"Why didn't you call then?"

"We didn't exchange phone numbers."

Yes, the most stupid thing I had ever done.

"You knew my address, Susan."

"We agreed to bump into each other someday, remember? Leave it to fate?"

I stood there, looking at her, completely stunned. I heard Marley again, "Is this love, is this love, is this love that I'm feeling?" This time I was sure that it was inside my head.

"Where's that black friend of yours?"

"Chris?"

"Yeah, Chris was his name. Is he coming later?"

"No, Chris is gone. He's left the country."

She stopped smiling. "Oh, that's really bad."

"Yeah, I really miss him."

"I believe you. But that's not what I meant."

"What then?"

She smiled again. "If he's not here, who's going to tell you to take me home with you?"

The second time she had used that line on me. This time I liked it even more.

"I guess I'll have to do it myself. When are you done?"

"My shift ends at two."

"I'll be waiting right here!"

* * *

I hadn't believed Nancy when she told me about falling in love at first sight. I would doubt until it happened to me, she said. Well, this wasn't first sight properly. Susan and I had spent a wonderful night together one year before. But my heart was beating now the same way it had with Catherine. That realization scared me. Catherine ended badly. I didn't need that shit again. But I remembered Paul. It might end someday, but it was worth trying, because between the beginning and the end there was the middle. And that middle could be really good. All I had to do was to stretch it for as long as I could.

I took her home that night, and she never left my life again. The more time we spent together, the better it got. She stayed over every weekend and many times during the week. My place was much closer to New York University than hers. It also gave us much more privacy. She shared an apartment in Queens with three other NYU students. Soon she had clothes in my closet, books on my desk, and personal objects all over the apartment. I loved it. What had I been missing all those years?

* * *

I had the impression that we were made for each other. We could talk about anything and everything, with the exception of my past. At first it was easy to avoid the subject. "I'll tell you that another day, Sue." But that day never came, and she started to get suspicious. What did I have to hide?

Shortly before Christmas we had a big fight. She caught me in a small lie and got really angry. I felt very bad because I didn't want to lie to her, but I couldn't tell her my story. We had been together for only two months. What if we broke up and she used that information against me? One call to the Feds and I'd be gone.

I decided to go for the twisted lie. "Listen, Sue, have you ever heard of witness protection programs? When people are given a new identity? I wasn't born Michael Edwards. That's my new identity. Michael has no past. That's why I don't talk about it."

"What's your real identity then?"

"I can't tell you! My life depends on no one knowing anything about my past."

"What have you done, Birdy?"

"Nothing! I'm a victim. My life is in danger. There's even a bounty on my head. Almost one million dollars."

That scared her. I felt sorry, but that was the truth.

"What about your family and friends?"

"I'll never see them again. It would be dangerous for me and for them."

"But they know that you have a new identity, right?"

"No. I just disappeared one day. They probably think that I'm dead."

She looked at me as if she considered me most despicable person in the world. "How could you do that to your parents?"

I sighed. My parents! Since when did they deserve any consideration?

"Listen, Sue, I didn't do anything bad. I'm the victim, okay?

I just want to stay alive. What's wrong with that?"

"You live a life of lies."

"I lie only about my past, and only because I have to. I didn't choose this, Sue. Why is it so hard to understand?"

She didn't answer. She sat down on the couch, still giving me the you're-such-a-bad-person look.

"Don't judge me, Sue. You don't have the right. What would you have done in my place?"

She sighed. "I don't know."

I sat close to her and took her hand.

"Listen, you have to trust me. The past is shit anyway. What we have here is real. The two of us. It's not a lie."

"Maybe, but it's scary. To know that you're hiding things from me. Forever."

"It's not forever. I might tell you someday. But not now."

She looked me in the eyes. "What if I don't like it when you tell me?"

I looked down. I didn't have the answer.

"You're not a criminal, are you, Birdy?"

How could I deny that without lying?

"Well, Sue, I had to break the law a few times until I got my new identity, but I'm clean now."

She gave me a sarcastic smile. "Now? And how dirty were you before you got clean?"

I closed my eyes. It was tempting to confess everything. I remembered Douglas warning me that sooner or later I would tell everything to the woman I was sleeping with. It was only a matter of time. The longer we stayed together, the harder it would be to resist. If it was bound to happen anyway, why not spare us the trouble and the agony? Why not tell everything now?

But it would be dangerous. I didn't really know her that well. Douglas popped up inside my head, "Don't be stupid, Pablo! Shut the fuck up." "But I really like her, man," I told him. "Still no reason to risk your brown ass," he answered.

Susan was looking at me, really angry, as if she could hear the conversation between Douglas and me going on inside my head. "How dirty, Birdy? You don't have to tell me the details. Just give me an idea."

"I dealt in drugs for a while. But I never killed anyone. Never raped anyone. Never shot anyone. Never hurt anyone." The moment I said that, I remembered the guy I assaulted inside the restroom. "Well, once I had a fight with a guy, and I beat him up really bad. But it was self-defense."

Another lie. A small one, but still a lie.

"And why did you have to do all this if the government was protecting you?"

Shit, I never said that the government had given me the new identity. But it was implied, wasn't it? A witness protection program was a government thing. I couldn't say that I did it myself.

I chose an ambiguous answer. "It took a long time to get the new identity. Until then I had to survive on my own. It was hell. Life on the streets is hard. If you knew my background, you'd be amazed that I'm still alive."

"I'd love to know your background. Why don't you tell me?"

I sighed.

"That was deep," she said.

I got angry. "I hate when people tell me that!"

"And I hate when people don't tell me what I need to know!"

"I'm sorry, Sue. I can't tell you anything about my past. I might do it someday, but I can't guarantee it either, so I won't even promise. I really like you. But if this situation is too much for you, I'll understand."

She looked at me, very sadly. "Are you saying we're splitting?"

"I hope not. But I won't tell you about my past. If you can live with it, fine. If not, well..."

She stood up. "I'm going for a walk. I have to think."

She came back two hours later and told me that she wanted to try to find a way to live with the problem. I asked her to move in with me. She could sublet her room in Queens in case we broke up. If we were living on borrowed time, I wanted to do it as intensely as possible.

"Aren't we moving too fast, Birdy?"

"Maybe. But my therapist always says that it's better to regret things you've done than things you haven't."

"How can you do therapy if you can't speak about your past?"

"Paul knows, Sue. I told him everything. He's helping me with that. A lot."

She hugged me. "Good to know that you're not alone with this burden."

After that we didn't talk about the issue anymore. But it never went away, the big elephant in the room called my secret past.

* * *

Susan had spent Thanksgiving with her family in Nebraska so that we could spend Christmas and New Year's together in New York. Paul and Betty Nelson invited us for Christmas Eve. Paul was very curious to meet Susan and Susan to meet Paul. They spent the whole evening talking to each other. Betty entertained me with her jokes. The Nelsons were becoming family to me.

New Year's Eve we were invited to a big party by one of my clients. We greeted 1994 with style. On January first we were still in bed when the phone rang at around noon. Susan got it.

"No, it's the right number. You're looking for Birdy, right?" She suddenly smiled. "I recognize your voice! Chris? Susan here. Remember me? Birdy's birthday party in 1992? Party service company?"

They talked like they were best friends. I wondered what Douglas was telling her, because she was laughing all the time. I could only hear her side.

"End of October... No, I did it myself. You weren't here to help... Not that uptight anymore..." Eventually she passed the phone to me. "Chris. From Cairo."

I didn't know what to call him. Douglas? Chris?

"What's up, man? Happy New Year!"

"Happy New Year, Pablo! Congratulations! Susan! Wow! I always knew she was the right one for you!"

"Your intuition, right?"

"Exactly!"

We talked for more than an hour. It was very expensive to call from Egypt, he said, but he was a multi-millionaire and could afford it. He told me about his travels in North Africa, riding camels in the desert and stuff. Now he was headed to Nigeria. Already one year on the road. It was taking longer than planned. He would need more than two years to finish his trip.

"But no one is waiting for me in Jamaica, Pablo. I can take my time. Any chances of seeing you? Why don't you take Susan on a trip abroad? We could meet in Asia in the summer."

"I'll think about it."

I would love to, but I was afraid of going through immigration and customs. Even for trips inside the country I avoided airports.

Too many security people. I felt safer and more relaxed driving. I took Susan on a car trip to Maine during spring break 1994. We liked it so much that we decided to spend four weeks there in the summer, followed by two weeks in New Hampshire with the Nelsons, who would be vacationing in Martha's Vineyard. Altogether, six weeks to recharge the batteries before she went to graduate school.

[5/8]

When we arrived in Maine in July 1994, we had been together for eight months, six of them living together under the same roof. I now trusted her enough to tell my story. It was a very difficult decision to make. What if my past was too much for her? What if she decided to leave me?

I spent many sessions with Paul talking about it. He made me see that waiting probably wouldn't change the outcome. He even quoted Shakespeare to me, that thing about the coward dying a thousand deaths and the brave dying only once. But a courageous death wasn't an option to me. I wanted to live happily with Susan.

Then Douglas called in June. He was in India and loving it. India was like heaven for an esoteric guy, with the whole meditation and good-energy stuff. All the fate and intuition he could eat. He was even learning yoga.

When I told him about my dilemma and my fears, he laughed and said, "You really don't trust life, do you? After everything that happened to you!"

"Could you talk to me in non-esoteric language?"

"Of course! You don't need to fear, Pablo. Nothing bad will happen. Fate has brought the two of you together. You're meant for each other. Is that clear now?"

I sighed and automatically regretted it. "Don't tell me that it was deep, Douglas."

"I don't need to, Pablo. You know it already."

I couldn't beat him in that game. That made me angry. "I've told you already that I don't believe the fate crap!"

He laughed. "Yeah, I remember. You believe in science. Quantum physics. Shit happening, leading to other shit, right?"

"Exactly!"

"All right, then. I'll give you the scientific version. That same quantum physics shit that put you and Winston together in that room, that put you inside that fast-food joint in Texas, that brought you to me: it also brought you and Susan together. What about that? Scientific enough for you?"

I sighed again. "All right, Douglas. Thanks for the advice."

"Thanks my ass! Listen to me, Pablo. Do you remember the story I told you about Marcia? The woman who left me because I was hiding?"

"Yes, I do."

"Well, man, I regret it to this day. Don't make the same mistake. Talk to Susan. Tell her everything. Stop hiding behind your fucking legends."

He was now talking in that annoying tone of voice he used each time he played the boss card. But he wasn't my boss anymore.

"I'm not hiding!"

"Whatever you call this thing you're doing right now, stop it. Tell Susan everything. She's the right woman for you. Marry her and have twenty kids. If you lose Susan, you'll regret it until you die. And I promise you one thing: I'll remind you of it every fucking day of your life. It will be hell!"

"Are you threatening me?"

"Yes, I am! Sorry, but I have to hang up now. Yoga starts soon. Take care!"

That settled the issue.

* * *

After Susan and I had been on the beach for about two weeks, totally relaxed and full of energy, I told her my story. At first she took it really well. I was relieved. But when she understood all the implications, she got scared. The government wasn't protecting me, but hunting me. There was no statute of limitations for murder. I could get arrested even ten or twenty years down the road. How could we build a future together? How could we raise a family?

I suggested that we emigrate. I was a coach, and she wanted to become a professor of philosophy. We could do that abroad. We had enough time to plan everything. She was starting her master's degree in the fall. She needed two years for that and would be finished in the summer of 1996. The PhD could be done abroad.

She didn't want to emigrate; she loved New York City. But it was either that or get used to the idea that any day I could get caught. We started analyzing possible emigration scenarios. Language proficiency was vital to our careers, so we had to move to an English-speaking country. Susan couldn't speak Spanish.

New Zealand was my favorite destination. It was warm and very far away. She hated the idea. Only sheep over there. She had left Nebraska for New York because she liked big cities. Her choice was London. Not my favorite city. I could live there for a few years, but not forever. She could do her PhD there, for example, and we'd move somewhere else afterwards.

She could do her PhD on a student visa. Unless we got married and I came with a spouse visa, I would need my own student visa. I could imagine doing a degree in psychology, but Michael Edwards had no school records, and I couldn't go to college without a high school diploma. Maybe Douglas's contact at the New York Department of Education could help me with that?

What if none of us could get a work permit after we concluded our studies? There was always Jamaica. Winston had the right connections; he would help us get a visa. Jamaica was close to America. We could come to New York whenever we wanted.

Would I be able to get coaching clients in our new country willing to pay me $500 for a session? I didn't want to be a poor immigrant. I had savings, but how long would the money last? In the past year and a half I had wired a quarter of a million dollars offshore. I could save much more if I worked full-time again. I wasn't doing anything productive with my free time anyway.

I could handle six sessions a day, three in the morning and three in the afternoon; 120 sessions per month, bringing $60,000. When Susan graduated in the summer of 1996, I could have two million dollars offshore.

Susan was surprised and a bit upset to hear me talking about that stuff. She knew that I made good money, but we never talked about the details.

"Five hundred dollars in forty-five minutes? Do you know how many hours I have to work to earn that kind of money? And I'm paid well above minimum wage at the party service."

"It can't be that much, or the clients wouldn't pay, Sue. I even have a waiting list. You could do it too, you know; it's not that difficult."

"Thanks, but I want to teach." She smiled. "So you'll have two million dollars when we leave? Unbelievable!"

"Enough to marry me?"

"Are you proposing?"

"Not yet. Just checking my chances."

"I might marry you someday, but not because of your money."

I laughed. "You don't need to fear that, Sue. The money is long gone."

She frowned. "You just said you had it offshore. Was that a joke? Are you fooling me?"

"Not talking about that money, Sue. I'm talking about the real money that I lost."

She looked pissed. "Which money? I thought you had told me the whole story. Have you being hiding the really bad stuff for the very end?"

I laughed again. "You know how cute you look when you make this face?"

"Don't stonewall!"

She looked even cuter now.

"Take it easy, Sue! I'm talking about my inheritance. Dad's fortune."

She looked relieved. "Sorry, Pablo. I forgot about your family. How many millions does your dad have?"

It was nice that Susan had started calling me Pablo. It felt good. I liked it much better than being called Birdy or Michael, even when she sounded pissed.

"Millions? You kidding me? Dad's worth a few billions! Difficult to tell how much exactly. Between three and five, I guess."

Her jaw dropped.

"It had to be divided by six children, but my share would be at least five hundred million. Half a billion dollars. What about that? But it's gone now. My siblings will inherit my share. You won't marry me because of my money, Sue."

When she could talk again, she asked, "What do you do with half a billion dollars?"

Only poor and middle class people asked that kind of question.

"Nothing. You just own it."

"You don't need it."

"Probably not. But it doesn't hurt, you know?"

"It's not a fair world! Some people are born rich. Others work their asses off but live and die in poverty. The wealth should be better distributed!"

I was used to that now. Susan was very left-wing, not a relationship Dad would approve of.

"Sue, find half a billion destitute people and give each of them one of those dollars. The money will be gone, but the people will remain destitute. Redistribution doesn't change anything."

She looked at me angrily. "Why don't you trade places with one of them?"

"Because I don't like poverty! I was poor for a few weeks, and I hated it. So I found a good-paying job. And if I could do it, anyone else can. This is the land of opportunity. You're American, right? You should believe in the vision thing."

She gave me the fuck-you look. That happened when we discussed politics. Not that I didn't agree with most of the stuff she said, but I liked to tease her. She hated the vision thing.

"How could your father get so rich? You can't amass this kind of money legally, can you?"

I laughed. "Dad has a license to be bad."

"A what?"

"When Douglas calls, ask him. He'll explain it to you."

"Tell me now!"

I explained Douglas's theory.

"He's right about that, Pablo. All criminals."

"Thanks, Sue."

* * *

The second half of our vacation in Maine wasn't always easy, but we both felt much better living with the truth. It was as if we could finally breathe. The two weeks we spent with the Nelsons in Martha's Vineyard were even better.

We returned to New York full of energy and hope, back to our routines. I had coaching clients and therapy sessions. Susan had graduate school and jobs on the side to complement her student loans and the money her parents sent her.

Only one thing broke our routine: getting news from Douglas. The fridge had no more places for postcards. I bought a world map, where I plotted his movement. He traveled around East Asia and Australia until Christmas 1994. He celebrated New Year's Eve twice, cruising the Pacific on a luxury ship. One day on one side of the International Date Line, the next day on the other side. "Decadent but cool," he told me later.

He got to Chile in January 1995 and covered Chile, Argentina, and Brazil until the end of March. He didn't go to Bolivia or Colombia. "No way I'll come close to the brown scum, Pablo." He moved directly to Central America in April. He called from Mexico in May, and we were expecting him in Jamaica sometime in June or July. Two and a half years on the road. Sometimes I envied him.

[5/9]

On Sunday, July second, the phone rang at about one in the afternoon. Susan and I were having brunch and trying to set our wedding date. I had planned to have that conversation on the beach. We were traveling to Maine the following day, where I was planning to propose. But sometimes plans failed, as I well knew.

We were packing together Saturday afternoon when Susan caught me hiding something in my suitcase. It was the engagement ring, but she thought that it was marijuana and started to make a big fuss about it.

Susan hated drugs, and I never smoked a joint when she was around. Douglas had always brought me more grass than I could smoke. When he left, I had a huge stockpile. Usually Paul and I smoked together after the Thursday therapy session. His office became the new Sweet Jamaica. Only the music was different; Paul preferred the Woodstock crowd: Joplin, Hendrix, etc.

Susan complained to Betty, hoping that Betty would stop us. But Betty was more relaxed about it. A guy thing, Betty told her. Susan should consider herself lucky. Many women had to put up with lots of guys in the living room watching ball games on television and making a lot of noise. Sweet Jamaica was much better. As long as there weren't any women involved, Susan shouldn't worry. Betty was a wise woman.

So we had a fight Saturday afternoon because of imaginary marijuana in my suitcase. Why would I bring grass, I asked, if I wouldn't have the opportunity to smoke it? We were always together, after all. But we were visiting the Nelsons on our way home. She accused me of planning to smoke joints with Paul once we got to Martha's Vineyard.

That made me angry. If she really believed that it was grass, she should get it and flush it down the toilet, I told her. She started searching. "In the white shirt's pocket," I said, to keep it short and stop her messing up my suitcase.

She found it quickly and blushed even quicker.

"The candlelight dinner is hidden in the other suitcase, in case you want to confiscate that too," I said, still angry.

She apologized long and hard. Couldn't we just forget everything? Pretend it never happened? I agreed, for lack of alternatives. But the genie was out of the bottle.

For that reason we were discussing the wedding date over brunch, even though I hadn't officially proposed yet. I wanted October sixteenth, the caveman's fourth birthday. It was a Monday in 1995. I had learned to cherish that day. Had I not been inside that restaurant, the caveman would never have come to my rescue. I would certainly have been arrested or killed.

Susan hated the suggestion. A Monday. And in three months? Not enough time to plan. When the phone rang, I was arguing for having a simple ceremony with only a few guests on that date, and throwing a big party in the spring. I saw a Jamaican number on the display and smiled. Finally!

"Douglas!"

"Pablo, my man, what's up? How's Susan?"

"Fine! She's here. How are you doing? How does it feel to come home after all this time?"

"Yeah, how do you feel about it?"

We both laughed.

"Have you finally found out what you're going to do with your life, Douglas?"

"I guess so. But we can talk about it later. Do you have a speakerphone?"

"Yes. Why?"

"Turn it on. Susan should listen, too."

"It's on now."

"Hi, Susan! What's up?"

"Hi, Douglas! Nice to hear you! When are you coming over here?"

"I don't know. Why? Do you need me there to tell Pablo to marry you?"

"No, he'll do it himself."

"How can you be sure?"

She blushed. I thought, you deserve it, honey.

"Tell him it's your intuition, Sue. Douglas believes this kind of crap."

Douglas laughed. "My educated guess is that you're pissed off, Pablo. Why?"

"Never mind, man. Let's talk about you. How long have you been there?"

"Changing the subject?"

Susan laughed.

"Recognize the pattern, Susan?" Douglas asked.

She smiled and answered, "Yes."

"He does it all the time, doesn't he? He sighs deeply and bang! He's gone!"

She laughed again. I was getting upset. My best friend and my future wife united against me.

"Don't let this trick irritate you, Susan. Stay on the subject! Like I'll do right now. So, Pablo, you told me that you guys were going to get married before you left the country. What are you waiting for?"

"I'm ready, man. I'd love to get married on the caveman's birthday, but Sue won't do it because it's a Monday."

"It's just too soon," she protested.

"The caveman's birthday? It's a great date! It's the day you guys first met, right?"

I had completely overlooked that fact.

"Yes! One more reason, Douglas. Thanks," I said, looking triumphantly at her. "There are many other good reasons as well."

"I don't see the point of hurrying things," she protested.

"You should do it before he changes his mind," Douglas said.

I gave her the victor's smile. Susan hated to lose an argument. She was now pissed. I could see that something bad was coming.

"Yes, Douglas, he can't wait to have a married woman around him again. He has this thing for married women, you know? Has he ever told you about Catherine?"

That was mean. Like Douglas, Susan always threw stuff back at me at the worst possible moment. She gave me a smile, meaning, what about that, honey?

I smiled back. I could be mean, too. "Sorry, but I like them much older, Sue. You're not there yet!"

She gave me the fuck-you look. Douglas laughed. I could

hear a man laughing on his side of the line. Who was that?

"You guys were really made for each other," Douglas said. "Are you going to Maine again this year?"

"Yes, we're leaving tomorrow," Susan answered.

"Changing the subject, Douglas?" I asked, tongue in cheek.

He ignored my comment. "So I was lucky to call today. Fate is on our side this time. There's someone here who's dying to talk to you, Pablo. I'm on the speakerphone, too. He's listened to everything."

Winston! That was dangerous! "Listen, Douglas, this line is not safe!"

"Don't worry, Pablo. It's over. You don't have to fear anymore. You're clean now."

"Now, yes. But there's still that thing in the past, remember?"

"I'm talking about the past. It's over! But I'll let Winston explain. He was afraid that you'd hang up if he called directly."

"Pablo, man, finally!" Winston said. "I've been looking for you for ages!"

It was good to hear his voice again. I hadn't talked to Winston in almost four years.

"I had to hide, Winston. Sorry."

"I know. But it's over now. I have good news for you: there's no one out there looking for you anymore! All charges were dropped! Even those two bounties on your head are gone!"

"Is this one of your jokes, Winston?"

"It's true, Pablo! It's over! Over!"

I froze. I felt dizzy and couldn't breathe well. My heart started beating fast. My hands started shaking. All of a sudden I had a flashback. I saw myself inside the fast-food joint in Texas, lying on the floor behind John's dead body, listening to the shots and the screams. It was a very vivid recollection. Dr. Clark once told me that sometimes anxiety attacks included flashbacks, but I had never had one before. I was scared.

Winston kept talking, but I could hardly follow.

"...hired private detectives. They tracked down one of the killers, who confessed everything and identified the other two. Then we..."

Another flashback. I was in my apartment in Stanford, watching the three delivery guys getting killed, blood coming out of their heads and flesh wounds.

"...who was hiding in Mexico. We had him kidnapped and brought to America. We delivered the three to the police. The guys were small fish and made a deal with the cops to..."

I looked at Susan. She was beaming with joy, too happy to notice what was going on with me. Now my whole body was shaking, like I was receiving an electric shock.

"...got the Mexican behind the whole operation, the one using your identity. The case was completely solved and all charges against you were dropped..."

Then it happened. It was like a volcano erupting. I burst out in tears and couldn't stop crying. My body was shaking so much that I had to sit down on the couch. Susan was talking to me, but I couldn't understand a word. All I could do was cry.

* * *

Later Susan told me that I cried for almost an hour. I was so exhausted afterwards that I fell asleep on the couch. My breakdown scared the daylights out of her. She called Paul, who told her to let me cry. I had to get it out of my system. She begged him to come by. Paul told me later that he was more worried about Susan than about me. She was freaking out on the phone.

The Jamaicans called again while I was sleeping. Susan told them what happened, got their phone numbers, and promised to call back some time in the next days.

I woke up at around four in the afternoon, and Paul was there. I told him about the flashbacks, the increased heartbeat, the breathing problems, the shaking, and the unstoppable crying. I asked if I should worry. He answered that no reaction would have been the worst kind of reaction. We could talk about everything later. Now I had to rest.

[5/10]

We drove up to Maine the following day and spent three weeks there. The first week was the hardest. I was in denial. I kept asking myself, why now? Why should my past come back when I had finally left everything behind? Susan and I were going to leave America for good in one year. Start a new life. Build a future. The past was dead and buried. If only I could forget that phone call and carry on as before...

Susan couldn't understand my lack of enthusiasm.

"It's great, Pablo! You'll have your life back!"

"I don't want that life back, Sue. I'm happy as I am right now. I like being Birdy the PSMT."

"You don't have to stop that. I'm talking about the future. We don't have to emigrate anymore. We can build our lives in New York. On a solid basis and without any fears. That's wonderful!"

"Yes, we can stay. That's great. If no one is looking for me anymore, then there's no danger. I can carry on as Michael Edwards."

"Michael Edwards is fiction, Pablo. He has no past and no history. What are you going to tell your children about your past? Will you lie to them?"

"What would we have done if Winston hadn't been successful? We would have carried on with our plan, wouldn't we?"

"But he was successful! You can't ignore that. The situation has completely changed. You have to face it, Pablo!"

* * *

I called Paul on Tuesday evening, at the time we usually met for therapy.

"You told me many times that you wanted to stop hiding, Pablo. It's your chance to come out of the closet and finally be who you are. Go for it!"

"But if I choose Pablo, I'll lose Birdy!"

"No, you won't! Birdy is the Pablo you always wanted to be. You just never noticed it. Birdy is just another name for you."

* * *

I called Douglas two days later.

"Pablo, remember Marley's song 'No Woman No Cry'?"

"What about it?"

"As Marley says, in this great future you can't forget your past."

"I never did. I just want to leave it behind."

"You can't. You're brown, man. Latin American. Multimillionaire. You have fucked-up parents. You had a shitty childhood. Your past is part of you. That's who you are. You should be proud of it!"

"I don't see any reason to be proud of that shit!"

"You overcame it, Pablo! You survived. You grew up. Your past is like a badge of honor."

"Are you proud of your past?"

"Yes, Pablo! Very proud of it. Life dealt me a very crappy hand of cards, and I made the best of it."

"Despite all the bad things that you had to do? Killing people indirectly and stuff?"

"I did what I had to do. I'm very proud of my past. You should be proud of yours as well."

* * *

When I told Susan at the end of the week that I had made up my mind and decided to go back to being Pablo, she was very happy.

"Great! I'll marry the real Pablo. I never liked the idea of marrying Michael Edwards."

"Don't get carried away, Sue. I haven't proposed yet."

"You'd better hurry up before I change my mind."

"No need to worry, Sue. Pablo has a lot of money. Half a billion. You'll do it for the money!"

"Is that what you think?"

"Absolutely."

"If that's the case, be warned: I won't sign any premarital agreement. If you divorce me, I'll take half of your money and give it to the poor."

"That would only kill Dad, Sue. You'd have to give the money to poor black people. That would kill both Mom and Dad."

* * *

The rest of the time we spent making plans for the future. My past was completely clean, but not my present, as Winston reminded me when I called him. Living under a fake identity was a crime. If I came clean and confessed everything, his lawyers would take care of the rest. I didn't need to fear any consequences, he said. There were many extenuating circumstances. When I heard that, I remembered Douglas telling me angrily that there were no extenuating circumstances and it made no difference if things were premeditated or not. I promised Winston to think about it and invited him to come to New York in the last week of July.

No way would I confess anything. Why open that can of worms? There would be questions. I didn't want to tell the Feds about the drug dealing. It would lead to Douglas and the clients. Why should I implicate them? And what would be the price to come clean? Only giving back the identity kits I had? What if they requested the ill-gotten money? I had one and a half million hidden offshore. I didn't want to give it back. I had earned it. Acting classes, coaching academy, putting up with people like Peter the bore, constantly watching my back, scary informal banking, drug wars, nightmares: I had earned every cent of it, and I was going to keep it.

I came up with a better plan: Michael Edwards would leave the country and never return. Susan would take one year off from graduate school and we would travel abroad. I would leave the United States using Michael's passport, and come back one year later as Pablo. By then most traces of Michael would be gone.

Before we went back to New York to meet Winston, Susan and I finally had that candlelit dinner. I proposed, and she accepted.

* * *

It was fun to talk to Winston again. He was surprised to hear about my plan, but he had to respect my wishes, he said. Now I was street smart; not the baby-faced Pablo anymore.

He told me the complete story of how he and Dad had cleared my name. Without Dad it wouldn't have been possible. Lawyers and private detectives alone couldn't do it. We needed inside information on the case that only the Feds had. Someone had to convince them to share that information with us. Dad had a lot of connections at very high places in America. A lot of people at the U.S. State Department knew Dad well. He had wined and dined every American ambassador in the past three decades. That helped a lot.

When I was finally clean in the fall of 1992, Winston started looking for Douglas. But Douglas left the country shortly after that. If only he had stayed a little longer.

"But how did you know that I was in New York, Winston?"

"Educated guess. Where else could you be? Douglas was the only guy you could go to. It was safe. None of your other friends knew about him. He was a hard guy to find, but we'd done this together once. And Douglas stopped calling soon after you disappeared. It couldn't be a coincidence."

Yes, that was my good old friend Winston: a smart and rational person. Educated guesses, no intuition shit. He updated me on his life. He was engaged and going to get married in December. His fiancée was named Alicia. She had finished medical school and was training to become a pediatrician.

Then he updated me on my family. A lot had changed. Some news was very difficult to believe. Dad and Mom had separated, after so many years! Juanita had divorced and remarried. Santiago's alcohol problem had become worse. He practically drank all day.

After I disappeared, Dad finally did what he had been saying for years that he would do someday, but never had the guts to: he retired. He let Pedro Junior and Diego run our conglomerate and take over the political activities. Dad dedicated all his time to searching for me. There was a lot of waiting involved, so he finally bought a luxury yacht for sport fishing, another thing he had talked about and postponed doing for years. He started cruising the Caribbean Sea, and made Kingston one of his ports of call since he had to see Winston regularly to plan their next moves.

He took Winston and his father William for a fishing cruise in the spring of 1993, and William loved it. The next time the two old men went alone. They liked it even more without Winston. Our dads hooked up very quickly. Two guys with similar personalities: both extremely rich, powerful, and bossy. William was a self-made billionaire. Dad didn't start from zero like William, having inherited a few millions from Grandpa, but he multiplied those millions many times over. Both didn't have wives anymore. Dad was separated. William was a widower. Winston's mother had died of cancer back in the eighties when we were still attending Columbia. They were now cruising the Caribbean Sea together many times a year. Pedro and William, best buddies.

Susan and Winston got along well. The only thing she didn't like was when we decided to revive Sweet Jamaica for one evening in Paul's office, shortly before the Nelsons left for New Hampshire. This time Paul had to put up with Marley.

Before Winston went back to Jamaica, he rented storage space in New Jersey in the name of the American subsidiary of one of his companies. We would need that for our stuff.

* * *

In the beginning of August, we went to New Hampshire. I had a lot of stuff to discuss with Paul before I left the country. He strongly advised me to face my family, especially Dad. Washing the dirty laundry was never pleasant, but I'd feel much better afterwards. I had learned to trust Paul's advice and decided to do it.

In the second half of August we staged Michael's emigration. We moved the furniture and everything else we had into storage, and I terminated the lease on my apartment. I closed my bank account and cancelled credit cards, gym membership, health insurance, magazine subscriptions, everything. If no one was owed money, no one would go looking for Michael Edwards after he disappeared.

My clients knew me only as Birdy, so I didn't need to get rid of them for good. I told them that my father lived abroad. He was now very sick, and I had to spend time with him, up to one year. About a quarter of them agreed to pause coaching and wait. The rest couldn't or didn't want to, but that didn't bother me. The clients I could keep would recommend me to many others in the future.

Susan and I left New York on a flight to Nassau in the Bahamas on Monday, September fourth, 1995. Winston had set up a BVI offshore company in his name and opened a bank account for it on the Cayman Islands. To that account I transferred all the money that I had in the three Caribbean jurisdictions. After that I closed the accounts and the offshore companies. We had to fly from island to island until everything was taken care of. Susan was outraged to see how big the offshore industry was. All criminals, she kept saying. We had a few arguments. But the beaches were nice, and all in all we had a good time.

* * *

After one week we went to Jamaica. I flew out as Anthony Harris, wearing my nerdy glasses. Officially Michael Edwards never left the Bahamas. It was great to see Douglas again after two and a half years. He told me about his career plans. He was rich now, having amassed more than ten million dollars. He didn't need to work for money anymore, but he needed an occupation. The only thing he really knew about was drug dealing, so he would use his experience to help rehabilitate small drug dealers; support them in prison, help them get a job when they got out, give their children a good education, and so on.

When Winston and William heard about Douglas's plans, they offered help. Many of the guys Douglas wanted to rehabilitate came from Trench Town. William wanted to give something back to the community where he had been born and raised. He set up a foundation and let Douglas run it. Startup capital was fifty million dollars, enough money to make a real difference. The foundation was named after Douglas's late father.

Douglas was very happy with the new life he was about to start; finally the chance to do good. He had lost a lot of guys in his ten years in the business, and was never able to help them. "Big fish like you and me almost never get caught, Pablo. Usually only foot soldiers get arrested." He couldn't make amends to his former foot soldiers, but he could help others.

"Doing some justice and working on my bad karma, Pablo."

"Come on, you don't believe this bad karma shit, do you?"

"Karma is a motherfucker. What goes around comes around."

I laughed. "If so, what about the guys you killed indirectly? How can you make up for that?"

"I don't know yet. Maybe you can help? What are you going to do about yours? When you figure it out, please let me know."

I wasn't going to start that discussion. "Hey, now you have a license to be good! How does it feel being the good guy, Douglas?"

"Very good. I miss my gun, though. I can't shoot you now for changing the subject."

* * *

Dad came to Jamaica one week after us. I had requested to meet him alone and on neutral territory. We stayed in Winston's beach house. Dad and I took long walks on the beach, talking about the past. We started slowly, clearing the minor problems first and moving gradually to the major issues, until I could tell him everything I had ever wanted to.

The really painful stuff I told him one evening after dinner. We were sitting alone in the living room; Susan had gone out with Alicia and Winston. Dad listened in silence, not even trying to defend himself. He recognized his mistakes and asked for forgiveness. That really hit me. I couldn't believe it. He had never before admitted any mistake. He had never before apologized, not even for the marble story. What had happened to him?

I told Dad that I needed time to forgive him. He said that he was seventy-one, and still had a few years to live. But he would like to be forgiven before he died. Could he expect that? When I heard that, I broke down crying. So did he. We cried for a long time, sitting far apart from each other in the living room. I couldn't bring myself to get up, go over, and hug him.

After that, things started to get better.

Dad explained why he and Mom had split. He had thought about leaving her many times, he said, but had never had the guts to. When I disappeared, he was devastated. Mom kept blaming him. He had sent me to America; he had agreed to Columbia; he had kept me there even when they found out that I was hanging out with blacks. It was his fault that I had turned bad. He never really believed that I had done it, but he felt guilty anyway. Mom was right: America had been his idea from the very beginning.

Winston was the only other person who also believed that I was innocent. When he made contact and told Dad about his plans to help me, Dad immediately invited Winston to come to our house to explain to the family what he had in mind.

Mom flipped out when she heard that Winston was coming. She had gone through so much already. Her son had become a criminal. What a shame! Everyone in town knew it and talked about it behind her back. She didn't need to be humiliated even more by having black people as guests. Once had been enough.

Winston came anyway. Dad put him up in one of our five-star hotels and brought Winston home for dinner to explain his plan. Dad insisted that Pedro Junior and Diego attend the meeting, but they came with very long faces. Like Mom, they didn't want to dine with a black guy.

Winston talked about hiring the best private detectives and lawyers that money could buy. He had already screened many investigative services companies and law firms, and made a short list of the best ones. He would hire them and control their work. The family didn't need to bother with that. But he needed Dad's help on the political side.

My brothers asked how much the operation would cost. Winston answered that he had no idea; a few million for sure. The retainer fees for the firms involved would add up to half a million dollars. Nobody could tell how many weeks of work that would cover. My brothers were outraged. Pedro Junior accused Winston of trying to rip the family off. The whole idea was a scheme to embezzle Dad's money. Winston could fool Dad but not the rest of the family.

Winston stood up to leave while Dad tried to calm everyone down. Talking in Spanish, he said that Winston was as rich as we were. He didn't need to rip anyone off. He was a good friend of mine and was only trying to help. Mom said that I had so many white friends in America. Why ask a black one for help? Black friends were the reason I had gone bad. That was the last sentence Winston heard before he left the room. His Spanish had improved a lot since his first visit, and he could understand everything.

Dad ran after him and apologized many times. He took Winston back to the hotel and continued the meeting there. Dad insisted on paying for everything. Winston, really pissed off, declined. He needed only political help. Only for that reason would he agree to work with Dad. But only the two of them. He didn't want to see the rest of the family ever again.

That incident was the straw that broke the camel's back. Dad was so furious that he didn't return home that night. He spent the night in the same hotel as Winston. The next day he drove Winston to the airport. He was still very mad at Mom, so he went to the beach house. The longer he stayed there, the less he wanted to go back to Mom. He never did.

Dad's estimate was that Winston spent at least five million dollars to clear my name. Winston never talked with Dad about money, but he once let it slip that kidnapping the killer in Mexico alone had cost one and a half million.

* * *

At the end of September, Dad, Susan, and I left Jamaica on the yacht. We cruised for a few days, and Susan loved it. I teased her a lot. "I always knew that you'd love having money, Sue. All left-wing people do." Those days at sea were a very good opportunity for Susan and Dad to get to know each other. Dad liked Susan from the beginning, despite her being left-wing. They had a few heated political arguments on the boat, but he was always respectful and polite. It was fun to watch them arguing. A Red in the family! Fate? I had to think about Douglas all the time.

[5/11]

It was a very difficult homecoming. My last trip home had been in the summer of 1991. I hadn't seen my family in four years. I had changed, and so had Dad, but the rest of the family was still the same.

Mom was angry at me because I saw Dad first and spent so much time with him. In Jamaica! Now Dad was also hanging out with black people. He did it on purpose, she said, only to embarrass her and stain her reputation. Whenever the Jamaicans were in town, Dad took them everywhere: to the finest restaurants, the country club, the yacht club. The whole family suffered because of that. Pedro Junior once had a very important business lunch in the country club's restaurant when Dad showed up with William, to everybody's embarrassment. Pedro Junior had to tell his business partner that Dad was getting senile, which he probably was. How else could one explain his behavior?

Mom told us everything about her ordeal. What a terrible time she had when everybody thought that I was a criminal. People started avoiding her. She had to cancel her winter salon evenings because nobody came anymore. She got no invitations to parties, either. A terrible year. And why didn't I come back after the problem was solved? That black friend of mine, meaning Winston, had said that I was hiding, fearing for my life, and that I would show up when there was no more danger. Dad believed him and spent millions of dollars to clear my name, but I never showed up. Never had the decency to express my gratitude. I told her that Winston had paid for everything, but she didn't believe me.

Mom didn't like Susan, especially the idea that we were going to get married soon. Why didn't I choose a Latino girl, Spanish speaking and Catholic? Well, at least she wasn't black. God was merciful, she said. He took that cup of suffering away from her. Her worst nightmare was to have black grandchildren.

Mom wanted to make a big celebration in our house, inviting everyone in town to greet the prodigal son. I told her that I would like to invite Douglas and Winston, and Mom made a huge scene. How could I invite black people to our house? Shame on me. If my friends weren't welcome, I wouldn't come either, I protested. Typical me, she said, always selfish, never thinking about the family. What would people say? I told her I didn't care. She gave up the idea and went for a family dinner instead.

Dad sat as his place as if he had never left, Mom at his side like they were still happily married and not separated. Weird thing. The only people happy to see me were Juanita and her kids. She brought along her new husband. He seemed much nicer than the first one. I was happy for her. Mom didn't exchange a word with the poor guy the whole evening. Juanita's divorce was a big shame for the family, she had told me a few days before.

Pedro Junior, Diego, Manuela, and their families treated me as they always did: with indifference. Santiago got really drunk. Nice family dinner. Susan was glad when it was over. Like most people, she also had a dysfunctional family, but mine topped everything, she told me afterwards.

* * *

On the Monday before the caveman's birthday, I went to a barbershop and had my hair cut and my beard shaved. In the afternoon I had pictures taken for my new passport. I applied for it on Tuesday, and Dad made sure that I got it on Friday. I needed my real identity back before I could get rid of the fake ones.

October sixteenth, the caveman's fourth birthday, was the perfect day to say goodbye to my fake identities. I went with Susan to the beach in front of our house, where I burned the two identity kits. Michael Edwards and Anthony Harris were gone forever. Now I was only Pablo. No more hiding. Ever again.

Two days later Susan and I left for Europe. Before we left, I told Dad that I didn't want to inherit shares in his conglomerate and stay in business with my siblings. I asked him to divide his fortune before he died and to give me my share in cash. He understood my reasons and agreed to do it.

While Susan and I were away, he asked his auditors for a fair valuation of his fortune. They came up with four billion two hundred million dollars. The conglomerate alone was worth two and a half billion. The rest was invested in financial assets and property at home, in America, and offshore.

He decided to keep 300 million in cash and property for himself and Mom, 150 million each. We'd get that after they died. The rest was equally divided by six, each kid getting 650 million. Pedro Junior, Diego, Manuela, and Santiago all inherited shares in the conglomerate and twenty-five million each in financial assets at home. Juanita and I got financial assets and property: hers inside the country, in America, and offshore; mine all offshore. I insisted on that. I had learned to love offshore financial structures.

It was a fair division. Juanita thanked me a lot. The other four got very upset. They would have gotten a much better deal if the division had happened after Dad's death, because they would control the auditors and make sure the final valuation was much lower, giving Juanita and me a much smaller share.

I didn't do it only for the money; a few million more or less wouldn't change anything. As Susan liked to say, you didn't really need that much money anyway. But it was a matter of principle. It was my birthright, and I wasn't going to let anyone take it away. Douglas had once said that Mom took away my birthright to watch the movie at the moment I was going to die. I never believed in the movie crap, but Douglas was right about the rest: birthright was birthright. My inheritance was part of my identity. I wasn't going to deny who I was anymore.

Much more important to me was the one and a half million that I had earned as the caveman. I had Winston wire it back to me. My plan was to buy an apartment in lower Manhattan with that money, or at least to pay for part of it. The apartment I had in mind wouldn't be cheap. I had destroyed all evidence of the caveman's existence, but I'd always have that apartment to remind me of him.

Dad's lawyers helped me set up a very complex legal structure using offshore companies and trusts so that I would never have to pay tax in America on income from my offshore investments after I became a permanent U.S. resident. I transferred twenty million dollars to my old bank account in America that had been reopened. Part of that money was for the apartment, the rest to invest. I would make at least $500,000 a year with my coaching activities. More than enough to live comfortably even after paying taxes. I would never need to touch my offshore fortune.

* * *

We came back from Europe in the middle of December for Winston's wedding in Jamaica. Dad attended it, too. Christmas we celebrated in Dad's beach house with him and Juanita's family. In January 1996 we left for South America.

During that trip I thought a lot about how I could show both

Winston and Douglas my gratitude. I owed them a lot. I thought about what Douglas was doing with the foundation. He was right: if you couldn't give back to the same people who helped you, then you gave it to someone else in need. When we came back from South America in April, I donated fifty million to the foundation, doubling its capital. Douglas, Winston, and William were very happy about it.

Douglas couldn't resist teasing me.

"Is that the solution you came up with, Pablo? Using money to buy you good karma?"

"If I've got bad karma, then it's big enough to take care of itself, Douglas."

* * *

Our wedding took place in Jamaica on Saturday, May eleventh. Susan's family and the Nelsons flew in from America. Dad and Juanita's family came, too. Both Winston and Douglas were my best men. We had a two-week honeymoon in Italy and returned to Jamaica to spend a few days before we boarded a plane to New York City.

The evening before we left we had a farewell dinner at Winston's place. Douglas brought his new girlfriend, Janice, a criminal defense lawyer he had hired for the foundation's legal team. They looked very in love. Would she be the one?

Douglas talked the whole evening about esoteric stuff. Janice agreed with everything. No wonder. Douglas would never fall in love with a woman who wasn't a believer. Surprisingly, Alicia agreed, too. Winston gave me many embarrassed looks, like saying, "Sorry, man." Even more surprising was Susan's behavior. The more Douglas talked, the more she found that the esoteric crap made sense. At the end of the evening I was giving Winston the same I'm-so-sorry look.

In the future Susan and I would meet the four of them for only a few days a year, hopefully not enough time to indoctrinate her. But Winston and Alicia would see Douglas and Janice a lot. It was only a matter of time until Alicia was converted. Then it would be three against one. I felt sorry for Winston.

Douglas, Janice, Alicia, and Susan talked the whole evening about fate giving us chances to make choices and other related nonsense. Apparently everything that had happened to me was supposed to happen. I had needed to go through that. So did Dad. We had needed those experiences to change.

What about Mom, I asked? If that was true, how come it didn't affect Mom?

Douglas couldn't explain. "It's not a science, Pablo." That much I knew already. Susan said, "Don't be sorry, Pablo. Who knows what fate still has in store for your Mom? Maybe she'll change some day." They all agreed. Only two of them had met Mom personally, Winston and Susan. But the others had heard enough stories. They all hoped that Mom would change for the better someday.

I hoped not.

In a world ruled by what Douglas called the quantum physics shit, where stuff happened randomly, one thing leading to the other, where no prediction was possible, where you couldn't rule anything out, where Nancy fell in love at first sight and Dad hung out with Jamaicans, it was very comforting to know that one thing would never change: Mom.

[Epilogue]

Next Thursday, March sixteenth, 2006, is my birthday. I'll turn forty. I'm going out with Susan. Candlelight dinner. The big party will be on Saturday. Two hundred and fifty guests are invited: friends, family, and a lot of clients and former clients. The Jamaicans are coming, too.

I continue to coach people, but I'm not known as Birdy anymore. It's Pablo now. I've also changed one letter in my job description: from PSMT to PSDT. Not self-motivation, but self-discovery. That's what it's all about: finding out who you are.

Meanwhile I charge $600 per session, but Susan still thinks that my fees haven't changed. She doesn't ask, I don't tell. Money is still a difficult issue between us, especially the fortune offshore. When I gave the fifty million to Douglas's foundation, Susan was happier than Douglas. "Fifty million gone. Only six hundred million left!" She doesn't know that meanwhile my fortune has grown to 765 million dollars.

Money has a tendency to grow. So does poverty. Therefore, there is no hurry to give away the money. I intend to get involved in serious philanthropy when I get older. Right now coaching takes all my time and energy.

People worry too much about material destitution, overlooking the fact that there is a lot of emotional and spiritual destitution out there. I'm very good at helping people overcome that.

* * *

Four years ago I became an American citizen, but I kept my old nationality. The kids hold both passports as well. We raise them bilingual. Susan has learned Spanish quite well since we got married.

Each kid has an Anglo and a Latino name. Our first son, born in 1998, is named Douglas Pablo. The second, born in 2000, is Winston Pedro.

We had planned to have more kids, but both pregnancies were very difficult. We almost lost the second baby and decided to stop. We talked about adopting a girl but somehow never did it. Taking care of the two boys keeps us very busy already.

Because of the children, it took Susan longer to finish her PhD, but she was done last summer. Since the fall she's been teaching philosophy as an assistant professor.

* * *

Alicia and Winston also have two children, a boy and a girl. Douglas married Janice in 1997. They already have four children, two girls and two boys, and are talking about having more. Douglas is a great dad. It's probably the role of his life.

We all meet every summer for vacations on the beach. The even years are black: we go to Jamaica and stay in Winston's beach house. The odd years are brown: they all come to my hometown and stay in Dad's beach house. Well, my house now. Dad left me the house and the yacht in his will. He died two years ago.

* * *

With the exception of Juanita, I have no more contact with my siblings. She visits us whenever she comes to New York or when we are spending time in my beach house. Mom never goes there because of the Jamaicans, so we go to her place instead. She still travels to New York every November to walk her fur coats. Each time we take her for lunch with the kids. She treats them well, but doesn't play the grandmother role.

Susan's parents would make wonderful grandparents, but they live in Nebraska, and we don't see them very often. The Nelsons became the boys' surrogate grandparents. The kids call Paul Grandpa and Betty Grandma. I'm very happy about it.

I forgave Dad in 1998, right after our first son Douglas was born. He came to New York to see us. He told me that he was very proud of me and of what I had made of my life. When he saw little Douglas, his eyes became misty, and he told me, "A son is a huge responsibility, Pablo. But I'm sure you'll be a great father. Much better than I was. I'm sure of it!" I couldn't resist. I gave him a hug, and we both cried. Susan cried, too. All that noise scared little Douglas, who cried the loudest.

* * *

Dad and I developed a good relationship in his last years. I'll always be thankful to Paul for encouraging me to do it. He retired three years ago. He was not even sixty yet, but he inherited a lot of money when his mother died. I never knew that he was from a rich family. He and Betty moved to the house they bought in Martha's Vineyard.

He finally has time to write movie scripts all day. It has always been his hobby, helping him relax after a long day of therapy sessions. He even has an agent in L.A. and managed to sell a script last year. It's being produced now.

He hasn't been as lucky with my story, though. He thinks that it would make a great movie and has already written three different scripts. But he can't find anyone interested. People say it's not a credible plot. Moviegoers would never believe it. Yeah, why should they?

Like people one day won't believe that New York once had garbage on the streets. My own kids laugh when I tell them that when I was their age, we could see garbage on the sidewalk. "Right, Dad," they say, rolling their eyes. Yeah, why should they believe? The city's administration managed to clean up New York. There's nothing subversive about the city anymore.

There's nothing subversive about me, either. I'm now a law-abiding, tax-paying citizen. Respected coach and family father. The caveman is gone. Just like the garbage.

* * *

It took many years for the city to get clean. I didn't enjoy watching subversion slowly dying. But one day in the late nineties I stopped feeling bad about it.

I was walking down a street not very far from our apartment when I reached a spot where the sidewalk was blocked by a lot of garbage and three empty garbage cans lying on their side. I asked myself, where did those garbage cans come from? And why dump the garbage on the sidewalk? To upset someone? To send a message?

I had to smile. Yes, a pocket of resistance! An anarchist soul out there was fighting the good fight. A garbage lover like me? In such a big city I couldn't be the only one mourning the garbage's disappearance. I wasn't alone after all. I had company. I was a member of a secret fellowship. I called it the "Fellowship of the Garbage Lovers."

At that very moment I realized that it must be the same with the caveman. Somewhere in New York other cavemen and cave-women must be carrying the torch and doing their subversive thing: uninvited, unwanted, uncontrolled, and unaccounted for. There was also a secret "Fellowship of the Cave People." There must be.

I found consolation in that thought. Actually, in that belief. Since that day I firmly believed in the existence of the Fellowship of the Cave People, even though I couldn't prove it.

* * *

Last week I finally got the proof. The most wonderful birthday present I could have ever wished. When I tell Douglas about it, he will certainly say that it was fate.

Subway station Rockefeller Center. Late afternoon. I was standing on the platform waiting for my train. I heard another train arriving on the opposite side and turned around to watch. The usual ritual: people getting out, people getting in, the platform getting empty. Then I saw a guy jumping up from his seat and running to the door. Once outside, he turned around and stood still, watching the doors closing and the train moving away.

I got goosebumps. Holy shit, was that guy losing his tail? Just like me in the old days? He turned around and walked in my direction. He didn't notice that I was observing him.

Our train arrived, and I got into the same subway car as he. He took a seat close to the door, as you should do when losing your tail. I chose a seat by the window. From there I could keep an eye on him inside the train, and later on I would be able to watch him on the platform.

I wondered if in my drug-dealing time another caveman had seen me losing my tail and recognized me as a member of the fellowship. If yes, had he had the same desire that I was having now? To go over to the guy, introduce myself, invite him to have a beer, and exchange war stories?

We traveled two stops. I was wondering, would he get off at the second stop or wait for the next? When it looked like he was definitely going to stay until the next station, he jumped up and left the car. He was quick. Had I been that quick?

He stood on the platform about six feet away from me, watching the doors. When the train started moving, he looked in my direction and our eyes met. I could recognize a spark in his eyes and almost hear the bells ringing inside his head. "They found you boy! You can run but you can't hide!"

But he noticed that I was smiling, and his eyes relaxed, as if he could feel that I was friend, not enemy. He smiled back as I passed by. For only a fraction of a second we were face to face, looking each other in the eyes and smiling. But it felt like time had frozen.

Things started moving quickly again. The train accelerated

and left him behind. I had to turn my head. Still smiling, I raised my right hand and showed index and middle fingers, giving him the victory sign. I had the impression that he laughed when he saw it. But I was too far away to be sure.

The train got into the tunnel. Suddenly I had that feeling again, the one that I had right after the shooting in Texas, when I realized that the killer wasn't after me and I was still on the run. That feeling that was so difficult to describe, that mix of relief, joy, gratitude, peace, and hope. Yes, the fellowship really existed! There were other cavemen out there!

Why was he losing his tail? What was he afraid of? And who was he? He looked very young. Early twenties, if not younger. Almost a kid. Young enough to be my son. All alone out there, looking out for himself.

I felt the urge to protect him, just like the mother Marley sings about in the song "High Tide or Low Tide." She is crying and praying to God to protect her child. "He needs protection. God, guide and protect us." I felt exactly like that mother. Weird thing.

I'm not a praying person. Millions pray to win the lottery every week, but only one person does. Was it luck, or was the person's prayer answered? And if yes, what about the other people? Were their prayers not good enough? How does God, if he is really out there, decide who deserves what? Impossible to know. And if almost all prayers never get answered, why bother?

The esoteric crowd talks about sending people good energy. The Age of Aquarius thing: peace, love, and good vibrations. I'm not sure if it works, either, so I've never done it.

That afternoon I decided to give it a try. What did I have to lose? That guy gave me the most wonderful birthday present ever. I would never be able to thank him personally. Why not send him good energy as a sign of gratitude?

I closed my eyes and said to whoever was in charge of the energy thing, "That kid needs protection. Guide and protect him. Stand by him through his troubles. Help him accomplish whatever he has to do. And when he's finished, please bring him back. Don't leave him out there. Bring him back! Like I was brought back!"

[The End]

Thank you for reading On the Run. If you enjoyed it, please consider telling your friends and posting a short review on Amazon and/or Goodreads. Gaining exposure as an indie author relies mostly on word-of-mouth. Your help is needed and greatly appreciated!

Izai Amorim
contact@izaiamorim.com

[Glossary]

Glossary of (almost) Extinct Communication Devices

Landline Phone

Telephone that used wire for transmission. A plug at the end of the phone cord was used to connect the phone to the wall jack, where the so-called telephone line (provided by the phone company) ended.

Pay phone

Landline telephone located in public places. Early models accepted only coins; later models accepted coins and cards. Pay phones in the United States (and in many other countries) had their numbers publicly displayed and could receive phone calls.

Pager

Wireless device used to receive messages. Numeric pagers could display only numbers; alphanumeric pagers could display text and numbers.

Answering Machine

Device used to record messages to a landline phone. Early models used tape; later models computer chips.

Fax Machine

Device used to transmit copies of printed documents (facsimiles) via a landline telephone line.